LOCAL RESISTANCE

LOCAL RESISTANCE

A World War Two Mystery

J.G. Harlond

www.penmorepress.com

Local Resistance by J.G. Harlond

ISBN-13: 978-1-942756-84-2(Paperback)
ISBN —978-1-942756-85-9 (e-book)

BISAC Subject Headings:
FIC006000 FICTION / Espionage
FIC002000 FICTION / Action & Adventure
FIC014000 FICTION / Historical
FIC022030 FICTION / Mystery & Detective / Traditional British

Cover Illustration by Christine Horner

Address all correspondence to:
Michael James
Penmore Press LLC
920 N Javelina Pl
Tucson AZ 85748

For

Antonia

With grateful thanks to Robin Makeig-Jones

The south-west coast of Britain, early March 1941

A huge bull dolphin broke the surface first. A living torpedo launched into the black night then disappeared back into the dangers of the wartime deep. The watcher on the strand felt his heart leap at the unexpectedness. He had been waiting, but not for this.

Then it came. A steel leviathan surging upward, periscope first, then conning tower and metallic flank breasting the surface. It stayed just long enough for two men to inflate a rubber dinghy and set it into the water, to row ashore and collect the waterproof package grasped so tightly in the watcher's hands.

*****

Part One
Home Front

Porthferris, Cornwall, March 1941

Chapter 1

Maisie Rose Hawkins pulled the sash window down as far as it would go. The wood was swollen after a week of persistent rain and was hard to budge. Leaving her hands on the upper rim, she took a deep breath. He'd be home soon. She gulped in the clean air and her last moments of peace. The rain became sharper, smacking her face: a warning. She tugged the window closed, slipped the catch and drew the curtains then, shutting out the dangers of the dark, she pulled the blackout material down and switched on her bedside light.

Once in the chilly bed, she turned off the light and tucked the sheet and woollen blankets under her chin. The darkness was absolute, an ebony cocoon. Maisie listened to the wind rattle the window and roof slates of the old cottage. No bombers, though, not yet, only the occasional clatter of rain and loose guttering. Something else that needed fixing, but she couldn't do it on her own.

"Maisie! Maisie! Open the door, woman!"

There was another, louder, clatter then a clang. Stan. Drunk as usual. He'd staggered into the dustbin.

"Maisie Rose!"

Maisie listened, knuckles as white as the sheet she gripped. Stones bounced off the cottage wall. He was aiming for the window. She pushed herself further down into her cold marriage bed and tugged the blankets over her head. He couldn't get in. She had locked and bolted the doors, front and back.

Under the blankets was a blessed silence, but even so, Maisie was taut, waiting. Then it started – a repeated dull thudding. He was kicking the back door.

"Ssh, you'll wake the house," she murmured, thinking of her sleeping daughter in the next room and her father-in-law, lying like a skeleton on a pallet in the living room below. "Ssh," she repeated, but made no move.

The banging stopped. Maisie held her breath, then gasped as a large stone hurtled through the bedroom window under the blackout blind and landed thump on her stomach like a punch.

"Open the frigging door, Maisie – it's pissin' down. I'll catch my death out here."

Maisie rolled over and looked at the luminous dial of the alarm clock: twelve-thirty. The pub had shut long ago; where had he been all this time?

The cottage was small – two up, two down – but they had two doors: a front door leading into the sitting room, and a back door leading into the kitchen. He had returned to kicking the back door. Soon he'd be scuffing off the green paint like Nipper, the terrier they'd had when they were first married. Nipper had scraped away all the paint and most of the woodwork in one corner by the time he died. Poor ol' Nipper, she thought. What a dog's life: no cooking, no cleaning for others, trying to make ends meet and hiding the housekeeping. A dog's life.

"Maisie!" Muffled threats and obscenities. A huge cracking noise. He was breaking the kitchen window. It was too small for him to get through, but he'd break it just the same; that was Stan's way.

"All right, I'm coming."

Maisie got out of bed and opened the wardrobe to put on her thick brown winter coat. It softened the blows. His grip didn't leave such big bruises. She'd have to keep her head down, though; Big Stan threw a nasty punch even blind drunk.

By the time she got to the middle of the stairs the noise had stopped. She crept into the tiny kitchen, feeling her way in the dark.

It was too quiet.

She tiptoed, barefoot on freezing flagstones, and stood behind the back door, trembling. Nerves, not the cold. Was he standing with his back to the wall, waiting to pounce? He'd done that before.

Turning slightly, she tried to see if he'd succeeded in breaking the window. A draught of cold wind said he had, but he hadn't been able to get through. She moved silently out of the kitchen and into the sitting room. The old man coughed.

"That Stan come home?"

"It is. You warm enough?" Maisie bent her ample figure over her father-in-law's make-do bed and tucked his blankets round him as if he were a child. Kissing his papery brow, she said, "Go back to sleep, Grandpa."

"If he'll let me. Noisy bugger."

Local Resistance

Lifting the side of a curtain, Maisie peered out into blackness. There was no moonlight, only rain pouring down in black waves. She felt the cottage shift under her feet. In her mind it was sliding down the hill, taking them down, down to the rocks and the shingle beach below, into the surging tide and out to sea. She was drowning in her own home.

Mentally shaking herself, Maisie dropped the curtain and by sense of touch selected the tallest bottle on the chair that served as a table beside the invalid's bed.

"Here, Grandpa, have a drop more of this – help you sleep better. I can't see a spoon, just take a swig. Pretend it's whisky."

"That the red stuff?"

Maisie held the bottle to the old man's lips and tipped it so he had a more than generous measure. "There we go, and a drop more for luck – help you sleep, my heart."

She held the bottle a second time to the old man's lips until he spluttered and pushed it away with a feeble hand.

"That's it. All right? You won't get disturbed now."

"He's gorn quiet."

"Mmm."

"You goin' to let him in?"

"Course I am."

"You don't have to, girl. Let him sleep it off out there."

"It's pouring."

"Sober him up. He don't deserve you, Maisie. My own son and I say he ain't good enough. Was a time, though, before the Great War, when he was a boy and we was working the boats together . . ." The old man began to wheeze in distress.

"Sshh, don't you fret now."

Old Joe Hawkins, who had once been a broad, well-muscled, sea-faring man, turned his face to the wall and began to weep. Maisie patted his shoulder then went to the front door, pulled back the bolt as silently as she could and stepped into the porch. There was an old pair of rubber boots and an umbrella under the hat shelf. She pulled on the boots then grabbed the torch they kept on the shelf. Stepping outside, she pushed up the umbrella and made her way round the stone walls to the back-door entrance.

Big Stan was splayed out face down, half on, half off the path to the back door. His arms out rigid beside him; heels in the air like a prostrate monk. Maisie pushed at a leg with a boot. He didn't move. She pushed a bit harder. Nothing. Dead to the world. *If only* . . .

She returned to the front porch, methodically put the torch and umbrella back in their places, removed her heavy coat, hung it up and kicked off the rubber boots. Then she closed the front door and bolted it again.

Grandpa was asleep, but his breathing was irregular. There was nothing more she could do for him so she felt her way back up the narrow staircase. Pausing outside her daughter's room, she peeped in the open door. It was very dark but she knew Ginny would have a hand tucked up under her chin like a baby, although she was old enough to have a baby of her own; her golden curls would be squiggled over the pillow. Maisie smiled, comforted by a moment of normality, and returned to her room – their room. Sitting on the side of the lumpy bed, she wondered if it was too late to reverse events, to open the door.

It was like a story, what was happening – going to happen. Another woman had taken control. The real Maisie Rose Hawkins was asleep, innocently asleep – like her daughter. Stan's own father had said "Let him sleep it off out there". So she would and, this being the case, the next step – the next part of the plan that was not *her* plan – meant she'd have to move fast.

Local Resistance

She pulled off her nightgown and dressed hastily in warm clothes; it was early March but the storm made it midwinter. Tying a dark scarf over her own fair curls, she returned to the kitchen. Slowly, she opened the back door: he was still there, face down in the mud and rain. Hadn't moved.

She closed the door, dropped the latch but left it unbolted. Now, she went back into the sitting room. Grandpa was fast asleep – wheezing, but calm. She pulled on a dry mackintosh and her rubber boots, picked up the big torch then, thinking what this might imply, put it back on the shelf and exited the cottage by the front door.

Leaning her tired body into the wind, Maisie trudged down the steep hill to the quay. Trees crashed around her; the harsh southerly gale whipping waves into a frenzy over the rocks below lashed her face, pushing her backwards. But she would not go back. Rain was good; it would obliterate telltale footprints.

Once she was on the quay, though, it was a different matter. Shaking with cold and nerves, she stopped and looked with horror at the black water crawling over the cliff path footbridge. The stream below the bridge was in full spate; swollen by the tide, it was gushing over the rough wooden planks. She grasped the slippery rail for support and tried to get her breathing under control. She had to cross the wooden footbridge to reach the path that zigzagged up the cliff to Cleve House and safety.

The gusting wind joined the sound of incoming waves slapping hard against the man-made harbour wall and the rocky outcrop to her left – crashing in, urging her to action. Then, amid the mayhem of wind and water, Maisie was suddenly aware of something – or someone – behind her.

"Stan!" Her voice rose high in panic on the single syllable.

"Stan?" Fear went to her knees, draining the strength to even stand.

Forcing herself to move, she stepped onto the bridge, desperate to cross the inlet and get to her one safe haven. She grasped the handrail but slipped, one leg shooting out sideways off the bridge; only her body saved her from the roiling water less than a yard below.

"Stan!" she called. "Help me!"

But no one came.

Crying with fear and the terror of drowning, Maisie clung to a slippery upright. "Help me, help me . . ." her voice choked on the words. "Help me, please . . ."

But no one came.

Gradually – oh, so slowly – Maisie got back to her feet and hand over hand edged backwards onto the quay. As she stood there once more, getting her breath back, she knew for certain a man was there: watching her. She felt she could hear him, feel his breathing.

A car swung down past the entrance to the quay, its hooded lights glinting off the puddled stone paving, then carried on up the opposite hill. And in that small instant Maisie saw a tall, thin man in a long raincoat with a sou'wester pulled over his face.

It wasn't Stan, but it was someone who could have come to her aid and had made no move to do so.

The awfulness of this thought forced Maisie to accept the danger she was in. She tried to remember if it was a spring tide. Would the water coming over the quay pull the little bridge away as it had done before? But what was she to do? Cross the bridge and risk the tide again? Or go back and take the longer route past the shops, and have to pass the tall man who could have helped her and didn't?

It couldn't be anyone from the village, anyone she knew. One of the locals would have rushed to her aid. The idea of a menacing stranger set her heart racing once more. Keeping her head down, she stepped backwards in the direction of the quay, then another step, and another. She turned. The tall man did not move. He did not speak; she did not speak. Then he turned and, striding fast, set off towards the main street.

Maisie had three choices now: to go home, to take the long way round and follow the man up Porth Hill, or risk the low bridge and then a surging gale on the exposed cliff path. Anxious to get to the safety of her employer's home, yet desperate not to have to see the tall man again, she decided to risk the bridge. But it was too late. A wave crashed up through the rails and fell, swirling into the torrent below. It would have taken her with it. Maisie turned and ran. Head down, staring at her feet, she followed the man up Porth Hill.

By the time Maisie got to Cleve House, she was mentally and physically exhausted. Letting herself into the vast old kitchen she stripped off her soaking mackintosh and boots, lit a gaslight, put on the indoor shoes she kept with her overall in the broom cupboard and set a pan of milk to boil. When it was hot she poured it into two mugs, stirred in honey and took the milk on a tray up to the main bedroom.

"I thought you might like some milk," she said, entering a darkened room.

"Maisie? I thought you'd gone home hours ago. What time is it?"

"Late."

Delia Metherall lifted herself onto an elbow, switched on her bedside light and blinked. "Your hair's wet."

"Still tippin' down."

"It's a dreadful night to be out."

"Worse if I'd stayed home."

"Ah," Delia nodded, "like that, is it? Have a hot bath. There should be enough water in the tank." She struggled into a sitting position and looked at her housekeeper. "Are you hurt?"

"No. Here – take this milk. I'm sorry to wake you. Careful, it's hot." There was a pause. "He's stretched out by the back door. He's . . ."

Delia took the cup. "He'll catch his death in this weather."

The two women looked at each other. Two women so alike in appearance so different in experience. Two women who were cousins, except one was illegitimate and lived in a tied cottage, and the other lived in a beautiful Georgian mansion with ten acres, coppices, a kitchen garden and a pond – now home to an evacuated preparatory school.

"Go to bed, Maisie. We'll deal with it in the morning."

Maisie Rose looked down into her cup and nodded.

"Ginny's there, isn't she?"

"Didn't wake up when he was yelling – she won't wake up to help him now."

"Was he shouting?"

"Roarin'," Maisie put a hand on her stomach, gripped the fabric of her dress.

Delia said, "Don't worry – if he wakes up he'll get himself indoors."

"And if he doesn't?" whispered Maisie.

"You worry too much. He went out for a drink and drank too many – as usual. You're safer here with me tonight – let him sleep it off."

"I shouldn't have . . ."

"What? Stayed here tonight to look after me because I've got a dreadful migraine and can't even see properly? I can't look after two small children on my own like this, let alone what needs doing for the school. I can't manage without you. Everyone knows that. Unless . . . Maisie, what do *you* want?"

Maisie shook her head, "Nothing. Not anymore. It's too late for wanting things."

"Perhaps you'd better let someone else see you in the morning."

Maisie Rose looked up. "What? You mean for –"
"An alibi. Exactly."

Chapter 2

The moment there was a hint of dawn around the blackout curtains Maisie trod softly down the backstairs, collected her still damp mackintosh, and then stepped back into her rubber boots and out of the scullery into a clear new dawn. The gale had blown itself out but the early morning was thick and heavy with moisture. She walked through the vegetable garden to the gate leading onto the cliff meadow. The latch was slimy and cold. She thought of her own back door. She ought to hurry; Ginny was the last person to deal with a crisis.

Risking the possibility that she would have to return because the footbridge had been swept away, Maisie took the path across the cliff meadow down to the village. A line of sandbags now marked the edge of the cliff, forming a dull outline with an occasional glimmer of silver from the rolls of barbed wire set behind it. The once wild place, open to merciless weather, now sported a concrete pillbox, turning it into a man-made garrison.

"Halt – who goes there? Stay where you are and don't move!"

Maisie froze. She had forgotten about the Home Guard lookout post. Had any of them seen her the night before?

Had anyone been on duty down on the quay? Was that who it had been? She should have mentioned it to Delia. Then something inside her advised her not to. Not to say anything at all until she knew more.

"It's me, Maisie Rose Hawkins. Who's that?" she called out.

"Maisie?"

"That you, Alf?"

Portly Alf Plowden the grocer emerged from the pillbox and slithered a few steps to where Maisie was standing. She wondered if he could hear her heart hammering against her ribs.

"What you doin' up here so early?" he demanded in a friendly manner.

"I got to get back to see to Stan's father – he's really bad."

"You been with Mrs Metherall, then?"

"Course I have. Where else am I likely to have been if I'm up here – Plymouth Ho?"

"Just doin' my duty, maid. Can't be sure of anyone these days, what with us being in the front line."

"Front line? Front line! You mean it's real?" Maisie looked about her in horrified disbelief. "The invasion's started?"

"No, no . . ." Alf raised a soft hand. "Not s'far as I know, but it *might* happen. We've been told to keep a special eye open and – other things – like that. Can't say no more, and I wouldn't if I could. Mum's the word." He tapped his generous nose with a sausage finger. "No point alarming folks."

As if in defiance of his words, there was a dull crump, crump of distant explosions. Alf turned and looked westward across the cliff top meadow. A vague purple light confirmed the noise of bombs. "That'll be Fowey harbour or St Austell catching it again."

Maisie put a hand to her mouth. "Oh, poor people. They'll have come out of their shelters by now, thinking it's safe to get breakfast. What they German's want, bombing little old places like that?"

"'Specs there be a few Germans saying same thing about us."

"'Tis barmy, Alf. People going about their lives best they can and . . ." Maisie paused, watching the sky and listening to the distant *ack-ack* of anti-aircraft guns. "Poor people," she sighed.

There was a silence between them then Alf muttered, "There but for the grace of God, eh?" He gave Maisie a paternal smile and touched her arm. "Nothing we can do. Off you go, maid, and watch your step down there. 'Tis proper tricky now we can't dig out they steps no more."

"Oh, right . . ." Maisie began to move away. She was nearly at the top of what used to be a roughly-cut terraced path leading down to the quay and beach when Alf Plowden called out behind her, "Hey! You shouldn't have come out of your house like that, Maisie Rose Hawkins; you've forgotten your gas mask again! You been told about that before. I've told you myself in the shop. You got to carry it with you at *all* times."

Maisie felt dizzy. She was still wobbly as she finally dropped down into the gully that opened into Porthferris Bay. A solitary gull mewed above, an unusually gentle tone. The upturned rowing boat her husband used or loaned for fishing trips was up, lying behind nine-foot posts that had been set the length of the wide bay to prevent enemy landing craft making use of the hard Atlantic sand. It looked like a coffin.

Would she get anything from the fisherman's guild? Had Stan paid his dues? She could sell this little working crab and lobster punt easily enough, and the bigger winkboat he kept in the cove beneath their cottage, but who would take on the trawler and his father's old mackerel lugger now all the young men were away in the forces?

Turning from the water, Maisie was thrilled to see the rickety bridge still in place and quickened her pace. Taking a deep breath, she crossed in a few strides and ran onto the quay.

A dog barked. She jumped guiltily, then, as if a baton had been raised, skylarks lifted into the air from the meadow above and dowdy sparrows twittered from village rooftops and railings. Her whole small world came alive with "glad-that-I-live-am-I" birdsong. Maisie smiled – she couldn't help it. Perhaps – at last – the storm had blown away all the bad things in her life.

"Mornin', Maisie Rose."

Maisie stopped in her tracks for a second time. It was the village milkman.

"Oh, Gordon! How are you, m'dear?"

"Middlin', middlin'."

Maisie edged round the loaded milk dray and paused to stroke the muzzle of the old horse pulling it. Watching her, the elderly milkman brushed his hands down his brown overalls. "Bad do last night," he muttered.

Maisie gulped.

"Devonport and Plymouth must have took another beatin'."

"What, bombers? In that gale? I thought bombers couldn't fly in storms."

"Hah! Dockyard must have got it. Falmouth as well, prob'ly. Bad do, bad do."

"I didn't hear them." Maisie paused and framed the truth out of what felt like a lie. "I was up at Cleve – that old house has got walls a yard thick." She hadn't noticed the bombers, not one. "Poor people," she said once again. "Your Walter all right? Still in the dockyard, isn't he? Not called up?"

"Reserved occupation. Don't know if it's better or worse than his brothers out on the water. My Peggy gets into a right state. Mind you, she never complains when he brings a bit extra home. Big tin of corned beef we got last week."

Maisie smiled then said, "Well, can't be stop stood here gossiping. Got to get Stan's breakfast, and his old dad was coughing fit to crack the walls yesterday. Ginny's no use as a nurse and no use with a frying pan, neither."

"But she's pretty as a picture, your maid. Prettiest girl I ever did see, and you was lovely in your time."

"Pretty is as pretty does," retorted Maisie, ignoring the unintentional slight.

The horse moved forward of its own accord and stopped outside the back alley for The Fisherman's Boot pub. As he reached up for a pint milk bottle, Gordon nodded over in the direction of Cleve House. "You got your work cut out with that there school movin' in. She not well again, or is it one of the little'uns?"

"She gets desp'rate headaches. I got my lot their supper and went back to spend the night, like I did last week."

"Funny place to have a school, if you asks me," Gordon said, tucking a smaller bottle into a pocket.

"What was in that, then, Gordon?" Maisie asked with knowing grin.

The milkman looked about him. "You want a third of a pint, maid?"

"Above the milk ration?"

Gordon shook his head. "Not milk – clotted cream. My Peg says it's a bugger to get out of the bottle, bein' so thick, but once you get the hang of it, it drops nice and neat on a scone for a proper Cornish tea. Mum's the word, though, eh? I don't want that bugger Bantry after me. Not that it's my idea. They thought it up at Glebe Farm. George Deakin's a Deakin at heart, if you knows what I mean?"

"My ma was a Deakin, too, Gordon. But making clotted cream's not allowed anymore."

"Best you tell George that."

Maisie grinned. "What do I do about paying?"

Gordon sucked in his breath as if she'd suggested something pornographic. "Can't do no bills, not with that rationing bugger Bantry poking his nose in the dairy office ev'ry two minutes. We'd best have an *arrangement*." He spoke the word as if it were sacred script.

"Tell you what," said Maisie, "you leave me a third of a pint like this on Fridays and I'll leave you some jam for the dairy. I'll leave a jar for you and Peggy as well, if you like, when I can spare one."

"Not that NAAFI stuff in a tin, is it, for the forces? I can't be doin' with that. All saccharine syrup and no fruit. I told our Walter he was doin' us no favours bringin' that rubbish home. Gives me the trots quicker than ol' Chester here can manage on the home stretch."

Maisie laughed. "No, Stan swaps that stuff for . . . I saved our sugar ration all last summer and made up blackcurrant jelly. I'll put some on the shelf in the outhouse. Best leave the cream there, too, out of sight – not that we ever get any visitors."

"Right you are. I got to move on now, maid. You look after yourself. You'm too kind for your own good."

Suddenly anxious to delay going home, Maisie said, "Peg still doin' for Dr MacManus?"

She wasn't one to gossip as a rule – would Gordon notice? *Not like her to hang around passing the time of day*, he'd say as he went about his round tomorrow – after the village had heard the news. *I thought it was a bit fishy. I see her of a mornin', you know, but not that early. Makes you think, makes you wonder.*

Maisie braced herself, her head full of unspoken, damning gossip. "I best be getting on as well."

Gordon touched his cap and Maisie set off up the high-hedged lane leading to St Chad's, the church hall and the glebe-land spinney. It was a climb she'd made a thousand times with full shopping baskets. These days the basket was a lot lighter, except on the days she collected their monthly rations. Some days she had a bag of Delia's finer linens to wash or stockings to mend. Today she bore only an invisible burden of guilt, but her calf muscles cramped and her right hip ached before she was as far as the hotel on the first bend. *Perhaps we should move into Cleve House,* she thought. *Delia's asked me often enough.*

The idea brought Maisie to a halt. She bent over to catch her breath. *I loved him once. Loved being at home for him. The climb was nothing then.*

Taking another deep breath, Maisie started again then stopped. Something had caught her eye. A curtain in the big bungalow up to her left twitched. The bungalow had been vacant since the summer of '39, as far as she knew. Maisie peered up at the windows then shrugged and started on her way again, walking more briskly up round the entrance to Bayview Hotel and on until she stood before her own small cottage set among rowan and hawthorn hedges and salt-proof rhododendrons.

There was a low, green-lichened latch gate, and a paved path that led to her front porch and round each side of the cottage to a set of steep, spade-made steps leading down to a tiny shingle beach. The steps were exactly the width of Big Stan Hawkins' gumboots, and treacherous when wet. He kept a boat in a sea-cave below. And a lot of other things she didn't ask about in a tunnel at the back of the cave that led into the disused copper mine beneath their hill.

But for all he used the path nearly every day, Stan never bothered to re-cut their cliff steps: they were as smooth as a playground slide in places. For a big man with a beer belly he was surprisingly agile, but Maisie had visualised him face down in an ebb tide more than once. Wishful thinking.

She put her hand on the open gate and paused to look about her, taking her time, trying to ignore the cold prickle of fear crawling down her back. If he was awake and could remember anything she'd get a bashing.

For a final moment she looked at her home, taking in its outward tranquillity, how sunshine glinted off the wet slate roof. Picture postcard, it was: an ancient yellow rambler rose was showing signs of new life around the porch; pansies and other early spring flowers crushed under the night's rain were jostling for breathing space in the tiny garden. She had lived here when it was her mother's home, and stayed here after she'd married Big Stan because she was pregnant with Ginny. In those days her mother had been there to protect her.

Maisie sighed. In those days she'd thought she'd be able to tame his drinking, blamed it on his war-damaged nerves. The gas-attack dreams eventually subsided, but not the drinking. Reluctantly she'd come to accept Stan would never again be the sweet-tempered boy who'd taken her out in his boat when they were courting – before the world went mad the first time. *Her* Stan Hawkins had died in some unnamed French field that was forever a hell-hole. Someone else had come home in his place.

Finally, as if in slow motion, Maisie walked round the back of the cottage.

Everything was the same, and not the same. It was no longer raining, and Big Stan was not stretched out face down in the backyard, drunk as usual.

Maisie lifted the latch and entered the kitchen.

"Oh, Ma, thank God you're back!" cried Ginny.

"What's wrong?"

"I heard a bang and I came downstairs and . . ." the girl started to sob.

"Just tell me slowly." Maisie put her arms round her daughter's shoulders and stroked her hair.

"Grandpa – his bottles are all over the floor and he's . . . Ma, I think he's dead."

Maisie ran into the sitting room; the old man was as she'd last seen him, except his left arm had swung out and swept the medicine bottles to the floor. His face was peaceful, and he was quite dead.

"Where's your pa?"

"Pa? I don't know. He didn't come home last night. He's not upstairs."

Maisie straightened up and looked at her daughter. "Didn't you hear him come in?"

"No. Oh, Ma . . ." Ginny started to wail.

Maisie went back into the kitchen, opened the door and stared at the mud that lay around the back step. Rain had washed away all trace of footprints as she'd hoped, but it had left no clue.

Chapter 3

Bob Robbins let the old police Ford Prefect chug up the steep hill. The wife hadn't reported the fisherman missing for three days – another half hour wouldn't make much difference. The lanky lad sitting beside him in a brand new constable's uniform stared out of the grimy windscreen, long artist's hands round his new helmet. There was nothing to look at, only high-banked hedges, the occasional five-barred gate. The boy was nervous. Bob couldn't see why – all they had to do was talk to the wife. In principle, it was only a matter of verifying the date and time the fisherman had last been seen. If it wasn't a straight-forward "lost at sea" he'd have to ask about bank details or post-office account, go over prior events and poke around a bit, but there wasn't much they could do unless something surprising emerged. The local area would have to be combed, but if he'd gone in the sea, which was most likely, the body would wash up sooner or later.

Bob drove on for another winding mile then, to break the silence, tapped the boy's arm. "Cheer up – may never happen." The boy gave him a dour look. Bob sighed, "Go on; tell me it already has."

"What I can't understand is how – with the whole world at war, people dying in battles and air raids everywhere – someone could go missing in a village like Porthferris."

Bob Robbins couldn't see the connection between the "whole world" and Porthferris, with its tiny harbour and seaside beach, but suspected the former was much on the boy's mind. "He's a fisherman, lad. Like as not he went overboard."

Arriving at the junction on the brow of the hill, Bob halted the car and looked at a felled tree lying at the side of the road. "Oh, now that'll make an *excellent* road block. Keep Jerry out of Cready and getting onto the main road for Plymouth *very* nicely."

"The Home Guard has been busy. That's a big tree," PC Oliver replied, failing to pick up the irony in Bob Robbins's voice.

The aging detective sergeant sniffed and ran a hand through his bristly white hair. Looking left then right, he said, "Well, they've succeeded in confusing me by taking the road sign up, I'll give 'em that. Which way do you think?"

"It doesn't make much difference. If you go left, we pass the old school house, the church hall, the vicarage and St Chad's, then the lane goes down past the cottage. I think the Hawkinses must live in the little place before the hotel – going down. If we miss it, we can go all the way down and come back up past the quay and the turning for what they call Inner Harbour, through the shopping street and back up Porth Hill – which is that road over there." He pointed slightly to his right. "Either way, both roads go down to the harbour and the beach and loop up round, back to this crossroads. That road there," he turned in his seat and indicated over Bob's shoulder, "is another way back to Cready, past a garage."

"Know your way around here, then?"

Local Resistance

"My parents have friends who used to vacation here. We used to go sailing with them. They kept a dinghy and a small yacht down at Porthferris harbour."

Bob mentally filed the social background alongside the plummy accent and crashed into first gear. "You can point out local landmarks, then, and give me any titbits of local info."

"I'll try. Can't say I've ever spoken to – as in talked to – any of the villagers except the fisherman, Mr Hawkins."

"The one that's gone missing?"

"I suppose so."

"Local people round here are all related one way or another, there's probably a dozen Hawkinses fishing this coast between here and Looe alone. Still, it'd be handy if you knew him – how do you, by the way?"

"Know him? Not sure I do. But if it's the man that's gone missing, it seems a bit odd. Odd that he's drowned, I mean. He used to help us with our boat. Got us out of trouble in a tricky current near rocks once, when we were youngsters."

As far as Bob was concerned his new assistant was still a youngster, but he said, "Stan Hawkins – you don't reckon he's got himself drowned, then?"

The boy gave a slight shrug. "It's possible, obviously. But he knows the coast better than – well, anyone we knew. His family's lived here for centuries. One of his ancestors stopped a pirate attack on Porth single-handed. Turks, he called them. I read up about it afterwards, about how white slavers and pirates landed along the coast here." The boy paused then said quietly, "I've never thought about it before, but I suppose what he told us was what first got me interested in history."

"That what you are going to study, when the war's over?"

"Hopefully."

"So how did you end up in the Police?"

"My mother's . . . Ah, we've missed it. That was the hotel, Bayview, and these houses here – the locals call them Vicky Villas – are Queen Victoria Villas. That big bungalow up over there is called Seabreeze. My people's friends own it. We boys used to camp in the back garden. Huge fun."

Bob drove on slowly in third then changed down to second gear for the hill was steep and they had reached the village of Porthferris itself. The young policeman continued his running commentary.

"Round here. That's Inner Harbour – it's a complete maze of cottages crammed in together behind the sea wall, and that's the Fisherman's Boot. There's another pub built into the sea wall itself – the Ship, I think, but it was empty when we used to come here. Carry on past the shops and post office, then follow the road up Porth Hill and we'll get back to the crossroads."

Bob coaxed the car up another steep incline and carried on round until they passed the church again, then slowed to a crawl past a spinney and turned back down Church Lane.

"There's a gate there, behind that car." PC Oliver tapped his grubby window.

Bob pulled into the side of the lane as best he could. "That Hawkins' vehicle, do you think?" he asked.

The boy gave another slight shrug and opened his door to get out. Shrugs irritated Bob but he reminded himself the boy was straight out of school – boarding school by the sound of it. He probably assumed everyone had a motor car.

The young policeman put on his helmet and said, "What exactly do you require of me, sir?"

"Nothing at all at the mo. I don't want to go in yet, not until we have a bit of a recce first."

"Oh, yes, sir, I didn't think about that. Sorry."

"No need to apologise, lad, and a bit less of the 'sir', if you don't mind; makes me feel like a headmaster." He paused and looked around. "Let's take a walk back up the lane. I think I spotted a track down to the sea somewhere earlier."

"There are lots. We used to bring our boat round to explore the little coves; they're only tiny but most of them have got deep sea caves. This area was famous for smuggling. Tricky, though. The tides are really fast and if you don't time it right . . . That's how Mr Hawkins found us that time."

"Round here, was he? In his fishing trawler?"

"No, it was what the locals call a 'winkboat'. They use them for setting crab and lobster pots, and for fishing. They've got a sail and a motor. I think the name might come from the winch for winding in nets: winch – *wink*. Not sure. Anyway, he kept it down here below his cottage."

"That'll be the one the wife says is missing."

Bob walked up the hill, looking to his right, over sagging wooden railings and a few yards of tall grass and high weeds, out to sea. Getting down to a beach from here would be tricky as well, but you'd be completely hidden from the road. He peered at the horizon, shading his eyes against the shimmer off the water on a rare clear day. A sudden tiny burst of colour emerged from grey thistles crowding among the railings. Bob caught the red and yellow, then the characteristic warning 'twsitt-witt': a goldfinch. He turned his attention to the grass and herbs as another goldfinch sang, making a mental note to return. The green cliff was excellent habitat: few people and plenty of bushes. He touched his left jacket pocket for his small binoculars, but he'd left them at home.

Turning back the way they had come, and taking care not to look at the boy, Bob said, "Let's sort out this name business. Remind me what you're called, lad, apart from PC Oliver."

"Laurence, sir."

"Did your mother know what she was doing choosing Laurence to go with Oliver? Never mind – ignore that. What do they call you in the canteen? What do you want me to call you when we're on our own like this – Laurence, Laurie, PC Oliver?"

The young man looked down at his shiny new boots. "At school I was called Oliver by the masters; sometimes Oliver Four. I have three – had – three older brothers. The chaps in my dorm used to call me Olly. But, if it's all right with you, I prefer Laurie. It's what my family call me."

"Fine. Laurie it is. Three brothers? In the forces?"

"That's why I'm here, in this uniform."

"Your mother?"

Laurie Oliver nodded his head. "Roger, the eldest, got it at Dunkirk. John is in a minesweeper. Sam's a pilot officer now, in the Air Force."

"And you're a rapid entry wartime recruit in the Cornish Constabulary. I see. Well, we'd best make a cracking career policeman out of you, then. Head of Scotland Yard by the time you're thirty suit you?"

The boy gave a sheepish grin.

"Thought so. Right, let's get started with this Hawkins business. Assuming you're right, that it's a bit odd that the chap's gone underwater, keep your eyes peeled and write down anything that looks a bit iffy. Make a note of what Mrs Hawkins says, and keep it legible, we'll need it later. We've got her statement from when she came into the station this morning and what Sergeant Mallett put in his report, but we'll need more details. She gave Mallett a couple of snaps. Have you seen them? Ah, but you know who we're looking for, don't you?"

"If it's the same man, sir, yes. He's a big man, dark. Erm . . . I don't know what more I can say, sir – sorry."

"Sarge will do, not 'sir'. Just call me 'Sarge' – it's what I was used to before I left to go into civvy street so I may as well go back to it. According to Mallett, the local Special Constable went straight to Hawkins' trawler in the harbour when the wife reported him missing this morning. There was no sign of him there, and his crew don't know anything. Not that Specials are much use on police business down here, they're more interested in checking no lights are left on for the blackout."

"Sarge," Laurie was cautious about using the term but clearly had something to say. "Did they check in the old mine? It's very close as the bird flies, or to get to by boat. Takes a good while to get round by car because you have to go up to the crossroads, where we came in, then onto the back road to Cready and down Smugglers Mile Hill round the woods. But if the weather was too bad to get back here, he might have moored his winkboat there and – erm – stayed there, I suppose." Laurie pointed at a line of jagged rocks like the spine of a great dinosaur creeping into the sea. "It's round that promontory over there."

"Why would he do that? Stay there for three days, I mean, instead of coming home."

Laurie Oliver flushed slightly pink. "Just a thought, sir – Sarge."

Bob scratched his chin then sauntered back down the lane, with Laurie Oliver a few paces behind. The car was still there. Visitor, most likely. He sighed, looked at his watch then opened the gate and knocked on the front door. The wife answered before he'd raised his knuckles for the second knock, giving him a bit of a start. At first glance she was very like his own wife, Joan. Later, as he watched her talking with the vicar, he decided she wasn't like Joan at all. But there was something.

"Mrs Hawkins? I'm Detective Sergeant Robbins and this is PC Oliver. We've come about your husband."

There were two men in the small living room, one of whom, Dr MacManus, Bob recognised from a recent accident outside Cready market. The other was the local vicar, a very tall, thin man – taller than Laurie Oliver – who unfolded like a clerical Pinocchio from a chair at the family dining table. They were arranging a funeral.

Seeing the vicar and the doctor together, Bob immediately assumed the fisherman had been found, an embarrassing mistake.

"No! Oh, no! Not my husband, Detective . . . Sorry, what do I call you?" Maisie Hawkins was pink about the cheeks, "I'm not used to the police, you see. We've only got Jimmy Beer here in the village, and he's only a Special . . ."

It's all about names today, Bob thought. "Call me 'Mr Robbins'." As he spoke he caught the doctor gazing at the woman with a protective eye.

PC Oliver was standing with his back to the door – round-shouldered like the vicar, for the ceiling was low – and gazing in turn, at a simply beautiful maiden – there was no other term for her – who was standing across the room by the opposite door. Bob huffed. Any minute now a batty white rabbit would rush through with a broken watch.

The vicar broke into his fanciful thoughts. "We are arranging a funeral for Mrs Hawkins' father-in-law, Mr Robbins."

"Which is why we have to find my husband," Mrs Hawkins said, as if this explained everything.

Did she only want him back for the funeral?

"Ah, yes. Well, you finish what you need to and PC Oliver and I'll take a stroll outside. There's a path down to the water, isn't there? Is that where the boat's gone missing from?"

"Yes," replied Maisie Hawkins, "but you got to be ever so careful. It's awful slippy, what with the rain and all. Ginny can show you. Get your boots on, girl, then show these gentlemen where your dad's path is."

The woman's words came out in a rush and she'd flushed puce red. She wasn't happy about his suggestion.

The girl sidestepped round PC Oliver, leaned against the wall of the tiny porch and pulled on a pair of wellington boots, then she opened the door and went outside without a word. Bob looked back at Mrs Hawkins.

"My daughter is a bit . . ." She gave him an apologetic smile. "She's . . ." She turned to the doctor for support. "Ned, can you go with them? You know about Ginny."

The doctor got to his feet but Bob waved a hand for him to sit down. "Thank you, sir, but we'll be quite all right on our own." Nevertheless, the doctor followed him out. "No, really, doctor, don't trouble. Better if we do this on our own. The young lady can come straight back the minute we know where to go."

"As you wish," the doctor muttered, forced to retreat.

Bob was cursing under his breath. He shouldn't have let himself get distracted thinking about Joan; he should have picked up on the dynamics in the room the moment they'd entered. It was obviously going to take longer to get back into harness than he'd thought. But then he'd never expected to be called back into the police, never dreamed when he bought a two-up-two-down in a one-shop, one-eyed Cornish village that he'd be returning to police work again. He blew through his ample cheeks and deliberately walked in the opposite direction to the way he'd seen PC Oliver follow the girl.

A narrow, paved path led past the back door to the cottage and past a broken kitchen window. Bob studied the window for a moment then continued past the outdoor privy and a woodshed, then round a large, well-protected henhouse and through a cottage garden given over to vegetables. There was evidence of recent work despite the rain. Then on, down a dog-leg turn to where the PC was standing, moon-faced, gaping at the girl.

The girl, Ginny, pushed a lock of wavy, fair hair out of her eyes and gave Bob a glorious smile as he approached, but didn't say a word. Then she turned the honey smile on the young PC and pointed vaguely at the boy's large feet.

"This is the path, sir," Laurie stated, as if divining the riddle of the Sphinx.

"Is it, now?" Bob couldn't keep the sarcasm out of his voice, but neither boy nor girl appeared to notice. "Thank you, miss, very kind. We can manage from here. You go back in and help your mum."

She stared at him for what seemed longer than was polite, making him wonder if she was deaf. Then she said "All right", and turned and skipped back the way she'd come.

"Whoa," said Bob, "if that one's not away with the fairies, I'm Father Christmas."

"She's the angel," Laurie Oliver said.

"What?"

"The angel. My brothers called her 'the angel' because Roger said she reminded him of one of the angels in our chapel windows at school. He and Sam were dead keen on her; used to sit on the quay when she was mending her father's nets. But actually, I don't think she's . . ."

"Got the wings *and* the halo?"

The boy looked confused. "I was going to say 'quite right in the head'."

"Mm." Bob nodded. "I got the idea."

He looked out to sea again, shading his eyes. A Midlander by birth, he could never quite get used to the sense of freedom and unexplored possibilities the sea offered. For a few seconds he was lost, studying blue on blue, then snapped back to attention. "Right, you seem to know these cliffs like a native – you first."

It was more difficult getting down than he'd anticipated, and PC Oliver's new boots lost their shine well before they reached the shingle.

"Looks like the tide is coming in," Laurie said, bending down to feel the dry, stony sand. "We had better be quick, sir – Sarge."

"Is this one of the caves you mentioned?" Bob asked, indicating a narrow cavern-like fissure in the cliff.

"Yes, but I don't think we have much time to get into it, sir." The boy threw up his hands. "It's no good, sir, I'm sorry. It's habit, you see – the 'sir' business. Could you bear with me for a while, until I get used to things?"

If Bob had been close enough he'd have given the boy a warm-hearted slap on the back. As it was, standing a good two yards away, he gave a crooked smile and said, "You take all the time you need. And as for having time to get into that cave, we can come back after high tide or tomorrow, earlier in the day."

He looked down and shook a ripple of blackened seaweed off a sturdy brown shoe then turned a large pink-striated pebble with the same foot. A small crab scuttled hastily into a moat around a rocky protrusion. Taking in the way sharp, misshapen rocks emerged from the shingle in almost parallel rows, Bob said, "If it's true what they say about the smuggling in these parts, and smugglers really used the caves along here to store their booty, they must have known the coast better than the backs of their hands."

In daylight one could perhaps take a reference from the cliff above to calculate where the tips of the rocks were lurking to rip your hull from under you; but in the dark it would be impossible, unless they used guiding lights. And whoever handled the guide lamps had to be on the cliff path itself – or up in the cottage. He tried to imagine what it would have been like on a stormy night, getting a laden rowing boat into this cove after fetching the tea, 'baccy and brandy from a ship further out in the Plymouth sea lane. It must have been very, very dangerous, and very lucrative, to make it worthwhile. But you'd have to be an expert or very greedy, or mad, or all three, to do it in a storm.

He ambled over to a line of jagged rocks and followed it down to the water's edge then back again. There was no way to determine whether the fisherman Stan Hawkins had been here since his wife had last seen him or not. She'd reported the boat missing, but that didn't mean he'd been in it, or fallen out of it.

The boy was right, though – the tide was coming in, and judging by the amount of fresh seaweed on the upper edge of the rough shingle the sea filled the cove at every tide. Although, yes, there was something. "What's that?" he asked, pointing at the entrance to the sea cave.

Laurie crunched across the rough, grey sand, peering at the cave then caught sight of what Bob was indicating and scrambled into the dark cavern. Pointing at a large metal ring in the rock wall, he asked, "Do you mean this?"

"Must be where Hawkins ties up his boat," Bob called.

Laurie reached out and took a short length of thick rope in his hand, saying, "Sergeant Robbins, you'd better look at this."

Joining him, Bob grabbed the short length of rope attached to the ring. "It's been cut," he said, "sawn off. Now why would Hawkins – or anyone – do that?"

"It's a bit odd, sir. It would have taken a good bit of time to saw through that, unless he had a special knife for the job."

"Fish-gutting knife, perhaps? Maybe. One of those nasty blades Home Guarders get issued now? Possibly. Come on, we'd better get back and talk to the wife."

Bob was pleased with their unexpected little outing until he was a third of the way back up the slippery terraced path to the cottage. By half way his heart was hammering in his head and he had no alternative but to stop and get his breath back.

"Go on up," he gasped, trying to stand straight so the Apollo in uniform could get past him and stride on up the cliff. "Go on, wait for me up there. Only," he raised a slightly trembling hand, "not a word about this when we get back to Cready, all right? If the Constabulary go calling old farts like me back to work when we should be sitting in our back gardens enjoying our well-earned rest, they can't complain about us not being fit. But I don't want it round Cready station that I'm decrepit. Got me?"

PC Oliver grinned. "Got you, sir. Not a word from me, scout's honour."

"'Scout's honour'," Bob muttered, watching with undisguised envy as the boy leaped up the remaining steps. "Sending whelps and pensioners out on proper police work . . . What do they expect? . . ." Bob chuntered on as he scrambled as best he could to the top.

Once on the level again, he paused and listened: the oystercatchers and turnstones that had flown off when he and Laurie descended to the beach had returned. He looked down but couldn't see them. *Perfect hiding place*, he thought to himself: *ye olde pirates and smugglers down below, and ye olde customs officers up here, and none the wiser.*

When he got round to the front of the cottage, Mrs Hawkins was in her porch saying goodbye to the vicar and the doctor, whom she addressed as Ned. Dr MacManus evidently had something to tell him, though, for as soon as they reached the gate he said something to the vicar, who set off uphill on his own; then the doctor coughed slightly and made a small beckoning gesture.

Bob nodded in response. "PC Oliver, can you go in and run through the details Mrs Hawkins gave the desk sergeant, please. I need to get something from the car." He joined the doctor and they walked out onto the road.

"Yes, sir, how can I help?" Bob asked.

"It's not exactly help I'm after," Dr MacManus replied softly.

Dr MacManus was a fair-haired, freckled Scotsman, paling to grey. Neither tall nor well built, he nevertheless had a no-nonsense air about him. Not a man to be crossed, Bob thought, and another non-local, like himself, which for no reason he could name he found reassuring. "Go on," he said.

"I only wanted to warn – ask, I should say – that you are gentle with Mrs Hawkins. She's had a terrible week of it. Not just a week, either."

Bob took an un-ironed handkerchief from a trouser pocket to wipe his brow, giving the doctor time to choose his words.

"I don't think I'm breaking any confidences if I tell you Stan Hawkins was not the best of husbands. And she's been caring for his father for months now, single-handed. The girl Ginny is a sweetheart, but not . . ."

"The full tea service? Mm, I'd rather picked that up for myself. So you're saying Mr Hawkins has taken himself off on other occasions?" Bob kept his eyes averted, stuffing his handkerchief back into the pocket of his brown tweed jacket. "Is that why she waited three days before reporting him missing?"

"Ah, as to that, I couldn't say. But I have had to *treat* Mrs Hawkins, if you see what I mean?"

"Treat her, sir?"

The doctor paused and gave a dry cough. "I don't think I'll be contravening my oath if I tell you she's had a cut over the eye that needed stitching." He coughed again, evidently torn between his role and oath as a physician and a desire to help the woman in question. "And terrible bruising, what she'd let me look at. A broken arm . . . She said she'd taken a fall down the stairs. The cut over the eye was another *accidental* fall."

"I see. Thank you, sir. I'll bear this in mind and tread carefully. You don't by any chance have any theories about where Mr Hawkins might have gone with his boat, or what he might have been doing, do you?"

The doctor looked away, "No, no, I can't say I do. It was very bad weather."

Somewhere in the distance there was a heavy booming noise. The two men exchanged glances. "Tip and run bomber," sighed the doctor. "I hope I'm not going to be busy this day. Why can't they drop their unused bombs over the water, it's close enough."

"Could it be that one of them did?" Bob said. "That might explain our missing fisherman." Although it didn't explain the sawn-off rope.

Dr MacManus got into his car and Bob, musing on the doctor's evasion regarding Hawkins' activities, returned to the front porch. Knocking a polite rat-tat on the open door, he went in.

"I'll put the kettle on again," Mrs Hawkins said, getting up from a chair at the table next to PC Oliver, who also got to his feet. Bob flapped a hand for the boy to sit, but kept his eyes on the woman, who was more at ease now.

"Bless you, ma'am, that might just save my life," he said with undisguised pleasure, then cursed himself for saying something so crass in a household that had just suffered one bereavement and was awaiting news on another. "Sod it all," he muttered to himself as he let his weight fall into a fireside chair.

Feeling eyes on him, he looked up; the angel-girl was staring at him. He gave an apologetic grin, deciding in that instant to drink his tea and be gone the minute he had answers to the questions concerning the boat and the cave. He'd come back and make a better job of it tomorrow, and bring the lad with him, show him Detective Sergeant Robbins might have left the police force nigh on ten years ago to work in insurance then take early retirement, but he still knew how to run an investigation.

When Mrs Hawkins returned with a laden tray he got to his feet and waited until she'd served them from an aged teapot. Refusing the offer of sugar and keeping his eyes on his cup, he said, "Is there anything else you can tell us, Mrs Hawkins? Something you may have forgotten this morning?"

She looked away, exactly as the doctor had done, and shook her head. "No. I wish there was."

"So the last time you saw your husband was three days ago in the afternoon? And he went . . .? Do you know where he was going?"

"No. He didn't – doesn't – tell me much. He did say he wasn't putting out in the trawler till the weather got better. I thought he'd be down at the quay doing repairs and the like. It's what he normally does in bad weather."

"And he didn't come home that evening?"

Mrs Hawkins looked at her cup as she stirred her tea. "Stan goes to the pub most nights. Every night, I s'pose. The landlord saw him out on Monday night and locked the door behind him. About ten-thirty-ish, he said, perhaps nearer eleven. He'd called 'last orders' and Stan was last to leave."

"But he didn't come straight home?" Bob rattled the question off fast, catching Mrs Hawkins with her cup to her lips. She set it back with a small clatter in the saucer.

"I've been trying to remember the last thing Stan said before he left the house, but I can't. I went back to Cleve House in the evening you see, to be with Mrs Metherall. Ginny was here, and his father."

Bob looked at the girl, who was now gazing across the small room at the mantelpiece. "And your daughter didn't hear or see him come in?"

Mrs Hawkins shook her head. "When I got back in the morning . . . Stan's father had passed away . . ."

Bob beat a quiet tattoo with the stubby fingers of his right hand and let an awkward silence hang in the air, then broke it with, "So after being at the pub your husband went out in his boat to do a bit of night fishing – in a storm?"

"His boat's not there, that's what I told Jimmy Beer, our Special," Mrs Hawkins replied. "I looked when I got back from the vicarage."

"From the vicarage?"

"As soon as I got in Tuesday morning and saw what had happened here . . . I dashed up to the vicarage. They've got a telephone, you see. I called Dr MacManus and came straight back. Then I sent Ginny down to the quay to fetch her pa, thinking he'd be on his trawler. But he wasn't there. So while Dr MacManus was here I went down to the cove in case he was there – t'was awful slippy. Stan's boat was gone."

"And the rope had been cut. Why would he do that, do you think?"

The woman looked at him with undisguised surprise. "The rope's been cut? I didn't notice. I just saw the boat had gone and . . . I was in a hurry to get back up here, in a bit of a tizz, what with one thing and another. I thought prob'ly the tide and the storm had taken it."

Bob let another silence hang in the stale cottage air while he sipped at his tea. Eventually he put his cup and saucer back on the tray and got to his feet. "We'll get a proper local search going. You'll let us know if you remember anything we ought to know. Just one thing – you said your husband has three boats. There's the trawler in the harbour and the missing boat here – where's the other one?"

"Where it usually is. He uses it off the beach, and hires it to holidaymakers sometimes. It's still down there, and the trawler's moored alongside the quay – the *Porth Rose* she's called. There's an old lugger in the harbour as well. It was his father's. But Stan hasn't been out in it since his father was taken bad a few years back."

"And we've got the names of his crew – that right, PC Oliver?"

Before the boy could speak, Mrs Hawkins said, "Stan usually went out with two of the Deakin boys from Inner Harbour; sometimes young Roy Braund from Victoria Villas goes with them, but he's still at grammar school. I've asked them all and no one knows anything 'cept that Stan left the Boot . . . like he usually did – does. And they've all looked. They got together yesterday with some others from the pub and they went off in different directions, but nobody's seen anything."

"Mmm," Bob looked out of the windows. "Did they go into the mine, do you know?"

Mrs Hawkins went rigid. "Prob'ly."

"Well, we'll have another look anyway. Can you give us the address, Mrs Hawkins, for the Deakin boys?"

"Third cottage on the left as you go into Inner Harbour from the sea wall. That one's Tommy's now. His brother's two doors up. Knock at any door, someone'll tell you. You can't miss them. They're identical twins – got white hair and white eyebrows. If anyone knows what Stan was doing, though, they will. If they'll tell you."

Bob gave her an inquiring look. "Like that, is it?"

The woman nodded in reply. "They're a close lot, the harbour Deakins, even when they've got nothing to hide."

"And you think they might have something to hide – relating to your husband?" Maisie Hawkins went pink. He gave her a moment to speak, and when she didn't, he said, "I'll talk to them, and if it's all right with you, PC Oliver and I will pass by tomorrow to have another look in your cove."

"Oh! But if the boat's not there . . . I mean, will that be morning or afternoon, sir? You see, I work over at Cleve House, as a sort of housekeeper, and then I've got my father-in-law's funeral to arrange."

"Of course you have. I'm sorry, but we can't leave it. Not to worry, he might be back by then. He's gone off on his own like this before, hasn't he?"

Maisie Hawkins clasped her hands together. "He sometimes goes into Plymouth if he's got a big catch. The trawler was fitted with an engine a few years ago . . . Means he can come and go easier. He sometimes puts in and stays there."

"Overnight?"

Maisie Hawkins looked away. "Sometimes longer if he's waiting for something to come in or if he's . . . I don't know, really."

"But the trawler's in the harbour, you say?"

"Yes."

"We'll have look at the casualty lists, anyway, just in case. Jerry's been busy over Plymouth again, despite the weather. Your husband may have got caught in an air raid."

"I did wonder." Maisie Hawkins met Bob's eye then, concentrating on removing the lid of the teapot and stirring the remaining leaves, she said, "Stan sometimes collects – goods – but he uses the trawler."

"Goods? Not fish?" Bob cocked his head to one side, trying to sense what Mrs Hawkins was reluctant to say. But instead of mentioning black-market goods he said, "I'm very partial to a bit of sea bass. Bit of a fisherman myself, with a rod, of course, not a boat. He'd take his catch in to Plymouth and return with . . .?" Maisie Hawkins put his cup and saucer on the tray. "On his own, or with the Deakin boys?" Bob insisted.

"A couple of the boys went with him, I suppose. Must have done, though I think he could manage the trawler on his own if he had to – with the engine."

Bob gestured to PC Oliver that it was time to go. "One last thing, and you'll have to forgive me asking this, but is there anything special that might help us identify your husband – if he's had an accident?"

"Only his left hand. I told the policeman at the station. Stan's only got the first two fingers and thumb on his left hand – from when he was in the trenches." She held up her own left hand, holding the third and small finger down.

Self-wound to get a "blighty", Bob thought, casting his mind back to the first war. Still, shooting your own left hand, whether by accident or design, was pretty nasty. He looked at the woman. "Yes, we've got that. Well, thank you for the tea, Mrs Hawkins." He turned and nodded a farewell at the girl, who gave a luscious, vacant smile in response.

Before he left the porch, Bob tried one last question. "One thing – put it down to me being an up-countryman, not a local – you said your husband does the odd bit of business in Plymouth. Has that increased lately, what with rationing and so on?" Trapped in the tiny porch, the woman had nowhere to look; he tried to hold her gaze. "No specifics needed. I shan't be asking awkward questions. I just need to know where he goes and who he meets."

"I can't tell you, really. He goes into Looe with most catches, sometimes into Plymouth if he's got a big load, like I said – it depends. I can't tell you who he meets there. You could ask, though. The Deakin boys crew for him, mostly. They might tell you more about the fishing side of things."

"And the other side?"

Mrs Hawkins put a work-reddened hand to her mouth. "We sometimes get – extras – you know, tins and the like."

"What, bartering? A crate of sprats for a can of petrol, that sort of thing?"

"I've never asked, to be honest."

"And you don't know if your husband might have any enemies."

"Enemies! Stan? No. I never thought . . . I mean . . . It doesn't make sense. How would he have got to Plymouth, anyway? We don't have a motor car, and he couldn't possibly have made it in that little old boat, not in the dark and the sea the way it was."

Bob registered the word "dark", and without thinking, patted the woman's arm. "Try not to upset yourself, my dear. I'll come back tomorrow and have another look round. Was this about the same time you saw your husband on Monday?"

Mrs Hawkins nodded; she didn't speak. Bob touched the brim of the hat he'd forgotten to put on – something else he'd got to get used to doing again – and closed the garden gate behind him. The woman waited in the porch until he was in the car.

As they set off, Laurie, who couldn't contain himself, said, "So what do you think, sir? Has he drowned or what?"

"Probably – but there's more to the 'what' than I'd like."

"How do you know?"

"Because Mrs Hawkins couldn't answer a single question with a straight answer."

"You don't think she – I mean – she couldn't have *murdered* him, could she?"

"Nah!"

"No, I suppose not. Nothing dramatic like that happens in a place like this. It's too small and quiet. So . . . I mean, can you tell me what it is that's strange about Mr Hawkins' disappearance, apart from the cut rope? Do you think she might know where he is?"

"No, but she's wished him dead and gone a time or two, I reckon, and she's suffering the guilt of it now. She's covering for him, though. Her hubby's up to a bit of smuggling. What was it in Kipling's poem? 'Baccy for the parson, brandy for the clerk?"

"Five and twenty ponies,
Trotting through the dark –
Brandy for the Parson, baccy for the Clerk.
Them that asks no questions isn't told a lie," Laurie recited.

"'Them that asks no questions' . . ." Bob sighed. "I wish. Why do I think that if we start asking questions in little old Porthferris we're going to find more than we want to know?"

"What, like brandy or buried treasure?"

"Don't be daft. Mind you . . ."

Chapter 4

As the car approached the crooked crossroad junction for the second time that day, Bob said, "Which way for the old mine?"

They turned down a steep hill bordered by high banks that turned sharp right as it levelled and led into the disused copper mine, Wheal Marie. There was a sturdy five-barred gate, but the expected "No trespassing" sign to indicate it was private property was absent. Laurie opened the gate and Bob drove the short distance to an open esplanade overgrown with tufts of grass and bordered by weather-defying hollyhocks.

He had been expecting a picturesque chimney and a tumbledown winding-house such as he'd seen further down the Cornish coast, but was disappointed. All that remained here was a wide door into the hill and a square stone building that might once have been a counting house. Various low brick walls overgrown with weeds suggested other buildings had once stood here, but the locals had evidently been helping themselves to building materials for generations and there was little left above knee height. There was certainly nowhere visible, apart from whatever lay behind the door in the hill, where a grown man could take shelter or stay hidden for three days.

Bob strolled across the open grassy space to examine a row of long stone tables where women and children had once broken and sorted rocks, then wandered to the quayside. At one time Wheal Marie had been a thriving enterprise; there were moorings for the various barges that had once transported the copper by sea to Plymouth, Looe or Falmouth, and brought in explosives and equipment. The mine was at the bottom of a steep hill too far from a main highway for road haulage, especially using horses. He stepped closer to the edge of the jetty. The moorings had been in recent use.

"Oy!" There was a shout from behind him. A giant of a woman and a raggle-taggle group of bony children were doing a quick march towards him.

"You can't come down yer – this is private property! You can't come down yer without permission." The woman's accent was as thick as Cornish cream.

Laurie appeared from behind her, surrounded by more children in various states of dress. "This is Mrs Cottle, sir –"

"Becca Cottle, not *Mrs* Cottle. It's Mrs Benjamin, if you must know. Who be you, then?" the woman demanded, coming close enough to Bob to jab a strong finger in his chest and nearly send him backwards over the quay.

Bob sidestepped out of danger. "Detective Sergeant Robbins, Cready CID, madam," he said, emphasising the "madam" and trying to distance himself at the same time, to no avail. The edge of the quay was still regrettably close. He sidestepped again then executed a nifty fox-trot turn to get out from under the woman's enormous bosom. If she noticed the "madam", it made no difference: she was on the attack.

"What you want down yer? We'm not doing nothing wrong. We got permission from the Colonel. My pa works for the Colonel – he gave us special permission, see."

"Colonel?" Bob queried.

"Colonel Waterson. Don't you know nothin'?" Before Bob could respond, the woman started again in fishwife tones. "Haven't you lot seen enough? Jimmy Beer's looked ev'rywhere, if it's Stan Hawkins you'm seeking. I told him, Stan hasn't been near the mine for at least a . . ." She bit her tongue and tried to button her gaping blouse.

"A week? A month?" Bob offered.

"Can't say, bain't nothing to do with me. I got things to do. I can't be talking yer all day." Becca Cottle Benjamin turned and began walking back the way she'd come.

As she moved, Bob noticed a once brightly-painted gypsy caravan parked under the shelter of the hill. Trying to catch up, he said, "You live here, Mrs Cot– er, Benjamin?"

"I do."

"Pretty caravan," he said, wondering if all the children lived there, too. "I'm new to the district, you see. I was curious to see how the old mine worked." As he walked he noticed tyre marks, not his own. The storm had smoothed them over, but another car had been here recently. "Thought I'd have a look round, see a bit of Cornish heritage."

"B'ain't no heritage yer, I told you. And you can't go in – 'tisn't safe."

"'Tisn't safe," piped a voice from somewhere below. A child with a gummy, green nose and red cheeks shook his head sagely and repeated, "Tisn't safe, mister. We'm not allowed in there. It'll crash in on your ade, see."

"Crush you up like an ol' eggshell," explained another of the brood with such bestial delight that Bob felt himself shudder.

He could think of no reply except, "In that case there's not much point us staying, is there?"

The children shook their heads in unison then raced for the gate as a pack, climbing up on the rungs to wave him off.

Bob felt ridiculous. He'd been outmanoeuvred by a blousy female and a group of small children, but there was no alternative except to tell Laurie Oliver to get back in the car and drive off.

Once out of the gate, Bob kept his eyes on the road and avoided conversation.

"Quite a harridan," Laurie said quietly.

Bob grunted in reply and Laurie Oliver was wise enough to stay silent until they were nearly into town, when he said, "Should we not have gone down to Inner Harbour, sir, to talk to the Deakin brothers?"

"I hadn't forgotten, but it's best not to knock on doors with that type. If they're the sort I think they are. I'll wander down to Porth quay later and have a chat with them about boats and fishing." As he spoke, Bob was formulating another plan. It involved a set of fishing rods and a folding stool for the Wheal Marie quay on the following afternoon.

But both plans were jettisoned within the space of a few minutes. As they walked through the police station door, Sergeant Mallett, the desk officer, lurched out at them. "You've got to get out to Kerrith Cross. Bloody Kraut plane dropped a bomb – missed the new airstrip and the RAF huts and landed on the village school. There's kiddies and teachers trapped inside – if they're still alive."

Chapter 5

When Bob Robbins knocked at Maisie Hawkins' door the next day there was no answer, for which he was grateful. He waited a few moments before trying again then wandered around the cottage to the back door. It was unlocked, as he expected. Opening the latch, he called out, "That you, Mrs Hawkins? Can I come in?" and knowing full well he had no right to do so, he entered the small kitchen. It was basic but spotlessly clean. He stepped back onto the door mat and wiped his feet carefully, calling out, "Mrs Hawkins." There was no reply so he went into the sitting room. It was as it had been the previous day: table and three wooden chairs, another chair beside the fireplace; two easy chairs in floral upholstery. He opened the heavy sideboard: plates and dishes, no alcohol – meaning Stan Hawkins did his drinking elsewhere. The grate was cold, clean of the previous night's ashes. He sniffed: not a trace of alcohol, pipe tobacco or cigarettes.

Standing at the bottom of the stairs, he said, "You up there, Mrs Hawkins?" then climbed the narrow staircase from the kitchen. Floorboards creaked on the landing. He opened one door – a pink room with a view of the sea, an old-fashioned jug and washbasin on a stand, a pile of girl's comic weeklies on a bedside table: the daughter's room. He went to the window and examined the view. From here she could look out to sea; she could also see the path running round the house and the top of the cliff steps, but she couldn't see the beach below.

He crossed to the other bedroom. The window was patched up with a piece of hardboard. Otherwise, it was immaculate. A double bed, somewhat sagging in the middle, a mahogany wardrobe that looked as if it belonged in another, bigger house. A washbasin used that morning – the linen towel still damp to the touch. Not much sign of a man about except a pair of carpet slippers on one side of the bed. He opened the wardrobe – mothballs, one tweed jacket, two pairs of men's trousers, a gabardine mackintosh and a woman's thick, brown woollen coat, the sleeves showing signs of wear, not new. He ran his hand over the collar, lifted the coat hanger and sniffed. The coat was slightly damp. He put it back as it had been, closed the door carefully and went back downstairs. It wasn't a poor household, no smell of poverty or neglect – on the contrary. But there was nothing to suggest an extra income, not a hint of luxury anywhere.

Bob tutted despite himself; he'd fancied Stan Hawkins as a wide boy, a bit of a spiv, using his fishing boats for more lucrative cargo than sardines. Perhaps the proceeds went straight into the till at the pub. Closing the back door, he went to the outhouse. It was full of washing equipment: a tub and mangle, a tin bath. He poked along the shelves – soap and soda crystals, a tin of rat poison, shoe polish and household bits and bobs. No bottles of whisky or brandy, no tobacco. A few large Kilner jars of home-made jam – and, yes, two large tins of factory jam: strawberry, untouched and dusty. He wasn't sure what he was looking for, but this wasn't it. He picked up the rat poison and opened it with a coin. The tin was full. "Didn't think so," he said to himself. "Still, only takes a pinch, a teaspoonful now and again." He replaced the tin and cast about for anything unusual. Nothing.

Closing the outhouse door carefully behind him, Bob made for the cliff steps. It hadn't rained for twenty-four hours, something he'd learned was unusual in this part of Cornwall, but the path was still slippery. Doing his best to stay upright, he scrambled down to the beach. The tide was on the ebb, leaving that unmistakable, fresh smell that never failed to lift his spirits. A cormorant was drying its wings on a rock not far out. Bob felt in his pocket for his small binoculars and trained them on the shaggy black wings now shimmering petrol colours in the sun. But he had work to do. He popped the binoculars back in his pocket and crunched across the rough shingle to the sea cave.

The tide had been right up to the entrance, but a few feet in it was perfectly dry. Bob hesitated; he wasn't keen on confined spaces. Then from behind him he heard boots crossing the beach.

"Sarge, are you down here?" called a plummy voice.

Bob returned to the daylight. "Right on time, boy. Find anything?"

"Yes and no. Constable Beer says there's another cove like this belonging to the hotel, which actually I already knew."

"And?"

"That's it, really. Nowhere else a boat could put in between here and the mine. After that, going east, there's only Whitsand Bay and the Tamar Estuary. He suggested we look on Looe Island. He says the currents would have taken a body out towards Looe Island from here, then down westward towards Falmouth."

Bob nodded in approval. "Good, so we know which ports to alert. You get onto that as soon as we get back. Got a torch with you?"

"Er, no, sorry, sir – Sarge."

"Drat – I left mine up in the car. Nip back up and get it, there's a good lad."

While he waited, Bob took out his small binoculars and studied the bushes and brambles on the cliff above for goldfinches. Finding nothing, he panned the beach area. Two parallel, razor-edged rows of rock formed a natural channel into the cove. At high water a rowing boat could get right up to the cave, but whoever was in it would have to be an expert.

When PC Oliver returned with the big torch they went into the cave. It was narrow, but high enough for Laurie to stay upright with his helmet on. The floor showed it had been in use: sand packed down hard, but there was nothing out of place – no boxes or tins, no sacks, not even a pile of old nets. Reluctantly, Bob went in further but a large, bulging rock blocked his way. He gave the torch to Laurie. "Take your hat off and see how far back it goes," he said, abandoning any hope of shifting his rotund bulk round the rock without embarrassment.

Laurie took the torch and scrambled further in then called, "It looks as if it's . . . Yes, it's been bricked up. There's a sort of wall." He scrambled back and handed the torch to Bob. "Have a look, sir."

"Nah, I'll take your word for it. You couldn't get much past this point anyway, could you?"

Laurie studied the narrow space. "Probably not – depends on what you want to hide. If you used small containers, a shopping basket for example . . . but I couldn't see anything except some old bricks."

"Meaning there could be a storeroom?"

"More likely to be the mine, sir. There are probably tunnels behind here – if you think about the geography of it."

Bob nodded. "Yes, probably. Well, we've done our bit. You've established which way a body would drift, and I've drawn a blank on the contraband. Let's go."

"What about the sawn-off rope?"

Bob rubbed his nose. "Have another look, see what you think."

Laurie examined the short length of cut rope then tugged at it. "It's got a proper knot, sir. It won't come loose when the tide fills the cave."

"Mystery," said Bob. "Maybe we'll find out one day. In the meantime, I've got a desk load of paperwork to get through. Come on, we'd better get you back as well. Mallett said he wanted you this afternoon. Looks like the missing Mr Hawkins has gone in the water and there's not much more we can do, other than send out to coastal stations and wait till he and or his boat's washed up somewhere."

"And the contraband?"

"Contraband – war profiteering? Nothing evident. It was only a hunch."

Chapter 6

"I've found a man!" Rosy-cheeked Ginny gasped out the words before she was through the door to their out-house laundry.

Maisie fed another sodden sheet through the ancient mangle; fingers deftly tucked out of the way, eyes focused on the rollers. Keeping her scarf-turbaned head low, she said, "What's that?"

"Ma, I've found a boy! Only he's a man, a real man."

Relieved, almost laughing, but still taking care to keep the chapped fingers of her left hand away from the heavy wooden rollers, Maisie said, "That's nice. Do I know him?"

"Don't think so. I never seen him before."

"What?" Maisie looked at her daughter, exasperated. "I haven't got time for nonsense, Ginny. Pick up that basket and hang out the sheets if you've got nothing better to do."

"No! Listen, there's a man lying in the woods. He might be dead." Ginny's halo of golden hair moved as she spoke.

Maisie took her attention from the mangle, straightened her back and without turning, she asked, "Where?"

"In the spinney. I was looking for flowers and mushrooms."

"It's too early for mushrooms. You be careful, some toadstools can poison you just by touching. My ma told me that." Maisie sighed. "Oh, never mind. Who is it?"

"A man. I told you, a man."

"What sort of man – young or old?" Maisie was trying to keep her voice calm, but her body was reacting with a conflicting and simultaneous sense of panic and relief. Could Ginny not recognise her own father after a week? "What's he like?"

"I think he's tall. Long. Thin. He's in the bracken – under a tree."

Maisie's skin went from hot to cold: *not Stan, then.* "If you don't know him and he's not from these parts, we don't need to worry, sweetheart – leave him be."

"Ma! Listen, he's lying there under the trees in the wet. He might be dead!"

Maisie wound the handle of the mangle until another flattened sheet doubled itself into the tin bath below then she looked up at her daughter. "What exactly are you saying, girl?"

"There's a man lying up against a tree in the glebe spinney. I think he's unconscious."

"Not dead?"

"Might be. I was looking for mushrooms and I moved some ferns and there he was, sort of hidden. He must be soppin' wet."

That would make three. Death always comes in threes. Maisie straightened the freshly rolled sheet in the tub then, digging her thumbs into the small of her back to relieve her laundry-day backache, she tried again. "Old or young, did you say? Or would you call him middle-aged?"

"Young. I didn't look that close. He might have – you know – been drinking beer like my pa. He's awful still . . ."

"Didn't smell, though?"

"Smell?"

"Dead creatures smell, Ginny – you know that."

"Oh, yes. No, there wasn't no smell."

Maisie turned around and poked at the next set of sheets in the boiler with a pair of wooden tongs. "Prob'ly one of the Stevenson boys, gone out poachin' with too much inside him. Never catch anything, they boys. Rabbit would have to leap into their arms and beg to be cooked . . ."

"Tisn't one of them – I know them. You going to come and look? We've got to do something, can't just leave him."

Oh, we can, Ginny, we can, thought Maisie. *We can leave him exactly where he is. I don't want to know who it is, and I certainly don't want any more nosy policemen poking around and asking questions.* Nevertheless, she dried her hands on a frayed towel and said, "How muddy is it? Do I need my boots?"

They walked the short distance up the asphalted lane to the glebe-land spinney in silence. Maisie's mind was racing: *Ginny might be wrong. It's always been a possibility, Stan lying dead drunk under a tree or the like. Ginny isn't the only one that comes up here. These days, everyone's after something to put in a pot. It would be strange, though, if he'd been up here all the time and half the village tramping round him, planting gin-traps and setting bits of wire.*

As far as she knew, the police had looked all along the coastline as far as they could walk in either direction then used local boats to check the rocks and accessible coves. Stan's three-man crew had taken boats out and poked along the rocky inlets where there were caves they weren't too keen on the police investigating. They'd even moored off tiny Looe Island and searched there. Regulars of the Fisherman's Boot had joined in the hunt and the local Home Guard platoon had, they said, scoured the woods around Wheal Marie mine and up here in the spinney. No one had found a sign of him.

Nor anything remotely strange except for the cut rope and his missing boat, which must have been stolen. Stan would never have gone out in that little boat at night in a storm. *Would he?* Everyone said he must have fallen *into* the water – under the influence. Like most boatmen, Stan couldn't swim. He might have missed his footing somewhere . . . All the possibilities led to him being washed up on a beach along the coast, not up here under a pile of wet leaves. Still, if they found him now, up here in the spinney, Ned MacManus could do a death certificate and she'd get her widow's pension.

Mother and daughter climbed the stile into the woods belonging to the parish church and tramped along a rough, puddle-littered path until it split in two. The left-hand fork led down to a wooded area belonging to the copper mine then on down to a row of abandoned miners' cottages. The mine, Wheal Marie, had shut down years ago but the land around it – for all that it was heaving with unhealthy minerals – was a godsend to families like the Inner Harbour Deakin clan and the Stevensons, who set rabbit traps and caught pheasants nesting in the thick undergrowth. *It'll be one of them sleeping it off.* Ginny wasn't too bright at the best of times.

But Ginny took the right-hand fork, not the left, and after a short distance left the path altogether. They were on a badger run, by the looks of it. Then Ginny cut off to the right again and began to wade through waist-high bracken and ferns.

"I left my basket so I'd find him again," she said. "Over there. See?"

Balanced on a fold of ancient fronded leaves was a shallow wicker basket, and slumped against the bole of an ancient oak was a long shape, a man half leaning against the tree, half lying on his side, fast asleep. Or dead.

It wasn't Big Stan. It was a much younger man with dirty blond hair. He had dark rings around his eyes; one was purple and swollen where he'd been punched. Maisie bent down and put a hand against his cheek. He was warm to the touch and lithe inside a brown tweed jacket and twill trousers. His brown boots were salt stained and made of soft leather – nothing like army issue, so probably not a deserter or a downed pilot.

"He's a foreigner," Maisie muttered. "Foreign, definitely foreign."

Despite the blondish hair he was swarthy, with a day's growth of black beard. He looked different to a dark Cornishman, and nothing like how she imagined a German to be. Getting to her feet, Maisie peered up at the branches of the trees for a parachute. She wandered deeper into the spinney, peering up and down, this way and that, looking for any sign of how the stranger had arrived at the oak and collapsed. There was nothing.

Unless he came by sea . . . She went back and put a hand on one of his boots. It was damp, but everything around them was damp. Slowly, gingerly, she checked the boy's pockets for a gun. The trouser pockets were empty, not even a handkerchief, but inside the jacket was a woman's red leather purse containing pound notes, half-crowns, shilling pieces and small change. She put it back and pulled the jacket closed.

"He's alive, isn't he?" asked Ginny. "I thought he might be. That's why I ran."

"He is for now; won't be for long if we leave him here." Maisie probed rough fingers between the man's damp collar and longish hair, resting a finger against the pulse in his neck. "We'd better get him into the dry. Doesn't look like he's hurt: the ground's soft, he can't have cracked his head. 'Tis strange, though." Maisie's Cornish lilt was stronger than usual.

"Why doesn't he wake up?" asked Ginny, hunkering down and patting the young man gently on the shoulder. "Wake up, sir. Wake you up, now."

Maisie knelt down in the damp and reopened his jacket. He didn't have a gun but there might be a bullet wound, it was wartime, after all: anything could happen these days, even down here in a little Cornish village. He was wearing a good quality shirt, dirty and muddy in places but there was no sign of blood. As she gently pulled the jacket from his shoulder, something glinted: a knife. A very sharp, open flick-knife. Maisie touched the thin blade then closed it and rubbed her thumb and forefinger up and down the ridged-horn handle.

"Might be a POW, I s'pose, unless he's staying at the hotel. He's a bit thin, though. They Italians working at Glebe Farm get a proper feeding, that I do know. Besides, POWs get blue overalls." Ideas and thoughts jumbled into words: how on earth did a stranger come to be unconscious under a tree in the middle of the glebe-land spinney? "He must have come up the path from the mine and got lost," she said, placing the closed knife carefully in her own coat pocket and rocking back on her haunches, staring at the man's face, trying to glean information from his features. Struggling to her feet she said decisively, "Whoever he is, he's some mother's son and we'd better get him back to the cottage into the warm."

"I'll go down to the village, get Jimmy Beer." Ginny had already turned to go.

"No!"

Ginny looked at her mother in surprise. "Why not?"

"Never mind why not. Go and get the big wheelbarrow. We'll get him home same way as we come."

"What about the stile?"

"We'll go through the churchyard, then. If Reverend Hughes sees us *he* can help. Come on, girl, move yourself. Boy'll catch pneumonia out here in this wet."

Ginny turned as if to go then stopped. "Ma," she said slowly, almost in a whisper, "suppose he's a German . . ."

"Come to spy on Porthferris? Whatever for?"

"P'raps he's on his way to the dockyard in Plymouth, or coming up here to meet someone."

"You're not so soft, are you Ginny? More likely he's a Frenchie come across on a boat or one of ours who's had enough of fighting." She paused, "Most prob'ly one of ours, a pilot or someone from a crashed plane that's got out through France. But we don't need to go making a fuss about him with Special Constables before we know what's what. S'posing he can't be doing with guns and war. S'posing he's in the same state your pa was, back in '17. All shook up with the shooting and that . . . Go and get the barrow, there's a good girl. I can't face having bobbies back in my house – not unless this boy here wakes up asking for snitzel and schnapps – then you can scream from the rooftops. Go on, off you go."

Maisie Rose waited until Ginny was out of sight, then she sat back against the other side of the big tree, bent her head to her knees and began to howl with frustration and relief.

Chapter 7

Maisie set the young man's vicious knife on the mantelpiece then struck a match and set it to a wooden taper to light the latest scrunched up government pamphlet on "mend and make do" in the grate. Standing back, she watched the paper flame then shrivel then waited until a spiral of sweet-smelling wood smoke drifted into the silent room. A bit of dry kindling cracked with a shot of sparks. She felt, rather than saw, the young man in the truckle bed sit bolt upright.

Afraid to startle him further, Maisie turned slowly to look at him. "I'm sorry," she said, "I didn't mean to wake you. But I'm glad you are. We were worried it was concussion. I was going to get Dr MacManus then I thought best not, could be awkward. You staying at the hotel? You want me to get someone? I can go down myself if . . ." Maisie stopped; she was gabbling with nervousness.

The boy – although Ginny was right to say he was more of a young man than a boy – lowered himself back onto his pillow using an elbow and winced.

"Careful now, you've got a lot of bad bruises. Looks like you been kicked around. Best not to move too much – prob'ly you've got cracked ribs. Wouldn't be surprised." Maisie took a step forward, hand outstretched then halted.

The young man stared at her through dark eyes. His hair was long and lank, and a greyish shade of blond, but there was a thick, jet black covering across his bony chest and his eyebrows were black too, which made her wonder if he'd been using hair dye, and if so, why. Maisie smiled at him then walked quietly across the small sitting room to the kitchen door. Taking care not to get too close to him, as one might do to avoid alarming a wounded animal, she smiled again and nodded reassuringly then went into the kitchen and stayed just behind the door, watching to see if he'd try to get out of bed; try to escape.

When he thought she'd gone, he waited, as if to be sure he was alone then lifted himself slowly, painfully onto his elbows. With one hand he pushed down the white sheet and soft beige blanket to check if he was wearing the trousers to match the gaping striped pyjama jacket. He wasn't. There were scabbed gashes on his legs; she hadn't wanted to cover them.

The young man pulled the covers back over his body and looked around, taking in his surroundings. Maisie tried to interpret how he would be seeing her home, noting in turn the narrow bed, the door to the porch, how light filtered through the thin curtains, the fireplace, her mother's old high-backed easy chairs re-upholstered in floral chintz, and the smaller one for Ginny in plain, forest green. He moved his head awkwardly, squinting at the glass of cloudy liquid on the chair by his bed, at the plate with two fat, golden squares of flapjack: something he probably didn't recognise. He didn't seem English. He'd been ferried across from France, most likely on a fishing boat, and set down under their cliff, left to find his own luck. Or maybe he was from Spain. People were starving in Spain, they said.

Maisie had never been abroad; she'd never even been to London, but she supposed the boy would look at his surroundings and the food on the plate and know he was in England – leastways, not in his own country.

He looked around again, probably for his clothes: they were hanging on the washing line at the back of the cottage, out of sight from the road. Maisie wasn't sure why she had thought that, but something told her he was to be kept a secret. This was no German spy; he was someone to be protected.

Awkwardly, the young man tried to shift into a sitting position. Pain in his chest sent him gasping for breath. He collapsed back on the pillow and closed his eyes. Maisie patted her cheeks with a strange sense of satisfaction and closed the door.

"You going to call Dr MacManus?"

Maisie jumped. She'd been so absorbed watching the boy, she hadn't realised Ginny was at the sink peeling potatoes.

"Don't think so. No need, really. Soon as he's better he can be off on his way."

"Are you going to tell that policeman that came about pa?"

"No! Gordon says he was here yesterday, when he passed by after his milk round, while we were up at Cleve. Nosing about my house while I'm out, he was. We don't need police round here again. Although I s'pect you'd like to see that young PC again, wouldn't you?"

Ginny turned and grinned.

"Well you can forget it, my girl. You'm too old for a boy like that."

Ginny looked at her mother – she didn't understand.

Maisie sighed. "We don't need any more men in this house, Ginny. Besides, how do we know he hasn't got away from the POW camp at Trerulefoot or that quarry at Treluggan? Not but he looks too soft to have been doing any labouring like that. Whoever he is, we'll get him mended and send him on his way, and that's that."

Later that evening, Maisie opened the sitting room door from the kitchen and looked in – fearing the boy was still there, fearing he was gone. It was time to close the blackout curtains and light the small lamp on the sideboard. She entered quietly, hugging a water-bottle in thick tartan flannel to her ample breasts, and went up to the stranger's narrow cot. Holding it out to him, hands slightly shaking, she said, "I brought this for you. It's dreadful chilly out for this time of year. Still, might be nice in a week or two, usually is for the village fête. 'Cept we had a dreadful thunderstorm last year, I was forgetting that. You all right, m'dear?" Words tumbled from her, but slow and low and calm, belying her internal doubts and panic.

Lifting the blanket at his feet, she tucked in the warm bottle then sat on the end of the makeshift bed as best she could and stayed where she was, studying him in the shadowy light. Before long he returned her look through thick black eyelashes and smiled. He had, Maisie thought, a heartbreaking smile, like a child wanting to be cuddled, like a lover wanting to be kissed . . . She got up, picked up the glass of stale barley water from the bedside chair and left the room.

The tears began before she'd closed the door. She let them roll unchecked down her cheeks and fall onto the warm front of her blouse. Salty water from a shell that had once been called "my darling Maisie Rose".

When Ginny came in through the back door, Maisie woke with a start. She had fallen asleep over the kitchen table, exhausted after days of interminable worry. Dragging herself to her feet, she filled the kettle at the stone sink, frozen to the bone from sitting so long.

"Ma, I think our man's outside, the front door was open."

Maisie looked round. "How do you know?"

"I was in the henhouse." Ginny put a loaded egg basket on the wooden draining board.

"So what did you do?"

"I shut it."

"You didn't you check to see if he was in bed first?"

"No."

"Well go and look now."

"What if he's gone?"

"He won't get far half-naked on a night like this. If he's not in the bed, open the front door again so he can get back in."

"What might he be doing – out there?"

"Looking for the privy, I expect."

"But it's here, round the back, not the front."

"Well it's as quick one way round as the other. Ginny, just do as you're told."

Maisie waited until her daughter had set off round the side of the small cottage then lit a gas ring and reached up onto a shelf for a pot of glycerine salve. As she waited for the kettle to boil she massaged the healing unguent into her rough hands, tracing the shape of her fingers in turn, turning the tight wedding band round and round, wondering what to do for the best.

Best for the young man, who wasn't in uniform but probably should be.

Best for Ginny, who needed a young man who'd treat her right. A young man with an obligation to her family. Someone who wouldn't get annoyed by her odd ways and the strange things she said. Ginny was a bit thruppence in the shilling.

Tea made, Maisie took two cups into the sitting room, lit the lamp on the sideboard then got a notebook and two pencils from the drawer. When the boy came back in, wrapped in the blanket like a prairie Indian, she beckoned him to the table. He looked grey with pain and weariness, but she patted the chair beside her and put the pad of notepaper in front of him.

He looked at her blankly so she drew two women's faces on the top page – a young girl with a wide smile and wavy hair, an older woman with wrinkles on her forehead. Under the faces she wrote *"Ginny"* and *"Maisie Rose"* in plain letters, then tore the sheet of paper from the pad and passed it to him. He understood well enough and drew a young man's rather long face with longish hair. He shaded in the hair with the pencil as if it were dark and gave himself a stubbly beard. It was an effective self-portrait.

"That's good!" Maisie exclaimed. "But what's your name? Write your name." She pointed at her name. "I'm Maisie," – she pointed to the kitchen – "she's Ginny. And you are . . .?"

The young man made his hands into fists and tapped the tabletop with his knuckles; his face was tight with tension. It dawned on Maisie that she might have an escaped convict in her cottage. Not a spy or a soldier but a convict from Dartmoor Prison or the jail at Bodmin. Perhaps he hadn't arrived by sea but was making his way *to* the coast. Unless he'd been dropped off somewhere below their cottage, in the tiny cove where Stan kept his boat, and had climbed the cliff then got as far as the spinney before he passed out. She looked at his drawing and then the hair on his head. It had been lightened with peroxide. Why? There were plenty of Cornishmen with black hair and swarthy features. There was no need to hide black hair in England – *unless you needed to change your appearance to get away from the police . . .* Maisie took a deep breath, "Go on," she said, "put your name."

The young man stared at her for a moment then wrote *"Giovanni"* in a beautiful, flowing script.

"Gi – o – vanni," said Maisie, pronouncing the name with a hard "G" and struggling with the syllables.

"Giovanni – Gianni," the boy corrected her, using the soft "G".

"Ah, 'Giovanni'," Maisie repeated. Then she realised what she was saying, "Oh, dear Lord, you're Italian!"

The boy gulped and hastily scratched out the name, saying, "No, no, no," and writing underneath 'JEAN' in capital letters.

"Jean?" Maisie asked. "That's a girl's name."

"Jean – Jan. *En français, Jean.*" The boy pronounced the name with a shushing sound.

Maisie shook her head, bemused. The boy smiled and wrote JAN again on the pad.

"Jan? Like in Janet?"

"No, Jean or Yan with a 'Y'. Yan. Like . . ." he looked around the room as if for inspiration and stopped at the wireless set. "John! John with a 'Y'– like Johnny Weissmuller!"

"Weissmuller! You *are* German. What you doin' here?" Maisie's voice rose to a screech. She pushed back her chair, anxious to separate herself from the enemy. "Who are you? What you doing here in my house?"

If the boy understood her, he was confused by the question. "You bring me."

"Yes, I know, but you were in a bad way and . . ." She was on her feet now, looking for something with which to protect herself. The poker was nearest; she grabbed it and waved it at him. He grinned.

"I am Yan from Poland, and Jean from France. Giovanni is Italian for Johnny, no? You call me Johnny, that's okay."

"Yanny, Janny, Poland and France and Italy, what sort of nonsense you talking, boy? How can you be from three places? I don't believe you." Maisie screwed up her eyes, trying to look fierce, and balanced her weight from foot to foot, ready to cosh him on the head if need be, but the boy's smile was disarming – literally. She dropped the hand holding the poker down to her side.

"My mother is Polish, my father is French, and I worked in Italy – easy."

"Oh – I see, well, that's a start. And now we know you can talk English as well."

The boy grinned again and gabbled something incomprehensible, then doubled over, holding his ribs.

"You've got a cracked rib – more than one, I think – proper broken, most like. I thought as much." Maisie moved to the makeshift bed and opened the covers, inviting him to get back in. "Come on, back to bed now. We can do more of this tomorrow." The boy gave her a strange look. "Get to know each other." She indicated his cup on the table. "Do you want that tea? It's cold by now, but I'll make another, if you like."

Yan or Jean grimaced.

"As you wish."

When Maisie got back into the kitchen she realised she'd still got the poker in her right hand. She looked at the iron instrument, wondering how it had got there, then placed it carefully behind the kitchen door.

The following day, after she'd retrieved Jean's breakfast plate, Maisie handed him the notepad and pencil and left him to his own devices. When she got home after her day at Cleve House she went straight into the sitting room. He was propped up against the pillows, half asleep. The notepad was on his legs. He opened his eyes and smiled. Maisie brushed her hair off her face with one hand and unconsciously smoothed her skirt with the other. Johnny-Yan-Jean handed her the notepad. He had drawn a series of intricate pictures showing him in a city with cars. The final picture was him with his head under the bonnet of a car.

"You're a car mechanic! Well, I never," said Maisie. "That might come in handy."

Chapter 8

"Have you heard what's happened in Saltash?" Delia asked as she came into the Cleve House kitchen. "Incendiaries on the town, and the devils got *all* the churches except the Wesleyan. Ezra Paddon will have something to say on that, I don't doubt. They were aiming for the bridge and kept missing."

"They were talking about it in the village this morning. I heard the explosions during the night. Thought it was close," said Maisie, wringing a dishcloth into a tight knot, then tightening it again with nervous fingers. "No one seems to know if the railway line is down, though. Mrs Prior said something about it being a prime target last week. Stands to reason, I suppose. Amazing they haven't got that old bridge down already."

"Mrs Prior's up here again," Ginny said as she laid three places for lunch at the kitchen table.

Maisie and Delia Metherall exchanged glances.

"She'll be talking to Mr Booth about her boy Simon, I s'pect. She was here the other day as well," Ginny continued.

Maisie looked across at her employer again and raised her eyebrows meaningfully. "Another one falls for Lord Byron Booth."

"Another one?" Delia replied. "Oh, glory, not me! I have Charles, who's a perfectly good husband – when he's at home. That reminds me – he says he'll be here on and off during the next few weeks. Didn't say why, but I don't care. He's been too lucky so far, not being posted abroad. Not that risking his life every night in London during the Blitz can be called luck. He says there can be as many as seven hundred German bombers over London at a time. They even send mines down with parachutes."

"You're gushing," Maisie whispered in Delia's ear as she passed her on the way to the oven.

"No, I'm not!" Delia went slightly pink and changed the subject. "Something smells good. What have you managed to concoct? I've been walking our woods with a nice woman from the forestry people all morning and I'm starving. They're going to fell some of our trees, but I can replant with young stock, and they'll send someone to help me do it, too. Isn't that splendid? One doesn't expect help from anyone these days. Oooh, toad-in-the-hole! What a treat!" Delia clapped her hands with delight as Maisie placed an open-topped dish of piping hot, baked yellow batter on the table. "With real sausages or Billy Baxter's breadcrumbs in battledress?"

"Real – Billy promises they've actually got meat in them. He didn't say what meat, and I didn't ask, but I've made do with one each here and mashed up a few to put in sausage rolls for the children's tea. All the St Dominick's little ones ever used to get was bread and scrape for tea, according to that Clapper woman, or whatever she's called."

"Maisie, one day your kindness will get you into trouble, and not only with Miss Claverham. And be warned, she doesn't approve of spoiling children with good food."

"Well, I do, so we've got another war on our hands. I put four eggs in our batter as well."

"Four eggs! We could be arrested!" Delia covered her mouth with both hands, genuinely shocked.

"We need our strength. You got to look after yourself if you're looking after others. I learned that the hard way," Maisie replied drily. Then, looking at her daughter, she said, "And that's another secret. Mind you remember it, girl."

"Why is it a secret?" asked Ginny placing a silver salt pot into the exact centre of the table. When no reply came she repeated the question then added, "Why is it *another* secret?"

"Because we've got too many hens," Maisie replied, riffling through a cutlery drawer for a serving spoon. "Another four chicks hatched this week, and we were over the twenty limit a month ago. I shall have to start supplying eggs to Alf's grocery or a shop in Cready if I get caught. I'm breaking Mr Nosy-Parker Bantry's egg law."

"What's wrong with supplying Alf Plowden? He'd pay you, surely," Delia said, sitting down to eat.

Maisie huffed. "It'd call attention, and Ma Bantry's in and out of that shop like a fiddler's elbow as it is."

"Why is there an egg law, Ma?" Ginny asked, pulling out her chair to sit down as well.

"Oh, s'pect it's because hens don't like laying eggs in wartime."

"Why don't hens like laying eggs in wartime?" persisted Ginny.

"Bombs frighten them," replied Maisie without batting an eyelid.

Delia bit back a grin. "Eggs are rationed, sweetheart, like tea and butter and Mr Baxter's sausages, and just about everything else in the larder."

"Our hens don't get frightened," Ginny said.

"That's because we don't get bombed. Jerry's not interested in little old Porthferris." Maisie dropped into her chair with a sigh.

"I don't see why Jerry – if that's Mr Hitler – is interested in England at all. He's got his own country to look after."

"Out of the mouths of babes and Miss Virginia Hawkins," Maisie said, spooning a generous helping of toad-in-the-hole onto Delia's plate.

"Not so much, Maisie. Are you trying to fatten me up?"

"Yes."

"Is that why our hens lay more eggs," Ginny continued, "and other hens ration theirs?"

Maisie raised her eyes to the ceiling. "Must be. And that's why we don't want people snooping round our cottage."

"In case they steal our eggs."

"Egg-zactly."

The pun was lost on Ginny.

Delia looked at Maisie and said quietly, "Actually, I'm afraid that's not quite true. Mr Hitler may be a lot more interested in Porthferris than you think, and all the other little harbour towns and inlets around the peninsula."

"But if he's going to invade he'll go up the Thames, surely, or land in Suffolk or Kent. You don't really think they'll cross the Channel this far west do you?"

"A fleet out of Normandy or Brittany, or the Channel Islands – it's not impossible. Our pilots have fought them off once in the air already; it may happen again. Why do you think the RAF are making new airfields down here?"

"But the obvious place to cross from France is to Dover, isn't it? Or to the east coast from Holland and . . . Ah, obvious. Too obvious. I see." Maisie paused then said, "But even so, Porthferris is just a couple of streets and a pub."

"And conveniently located between Falmouth and Plymouth. They won't get many boats in, but even a couple would enable them to land men who could get up to the Plymouth-Truro road, especially if they coordinate coming ashore in Looe and Fowey and other small harbours like ours at the same time."

"God almighty – an invasion," Maisie whispered.

"Has to be faced – we're really very vulnerable down here. One fifth-columnist in the village to ease their way in and . . . well, what could we do?"

Maisie felt a chill run up and down her spine. She stopped eating, but Delia didn't notice.

"Our local defence volunteers wouldn't stand a chance," Delia continued. "Can you imagine Billy Baxter and roly-poly Alf Plowden scrambling like snipers over the roof tops of Inner Harbour . . . Maisie, are you all right?"

Maisie shook her head. *A fifth-columnist. Someone in the village.* With frightening clarity she saw the outline of a tall man standing in the pouring rain on Porthferris quay. Who had it been? And why on earth had he been there? Because he hadn't just come out of the Fisherman's Boot, that was certain. Then another very disturbing thought pushed its way into her mind: the stranger in her cottage. She took a deep breath and tried to contain the impulse to pull off her pinny and rush straight home. What had she done?

"Are you all right, Maisie?" Delia repeated. "You've gone white as a sheet."

"Mm . . . I was just wondering . . . I mean, it's real, isn't it? That we could go the same way as France and Holland and Poland. Has the Major told you anything?"

"Charles only tells me what's common knowledge in London. His job is fearfully hush-hush. But he did say . . ."

Maisie had stopped listening again, thinking about the stranger lying in the truckle bed in her sitting room. He was a spy, and she was a fool. And all because she didn't want to contact the police in case the detective with the all-seeing eyes came back and started asking awkward questions again.

Delia looked at her and smiled. "Going back to the subject of eggs, I've been thinking, we've got room here for a secret piglet or two."

Maisie pulled herself back to the present. "What, with all they St Dom boys running all over the place? That piglet'll stay secret about ten minutes. Simon Prior will let it out, or cripple it with his blasted catapult."

"Actually, it doesn't have to be a secret. Anyone can keep a pig if they want to, can't they?"

"Fisherman's Boot has got a pig club. They've rented a sty up at Pew Pewsey's farm."

"I think you can keep a specific number of pigs for private consumption, and after that you have to share the meat, like eggs, or have the animals slaughtered by the Ministry of Ag," Delia said.

"Pew'll slaughter them for you, so long as he gets his cut. And who's going to say how many pigs you've got, or that you've got to share it with strangers?"

"Archie Bantry."

"Oh, Chief Food Inspector Bantry – him again!" Maisie smacked the table. "He was here yesterday afternoon, after you went into Cready, wanting to see your pantry and what the St Dom boys were getting for their supper."

"He told me last week he's been 'promoted onto' another committee: Parish Rationing and . . . can't remember. Agricultural something or other."

"Makes my skin crawl, that man does," Maisie said. "There's something altogether not right there."

"No, perhaps not. I can't see what pleasure there is in telling tales on fellow villagers."

"We're not fellow villagers, though, are we? He's from upcountry, got no family in this area at all, far as I know."

"There's pictures in *Picture Post* of pigs on bomb sites," said Ginny.

"In London, Ginny, not round this way," Maisie replied.

Delia smiled at Ginny and continued her conversation with Maisie. "Did you show Mr Bantry what we've got in the larder? How we keep the children's rations separate from ours?"

"I did. Good job we decanted all that NAAFI stuff into jam jars with grease-proof paper – he picked up every single one and counted them."

"Glory, I hope you told him it took you days to make it all? We'd better label them: *Porthferris yellow plum, September '40.*"

Delia's tone was light but Maisie put her hand to her mouth, remembering Stan had brought the tinned goods up from Saltash. Got them off a man who got them off the back of a lorry in the Navy dockyard. They would miss those extras: the corned beef and Camp coffee, the bars of soap and tinned peaches. A thought occurred to her. "What about the tea we got from – wherever it came from?"

"It's all in tea caddies around the house. I put some in the library behind the Dickens novels, and Trollope as well – seemed appropriate. The coffee is in separate, sealed bags in the old haricot bean crock, and there's Kenyan ground coffee in packets under the brown sugar as well. If Bantry comes back I'll have to swear I've had it since before the war started."

"Should be all right. You're the only person I know that goes in for real coffee. What a state we're in, though, having to account to a local busybody for what's on our larder shelves. They'll tie us up so tight with their rules and regulations, we'll have to get a licence to make rock buns before this war's over."

Delia gave Maisie a sharp look. "Calm down. Having a few extra pots of jam isn't a crime."

"'Tis, though, and they can fine you. We'd best be more careful. Alf's already had a run-in with Bantry over ration coupons and selling more than he's allowed. Bantry's threatened to report him and there's a hefty fine. That detective was right onto it, asking me what Stan was transporting in his boat."

"What did you tell him?"

"That we sometimes get extras by Stan . . . bartering. The detective said something like 'What, sardines for petrol?' and I sort of went along with it."

"Ooh, Maisie, that's a bit of a stretch. I can't see how you can call it bartering."

"Stan wasn't the only one in Porthferris doing it, and no one's bothered about it before." Maisie put down her knife and fork, unable to eat another mouthful; she'd used the past tense with Stan's name again.

"That's because it isn't a bit of duty-free smuggling anymore. They call it 'war profiteering' now."

Maisie grimaced, but before she could say anything, Ginny said, "We could keep it in our backyard with the hens."

"Keep what?" Maisie asked, taking her plate to the draining board and returning with a dish of stewed apples.

"The pig," said Ginny looking at her mother as if she were dense. "Our man could look after it."

Maisie glared at her daughter.

"What man?" Delia asked.

Maisie caught her eye. "Remember when Ginny found that little, old woman in the scullery?"

Delia nodded, understanding: Ginny was a bit simple.

"She's still there," said Ginny. "I saw her this morning. She's got a hunchback and a white cat."

Chapter 9

"We've got another new resident," the butcher said.

Maisie's head shot up. She had been scrabbling in her bucket bag, making room for her meat ration. "Where? Who?"

"I've got a bit of bacon fat and a marrow bone to spare as well, if you like."

"Oh, yes, I can make a good broth with that. Thanks, Billy."

The butcher wrapped Maisie's treats in newspaper and leaned over his counter with a wink. Maisie gave him a wary smile. He'd been sweet on her since they were in the same class at school. She could have married him, except Billy had looked like an over-fed gargoyle at eighteen. Still did.

"You all right, maid?" he asked. "Not – you know – feeling the strain? Can't be easy."

Maisie sighed, "Not easy at all. I wish Stan would just come home – or let us find him . . . wherever he is."

"'Tis a rare old mystery, I must say."

Maisie nodded then tried a phrase she had to practise with other shop keepers. She was deliberately starting with Billy, knowing he had a soft spot for her. "Billy, can I take something on Stan's rations – in case he comes home?"

The butcher narrowed his eyes. "D'you know something you're not saying, girl?"

Maisie smiled but she didn't have it in her to lie. "I can't say, Billy. But would you? Where's the harm?"

Billy gave her another sharp look. "You mean he's holed up somewhere safe, the lazy bugger, keeping out of the way while the rest of us carry on and do our bit. We might be too old to join up proper, but we got important things to do down here." His tone was sharp and cold. This was a Billy Maisie had never seen before. He must have caught her look for he checked his words and started again, but without his usual banter, "Bit of salted ham do you?"

"You're a saint, Billy, whatever you can spare. How much do I owe you?"

"I'll put it on the tab. Pay me end of the month."

"Have I reached my one and tuppence yet?"

Billy gave her a slow wink. "Maybe, maybe not. Depends what comes in this week."

"You mean not your own stuff, what you cut up here?"

Billy shook his head, then tapped the side of his bulbous nose.

"Oh, yes! Sorry, I'm not thinking. Thanks, Billy. What were you saying about a new resident?"

"Miss Maud Lily Pettit. Moved into that big bungalow they Londoners used afore the war started."

"You mean Seabreeze, at the bottom of my hill?"

"You'll prob'ly see her on your way back. She's 'very fond of gardening', she tells me."

"Makes sense, I s'pose. People getting out of London. Must be terrible up there, living like moles 'n' maggots in they nasty shelter places."

"Plymouth's worse: people trekking out to the moor of a night in case they're killed in their beds. We've been lucky, and no mistake – so far." Billy rolled the last marrow bone into a sheet of newspaper and handed it over the counter, saying, "I heard they're using the old house where St Dominick's school was – the one that's moved into Cleve House – for families with children, and turning the grandparents and old ones away. Leastways, that's what I heard. Could be a pack of nonsense; people get things mixed up. But Mrs Watts was telling me . . ."

Maisie stopped listening. Something Billy had said about a building jolted her memory and sent her mind scampering across new possibilities. She waited until he had finished parcelling the rest of her rations, then, as she was putting them into her bag, keeping her head down, she said, "Do you know if the old cottages belonging to the mine are being used again? Apart from Granny Steamer's place? I know there's no water or electricity there, but they've still got roofs and walls. People could live there right enough if they needed somewhere desp'rate."

"The cottages going down Smugglers Mile Hill? No, they're all derelict. We've looked there, if you're thinking about Stan. We did a Home Guard exercise as a practice. You'd have to be proper desp'rate to even try camping in there. The entire row is a ruin."

Maisie sighed, "Never mind. Oh, that reminds me, I've got a couple of windows still need fixing. Can you ask your brother-in-law if he's got any spare glass?"

Billy gave Maisie a knowing look. She averted her eyes and said, "Oh, you know, Billy, don't ask. I was hoping he'd be home to do it himself – but . . . Well, thanks for the extras –"

"Tch! No extras here! You watch yourself: careless words cost rations in this village. Archie Bantry'll be after us." Billy Baxter was suddenly serious. "Talk of the devil. Quick, get that meat out of sight," he hissed. "His informer's here."

The doorbell tinkled its warning.

"Morning, Mrs Bantry. Nice day."

Local Resistance

As Maisie reached the bend in the steep lane and looked out to sea, two Beauforts flying parallel broke the horizon and headed towards her, silencing the birds and freezing her to the spot. They'd be on their way back to St Eval after a raid over some occupied French harbour or out at sea. Watching and waiting, Maisie couldn't decide if having airbases in Cornwall was reassuring or otherwise. As they passed overhead, however, they brought her to a decision; she had to get the young foreigner out of her house. She'd tried to convince herself he wasn't a spy or a deserter, but now she was telling lies to feed him, and she hated telling lies. Billy Baxter had noticed she wasn't being straight with him and that titbit would be round the village within an hour.

The minute she opened the back door, Maisie hoisted her shopping bag onto the kitchen table and went straight into the sitting room. The stranger with the funny names was propped up on his pillows, gazing out of the open window.

"All right, Yan or Jan or Jean or Gianni, or whatever your name is, out of that bed. On your feet, you fraud."

He looked at her, surprised at her tone.

"Come on, admit it, you're shirkin' – pretendin' you're a damn Frenchie and hiding from proper men's work. Well, you're not doing it in my house. Get up!"

She grabbed the clean clothes she'd left neatly folded on the sideboard. "Come on, Ginny and me can't be living in that flaming kitchen every day. This is my house, and there's no room for strangers eating our rations and taking up space."

She looked at the red purse she'd found in his jacket now lying propped up against the clock on the mantelpiece. It contained twenty-five pounds, fourteen shillings and sixpence halfpenny: a lot of money. She'd been through the different sections at least five times, looking for anything that might suggest an identity or a location: a bus ticket, a betting slip . . . But there was no clue to where he'd come from – nothing to confirm he was French or Polish or even Italian, nor, to be honest, a spy or a layabout playing a joke on her to get a warm bed and free board.

Nevertheless, she said, "I'm not feeding you another morsel," and turned to gather up his clean clothes and shove them onto his chest. "Not until you get yourself a ration book, then get yourself out into my backyard and start digging our veg patch and cleaning the hens. Then, maybe – just maybe – I'll be in a better frame of mind to take you in as a *paying guest.*"

The young man looked at her with alarm and struggled painfully out of the low cot. Ignoring his discomfort, Maisie marched back into the kitchen.

When she returned later, he was standing by the table fully dressed. She put out a hand, and left it apologetically in mid-air. "Sorry," she said. He looked at her hand. "I'm sorry – it's that I'm that worried and . . . it's . . . it's all too much, you see." Maisie bit her lips, willing herself not to cry.

Gently, he took her hand between his palms.

"I'm sorry," she repeated. Unthinking, she reached up to give him a peck on the cheek. But their lips met.

It took her utterly by surprise. She pulled back out of reach.

The boy shrugged.

Maisie stared at him, then moved closer.

He kissed her again. And she let him.

Chapter 10

Maisie noticed the newcomer, Miss Maud Lily Pettit, well before she was within speaking distance. She generally passed the bungalow named Seabreeze at this time in the morning and today Miss Pettit was standing by the garden gate.

As Maisie approached, the spinster began to wave. It looked as if she were wearing lace gloves, but when Maisie got nearer she realised the hands were simply delicate: blue veins on very white, white skin. The woman had never done a hand's turn in her life.

"I say! Yoo-hoo!" Miss Pettit called.

"Sorry, my dear, I was daydreaming. You're Miss Pettit, aren't you? Or is it Mrs? – begging your pardon." Maisie chose to play the yokel: an easy way out of anything serious, and something warned her to be on her guard.

"It's 'miss', I regret. Victim of the Great War, if you know what I mean?" Miss Pettit extended a mauve sleeve across the low gate, then rapidly withdrew it and began to fiddle with the latch and stood back invitingly. "Have you time for a cup of tea, Mrs Hawkins? I have no coffee left, unfortunately, which is what I usually drink at this hour. I do so miss it, but one must not complain with our merchant fleet being so brave and taking such terrible risks to bring us our little luxuries. Forgive my familiarity – our local butcher gave me your name. Such a nice man, for a butcher."

Maisie tried not to smile and filed the snippet for Delia later. "Thank you, that is kind, but I must be getting on up to Cleve House. I've got to do their dinner," she said, emphasising the sound of the *r* in dinner.

"Ah, you work at Cleve House – as a cook? Mr Baxter did not tell me that. It is a school now, I understand."

"For the duration. I do the cooking, just while the war's on, and look after the house like always."

"It is a very fine house. I peeked a look from the road. Georgian or early Victorian?"

"I really couldn't say. 'Tis proper draughty in winter, whatever it is."

"But it will go back to being a family home – for the Metheralls?"

"Oh, yes. I should think so; it belongs to Mrs Metherall, really. It was her mother's family home."

"And Mr Metherall . . .?"

"Major Metherall he is now."

"He's abroad? In the desert, perhaps?"

"No, no – he's in London working for the Min –" Maisie caught herself just in time. Miss Pettit was obviously an expert gossip. Looking off down the lane, she made to move on. "I'm sorry, my dear. I would like to stop and chat, but I do have to be getting along."

"Yes, of course. Forgive my curiosity; it's just that I am so anxious to fit into your little community."

Another snippet for Delia. If Maud Lily Pettit had any idea of some of things going on in their "little community" she'd have a lady-like fit.

Miss Pettit held up one of her delicate hands as if to prevent Maisie leaving. "Look, Mrs Hawkins, it's simply that . . . Oh, how embarrassing. I was led to believe you might be interested in coming in to – er – help me – once or twice a week."

Maisie watched the woman's face carefully, thinking Billy Baxter needed a talking to. "Oh, I'm sorry – I can't. I've got that much to do already. My daughter Ginny is good with a mop and duster, though. Would you like to try her out for a week or two? See how she gets on?"

"Oh, yes, do send her along. Could she start tomorrow?"

"First thing in the morning? Or a bit later on?"

"Oh, later. I'm no early riser, not anymore. Ten o'clock will be fine. 'Ginny' did you say her name was?"

"Virginia. We call her Ginny."

"Splendid. I look forward to meeting – Ginny – tomorrow."

"And was she wearing mauve?" asked Delia with glee.

"I think she'd call it *lavender*."

Delia giggled, "And pearls?"

"Single strand at the throat: over lace, not on the skin."

Delia grinned. "I wonder who she is."

"Miss Maud Lily Pettit, according to Billy Baxter, who knows more about us than we do ourselves most of the time and, it appears, he's told her the lot. That's another nosy, old biddy we've got to watch out for. Wanted to know about Cleve House, she did; knows about your family already."

"Perhaps she knew my mother, or maybe the people who had the bungalow before told her. They came here for drinks a couple of times. What were they called, I forget?"

"The Oakleys."

"That's it. Maybe one of them told her about us. We have met them on and off over the years."

"S'pect that's it, then. Now, I can't stand here chatting if they nippers are going to get their midday meal. You sit down here and talk to me while I'm at it." Maisie pulled out a chair and pushed Delia into it gently. "I've only got the spuds to do; mince is all cooked, ready for their cottage pie. Do you think I could risk putting a bit of cheese on top to cheer it up? Beryl Deakin let me have some of their dairy cheddar last week. I've been keeping it in your side of the pantry, but there's enough for the little ones to have a sprinkling on top of the mash."

Delia nodded, but said, "Meat *and* cheese on the same plate is a bit extravagant. And think of the people who'd get into trouble if Mr Bantry walked in. You were right about getting fined – I asked Charles. He says it's £530! Or was that selling goods without coupons? Whichever, it's pretty stiff."

Maisie stopped in her tracks. "I didn't know it was that much! No wonder everyone gets the jitters when Bantry or his missis walks into a shop. Can we be fined for receiving, though, if it's a gift?"

"Probably."

Maisie sighed. "Stan got some of our stuff off the back of a lorry in Devonport, I do know that. Always said he'd found it washed up on the beach, but I knew what he was up to – more or less. Don't know what *they* got in return, though. Wasn't money, that's for sure. That's why I got twitchy when that detective cottoned on. I'm glad I didn't know it was that serious – I'd have given us away with fright."

"I hope you told your detective tins wash up on Cornish beaches all the time. Remember all those shoes that year? And the oranges?"

"And that whale! Bigger than a trawler, it was. Lor' how it did stink." Maisie laughed, then suddenly went quiet again. "What you were saying the other day, about German boats coming into Porthferris? It's possible, isn't it?"

"Charles thinks it'll be a combined attack – if it comes. They'll invade along the Kent coast *and* down here at the same time, and up in Scotland. I don't know if I'm allowed to tell you this, but if it does happen, and they do land nearby, we've made special arrangements here. You and Ginny must come to us immediately. I'm not joking, Maisie. This is horribly serious."

"You mean . . .?"

"I mean we have a safe hiding place organised. But this is our secret: there isn't room for the whole village!"

Maisie turned and looked at Delia. "Oh, my God," she murmured.

Delia nodded, then got to her feet and said, "Well, come along, chop, chop. Those cuckoos in our nest need feeding. Give me something to do."

For a while the two women worked together in silence, then Maisie burst out, "The world's gone mad. My whole world's turned itself inside out and back again, and I don't know which way is up anymore: Stan going off like that; Hitler packing his case to come and stay in Porthferris . . . 'Tis all as barmy as barmy."

Delia gave a wry smile. "Something will sort itself out sooner or later. Let me finish this and we can make a start on what Mother Nature designed us for."

"Washing pots and pans? Mother Nature has a lot to answer for," Maisie sighed.

"You wash, I'll wipe."

When the cooking pots were nearly all dry and on their shelves, Delia said, "I forgot to tell you – Pew Pewsey came over to bring some veg. He says we can go up there this afternoon and choose which piglets we want. But not to keep there because nosy Bantry's learned to count on his fingers – Pew's words, not mine."

"You thought where to put them?"

"In the old herb garden so they come ready stuffed."

Maisie looked at Delia's innocent English-lady face and started to laugh. Then she was serious. "It's getting worse, isn't it? First they Anderson shelters and then the rationing. Now we're stocking up to go into hiding. We won't end up like poor old France or Holland, will we? I couldn't bear it."

"Charles says . . . No, sorry, I can't say any more, except people are in place. He says Aubrey . . ."

"Aubrey! Who's Aubrey?"

"Aubrey Chatwynde."

"What, that chap that's taken over the Fisherman's Boot? I thought he was too posh for a village publican. Stan said he used to work in London. Jeweller or something. I thought it was odd."

Delia pulled on a cardigan and said, "Forget it, Maisie. You'll get me into terrible trouble if Charles finds out I've been talking to you. Look, why don't you and Ginny move in here now? Stan's not an excuse anymore. Please come."

Maisie shook her head. "Can't. Not yet."

"Why ever not? What is there to keep you up at that cottage now you haven't got to wait on Stan and his father hand and foot? Think of all the time and energy you'll save not having to climb that hill every day."

Maisie made a show of straightening the gingham tablecloth, her cheeks burning crimson.

Delia said, "All right – I won't nag. Just come when . . ." She paused, noting the stiffness in Maisie's neck and back. "I'll go and check the fence around the herb garden for the piglets."

"No! Not there." Maisie swung round, fully engaged. "We need every bit of green with any sort of flavour we can find, specially if we're going to end up having to feed ourselves altogether."

"Where, then? The front rose garden?"

"Save all that pruning you do."

"It'll be visible from the road."

"Keep the gates shut."

"I'll have to fence it in. Make it Simon Prior-proof," Delia said, nodding her head meaningfully. Simon Prior was verging on the delinquent.

Maisie caught her meaning and said, "Best you make it too high to see over as well. We don't want Archibald Bantry popping his head over for a sniff of your roses and getting a snout longer than his own in his face."

Delia grinned. "Archie Bantry can inspect us whenever he likes; we have nothing to hide – much."

The two women collapsed in schoolgirl giggles, laughing until tears sparkled in their eyes, but it was nervous laughter, and Maisie knew it.

Chapter 11

"Well, how did you get on? Did you break anything?"

"No! Miss Pettit says I'm her 'little treasure'."

Maisie rolled her eyes and put the remains of the cottage pie in front of her daughter sitting at the Cleve House kitchen table.

"Can I have some butter?"

"No, you can't be taking Mrs Metherall's rations, and the children's stuff isn't supposed to be for us."

Maisie poured herself a cup of tea and sat down opposite Ginny. "Come on, then – what's it like at Seabreeze?"

Ginny took a mouthful of floury potatoes before looking into her visual memory and reciting what she saw there. "First, I did her carpets with the vacuum cleaner like you showed me, then I ran a duster over a cabinet with glass doors. It's got fancy hinges and the handles on the doors are like stirrups. I shook the duster out of the window and started on the inside. It's got three shelves. The top shelf is empty. On the lower two shelves there are little tins and boxes. Miss Pettit likes little boxes. There's one that's ever so pretty. It's black with pink flowers on it and it's ever so tiny – like this." Ginny made a circle with the fingers of her right hand in her left palm.

"Sounds like a snuff box," Maisie said.

"That's what Miss Pettit said. 'They're snuff boxes, Virginia,' she said." Ginny took another mouthful then said, "Ma, what's snuff?"

"A sort of tobacco, I think. Men used to stuff it up their noses."

"Ugh." Ginny made a face.

"People collect snuff boxes. It doesn't mean Miss Pettit puts it up her nose." Ginny started to giggle. "Go on, then what?" asked Maisie.

"I picked up a gold box. It's like the locket Mrs Metherall wears on Sundays sometimes. 'That's pretty,' I said and I wiped it carefully and put it on the table so I could wipe the shelf underneath. The next box was silver; I needed the silver cloth for this one . . ."

For a few minutes Ginny recounted each and every move she had made while cleaning the cabinet, and Maisie half listened and half made a list of meals for the following week.

". . . some are wooden oblongs with draw lids covered in shells. One said 'A present from Ilfracombe'." Ginny struggled with the syllables saying, "Il-fra-come-bee."

"Ilfra-*coom*," Maisie corrected the pronunciation. "It's a seaside resort in North Devon. What about it?"

"It's on a shell box. There's a greyish sort of powder in it, like talcum but not white. I put it down and peeked inside the others, and do you know they were *all* dirty inside! All of them! 'Oh, dear,' I said, and I set to wiping out the insides of empty pots that had bits of grey dust in them. The bigger shell boxes have got dry crumby stuff in them, like bits of old leather. The one that said 'A present from Eastbourne' had whitish talcum, but it didn't smell flowery, not a bit. The one from Whitby had whitish-grey stuff and it was at least half-full. 'A present from Ilfracombe'." Ginny pronounced the place name slowly, still struggling over the syllables, then continued, "I was doing that one when Miss Pettit came into the sitting room and slapped her hand to her mouth like she'd had a nasty shock or something. 'Oh! No! You don't need to do those! That cabinet should be locked,' she said. 'So how am I going to clean it?' I asked, and she said I wasn't to. Not ever."

Maisie got up and washed her cup and saucer at the sink. "They're probably valuable. She doesn't want them dropped, most like. I can't see Miss Pettit taking that nasty snuff, though."

Ginny looked up and sighed. "I was careful, Ma, real careful."

"Course you were, sweetie," Maisie said, kissing the top of her daughter's head. "Now, eat up. I've got my hands full this afternoon."

"Miss Pettit sounded like Miss Claverham. Like a cross schoolteacher. There's one little box that looks like a lump of rock with barnacles; she says it's from the Rock of Gibraltar. Where's that?"

"Gibraltar? Off the coast of Spain, I think, but I haven't got time to be telling you about place names. Finish that up quick. I need you to get started on the children's tea. The important thing is, you managed without me all right."

Ginny gave her mother her joyful, vacuous smile. "Miss Pettit says I'm an '*absolute* treasure'."

Maisie couldn't help laughing: Ginny had captured Miss Pettit's funny little voice perfectly.

That afternoon, as Delia and Maisie Rose rounded the high-banked, narrow bend, a cyclist riding hell for leather nearly knocked them sideways into the hedge.

"Hey!" shouted Maisie.

Watching the retreating figure, Delia said, "That was Archie Bantry."

"Never! He couldn't pedal my sewing machine."

"It was."

When they reached the entrance to Home Farm, Pew Pewsey confirmed it. Standing on the inner side of his five-barred gate with a long-handled axe in his hand, he was snorting and stamping the ground like an irate bull. An underfed, wrinkled, aged bull, but an angry male nevertheless.

"Good afternoon, Mr Pewsey. Was that Mr Bantry on a bicycle?" Delia asked cheerfully, eyeing the position of the axe held aloft and exchanging glances with Maisie.

"That bugger ever set foot on my property again I'll chop his head off and feed his bollocks to my pigs. I told him: 'Set foot on Home Farm again, you friggin' old, nosy parker sod, and I'll have my missus cut off your willy and stuff it in a pie.' Nosy sow's dollop."

"Gosh," said Delia quietly, "I think he's cross."

Maisie put a hand on Delia's arm to stop her going any nearer and called out, "Shall we come back another day, Mr Pewsey?"

"Come in, go home, drop down a sodding mine shaft, do as you bloody please."

"Right, we'll take that as a 'Not today', then," answered Delia, her clear, well-spoken syllables floating in the Cornish air right over the angry farmer's head. "But please remember to keep two piglets for me."

Pew Pewsey made a growling guttural noise which the women decided was some form of acknowledgement. Then, arm in arm, trying not to run, they strode hastily back down the slimy, cow-patted lane.

They didn't stop to breathe until they were safely round the bend and out of sight, then they burst out laughing. That was when old man Pewsey caught up with them, axe still in hand. Maisie thought her bladder would burst.

"Come back, come back, you daft wimin. Ethel says we'm s'pecting you."

"No, it's quite all right," called Delia, gathering her senses faster than Maisie. "You're obviously busy – I'll come along tomorrow."

"Suit yer soddin' self," grunted Pew Pewsey. He gave a great harrumph and turned back the way he'd come.

"Start walking," muttered Maisie, "in case he turns back. They're all as loopy as crotchet doilies, that lot. His Ethel cleans her teeth with Vim."

Delia stopped and stared. "The stuff you use for the bath? I wondered how she got them so white."

"Keep moving," hissed Maisie.

At the bottom of the hill they met another cyclist.

"Benjie Benjamin, what are you doin' here?" asked Maisie.

"On my way to Home Farm."

"Oh-ho, not a good a day, Benjie. I'd turn round and try again next week if I were you."

"He's got an axe," added Delia.

"He's always got an axe, daft bugger. Kept one of they Land Army girls up a haystack two whole days last week. Said he'd chop her hands off for dropping pigswill outside the sty."

"Glory, would he?" Delia's eyes were like saucers.

"Like as not."

"Well, there you are, Benjie. Turn round and save yourself for the future." Maisie was only half-joking.

"No, I got to go. I went down to Becca's caravan for a bite to eat and then we had a bit of a cuddle and . . . Well, I'm late, so there'll be hell to pay. I'm working up at Home Farm, see."

"Working! You? At Home Farm? You poor devil, how did that happen?"

"Labour Exchange. They're onto me. Started asking questions about why I hadn't joined up and 'past experience', and where I'd been working. Had to walk up and down their office so they could see my limp. One of 'em even wanted to see my club foot. 'Twas proper 'barrassing taking my boot off and all. And, worse, the council offices have twigged onto my girls and all the little ones. Somebody's tipped them off 'cuz they knew about the kiddies' milk rations and where my girls are living and everything."

Maisie put a hand to her mouth. "That's awful. After all these years. You'd think people would have the decency to keep quiet about your girls. Not as if it's doing anyone any harm. Two of your boys joined up; they're doing their bit. Isn't that enough?"

Delia edged behind Benjie, a round-bodied, bald-headed man in ill-fitting corduroys and threadbare jacket now standing beside what passed as a bicycle in that it had a chain, handlebar and wheels. She wrinkled her face at Maisie and mouthed, "What?"

Maisie responded with a shake of the head and mouthed back, "Later".

Benjie lifted his greasy cap and wiped his forehead on something resembling a man's handkerchief. "So there we are. I be labouring for Pew Pewsey. He says they Land Girls got no idea so he needs help."

"But he's paying you?"

"Labour Exchange think so. I haven't seen a brass farthin' yet, though." Benjie blew his nose then wiped his brow again, sniffing with sorrow.

"Bit of a muddle, is it?" asked Maisie gently. "Pity you married the last one."

"But she was asking all the time. Said it wasn't fair, the other two had their special days, why not her?"

"Have the council – um – twigged about them being your actual wives, Benjie?"

"Can't say. Prob'ly."

"Oh, dear." Maisie nodded gently and patted him on the back. "Give them my love, Sal, Molly and Rebecca."

Benjie checked his bicycle clips and slowly edged a plump leg over what remained of the saddle. He was about to pedal off when he put a foot back on the ground. "Maisie Rose, tell your Stan I'm free if he needs me. I know I wasn't much help on the last run, but I'm better now – working up at the farm's getting me fitter. I can manage the heavy stuff now. I shan't drop it."

"That's a bit difficult, Benjie . . ."

"Oh, bugger, yes, I forgot. Sorry. Still no sign of him?"

"No."

Benjie grimaced and pushed off, veering left, then right before he got his balance and started tacking uphill.

Delia waited until he was out of earshot, then said, "What on earth was all that about?"

"You don't want to know."

"I most certainly do. Who – for a start – are Sal, Molly and Rebecca?"

"Benjie's wives."

"As in wedding wives, or common-law?"

Maisie gave a slight shrug. "As far as they're concerned he's married them – proper little ceremonies."

"I was afraid of that. Do they all live together? One big, happy family?"

"No, that's the problem. Sal and Molly live in separate cottages in that row past Paddon's garage. Becca's in an old Romany caravan in the grounds of the old mine. You wouldn't get me down there, I'll tell you that. They say that ol' mine's haunted – noises and bangs in the night, they say. Even Stan kept out of it, except for our tunnel. It joins with a tunnel from Bayview and goes right into the old workings. There's a way out on the hill above the old engine house, but I've never been in it. Stan tried getting out that way once, said it was proper dangerous."

"It can't be very healthy down there, either, what with the metal deposits in the soil and all the damp."

"No, but if anyone can survive down there it'll be Becca Cottle."

"And somebody has told somebody who's checked names against free milk lists, or the grocer's egg-count, and put three and three together. I suppose there's a whole brood of children."

Maisie nodded. "Ten or eleven, I think. Nurse Brown delivered the first two or three; now they look after themselves – rally round at delivery time, you know. Dr MacManus keeps an eye on them, of course, makes sure the little ones get their jabs. And Reverend Hughes has got Becca on his Parish Relief register as being 'homeless'. Like you say, Sal and Molly will be on the grocer's list, and getting milk for their little ones."

"So our local midwife, Dr MacManus and Reverend Hughes know all about – what? – one, two, three of the wives? And none of them have said anything to the authorities?"

Maisie shook her head. "It's not as if they're doin' any harm, and two of the older boys joined up, that I do know. One of them was at Dunkirk, but he got back all right. We were that pleased. Sal's one of Beryl Deakin's half-sisters – on the Braund side of the family, and Molly's one of Stan's cousins."

"But how did they manage about their children's birth certificates? How do people like that . . .? Sorry, ignore that. At least Benjie's got work now."

"If Old Man Pewsey don't get him with his axe, or Ethel don't poison him with one of her pies."

"But if Reverend Hughes knows that Benjie is a bigamist – can one say 'trigamist'? – why hasn't he . . .? No, no of course – the children would suffer. So, basically, lots of people know and nobody has ever bothered about it, until now. You don't think the odious Bantry is involved, do you? He's on our Parish Council now. If he twigged about Rebecca, Reverend Hughes wouldn't have any choice but to . . ."

"Hilda Bantry, more like. She virtually runs that church with her committees and rotas. Mrs Hughes has never got over losing their baby. She forgets things and . . . well, Mrs Bantry doesn't."

Delia sighed. "I met Mrs Hughes in Cready last week, outside the library. Found her, would be a better description. She couldn't remember what she was supposed to be doing. I brought her back with me, poor woman. What have two such perfectly nice people ever done to deserve losing their only child like that?"

For a while the two women wandered along the lane back to Cleve House in silence then Delia suddenly said, "What was that about Stan and the heavy lifting?"

Maisie sighed and paused at a gate. She looked out across the fields to the sea and harbour below, where her husband's fishing trawler and crab boat were still moored, and shook her head, unable to speak.

"Sorry," – Delia came to stand beside her. – "I shouldn't have asked. What sorrows and secrets we're obliged to keep these days."

Maisie turned and gave her a weak smile, then a thought occurred to her. "Delia, if Pew Pewsey's got Benjie working on his farm, do you think you could use an extra man at Cleve House as well? To do the heavy work? Keep your car in working order and so on?"

"My car?"

"No, well, just a thought. We could do with a handyman, that's all, and . . . maybe you could get a POW or someone like that. Someone safe, of course, no one dangerous. I didn't mean a prisoner in that way, like a convict."

"Ah, you mean like foreign internees. No, I shouldn't like that, not with all those children about. Besides, Charles . . ."

Biting her lip, Maisie waited for Delia to finish what she was saying, but all Delia said was, "Come on – children's tea time soon."

Chapter 12

Old Mr Humphrey of Victoria Villas huffed and puffed at the church organ pedals, his arthritic hands plonking down, missing and striking random keys, lifting rare chords from the ancient instrument as parishioners got to their feet and wandered, blinking, into the bright daylight. Reverend Hughes was in the horseshoe-arched porch, pressing familiar hands and making the usual platitudes until it was Miss Pettit's turn. Maisie and Ginny halted behind her.

"I'm so glad you were able to join us," Reverend Hughes said, bending from his lofty height to address the small spinster. "I noticed you one evening last week, entering the churchyard, but I regret I was on my way to a meeting and late as usual. Is there a grave you are interested in? I'm sorry, I don't know your family name."

"Pettit was my father's surname. I am Maud Lily Pettit, Vicar."

Reverend Hughes shook Miss Pettit's dainty hand a second time. "Very pleased to meet you, Miss Pettit. I hope you will take an active part in our church community here."

Maud Lily Pettit inclined her head in regal acceptance then said, "I no longer have a family that I know of, Vicar, but cemeteries are a little hobby of mine. Graveyards are so interesting, especially country churchyards. Generations of local residents, like in the poem."

"'Each in his narrow cell forever laid the rude forefathers of the hamlet sleep'. Thomas Gray expressed it so well."

Ginny caught the cadence of the pentameter and continued in a rhythm of her own making: "Appleby, Baxter, Plowden

Braund, Chapman and Cutler,

Dymond, Deakin and Drury,

Eckwith, Fulford and Gardner,

Hawkins, Hope and Hopkins,

Iddesliegh . . ." she paused and tapped the side of her head with the heel of her left hand then continued, "Parsons, Pewsey, Pluckrose and Rouse."

"Ginny!" Maisie tugged on her daughter's sleeve. "Miss Pettit and the vicar don't need you reciting the war memorial."

"On the contrary, Mrs Hawkins," Reverend Hughes beamed, "it is a prodigious feat. I wish I had Ginny's recall."

"They're on the church wall," Ginny stated bluntly, "next to the font."

"Goodness, and you remember all the names? How clever." Miss Pettit gave a moue of appreciation.

Maisie wanted to say *It's because she's got nothing else in her head,* but she didn't. Ginny's strange memory was as much a mystery to her as it was a surprise to their listeners.

"So there you are, Miss Pettit, a list of our local residents." Reverend Hughes led them away from the door where they were blocking the exit out into the churchyard.

"'Cept they're all dead now," added Ginny in a matter of fact tone.

"Yes, but we have their families here still, and new residents like Miss Pettit. And here are Mr and Mrs Bantry, some more new residents. Although, like my wife and me, not so new anymore."

Out of the corner of her eye, Maisie noted Billy Baxter and his wife coming to join them, but the moment Billy caught sight of Archie Bantry he tugged Edna in the opposite direction. Archibald and Hilda Bantry joined the vicar's group. Reverend Hughes had apparently failed to speak to them as they'd left the church.

Seeing Archibald Bantry in profile shaking hands with the vicar, Maisie felt the skin on the back of her neck freeze. He wasn't wearing black, and it wasn't a cold, stormy night, but this was the person on the quay who could have helped her and didn't and – worse, far worse – who knew what time she had gone up to Cleve House on the night Stan disappeared. Putting a hand under Ginny's elbow, she urged her away from the group.

Archie Bantry, a lean man with a nose like a brass tap, looked at her with narrowed eyes. She made an attempt at a smile. He inclined his head slightly in acknowledgement and Maisie's world stood still. Voices droned around her, but she was lost in a stomach-churning blackness. Then Mrs Bantry stepped into the hiatus and the day came back into focus.

Hilda Bantry was nearly as tall and angular as her husband. She didn't look particularly unkind or unpleasant in her fawn coat and hat, but Maisie had heard the sharp edge of her tongue on more than one occasion as she fulfilled her cleaning and flower duties on the church roster. They looked a sad sort of couple, standing together as if they'd found each other by accident.

Reverend Hughes began introducing Miss Pettit to them. Trying to control her inner panic, Maisie was astonished to see how Miss Pettit's animated face glazed over as she was presented, as if donning a mask.

"Mr and Mrs Bantry, from Prince Albert Villas – Miss Pettit, who I believe now resides in Seabreeze bungalow. Is that not correct? Mr and Mrs Bantry live next door to Mrs Prior, who runs our Sunday school. Mr Bantry is an important person in our community nowadays, he tells me – the County Agricultural Committee, isn't it?"

"That is correct, Vicar, food and rationing inspection, and County Agriculture – just doing my bit for our war effort." Archie Bantry looked directly at Ginny and narrowed his eyes again, then turned a serpent's smile on Miss Pettit, who stepped back a pace, perhaps without realising it. His large, right hand shot from his sleeve. Maud Lily Pettit reluctantly extended her small, gloved hand to him, then to his wife.

"But we know you!" stated Mrs Bantry. "In Ilfracombe, before the war – remember? We used to stay at the Strand every summer. Didn't you live there for a while with Mrs – what was her name? The elderly lady with a stick and a rather unusual name. She had a companion who . . . Oh, goodness me, yes."

"Crabtree-Goatley, or something of the sort," supplied Mr Bantry. "I was just thinking the same."

Miss Pettit gave a brave smile in face of the double-barrelled sights of the Bantrys. "Ilfracombe? No, I fear you are mistaken. I have never been to – North Devon, isn't it? I was abroad until war broke out. Rescued off the Rock of Gibraltar by our Royal Navy. Very exciting. I have been to Torquay, many moons ago, when I was a girl. That's in Devon."

Mrs Bantry pursed her thin lips and gave Miss Pettit a hard look. "My mistake, sorry."

"No apology required. We spinsters are much alike – white hair, white gloves in summer, navy-blue from September to May." She held up a hand and wiggled her fingers. "Blame ladies' outfitters and haberdashers – they offer us little choice. Now, do excuse me. I must be trotting along. Goodbye."

The party broke up and Maisie ushered Ginny down the church path to the lych-gate. Behind her, she heard Archie Bantry say loud enough for all to hear, "That young woman is well into female conscription age. She should be doing essential war work on the land or in a factory, not taking up our time on a Sunday with her nonsense."

"Oh, Archie, charity, charity – the girl's a simpleton," his wife replied.

"Not if she can read, she's not."

Maisie sighed and took her daughter's hand. The odious Bantry was right, and it was getting more and more difficult to keep Ginny at home. Dusting for Miss Pettit and washing up for Delia Metherall did not count as essential war work.

As they reached the turn in the lane to their cottage, Ginny said, "She has been to Ilfracombe. She's got a shell box that says 'A present from Ilfracombe' – I told you. She's got all these little pots with lids. Snuff boxes you said. She said they belonged to her father, 'cept some of them look new to me. She says they're for tobacco snuff, like you said. But they don't smell like tobacco. Not like Grandpa put in his pipe. It don't look like tobacco, neither. Tobacco isn't grey. There's bits in the shell boxes. The ones from Ilfracombe and Eastbourne smell like bad mushrooms. Where's Eastbourne?"

Maisie was only half listening; her mind had raced ahead. Their garden gate was open. So was the front door. *Someone coming in, or someone going out?* Either way, her heart lurched.

Yan, Jean, Gianni, whoever he was, had left. His clothes were gone. The soft boots she had so carefully cleaned, the cracks lovingly rubbed with saddle grease she'd bought specially from the hardware store, were gone from by the door. The jacket wasn't on the peg. The red leather purse she'd put back on the mantelpiece was no longer there, nor was the flick-knife.

"How will he manage without us?" Maisie whispered.

Ginny's face was white. "He's gone," she said in disbelief.

"Ah, well . . ." Maisie shrugged off her coat, but Ginny stood stock still in the doorway.

"He can't go. He's going to marry me."

Maisie turned and stared at her daughter, then sank into the nearest chair.

"Like that, is it? Another cheating male. They're lying devils, the lot of 'em. So who is he and why's he here? Did he tell you that in English?"

"No."

Maisie took off her church hat and threw it across the room. "Go and put the kettle on and make a cup of that disgusting coffee out of a bottle. I need to get my thoughts together."

Ginny crossed to the kitchen then popped her head back round the door. "I 'spect he'll be back dreckly."

"For free board and lodge? Not this time, he won't." Maisie stood up and tore the blankets and sheets off the truckle bed that had taken up most of her living-room since her dead father-in-law had started wheezing with the winter wind. She tugged them into a pile on the floor and kicked the bed over with an angry foot.

"Here," she called, "Ginny, fetch this and burn it — it'll be full of his germs." She flung the pillow at her daughter. "When did he say he wanted to marry you?"

"Yesterday afternoon."

"Yesterday! When?"

"I didn't look at the clock."

"Ginny! What I mean is: did he give you a date – for the wedding?" Even Maisie forgot how literal her daughter was at times.

Ginny cocked her head from one side to the other as if trying to remember. "No."

"So sometime yesterday afternoon, while you were here having a cuddle with our Mr Suspicious and I was cleaning floors up at Cleve House single-handed . . ." Maisie took a deep breath – what was the point? "Let's forget what he actually said, although I'd dearly like to know. Just tell me what *happened*."

"Happened? Like in what he did?"

"Yes."

"He liked to kiss me when I took him his meals."

"Just kissing?"

"We cuddled as well, in the night."

"In the night!"

"He said my bed was warmer than down here."

"I'll bet. So more than just kissing?"

Ginny hung her head then she looked up, bright eyed. A glorious smile spread across her lovely face. "Shall I have a baby? I'd like a baby."

"God help us," Maisie gasped, and burst into tears.

Chapter 13

"I saw three ships go sailing by, sailing by. I saw three ships go sailing by on Christmas day in the morning . . ."

Maisie hummed the words to herself as she gazed at a rose-pink dawn seascape through Ginny's open back bedroom window. It was May, not December, but the tune persisted. She tugged the sash window down further and leaned out for a better look. The first vessel was a fishing trawler: it was followed by two smaller, military-looking launches.

"Looks like your pa's trawler out there," Maisie said.

Ginny murmured something inaudible from the bed.

"I ought to let the twins use Porth Rose." Maisie studied the smaller boats for a moment longer. "No point her being tied up and they needing every bit of money they can get. They *are* Navy vessels. Can't think why they're in so close, unless they're trying to get into Wheal Marie quay." Maisie gripped the top of the window, "Ginny, you awake?"

"Mmm."

"Have you heard if the mine's open again?"

Ginny raised herself onto her elbows. "No one's there, 'cept Becca and her little ones. She's got a caravan like a gypsy. It's ever so pretty, all painted green and red."

"I know, and good luck to her, damp, draughty old thing." Maisie turned and looked at Ginny. "How do you know it's green and red?"

"She showed me."

"When? When were you off on your own down there? I've told you a hundred times not to go wandering about on your own anymore. There's men stationed on that new airfield . . ."

"I wasn't on my own."

"Then who were you with? Becca?"

"Yes." Ginny brushed her hair off her face with her hands, started to get out of bed, then lay back again.

"And?" Maisie had long accepted that her daughter wasn't quite right in the head, despite learning to read and write – to a certain extent. She didn't have a very high IQ, but Ginny was perfectly capable of being devious. "Is that foreign boy still around, then?" She squinted at Ginny's face. The girl responded with a wonderful smile. "So that's the way of it. And where is he, exactly?"

"With Mr Paddon."

"With Ezra Paddon, at the garage! S'pose it makes sense if he's a mechanic like he said. Who'd have thought it? Old man Paddon's the meanest devil I know, bible-bashing, old sober-sides. Wonder how your Yanny-Jan-Gianni wheedled himself into that job."

Maisie bent down to pick up Ginny's cast-off slip. Keeping her face averted, she said, "You remember you're going to tell me when your time of the month comes?"

"Yes," Ginny replied.

Maisie let out a sigh and turned back to the window, wondering if it was too late to tell Ginny about birth control, but as she looked out again at the trawler and Navy launches another thought struck her. "I hope they sneaky Deakin boys haven't been selling your pa's stash of tins and bottles, and those American cigarettes. We better get down and sort it out, bring what we can up here. Come on, they'll have helped Stan put his last load of goods into the tunnel; they know what he's got and where it is. God almighty, I should have thought about it before. If that detective gets a whiff – or Bantry – we're in trouble."

"He was on the quay."

Maisie paused. "Who?"

"Mr Robbins with the white hair."

"When?"

"Day before yesterday. He said 'Hello, Miss Hawkins, nice day' when I crossed the bridge to go up to Cleve House."

"So he's still sniffing around, then." Maisie had very mixed feelings: on the one hand she wanted Stan found; on the other, she wanted him gone forever, with or without a widow's pension. For a moment she lost track of what she was doing, then the Navy vessels caught her eye again. "I hope they aren't Military Police launches out of Plymouth. If they find Stan's NAAFI tins and stuff they'll fine me, and if I can't pay – which I can't – they'll most like send me to prison. Come on, we got an hour before I have to start on all they sandwiches for the tea party. We'll get what we can now and empty the tunnel as soon as we can tomorrow. That way if the Deakin boys come back . . ." Maisie pulled the covers off her daughter, "Up!"

Ginny swung her legs out of the bed, saying, "What about the other man?"

"What man?"

"The man that comes down to Pa's cave."

"What man? I thought it was only your pa's crew that used the cave."

"A tall man comes down from the road. The Deakins use their boat. He's thin, not like the Deakins – they're all little."

Maisie's mouth went very dry. "Tall – like Reverend Hughes?"

"Mm." Ginny was vague.

"When does he come? Every night? Every week?"

"Not every week. When there's a bit of a moon, but not when it's full. That's how I see him."

"Oh, hell!" Maisie shouted.

"What's the matter, Ma?" Ginny asked.

"Nothing. Everything." Maisie pushed the window up and went to the door. "If we hurry we can get a good load up in baskets. I'll use that funny American ham stuff for my sandwiches; it'll come in handy today. Get yourself washed and dressed, girl. We got a lot to do. Ned MacManus is coming at eleven to pick us up, and sandwiches have got to be done by then."

Carrying a large torch and a wooden mallet in her shopping basket, Maisie slithered down the cliff path as fast as she could, with Ginny behind her carrying an empty wicker laundry basket. The tide was out, which gave them plenty of time, but knowing Ned MacManus would soon be arriving, and anxious he should know nothing of what they were doing, Maisie was in a hurry.

"So who is it that comes down here at night, then?" she asked Ginny as they clambered into the seaweed-smelling cavern. But before Ginny could answer Maisie let out a groan. "Oh, no, you're right. Someone's been here." She focused the torch on the back of the cave: "Look."

Behind the bulging rock that made getting in and out of the storage tunnel so awkward, the brick wall had been opened and not all the bricks replaced. Maisie turned back to Ginny. "Who is it you've seen coming down here?"

"I don't know," the girl replied.

"Might be one of your pa's Plymouth mates, I suppose." She put her shopping bag beside the wicker basket on the rock and began tugging out bricks to get into the tunnel. "Whoever it is, he's thin as a rake. Unless it's children. I wouldn't put it past that Simon Prior to be running a black market racket, even at his age. Blast!" The nail of her right forefinger had torn down to the quick. "You have a go. I can't get in there yet."

Ginny edged round the rock and began pulling out bricks, placing one on top of the other like a small child's tower.

"Oh, for God's sake, Ginny!" Maisie pushed round her and sidled as best she could between the cave wall and the remaining bricks then panned the narrow space in front of her with the torch.

It looked like precious little was left. Using the torch beam she tried to decipher what was written on the boxes. The spam stuff was still there – nobody wanted that – so were the condensed milk and cans of kerosene, but someone had been at the cigarettes – a box was open and half empty, and all the liquor bottles had gone. She couldn't say for sure because she didn't know how much had come in, but a lot had been removed. And then she smiled, "Good!" she laughed. "Let 'em have it. Better for us: they can't fine us for what we haven't got – I hope." Balancing the torch on the top of one box, she opened another and began handing tins to Ginny. "Put these in your basket, take them up to the kitchen, then come back down for another lot. We'll load those sandwiches for the village tea and get rid of as much as we can this afternoon. That way I don't have to worry about neither Detective Nosy Robbins nor Mr Nosy Bantry – you sure it isn't him you've seen?"

"Don't think so." Ginny put the basket next to Maisie. "Shall I put the tins in the kitchen, Ma?"

"Course not! No, put them on the floor in the outhouse in case someone comes round before we're ready."

Between them they filled the wicker basket with as much as Ginny could carry then she manoeuvred it out backwards through the cave.

To conserve the battery, Maisie switched off the torch and perched against the large boulder to wait. As her eyes got used to the dark her other senses became more acute. She listened, but there was no drip-drip of water, no scrabble of rats to frighten her. After a while, feeling braver, she got to her feet, lit the torch and clambered through the brick wall, then started down the tunnel. After Stan's boxes, it was empty. Bent double, she reached the junction where it joined the Bayview tunnel. She stopped, put out the light and listened again. Nothing. Not knowing what she was expecting, whether to be relieved or not, she made her way back to the boxes and started to fill her shopping basket with condensed milk and a canteen-sized tin of jam, hoping she'd have enough bread to use it all up for the Porthferris Tea Party. The kerosene could go in the outhouse.

"I'll pass as much as I can to the twins," she said aloud, "then I can forget this tunnel and everything that goes with it."

Hearing her own voice in the still atmosphere, Maisie remembered what she was going to listen out for. Stan had mentioned bumps and bangs in the old mine more than once. People in the village reckoned it was haunted. Stan had said that was a ruse for keeping people out, but then he'd heard it himself. Maisie went to the gap where the cave met the tunnel and stood there, waiting. A chill prickled round her neck; she felt her stomach do a loop the loop. She turned and scrambled as fast as she could back to the beach, gasping for fresh air.

As she waited in the sunlight, her thoughts returned to what Ginny had said: someone, perhaps more than one, was coming down here at night, and walking right round the side of their cottage to do so. "I should tell that detective," she murmured, wandering back towards the cave, looking for some sort of clue in the broken shells and shingle under her feet. When she looked up she was facing the mooring ring and the severed rope. "Whoever would do that to steal his boat?"

Then Maisie remembered finding a very sharp, open knife in a complete stranger's jacket. "Oh, my God," she gasped. "What is going on?"

Maisie was spreading margarine on the last slice of bread when it dawned on her that if a man was coming down their side path to get to the sea cave, presumably to collect Stan's brandy and tobacco, there was probably someone already there to help him: the Deakin twins coming in by boat most likely, and taking the money for the goods. When Ginny came back from stashing the tins in the outhouse, Maisie said, "If someone's coming down from the road to get to the cave, is there someone already down there?"

"Johnny's there." The reply was matter-of-fact.

Maisie sighed, "Jan-Yan-Johnny? Of course he is. That explains it." She turned and looked her daughter in the eye, "You are *not* to see him again, understand? Not in the daytime, nor in the evening – never. He's not welcome here *ever* again."

Chapter 14

The May Day Fair in Porthferris was a tame relic of a pagan festival. Having lost its original meaning it was now a daytime village bun struggle with horseshoe throwing and cricket on the meadow backing onto Cleve House. A special tea party was held in a boathouse on the quay for the children of local fishermen and members of the East Cornwall Seafarers' Guild. The Guild provided for widows and gave family support during periods of bad weather, but they couldn't help Maisie until a death certificate proved she was indeed a widow.

Trestle tables in the boathouse were heaped with food, and children were treated to an amateur Punch and Judy show in a make-do puppet theatre. Punch and Judy were still immensely popular, the string of sausages now having a special comic significance for the adults.

Ginny was stationed at the tea urn, with careful instructions that she recalled and recited word for word from previous years. Maisie took charge of the sandwiches provided by village households and mixed in her own overloaded contributions with those more meagrely scraped with fish paste or ketchup. There were cakes, too, some with dried fruit and nuts, some with butter icing made from carefully rationed margarine and sugar or illicit Glebe Farm clotted cream.

Mrs Bantry had positioned herself along a workbench at the back of the boathouse, guarding various plates of colourful jellies. Maisie joined her, looking round with satisfaction. "Nigh on three years of war and rationing but we aren't going short. Our little ones will get their tea same as always. Someone should tell that Mr Hitler he's wasting his time trying to starve *us* out."

Hilda Bantry eyed her suspiciously and pursed her thin mouth. Maisie gave a little shudder. Then, looking across to the huge, open double doors, Mrs Bantry said, "What a disgrace! You would think private school pupils would know better!"

A sudden rise in the noise level indicated the entrance of the St Dominick's boys and one girl, Delia's daughter Libby, joining the local children. They arrived in a crocodile led by Mr Booth with Miss Claverham, known to all as 'the Clapper' for her means of obtaining attention. Once released from their teachers' control, however, there was a general pushing and shoving and yelling as boys veered off and helped themselves to fistfuls of sandwiches before Maisie could reach them. She soon found herself applying the rationing rules she so hated. "One at a time, one at a time! George Drury, take those sandwiches out of your pocket . . ."

Aubrey Chatwynde, landlord of the Fisherman's Boot, stepped in to help, sending overexcited miscreants off with a good-natured wallop. "Sit down, boys. Sit at the table and wait to be served like gentlemen, please. This is not a jumble sale. That's it. Sidle along the bench, and no kicking under the table." He snapped two fingers onto an ear and bent down to speak in hushed but menacing tones to a very red face. "That is enough. If you can't behave like a decent human being I shall throw you in the sea like a bad fish.

Understood?" His blazer and beige slacks lost their immaculate appearance as the culprit's palms begged for mercy.

Maisie watched, smiling, seeing why he was such a popular Home Guard platoon leader, and why he had been accepted so readily by the Boot locals, despite their mimicking of the posh voice and snide remarks about the spotted handkerchief in his top pocket.

Once the sandwiches had been devoured, Maisie supervised the passing of other plates containing pasties and buns along the tables. Miss Claverham made occasional feeble efforts to prevent boys getting up and running around, but it was a losing battle. The other teacher, Mr Booth, had completely disappeared.

Aubrey Chatwynde returned to her side. "Anything I can do?"

"No, we're fine now. Thank you, Mr Chatwynde. It's very kind of you."

"My pleasure, Mrs Hawkins, but I'd appreciate a task, however minor. Being here is a visible means of justifying my absence from the cricket match. I'm utterly useless with a bat and ball."

"Skill doesn't come into cricket up on that ol' meadow. You're lucky to stay on your feet at all up there, what with the wind and all they rabbit holes."

Aubrey Chatwynde laughed. "Not quite Lords, is it? I don't suppose I could offer you a glass of sherry to replenish energy?"

Maisie Rose grinned. "You certainly could."

"Come across to the pub, then. There's something I wanted to talk to you about as well, it'll be —"

"Mrs Hawkins, Mrs Hawkins!" Hilda Bantry interrupted them, edging in and eyeing the empty plates suspiciously. "Oh, they have all gone. I should have explained to you that each child may only have *one* sandwich and *one* slice of cake, or a pasty and a bun *or* cake – but *not* all three. I see it is too late."

Maisie took a deep breath and said pointedly, "A special occasion today, Mrs Bantry. The Porthferris tea party is always a special treat for the little ones."

"A special treat, indeed. For adults as well, I would say. Cream cakes, jam doughnuts, and some of those sandwiches were overflowing with ham."

"Spam, I think, not ham."

"Whatever it was – it is a disgrace."

"I don't see the harm, Mrs Bantry. We've made it all and brought it ourselves. Share and share alike, it's what we always do."

Mrs Bantry narrowed her squinty eyes and glowered about her.

"The cream cakes will be from Glebe Farm Dairy," Maisie continued. "It's a tradition down here with us. The dairy always sends us cream and cakes for the tea party."

The 'us' was not lost on Hilda Bantry, and Maisie cursed herself for encouraging peevishness. Out of the corner of her eye she glimpsed little Miss Pettit and called her over, hoping to distract the Bantry woman with a fellow Londoner, or wherever they came from.

"Miss Pettit, I am glad you could come. Have you had something to eat, my dear? There's scotch eggs somewhere, for the adults. Sandwiches have all gone, I'm afraid. It's for the children, really, but we adults always have a good time. Heaven knows, we need a bit of fun these days."

"Too true, Mrs Hawkins. I'm afraid this week's news has been particularly depressing." Miss Pettit could barely make herself heard above the din.

Hilda Bantry surveyed the small spinster coldly, then said, "That's a pretty brooch you're wearing."

Maud Lily Pettit slapped a hand over the brooch on her jacket lapel. "Oh!" she cried, then gave a wan smile and tapped it, leaving her left her hand covering it. "My beau gave it to me – when he was home on leave, before –" she paced her words, sighed gently, and said, "the Somme. We were to be married. I treasure it."

There was an awkward silence until Aubrey Chatwynde gave a polite cough. "Well ladies, I'll leave you to discuss your bangles and brooches. No place for a chap like me."

"But you worked in Hatton Garden, Mr Chatwynde, didn't you?" Maisie said.

"And who told you that, I wonder?"

Maisie couldn't remember if it had been Stan or Delia, but she caught the warning look in Aubrey Chatwynde's eye and flapped her hands in the air, "No idea." She turned back to Mrs Bantry now, all charm. "Have you had something to eat as well, Mrs Bantry – after all your hard work?"

As Aubrey moved away he cocked his head in the direction of his pub and held up an open hand with five fingers. Maisie nodded, then said, "Try one of Mrs Pewsey's big scotch eggs, Mrs Bantry, if there are any left. The smaller ones have got eggs from my hens. The sausage meat comes from our local butcher. All bought with saved up coupons, so nothing for you to worry about."

But Mrs Bantry was still focused on Miss Pettit's brooch. "Gold, diamonds and sapphires, is it?" she demanded, edging closer to the older lady.

"Oh, I'd like to think so, but, no, it's almost certainly paste, and . . . er . . . perhaps an amethyst." Reluctantly Miss Pettit removed her hand.

Maisie looked at the brooch. It was a small bunch of flowers with gold stems and leaves and pretty blue petals around what looked like diamonds. She knew nothing about jewellery, but the brooch did indeed look very expensive.

"I've seen one *exactly* like that before," Hilda Bantry stated, "in Ilfracombe."

Miss Pettit smiled again and turned to Maisie, but something caught her attention. "Oh," she squeaked, "is that a Punch and Judy show?"

"Billy Baxter, our butcher, and Alf the grocer do it every year. Not sure how they'll squeeze in this year, though – Billy's got such a corporation on him," Maisie laughed.

"One notes few people in this village have had to tighten their belts, despite the government urging us reduce our diets," Mrs Bantry replied.

The woman's voice reminded Maisie of railway announcements: someone trying to speak 'proper' without a trace of emotion. She wanted to shake the miserable woman until her hat flew off and her grey hair fell out of its sad little net. Instead, she said, "I'd best go and help get the kiddies organised for the show."

Extracting herself from behind the empty trestle table, Maisie wandered across the boathouse, checking on children still stuffing themselves with cakes and buns, and making sure Ginny was still in place at the tea urn. Then, slipping behind the puppet theatre, she opened a side door and ran across the quay to the Fisherman's Boot.

Once inside, she took one look at the landlord and said, "Could you make it a schooner of sherry, Mr Chatwynde, please?"

"Coming up. Dymond's Bristol Cream, in a bucket if need be. Make yourself comfortable over there."

Maisie hadn't been inside the pub since Christmas. There had been changes. Pretty curtains now hung at the windows, and cushions had appeared on the window seats. She went across to take a closer look at the fabric and caught a glimpse of a figure scurrying past. Through the old leaded panes she could only see it was a small person in blue, but she knew it was Miss Pettit hurrying back to her bungalow.

"Poor old biddy," she said as Aubrey Chatwynde put a large sherry on the table by the empty fireplace. "That Bantry woman's got it in for her. Seems to think Miss Pettit is someone she knew in a hotel years ago – won't let it go. We had a terrier like her once. Silly thing got stuck down a rabbit hole and the stoat that Stan had set earlier bit his ear off. Although . . ." Maisie paused, "I think Miss Pettit is quite a wily one on the quiet, so she might escape."

Aubrey Chatwynde, with a stiff whisky in his right hand, seated himself across the small round table opposite Maisie. "Your very good health, Mrs Hawkins. To happier times, eh?" They clinked glasses then he said, "I'm glad you mentioned Stan. No news?"

Maisie shook her head.

"We all keep an eye out for him, all my regulars, that is, up and down the coast. We haven't given up: we'll do our best for you."

Maisie set her glass down before her shaking hand gave her away. *He's about to tell me he suspects*, she thought. *He saw Stan leave that night. How am I going to react? Sad or surprised?*

The surprise was genuine.

"It's about Stan's boats . . . Do you think you could let us use them for a couple of weeks? Maybe a bit longer, maybe less."

"You mean for the Home Guard? Whatever for?"

Aubrey Chatwynde gave her a crooked smile and a knowing look.

"Ah, that," Maisie said. She picked up her sherry again, feeling a warm glow of satisfaction, enjoying the moment. It was lovely to be sitting down, and to be treated as a woman in her own right for a change. "Mr Chatwynde, do you think you could . . . um . . . Well, as it's my husband's boats you'll be using, could you do something for me?"

Aubrey Chatwynde's face clouded, as if she was interfering in carefully laid plans. Maisie was suddenly embarrassed, "Never mind – I'll ask the Deakin twins."

"Tell me what you need first."

"It's Stan's sea cave . . . Do you know about the sea caves?"

Aubrey Chatwynde grinned and nodded.

"I need someone to help me empty . . . There are some things in our sea cave – they must be getting very damp, and I can't use them."

"Perishable?"

Maisie nodded.

"Tobacco?"

"Cigarettes."

Aubrey Chatwynde grinned again. "I'll come and fetch them myself. Would they fit in the boot of my little roadster?"

"Prob'ly. There's other things as well. Ginny and I have got the tins we need up, but there's still some kerosene and all sorts down there. I can give you first dibs if you like."

"I like." Aubrey Chatwynde raised his glass, then he asked in a different tone, "How do you know you can trust me not to say anything, though?"

"I don't, not really. Except I thought Stan might be getting some of it for you."

"Sometimes." Aubrey Chatwynde raised his glass and met her eye. "Deal done."

For a few moments they sat in companionable silence then Maisie, warm with sherry, had a thought. "If I came in for a drop of sherry – now and again – do you think anyone would mind? I'd like a bit of company of an evening – now and again – that's all."

"Mind? Why would they mind?"

"Well, a woman – on her own – you know what I mean?"

"You wouldn't be the only unaccompanied woman in the Boot of an evening, I can tell you that."

"No! Who else comes in?"

"Miss Pettit."

"Never!"

"As you said just now, there's more to Miss Pettit than meets the eye. The way, I strongly suspect, there is a lot more to Maisie Rose Hawkins than she would like people to know."

Maisie gaped at the well-dressed, well spoken man in front of her and felt her face flush red. What was he suggesting? Had she just made a monumental mistake? Was this the man she'd seen on the quay that night? Or the person coming down by their cottage to the cove from the road? Or did he want to use the boats because he already knew about Stan's tunnel and simply wanted to get what he'd asked for, and had perhaps paid for up front? She knew she should say something about money, but she couldn't bear to mention it. With a slightly trembling hand, Maisie picked up her schooner glass and took a long sip of thick, sweet sherry, willing Aubrey Chatwynde to say nothing more.

He didn't, on that subject. He shifted onto the chair at her side and said very quietly, "Could I ask you to call me Aubrey?"

Flushed with sherry and a confused sense of contentment, Maisie Rose left the Fisherman's Boot and began to cross the quay, back to the boathouse, but halfway across she stopped in her tracks. Standing by the repaired footbridge over the inlet was the angular, hatless figure she had seen that night in March. It had been almost pitch black then, and she had only seen him for a split second, but her feeling when she'd seen him again at church were confirmed. It *was* Archibald Bantry.

She started to run. Dashing between children and parents, Maisie collided with the stocky police detective, Bob Robbins. "Oh!" she gasped, putting both hands to his chest.

"Mrs Hawkins," – the detective touched the brim of a hat he wasn't wearing – "I was hoping to see you."

"Have you . . . have you found him? Where?"

"No, no, I'm sorry. We put out his description to all stations, upcountry as well, but we've had no leads at all, I'm afraid. I'm here off-duty. I'm thinking of taking up sea angling for the summer months. Came down for a look at Porthferris Bay. Didn't know your fête was on – jolly event by the looks of it."

Maisie looked at his round face. He had widely spaced eyes that gave him a kind-natured expression. His bristly, white hair ruffled in the breeze off the water. Then she realised he'd caught her looking at him and said hastily, "I must get back to my post."

"I'll walk with you. I thought you might give me a few tips about the rocks along here. The best places to set up my gear and so on."

Maisie went limp with disappointment and relief, and without thinking said, "You can use our cove if you like. The current runs up round from the bay pretty fast there – you should get a decent catch, all right." She chattered out the words, then cursed herself for foolishness. Hadn't she been anxious to avoid having this very man anywhere near her cottage ever again?

Chapter 15

"Have you heard the news?" Delia gasped out the words the moment Maisie arrived to start her morning duties.

"I've stopped listening to it – it's too depressing."

"Dr MacManus says we've got measles! I had to call him out. Miss Claverham said two of the boys were queasy after the tea party and we put it down to greediness, but at bedtime time they were covered in a rash. So we got them into the sick bay and I called Dr MacManus. Oh, and – guess what? – Mr Booth was nowhere to be found." Maisie donned her apron while Delia prattled on. "Did you see him with Mrs Prior at the fête? Not very discreet, are they? The problem is – about the measles – Charles is due to arrive any time this week. He says he's got to come and sort things out here. Not us at the house – other things. Don't ask: I've no idea. But if we're in quarantine he shouldn't come. I don't know whether to warn him or simply let him come and find out, and then . . ." Delia's voice was rising in pitch.

Maisie was surprised. It wasn't like Delia to get so agitated. There was something more significant than measles going on, that was evident, but she wouldn't ask. She'd got enough problems of her own.

"If he does come, I'll get a piglet slaughtered," Delia continued. "We can have a sort of hog roast to celebrate, and it might make up for having the delightful odour of rural pig sty in the rose garden, not to mention forty small boys up to mischief wherever they can find it. That Simon Prior needs a talking to – he's the ringleader."

As Delia paced around the kitchen, Maisie set about her daily chores, then she stopped and said, "You mean no one can leave Cleve House while there's measles here? Can't I go home? That police detective is coming this afternoon to use our cove for his fishing . . ."

Delia raised her perfect eyebrows, "Is he, now? And is this an off-duty arrangement?"

"I s'pose so. Oh, no! Nothing like that." Maisie sat down on the nearest chair with a thump. "I've got to get home of an evening, Delia, to keep an eye on Ginny. It's not only for that detective chap. He'll be fishing off our cove, which is all my stupid fault, I know, but I need to keep an eye on him, as well for other reasons. He might find the tunnel. We left the bricks loose because I was in such a hurry with the sandwiches, and there's things still there belonging to . . ." Maisie gulped for breath, "other people. I told – someone – about it, and he says he'll take what I've got, but then last night I thought 'what happens when Stan comes back and finds it's all gone?' or worse, he finds there's a policeman there? So I need it to look like what it is, with the detective, I mean, just a coincidence that he's there – in case Stan comes back and finds him and blames me. He'll be angry enough without . . ."

Delia was standing still now, staring at Maisie. "Maisie, you've got to get it straight in your head. You did not cause whatever has happened to Stan. He was drunk; he slipped down your cliff path and somehow fell in the water, or whatever he did. I honestly don't think he's ever going to return."

"I left him out there in all that rain. I was *hoping* he would die. Now I think he must have got trapped in the old mine somehow and a tunnel caved in and . . . and it's all my fault. There's cigarettes and kerosene and I don't know what stacked in the tunnel, and Ginny says strangers are coming down from the road to get it, and there's prob'ly more in the mine – only how the police never found the tunnel is a mystery – which just goes to show they didn't look very hard for Stan, so he could be there. I know I ought to tell that detective so he searches again, but I just can't, because they'll send me to prison and then what'll happen to Ginny?"

"Oh, Maisie, Stan can't be in the mine. The police searched there, and our Home Guard. And *hoping* isn't a crime. Leaving a drunken sot of a husband, who everyone knows treated you badly, to sleep it off by his own back door, isn't a crime. Stay there in that chair and I'll make us some proper coffee."

"But it *is* my fault! If I'd opened the door and let him in –"

"He'd have given you a bashing."

"It wasn't always like that."

Delia clattered about with the percolator and her clandestine ground coffee beans and let her much loved housekeeper say what had to be said.

Maisie had reached the end of her tether. In gulping sobs she let go of months of pent up guilt and worry. "His poor dad – I gave him extra medicine. I wanted him to sleep, I didn't mean for him to die. Ginny's no use. I can't trust her with anything, and now she's courting and soon as not there'll be a baby and I'll have to bring it up, and there's no room in our cottage and I haven't got a pension or Stan's money coming in. He brought home a good bit of cash now and then. I'll be washing sheets and mopping floors for other people till I drop dead. If that boy had been decent and stayed . . . But he didn't, he just upped and walked out without a by-your-leave, and now I learn he's been taking Stan's stuff and probably selling it, so that means there's more people in the chain. And he's been seeing Ginny, though Lord knows when, because she doesn't come back late at night or anything like that, so she might be inventing it, and I don't know what to tell her about you-know-what that she'll understand, except that she mustn't see him . . ."

Delia abandoned the coffee pot and stood beside Maisie, cradling her into her body for comfort. "Sshh. There's nothing to be done. Let it go, Maisie."

"Every time I go home I wonder will Stan be waiting for me, sitting in his chair with his belt in his hand. Every time the door opens I get the jitters . . ."

"Sshh . . . You're all right." Delia gently rocked Maisie in her arms.

". . . and now that detective's come back and says he wants to go fishing on our beach. Fishing for information, more like. I said he could, then I remembered we hadn't emptied the tunnel in the sea cave or bricked it back up proper." Maisie took a deep breath. "Dear Lord, it's all such a mess and there's no end to it. And then I go saying nice things to him because he's got kind eyes and I like his roly-poly face." Maisie howled with distress.

Gradually she began to relax, and Delia said, "Perhaps these measles are a blessing. Stay here with me. You've got your own room and there's space for Ginny. Please come."

Maisie separated herself and wiped her eyes on her pinafore. "I can't. I got to get back for Ginny. I'm not happy about her being on her own now and she's never had measles. They say it's nasty when you get older, and she might be . . . Not that it would make much difference, but . . . Can I telephone Miss Pettit to warn her? She'll be there by now."

Part Two

Home Guard

Chapter 16

Charles Metherall, wearing an open-necked shirt and a pair of old cricket trousers, took a fond look at his sleeping wife and closed the bedroom door quietly. Passing his children's room, he was tempted to look in, but he didn't want them with him on this particular morning stroll down to the harbour: he had work to do.

Standing outside the front door, he inhaled deeply and caught a whiff of pig. He grunted, not unlike one of the porkers, with mild disgust, but spread his arms in a long, satisfying stretch nevertheless. The open sky was a delight after months cooped up in a London office and a cramped bed-sit. He was a country boy at heart. It was what had first attracted him to Delia, her honest dislike of the metropolis. He strode round what remained of the Cleve House garden, ignoring the pigsty and the general havoc caused by turning their family home into a prep-school playground, and headed out across the springy grass towards the edge of the cliff.

There was an ugly concrete pillbox set on the headland and a row of sandbags and rolls of barbed wire along the top of the cliff, but the view out to sea was otherwise unchanged.

He went nearer the edge and looked down. The wide sweep of Porthferris Bay with its holiday brochure golden sand and tide pools was now disfigured with wooden posts to prevent landing craft getting in. Barbed wire hung down over the brambles on the cliff and, worst of all, as far as Delia and the village were concerned, mines had been laid the full length of the strand. There'd be no sandcastles here for a very long time. He thought of Churchill's speech in the House of Commons – ". . . We shall defend our Island, whatever the cost may be, we shall fight on the beaches . . ." – and shuddered.

To the right, green cliffs thick with briars blocked off the worst of the westerlies; to the left, set between natural rock walls, was the tiny harbour. It was very small, but if the Germans synchronised landings in Looe and other small ports along the coast it would be an ideal spot to establish a foot, or jack boot, in the door, as they had done on Jersey.

Charles sighed and lifted his head to the air once more; it was too glorious a day for gloomy possibilities, an English May morning at its best. Despite the evacuated prep school, Cleve House was still a family home, and Porthferris Bay and the rest of the Cornish coastline were free from Nazi occupation. He swung his arms up and did a couple of PT jumps for fun.

"Cap'n, cap'n!"

A filthy cap on a bird-nest head popped up from the gulley path. Charles dashed his arms to his side. *What on earth?* "Ah, Harry, it's you."

Mad Harry Deakin hopped across the tufted grass from the cliff path to stand next to Charles. The Army major took a side step; even up here with a brisk sea breeze Mad Harry stank like a crate of kippers left in the sun.

Mad Harry doffed his cap. "Morning Cap'n."

Charles didn't bother to correct him. Harry called anyone of any rank Cap'n. He'd gone to sea as a young boy in the merchant fleet before the Great War and stayed away during hostilities, working barges in the China Seas they said, although nobody really knew. All that mattered as far as the village was concerned was that Mad Harry *hadn't* been in the trenches *but* he had returned in 1919 completely cuckoo. Initially, he'd set up home in the abandoned parlour of the Old Ship in Inner Harbour and had turned it into a foul-smelling hovel within days. During the worst of the winter weather he got himself inland to the Glebe Farm barn, where he could keep warm and drink milk straight from cows' udders. His other Deakin cousins helped him make a few shillings catching and selling crabs in summer. Otherwise, he lived off what he could cadge, sleeping in sea caves along the coast and talking to himself non-stop in a language no one recognised, perhaps of his own inventing.

Mad Harry garbled a few words now at Charles, who looked down at the filthy little man and said politely, "Sorry, didn't quite catch that, Harry."

"Germans, Cap'n. Here again, they are."

"Well, no. Not here, as in here in Porthferris, but, yes, too close for comfort, eh?"

"Here, they was. Last night. I see'd 'em. Up they come." He raised an arm and poked a long-nailed forefinger up into the air. "Up they come out the water. Trickly, trickly and over the quay, scrambly, scrambly. I see'd 'em."

"Did you? Good for you. Well, I must be going Harry, I, erm . . ."

"Give us a gun, Cap'n. I'll shoot the buggers next time they come up trickly, trickly, scrambly, scrambly."

"Sorry, can't oblige there."

"Shoot they and they barrels. Barrels and bags, barrels and bags. I see'd 'em, shiny bright in the moonlight! Ping,

ping!" Harry imitated the sound of bullets on metal using a grime-encrusted hand as a pistol.

"Absolutely. I'll see what I can do – in the pistol department, that is."

"You get me a gun, Cap'n. I'll shoot they buggers in the ade. I done it afore yellow buggers they was, on our boat, scrambly, scrambly, after our gear. Peeuuw, peeuuw." Harry's hand released another volley of bullets. "That showed 'em."

"Good. Yes, must be going, old chap. I'll see what I can do." Charles fairly sprinted across the grass and down the path to the harbour. Harry's whiff was worse than Delia's precious pigs.

Down on the quay, Charles took stock of the changes with satisfaction. Two machine gun posts had finally been set up in strategic positions at the junction of Porth Hill Road and Church Lane: one facing the main road uphill, where it could be used against transport trying to reach the quay; the other, sea-facing to protect the small harbour.

On the hillside, coming down from Bayview and just below Seabreeze in Church Lane, there was a four-inch naval gun in a concrete housing with double doors and a corrugated tin roof. Delia had described in glee what had happened the first time it was tested: apart from blowing its roof sky-high, there had been chaos in the village as people had collided in shop doorways, some running in for cover, others running out in case the buildings collapsed. Many of the shops and the cottages in Inner Harbour had sustained cracked windows. Curiously, the ancient leaded panes in the Fisherman's Boot had been unaffected. Everyone had applied to the Parish Council for repairs, and Reverend Hughes, acting on the villagers' behalf, was involved in a long-winded affair with Cready Town Council, who, uncertain what to do, had apparently applied to the War Office, presumably for compensation, although no one could say for sure. It was the stuff of village life.

Apart from the machine gun posts, the Home Guard had created a sort of tank trap in the freshwater stream leading into the beach, but had managed to leave the small footbridge in place. Chatwynde's platoon had also been busy drilling holes through the high sea wall protecting Inner Harbour and the lower quay wall across the quay car park, so they could pass heavy-weight chains and cables through to form barriers. Charles thought it unlikely they had a chain long enough and strong enough to be of any use, but they had done as instructed. Above the village, before Albert Villas to the west, imitation bombs had been painstakingly attached to cables that could be stretched across the road if need be. He didn't think for a minute any of it would deter a full-sized tank, but it might slow down the invader's progress sufficiently to enable Regular Army troops to come into action.

It was all very Heath Robinson, but it spoke volumes about the changing attitude to the war in the village. The earlier, pointless, moaning about rationing and the unfairness of the coupon system had given way to the reality of conflict, and the very real threat of invasion.

Charles crossed the empty quay and nipped down a narrow alley to rap three times at the Fisherman's Boot back door. Aubrey Chatwynde, elegant in a burgundy dressing gown and cream silk cravat, opened it and let him in.

"Tea or coffee?" he asked without preamble.

"Tea, please. Mm, what's that wonderful smell? God what a relief after Mad Harry."

"Fresh bread – bake my own. Keep it in the airing cupboard overnight, and as long as I can get proper butter I breakfast like a lord every morning. Come into the kitchen."

Charles settled himself at the table and looked about him.

Local Resistance

"Passed Mad Harry, did you?" Aubrey asked as he busied himself with an already boiling kettle. "Coming or going, was he, or didn't he know?"

Charles pointed a finger at his head, "Chap's bats; talks in rhyming riddles as far as I can make out. I must say, you've done this place up a treat. It was a real spit and sawdust dive when I checked it out last year."

Aubrey took care of himself, that had been evident when they had been brought together for their first meeting in London, but he hadn't anticipated quite such domesticity. No doubt Aubrey also cooked French-style casseroles and prepared fruit compotes with petit fours – the penchant for good wine and fine malt whisky he already knew about. Now, he wondered if Aubrey wasn't a bit too visibly womanish, although he was an excellent platoon leader and got results, as the preventive measures in the village demonstrated. His dossier said he'd been active behind enemy lines in Belgium, then in France, during the last war and, more recently, undercover in Spain, but there had also been hints of a distasteful scandal in London immediately prior to him being offered the post in Porthferris. Perhaps the task of setting up a Special Operations Auxiliary network, for which he himself was partially responsible, had been a useful way of getting Aubrey Chatwynde out of the capital.

Lost in speculation, Charles jumped slightly as Aubrey set a beautiful Crown Derby teapot on the table, saying "It has been confirmed, then? There are plans to come ashore along the Sussex coast and up through Penzance and Falmouth simultaneously?"

"Yes, as we feared," Charles replied. "It's 'Operation Sea Lion: the Extended Version'. Last report included place names on the Lizard. Silly devils have been using English picture postcards of holiday resorts and leaving them lying around on desks in Berlin; can you credit it?"

"They'll go for Plymouth first, though, surely? Take the dockyard at Devonport – stands to reason," Aubrey said, pouring tea into his own cup.

"I'm not so sure. They've got hold of map references for West Country airfields – presumably to back up seaborne troops. We've also received photos of the new landing craft they are building: it's called a *Siebelfähre*, designed for shallow water. Good job you've nobbled our beach, it's ideal for that."

Aubrey met his eye, "Not an adventure story anymore, is it? No indication when?"

"No, more's the pity. Aubrey," Charles looked away, paused and put his hands on the edge of the table, "our Berlin contact tells us someone hereabouts is providing the Fatherland with local map references."

"What, someone from round here?"

"East Cornwall, for sure. Unless it's someone with an ample petrol allowance or there's an RAF leak. Berlin is getting gen on the new airfields Bodmin way."

Aubrey shook his head in disbelief. "That is very bad news."

"Indeed. The worst part is that we have to play a double-game very soft and low here, because if the Germans get any inkling their plans are getting back to us their spy will go to ground and we'll lose the scent."

"Not to mention your man or woman in Berlin getting a bullet in the head. Quite. So what do you want from me? Do I get my special Auxiliaries action-ready to go in situ?"

"Not yet, not until you get a signal from your Plymouth contact – or directly from me, if need be."

"Ah, by the way," Aubrey busied himself pasting butter on crumbly bread, "I've got a new boy needs sending for English training. He's young, fit and red-hot. I'd like to get him into a course at Coleshill as soon as possible. Can you arrange it?"

"English training – what do you mean? Why isn't he in the forces?"

"He's half French. Turned up via San Sebastian. Only he's actually more Polish, really, called Jan Kowalski. Also passes for Jean Blanc and Gianni Bianchi. Jew, of course, which keeps the edge on his attitude."

"Italian, why isn't he interned? Ah, because he's half French, half Polish."

"He worked in the Turin car factory for a time, which is very handy; we've only got Paddon senior for anything related to motor engines. Speaks Italian like a native. Bit of a commie, that's what he was doing in the Turin car factory, I suspect: raising communist consciousness. But we need his skills whatever his religion and politics."

Charles watched Aubrey as he spoke. There was something behind his words. "How did he get here, to Porthferris, via San Sebastian?"

"Fishing vessel. They chucked him out at the landing for Wheal Marie."

Charles slammed a hand down on the table. "Damn it all, Aubrey, I thought we agreed that mine was off limits to everyone, no matter what!"

Aubrey raised two soft palms in surrender. "It's all right – they were Basque Spaniards. It's not as if we'll ever need to use them again."

"How did this Jean-Gianni know where to come?"

Aubrey got up and went to fiddle with the kettle on the gas stove. "I told him."

"You sent him a map!"

"No, don't get aerated. He's been on my books for a while. I knew him in London if you must know – before the war – and he needed to get out of France p.d.q."

Charles eyed Aubrey suspiciously, "Before the war?"

"I mix with all sorts, Charles, part of my useful charm. Shall I make a fresh pot or have you enough there?" Aubrey pointed at Charles' cup.

Charles sighed: Aubrey had more experience in working agents than he did and he recognised when he was being outmanoeuvred, so he gave in and said, "Tell him to forget his Italian or he'll be interned on the Isle of Man. You have checked him I out thoroughly, I hope?"

"That's your department now, old boy. I've been rusticated from that role."

"Mm," Charles pursed his lips, noting Aubrey's neat twist of responsibility and trying to ignore his irrepressible good humour. "But I must stress caution. Mistakes happen through goodwill. There's a loose cannon in the south of France as I speak. Last seen sharing a bottle of Beaujolais with Nazi officers. Could be deep cover. I only hope it is. That's the trouble with wartime recruiting, we don't know, can't know, the prejudices and backgrounds of all our operatives to even guess when they might turn on us."

"Do you know the chap involved – in France?"

"Not personally. Taken on in Paris – said he was British, but he pulled the wool over our eyes good and proper." Charles stopped and took a bite of the delicious bread. He was talking too much; Aubrey had this effect on him and, hopefully, on other people.

"What was this turncoat in France supposed to be doing, getting grounded Flight Officers out of the mud and across to Spain?" Aubrey was trying to cut more of the doughy bread in neat slices.

"He was. Now he's reporting to the enemy. Bastard."

"You'll find him soon enough."

"God help him when we do."

"Here, try this." Aubrey pushed a pretty jam pot across the table. "It's rhubarb marmalade, made by your very own Mrs Hawkins."

"Really? I hope it didn't come out of my wife's stores."

"Don't be churlish, Charles. Mrs H made the stuff herself – she told me."

Charles took a spoonful and dropped it on his plate. "Why do you want this Jan-Jean-Gianni boy sent to Coleshill if he's already got the tricks we need?"

"Bit awkward," Aubrey said between mouthfuls. "I've got him working at Paddon's Garage. Ezra's one of our Special Auxiliaries and knows the score. We all call the boy Joe, by the way. As Ezra's son's deaf, we've got Joe with him in the garage workshop working as an ex-school pal sort of thing. Joe's got an accent worthy of a Hollywood B movie bad guy so hopefully if people assume he can't hear he won't need to open his mouth and put his foreign foot in it."

"What's wrong with having a Polish boy working in a Cornish garage? Ah, I suppose people will wonder why he isn't in uniform."

"That, and the not minor issue of the fact that he is pretty unreliable self-discipline-wise – treats the whole affair as a lark. Treats life as a lark, if you ask me."

"Bodes ill, Aubrey. Is he worth it? Surely Ezra can show them how to spike an engine, and I can't see explosives being a problem – we've enough ex-miners and quarrymen in local Home Guard platoons around here to explain about explosives in standard training."

"You are right in that respect. It's the silent-night techniques . . ." – Aubrey made a cutting motion across his throat with his knife – "and tricky wiring that we need him for. He can sabotage a vehicle in the blink of an eye – far more imaginative than old Ezra. He understands English well enough, and what we're up to, but he plays his deaf and dumb role over the top when he doesn't want to do something." The kettle on the gas ring began to whistle and Aubrey got up to replenish the teapot. Speaking with his back to Charles, he continued, "Unfortunately, Jean has been having a bit of a fling with one of our young ladies so I'd prefer to get him out of the way for a while. A proper training course at Coleshill should serve to improve his accent and teach him more about the way the English go about their business."

"A local girl? Oh, Lord, no! That could lead to all sorts of problems. Who is she?"

"Your housekeeper's daughter."

"Ginny Hawkins! But she's simple. What in heaven's name does he see in her?"

Aubrey returned to the table and raised an eyebrow. "Have you seen her recently?"

Charles sat back, shocked. In his mind Ginny was still a child. Then he sighed, remembering how his own two children were growing. "You're right, she is quite a looker, now I think about it. As to being simple, half this village are as dippy as Daffy Duck! But he can't be walking out with Ginny. That can't be right."

"Seems it is. I've been – um – talking to her mother."

Charles gave Aubrey a crooked smile, "Have you, indeed? Does this explain the marmalade? It is delicious, by the way."

"Told you. Yes and no regarding the gentle Mrs H. She's good cover for a single pub landlord with a posh accent and a predilection for silk cravats, I'm afraid. Your housekeeper has her own secrets too, though. She's not likely to go gossiping about anything I may say by accident."

Charles sighed, "Secrets? You know she's Delia's cousin, don't you? There's a family scandal for you. Delia's uncle Frank got a bit too frisky with a local girl after a midsummer shindig. It went on all of his vacation until he packed his bags and left for Cambridge and she arrived on the doorstep with a bun in the oven. My wife's grandmother was far too generous, of course. Paid the mother off, provided that cottage for her to live in then took the child, Maisie Rose, in at fourteen to work as a maid in Cleve House. Cleve House belongs to my wife – you know that, don't you?"

"Skeletons in wardrobes – every family has them. Does your wife know? It's not impossible that she doesn't."

"Oh, yes. Delia and Maisie Rose Hawkins are closer than cousins: sisters under the skin. Not that Maisie Hawkins makes anything of it: quite the opposite in fact. She's a good woman and we do what we can for Ginny. The husband was a bad lot. No news about him, I suppose?"

"No, and that in itself is a mystery. Stan Hawkins knew this coast like the back of his ham-sized fist, and I don't reckon he was the sort to run off. Not while there's a war on, anyway. Everyone knows everything about everyone round here, but no one has a clue about Hawkins, which is very odd."

"Everything about everybody – I hope not!" Charles interjected, genuinely concerned. "I've told you, we don't need anyone knowing what you're up to or what'll be happening at the mine."

"Calm down, Charles. I play the London toff, ex-Hatton Garden, possibly a bit of a rogue – that why he's here – to a T."

"Why Hatton Garden?"

"Gives them something exotic they can recognise, and I do know a bit in the jewellery and antiques line: my grandfather was a silverware specialist. My stepfather has a shop there, too."

"Really? Why didn't I know that? Well, whatever works, but don't get in too deep with the local community. We don't need any emotional involvement or complications if – when

– we have to move into the next stage. We may need you to go up to the north coast, sort out Bude then move on up to the Exmoor coast area. I've got a new Patrol Leader from Tavistock starting who'll monitor the Devon border. They've got a lot of Home Guard volunteers round that way so his Special Auxiliaries can set up new bases without drawing too much attention, like you have achieved here. Well done on that score, by the way."

Aubrey nodded in reply then said, "Does your wife know you are not on leave?"

"No."

For a moment the two men sipped their tea, then Aubrey cut some more bread and pushed the dish still laden with bright yellow butter across the tablecloth. "Help yourself – plenty more where that came from."

"You're lucky. A special arrangement, or did it drop off the back of a lorry outside your front door?" Charles laughed.

"I keep George Deakin at Glebe Farm Dairy in good spirits; he keeps me in the odd pat of butter."

Charles shook his head. "Seems like the whole village is up to something, my wife included. Each time I get down here, Delia's got some new little scheme or another."

"Reciprocity, Charles. It's what makes the South Sea Islanders so content. Ask Mad Harry."

"South Sea Islanders!" Then Charles changed his tone, "Joking aside, you'd better take care. I hear Mr Bantry is on a mission to turn Porthferris into a law-abiding community. Hearing about rationing scandals will encourage him to come too close, and we don't need people like him nosing about. Or him reporting to Weights and Measures and bringing the police in as well, the fewer who know anything about anything, the better for all of us.

Aubrey wiped his mouth. Taking his time, he said, "I have no evidence, but I've got my doubts about the upstanding Mr Bantry."

"Because he's too upstanding? Proper nosy-parker, and his wife too, according Delia."

"Precisely."

"Keep an eye on him if you can, although I assume he doesn't come into your charming hostelry. I'll run a background check when I get back to the office."

"Might be better: just in case. Have you time for another cup, Charles?"

"No, I thought I'd call in at Bayview for a cup of coffee."

"Ah, yes, good idea. Curious fellow, Cyril Waterson. He was in the Hindu Kush, you know, *during* the last bash. Joined the Local Defence Volunteers on the first day they started for this one. Fussy old duffer, but it's a bit of an act. Chaps all call him 'The Colonel', although I suspect he may have blotted his copybook somewhere along the line and got cashiered before he made full colonel. My conjecture is opium. Not that I care a jot. His wife's nice, though. Very quiet. One of those dowdy, silent types. Nothing like the usual Colonel's mem."

"I know. She was born here. Bayview and the mine belonged to her family, not his."

"Waterson has a finger in various local imports, did you know?"

"I do now." Charles raised a questioning eyebrow.

"Oh, come on, Charles, you can't expect me to reveal my sources," Aubrey blustered.

"Excellent tea, by the way. Thank you. First quality Darjeeling with a touch of Orange Pekoe: your own mix?"

Aubrey gave a mincing shrug. "One can't immerse oneself entirely in a small community without taking advantage of some of its more entertaining aspects. Besides, I have to keep my hand in with import and export. This war can't go on forever."

Charles shook his head in mock despair and the two men finished their breakfast with companionable chit-chat.

Business with Aubrey concluded, Charles stepped back into the bright morning sunshine, returned to the quay and stopped to look down at the two trawlers resting in the greenish mud below. Stan Hawkins' *Porth Rose* was looking neglected despite signs of recent use; someone had left a pair of yellow yachting boots on deck. He took a deep breath – only one person in these parts would be using yachting boots on a trawler: it was a foolish oversight. Turning, to go straight back into the Fisherman's Boot to give Aubrey a sharp word, Charles noticed the quay standpipe was running. Apart from strutting seagulls pecking at invisible debris, there were no one about, nobody crating fish or rinsing buckets, but someone had left it running. He turned off the tap and as he did so he was hailed by another of the Deakin clan, arriving on the quay to start his day.

"Morning, Major. Fine day. You want to go out later? I got my gig if you fancy a turn along the bay."

"No, thank you, Tommy, but it's a nice idea. Maybe Saturday. The children might enjoy a bit of trip – if it's safe?"

"What, 'cuz of they mines? They'm on the beach, but the harbour's clear. Leastways we haven't been blown out the water yet. There was a seaplane dropping mines across the mouth of the Fal last week, but Jerry isn't interested in us – we'm too small."

Charles was stunned by the boy's callous attitude. Having survived weeks of nightly bombing during the London blitz, dismissing air raids and mines appalled him. German vessels could creep into any small fishing harbour and take over the entire community before they'd got out of bed. Tank traps and naval guns weren't much use if the locals were going to help them come ashore. He sighed with annoyance, but said, "You be careful, Tommy."

"I know, sir, 'there's a war on'."

Chapter 17

The double gates to Bayview Hotel were closed but the side entrance, half-hidden behind towering rhododendrons, was unlocked. Charles walked down the short gravel drive, waiting to be challenged, but the place appeared deserted. He knew it was not, because he had seen reports from military observers stationed on the top floor of the requisitioned building. Wrens and other naval personnel were monitoring ships coming in and out of the English Channel and paying special attention to anything that might be crossing from Brittany or Normandy, innocent-looking trawlers and pilchard luggers included, although they'd missed the Polish-French boy's boat, that was clear.

Bayview was a double-fronted, Victorian-gothic monstrosity built as a private residence on the labour of copper miners, who had scraped at lucrative seams running along this part of the coast and tunnelled ever further into nearby hills in the hope of finding more. It had been converted into a hotel in the early thirties.

The main door was open. Motes of dust bounced in a ray of sun. He passed through into the hall, empty except for the obligatory aspidistra, and noticed a brass bell on the reception desk. There was no sound from anywhere, but a distinct odour that took him straight back to his school days: lavender furniture polish and brown Windsor soup.

A small, sharp-featured woman wearing tortoiseshell spectacles suddenly appeared like a jack-in-the-box from under the reception desk. The two jumped simultaneously.

The small woman – her shoulders barely came to the height of the desk – put her hand over her heart and said, "Oh, my!" The intonation was what Delia called "achieved pronunciation". "Can I help you, sir?" she added, getting her apparently fluttering heart under control.

"I'd like to speak to Colonel Waterson, if I may?"

"Certainly, sir. Who shall I say wants him?"

"Major Metherall – we have met."

"Certainly, sir. I shan't be a moment."

Charles waited until the woman had made her exit, then took a hasty look into the two rooms leading off the entrance hall. There was no sign of anyone.

"Major Metherall, good morning." Cyril Waterson appeared from behind the stairs with a tea towel, which he hastily deposited behind the reception desk before offering his hand.

"Colonel Waterson, hello. I was trying to remember when we last met."

Cyril Waterson screwed up his ample face until his florid cheeks merged with bushy white eyebrows. "Christmas '38, must have been. Time flies. What can I do for you?"

"Official visit, I'm afraid. Can we have a little chat somewhere?"

"Got you. May I offer you a cup of coffee or tea?"

"Coffee, if you have any?"

"Come through to our sitting room. We shan't be disturbed there." He lowered his voice and whispered, "I've got some of the real stuff, by the way. Grind the beans myself." He turned his head and tapped the side of his generous nose. "Mum's the word, eh? Afraid we have become secret drinkers," he guffawed.

Charles said nothing, knowing his wife was probably getting their "real" coffee from the same supplier. He followed Waterson down a short, dismal service corridor into what must have once been a morning room. It had a French window and was decorated tastefully in primrose yellow. "What a lovely room," he said.

"All my wife's work. I stick to the greenhouse, when I'm not filling in forms. That blasted rationing chap was here again yesterday, wanting evidence that this was now a military establishment. I told him it was none of his damn business what sort of establishment we were and sent him packing. Sorry, I get a bit heated these days, old age and a dicky heart to boot. I'll get the percolator on. Make yourself at home."

Opening the doors of the French window, Charles looked out over a wide terrace and a well-stocked garden. Most of it was given over to neat rows of fruit bushes and vegetables. Unless he had professional help, Cyril Waterson was a busy man.

After a few minutes he heard low voices whispering in the passage, then Mrs Waterson held the door open as her husband brought in a wide tray with a complete coffee service and a plate of biscuits.

Charles crossed the room to shake Mrs Waterson's hand. She was, as Chatwynde had described, the dowdy, silent type, the dullness of her clothes out of place given the elegance of her morning room. He wondered how she had fared as the Colonel's lady; the entertaining must have been a strain. It crossed his mind that Waterson's dubious military past might have been more to do with his wife than him.

"You remember Major Metherall, my dear, from Cleve House?"

The woman smiled, retracted her hand from the briefest of shakes, then muttered something and disappeared.

"You know all about our new clients, I suppose. It's not dissimilar to hotel life," explained Waterson, "tight daily schedule: people to feed, rooms to clean."

"You're full, then? I understood it was only a skeleton observation crew."

"Not full – there are a few vacant bedrooms. They keep to themselves up on the top floor pretty well and fix their own suppers, which is a blessing. We let them use the grounds, and our little beach if they fancy a dip. It's not ideal, but to be perfectly honest, Metherall, this war hasn't been all bad news on a personal front. Hotel life is not to our taste. At the time, when Olwen inherited the house, it seemed like a good idea, a godsend, really. We set up in good hopes of, well, having a full staff to do all the running around, don't you know. Then I took a bit of a beating in an Indian railway scheme in '39 – put my trust in a tomfool Englishman who'd never been out of a Berkshire office, although I didn't know it at the time. Only found out by chance from other sufferers. Archibald Bantry – not a name to forget. He was supposedly in charge of the accounting – counting it into his own bally pocket more like. Then, would you ever believe it, he turns up on my doorstep wanting to see our kitchen and ration coupons! It's that bally rationing chap. 'Food inspector', he called himself. I tell you, I thought nasty coincidences like this only happened in novels. Pity we didn't inspect *his* bloody accounts – would have saved us all a packet." The colonel paused for breath and wiped an oversized pocket handkerchief across his brow. "Sorry, I get a bit heated."

"No need to apologise. Are you sure it's the same man?"

"It is – I asked him. Said he was only an employee, not in charge of anything so I couldn't blame him for what happened. Five minutes later he changed his tune and swore he'd lost all his savings in the scheme and had come down here to . . ." Waterson had lost his drift; he waved hand in the air. "But it's the same blighter. Oh, yes, and he's living here in Porthferris! Here! As if life hadn't served us enough blows."

"You hadn't come across him at church or in the village, then?"

"We're RC – go into Cready when we have to. Neither of us are what you'd call religious. What's curious, though, I've been doing my bit with the Home Guard – 'Dad's Army', as we're called – and never set eyes on him. Sorry, got a bit diverted." Waterson handed Charles his coffee. "You're here to talk about the top floor not my personal history. Sugar?"

Charles stirred an abstemious spoonful into his cup and took an appreciative sip before saying, "Actually, it's not about the observers."

Cyril Waterson looked at him with horror. "No! No, you can't, please, no. It would kill my wife and God knows we're already . . . No, don't billet troops on us, please. We'll take a couple of evacuees. A whole family. Would that do?"

"I'm not here for anything like that, sir." Charles paused before saying, "When we have finished this excellent coffee could we take a turn in your garden?"

Cyril Waterson looked at him questioningly, then immediately put down his cup and strode towards the French window. "This way."

Charles followed him out, shading his eyes from the sun and the glint off the sea. What had probably once been an immaculate croquet lawn surrounded by warm-climate shrubs was now a well-tended lettuce and radish bed. "You keep busy outdoors."

"Caleb Cottle's work . . ."

They were interrupted by frantic barking and a portly Jack Russell terrier bolted out of a laburnum bush to challenge them. Colonel Waterson bent down with some difficulty and smoothed its head. "This is Patch," he said. "Means Cottle's here today. We'll go into one of the greenhouses. Cottle comes in three or four times a week and does a few hours. Not a stickler for routine but he does the job and gets results. My wife and I do our bit, too, of course. Olwen does a sterling job with these lettuces, radishes and cucumbers. Cottle deals with the heavier work. Come and admire my tomatoes." He led the way under a wisteria trellis to a medium-sized greenhouse. The terrier watched them go then returned to its private identification of garden wildlife.

There was an unmistakable musky odour of warm tomatoes mixed with the remains of paraffin from winter heating and an overlay of cigar smoke. The colonel closed the glass door behind him and, standing with his back to, it said, "Right, then – what's afoot?"

"We would like to take over Wheal Marie mine completely, sir, on a strictly formal but very hush-hush basis – for the duration." Charles pulled a somewhat crumpled buff envelope from his trouser pocket. "Read this first, then I'll explain. One thing, before you open it, I must insist that this is absolutely, entirely between us. If – for any reason – we do not come to an agreement you *cannot, must not*, ever say a word about it. We shan't require you to sign the Official Secrets or invoke the Emergency Act, but your word as a British officer –"

"Can be taken for granted, Major." Cyril Waterson slit the envelope with a knife from the potting shelf.

"I see," he said at last. "You need Wheal Marie for the location: makes sense. Shall you also need me – us? I mean, are we to be involved in any way?"

"No, no. On the contrary, we request that you do not even visit the grounds."

"What do I tell my wife? The mine belonged to her father's family. She's the one who'll have to sign papers – if the War Office wants to buy it."

"No, it's not a matter of purchase. We only need your permission to use the property for an OB."

"OB?"

"Operational Base. Our Special Auxiliaries will go underground the moment the alarm is raised. In this case, literally. But we need to create a proper bunker first. And for that we need your permission, and your utter silence – under *any* circumstances."

"*Any* circumstances?" Colonel Waterson raised his bushy eyebrows. "Serious stuff, eh? What about Gladys? Gladys Fogarty, our receptionist-cum-housekeeper – you met her when you came in. I'd be happy to see her go, to be honest, but she's Olwen's bosom buddy these days. They sit up in her room for hours on end every evening listening to wireless programmes. Smoke like troopers, the pair of them. Or is it trains? What do I tell her?"

"You don't need to tell anyone anything, Colonel. Please don't, in fact. We do not want people in the village to start asking questions. What people don't know they can't pass on: it is absolutely vital that all this is kept secret."

"A tall order, in this village."

Charles grimaced. "I know, but if it does become common knowledge, and if Jerry does land, the OB and the Auxiliaries are entirely jeopardised – not to mention the danger of reprisals. You'll have heard what's happening in France where individuals or the Resistance have opposed the Germans and a local with a grudge has informed on them."

Cyril Waterson went very quiet, then nodded gravely. "I see – those 'any circumstances'. In that case, I shall say nothing to Olwen. Ironic, really," – he shook his head – "all the poor girl ever wanted when we were abroad was to return to Cornwall for a quiet life."

"You can say 'no' to this, if you prefer."

The retired colonel shook his head. "King and country, what?"

Charles smiled. "Thank you."

Waterson read and re-read the short letter. Charles waited, then said, "Given that Wheal Marie is in effect abandoned, you might put it about that it is unsafe, if asked, that's all."

"It is. Didn't you know that?"

Charles gave a wry smile. "We'll be bringing in sappers to strengthen shafts and create a living area. Am I right in thinking there's a tunnel leading through the mine to your cove here?"

Cyril Waterson suddenly went coy. "Ah, our sea cave, mm . . . There may be a tunnel . . . It would have been an air vent, I suppose. Can't say I've ever tried to explore it, myself."

Charles turned his head to hide his amusement. If Cyril Waterson was using his sea cave for incoming goods, the way Delia said Stan Hawkins used his, he was going to be very busy clearing it out for a day or two. "Could I beg a couple of these wonderful tomatoes?" he said to change the subject.

"Certainly, take a bag home. I've actually got some paper bags somewhere: collector's item, these days."

The colonel got down on all fours to peer beneath the potting bench. As he shifted empty plant pots aside and scrabbled about, Charles glimpsed a cardboard box labelled "Senior Service", then a large wooden box of "Havana Finest Cut". Waterson shoved the triple-layered cigar box to one-side, revealing rows of tins with red labels that Charles thought might be pilchards or soup, or fruit in syrup – and, if so, why on earth weren't they in the kitchen where it was cooler? And why keep cigars here? Charles didn't smoke often and never bought cigars himself, but something told him they shouldn't be in such a dry environment. There were other cardboard boxes of varying sizes, but nothing else was visible.

"Sorry," Waterson gasped, "all used up – no bags left – have to be newspaper."

"Let me have a cardboard box. I'll bring it back later," Charles ventured

"Box? No boxes here." Heaving with the effort, Waterson shifted his very ample backside to block Charles' line of sight.

Charles hid a grin and tried to make out what was on the shelves on the opposite side of the greenhouse.

Waterson finally struggled upright with a yellowed newspaper and said, "What about the woman in the caravan?"

"I'm sorry – what woman?"

"Caleb Cottle's daughter. She's got a caravan and a horde of brats down on the Wheal Marie site."

"Ah . . . that's awkward. I'm afraid you're going to have to evict her."

Waterson gulped. "I'd rather face snipers in the Hindu Kush than try to do something Becca Cottle won't like."

"That bad?"

"Worse. Boadicea reborn, an Amazon with both huge . . ."

"I get the idea. But she'll have to go – for her own safety, and that of any children she's got down there."

"A tribe."

"Goodness. Well, thank you for everything so far, Colonel. I'll keep you posted."

Chapter 18

Having finished most repairs to adjacent buildings, the Porthferris Home Guard found an excuse to test their heavy guns again. The first retort shook the bungalow named Seabreeze so badly the front windows, which were already cracked from the previous occasion, fell out. The second gun shattered the glass in the rosewood cabinet.

Maisie and her daughter Ginny were walking down Church Lane at the time. Miss Pettit came trotting out of her gate, hands all aflutter as if she had been fully expecting Maisie to be there to rescue her.

"My cabinet! My cabinet! What is to be done? What is to be done?"

Maisie, whose own heart had a skipped a few beats, was none too calm herself, but she managed to say, "There, there, don't you fret Miss Pettit. Ginny's here now – she'll clean up and I'll ask Mr Baxter if he can speak to his brother-in-law. He's got a builder's yard in Cready. They'll get someone to do your window, don't you fret."

She turned to her daughter. "Go in with Miss Pettit. Get a brush and pan and sweep up the glass, then close the curtains and the blackout to keep out the draught. Do round Miss Pettit's cabinet before you close the curtains so you can see the bits of glass – they'll be all over the carpet I expect."

"Oh, yes, do! Oh, but no! No! My little boxes! My little boxes! I must put them somewhere safe first. That is a priority."

"Ginny can help you with that, my dear. You leave it to Ginny."

"No! That is, thank you, but no, I . . ."

"Look here, Miss Pettit, shall I come in and give you a hand?" Maisie was already through the gate and at the open door before Miss Pettit could respond. Pushing Ginny in front of her, she hissed, "Get the dustpan and hand brush, and bring me something to put broken glass in."

"My little boxes! Don't touch them. Don't touch my little boxes." Miss Pettit had followed them indoors, but she was in more of a tizz now than she had been before.

"There, there, Miss Pettit. You calm down. Ginny and I'll sort you out in no time."

Miss Pettit wasn't listening. She went straight to the sullied cabinet and opened the door frame with a key kept on a chain around her neck, then scurried into her bedroom and returned with a sheaf of crumpled tissue paper, which Maisie assumed had been pulled from a chest of drawers. Ignoring shards of splintered glass, she put the paper on the floor by the cabinet, then stood up to start the removal and wrapping process for her precious little boxes. The sudden change of position made her dizzy and she reached out, grasping Maisie's arm for support.

Maisie manoeuvred the frail spinster into a fireside chair. "There you go. You sit down and let me get on with it. What is it you want doing first? These boxes can wait till we've got your floor clean, you know."

Miss Pettit was quiet for a second or two but then she caught sight of something. "Oh, that's the Hampshire box. No, leave it alone, Mrs Hawkins. Please don't touch it. I can do it. Please, let Ginny do my floor and then I will do the rest. Oh, dear, it's all such a shock. Oh, dear, oh, dear."

"Don't you worry. You sit there and we'll be done in a jiffy."

Maisie gently moved the tissue paper from beside the cabinet, then looked at the shelves to see what all the fuss was about. What Ginny had described to her, though, weren't snuffboxes at all. Small containers, enamelled tins, pretty pots and whatnots, draw-lid shell-box souvenirs, various knick-knacks for collar studs and pins, but no real snuffboxes; they were all too big to fit in a gentleman's waistcoat pocket. Ginny returned with a broom, dustpan and handbrush, but Maisie decided to say nothing until they were out of Miss Pettit's hearing.

While they worked, Miss Pettit chattered away to herself about wrapping the various boxes and putting them somewhere safe. From there, she went into a monologue that to Maisie – who was only half listening as she moved the glass into small piles for Ginny to brush up and place in a bucket – sounded like excerpts from the woman's life history.

". . . she could have helped when his poor wife was so ill and their little boy died of the whooping cough. Her own daughter-in-law loathed her most, of course, and she had good reason. What sort of woman denies her daughter-in-law her dear husband's belongings after he's been killed in a road accident? Poor girl, alone like that. I know. I know what it's like. They had the same first name, mother-in-law and daughter-in-law: Martha Collins. She was living in lodgings and her mother-in-law was queening it in that great house in Alton. I never liked Hampshire, especially not Alton."

Maisie looked round. "All done? Not quite, my dear. We'll be clear d'reckly, then you can see to your souvenirs. I got most of this glass up now."

Miss Pettit, however, was still elsewhere in her thoughts. "I did the right thing there. It couldn't be allowed . . ."

The spinster paused and raised a finely wrinkled hand, pointing to a shelf as if choosing a cake from a shop window selection. She was pointing at a hinged box not unlike a mustard pot. "That one is Scarborough," she said. "Miss Littleworth, and she *was* of little worth. If I had known it was paste beforehand, I wouldn't have bothered . . . The next one is Gibraltar. Rather tasteless. In the end I didn't need it. Mrs . . . what was *her* name: Golding – Gould – no that's the nice man in Hatton Garden. Such a gentleman: never asks questions, except with that nasty paste necklace, of course. He didn't like that one bit. I did tell him it was all a mistake. Golding – that was it. Fancy keeping all that English money in her hotel room then trusting me to bring the packet aboard the Navy ship." Miss Pettit giggled like a girl. "I should quite like to return to Gibraltar, a pleasant climate, although it was *such* a nuisance people asking for one's identity papers all the time. That was quite a trial, the passport business. And now *we* have identity cards and these horrid ration books with names on as well – one simply isn't free anymore." She gave a little sigh and turned to look out of the unglazed front window. "I shall have to stay here now. That reminds me – I must do those deeds."

"You don't want to be troubling yourself doing good deeds for nobody today, my dear," Maisie said, struggling to her feet and rubbing her knees. "You stay here, get your breath back, and I'll send Ginny down to get you your shopping." Maisie bent over the delicate spinster's chair. "Is there anyone we can contact for you? You shouldn't be on your own like this."

Miss Pettit looked at her, then away, without saying anything.

Local Resistance

Maisie helped Ginny get the last of the glass into the ash bucket and prepared to leave. "I've got to go now, my dear," she said, bending over Miss Pettit again. "The children's lunch will be very late if I don't get a move on. I'll call in at Billy Baxter's shop and ask about the window for you, all right?"

Miss Pettit looked up wanly; she was obviously still shaken. Leaving Ginny to finish setting the room to rights, Maisie bade farewell and set off for the village.

Billy Baxter, flushed from being involved in firing the first gun, kept her trapped for a few minutes, reliving each and every move he'd made that morning. Finally, he agreed to find someone to do the Seabreeze window, and as she needed nothing from his shop – everything having been delivered to Cleve House the previous day – Maisie called in at Alf Plowden's grocery to see if there was any chance of getting some soft brown sugar. There wasn't, but he did have raisins and sultanas. They chatted for a few minutes while he made up her package, then she crossed the street and entered the stationers to purchase Toby and Libby Metherall's comics and some crayons for Miss Claverham. She was astonished to find Miss Pettit at the counter. Small and elderly she might be, but the old biddy wasn't that frail or in that much of a tizz after all.

The doorbell tinkled again and Mr Bantry came in behind her. Miss Pettit turned to see who had entered and such a look came over her, Maisie thought it was as if she'd seen the devil himself. Then the little woman changed her expression in the blink of an eye and gave him a bright, welcoming smile, as if the shop was her private parlour and Archibald Bantry her honoured guest.

Gripping her shopping bag with its secret dried fruit, and doing her best to keep her own expression blank, Maisie half turned to greet him herself, "Morning, Mr Bantry. I hope you are well, and Mrs Bantry."

The tall, spare man lifted his trilby in reply then, without a word, reached a long arm across the side counter to pick up a box of Cornish Cream Fudge.

Mr Jones, the stationer, was folding coloured tissue paper. As he tied it up with soft string, he said, "That's the last of it now, Miss Pettit, I doubt we'll get anymore, neither."

"No, I expect not. Oh, and I also need some red ink, please," Miss Pettit replied.

The ink proved more problematic. It needed to be a special sort of red, and Miss Pettit had to do without. As she delved into her lizard-skin handbag for her purse, Maisie felt Mr Bantry peering around her, watching the spinster's every move. Maisie was suddenly reminded of the embarrassing incident at church, when he and his wife had insisted they had met Miss Pettit whilst on holiday somewhere.

Miss Pettit fumbled with her money and coins fell to the floor. Maisie bent down to help her pick them up, revising her opinion of the state of Miss Pettit's nerves once more. The Home Guard had a lot to answer for; breaking the poor woman's windows. The contents of the change purse were finally tipped onto the counter for the stationer to pick out the coins for her purchases. Before he had even rung up the price on the till, however, Miss Pettit had sidled round Maisie and Mr Bantry to get out of the door, forgetting her tissue paper in the process.

Mr Jones passed the light package to Archibald Bantry, who handed it to the spinster with a bow. "Here you are, Miss . . . Your name – so sorry, we have been introduced, but I quite forget."

Bantry's villainous smile sent a shiver down Maisie's back, and surely he had heard the stationer address her earlier.

"Pettit. Miss Maud Lily Pettit."

"Ah, yes, and you're living in the village at . . .?"

"Seabreeze – I acquired it this year. From Mr Anthony Oakley. Did you know him? They lived in Croydon."

"Lived?"

"Well, no, still live, I expect. Such a delightful place to be during this horrid war, don't you think? Porthferris, not Croydon, of course, too many bombing raids – too near London. Lovely house quite destroyed – in Croydon. One cannot sleep in one's bed . . . Not like here. Although today, well, quite a shock . . . Thank you, most kind." She took the tissue paper and tucked it under her arm. "That gun this morning has . . . Oh! How lovely – Cornish Cream Fudge! You are lucky to get that."

"A small gift for my wife." Archibald Bantry's lips sliced into another semblance of a smile. "Her birthday."

"Mrs Bantry has a sweet tooth?" Miss Pettit enquired with an unexpected calm.

"We both do." Mr Bantry's claw-like fingers closed more tightly round the box of fudge, perhaps fearing Miss Pettit was about to make a grab for it.

"Me, too," she said innocently. "I used to love fudge. I didn't know it was still made, what with the milk and sugar problem these days. But you know all about that, Mr Bantry, better than I."

Maisie looked from one to the other: something was going on here, and, surprisingly, Miss Pettit was in control.

"Well, now we are virtually neighbours, Mr Bantry," the small woman was saying, "I wonder if I might invite you, and your wife, of course, for tea. Would Sunday, suit you? I should have a new window by then. I regret I can't extend my invitation to luncheon – my coupons don't go that far." She gave a girlish laugh. "Do say 'yes', it would be such a pleasure to have company." Before Archibald Bantry could reply she suddenly added, "And you, Mrs Hawkins. I must show my gratitude for all your help today."

Maisie's heart dived: nothing and no one would get her in a room with Archibald Bantry. "That's very kind of you, my dear, but I'm busy at home on a Sunday – what with me being busy all week at Cleve House, you see."

Mr Jones behind the counter gave a polite cough and held up the two comics Maisie collected each week. Edging round Miss Pettit, she said, "You'll have to excuse me, I've got to get on."

As she was paying for the comics and crayons, Maisie was aware that Miss Pettit was still talking to Archibald Bantry, but she didn't pay any attention to the rest of their conversation and for a second time that morning made her farewell.

Chapter 19

On the second Friday in May, Charles Metherall, back in uniform, left the Cleve House grounds by the side gate, intending to enjoy a drink in the local pub before returning to London the next day. There was a persistent drizzle, so instead of crossing the soggy meadow he made for the path that joined the narrow lane serving the back gardens of Albert Villas and set up a brisk pace down to the village. Coming out from under a big oak now in full leaf, he was surprised to see another figure ahead of him. A figure he recognised by its limp, Byron Booth, as Delia called him, whose frequent absences from school duties were a matter of intense kitchen gossip. Out of sheer curiosity, Charles followed at a distance.

Mr Booth hesitated at the second back gate of the villas and did what Charles could only describe as a "furtive recce" then he opened it, closed it carefully and disappeared up the path to the back door. Just before reaching the gate himself, Charles stopped and waited. The back door opened and a woman, Mrs Prior, welcomed her visitor with the brief, affectionate kiss of long-time lovers.

Charles was furious. Commander Prior was at sea on a destroyer; the man's life was in continual danger fighting for his country, and what was his wife doing in his absence?

Playing Hollywood kissy-kissy with a classroom Lothario who couldn't even walk properly! Then he laughed – *At least it's not my wife.*

Musing on what he had seen, Charles strolled at a more leisurely pace down to the harbour. But as he came out of the short cut onto Porth Hill road he was forced to stop and take cover against a garden hedge as Plowden's Grocery van, with a make-do Red Cross flag on a broom handle sticking out of the passenger window, veered madly uphill, belching out precious commercial fuel. The end of the broom, with what might have once been a pillowcase, narrowly missed his nose. No sooner had it passed than he was forced back into the hedge as a vehicle bearing the words "W.M. Baxter, Master Butcher", chugged up the hill in pursuit. Its back doors were hanging wide open, and a young man in Home Guard uniform was clinging to a meat hook for dear life.

It was all so Keystone Cops and unexpected that Charles started to laugh. He was still chuckling when he reached the quay and a man in a baggy khaki outfit on a large bicycle with a small dog in its handlebar basket free-wheeled past him and with practised ease propped his velocipede against the wall of the Fisherman's Boot.

"Evening, Cottle," Charles said, as the terrier jumped down of its own accord.

"Evening, Major," Cottle grunted, making something of a salute then standing aside so the officer could enter the public house before him.

Blossom Deakin, one of the Inner Harbour Deakin clan, was behind the bar. Caleb Cottle slipped into a bentwood chair along the fireplace wall while Blossom pulled a pint without asking and looked at Charles enquiringly.

"Evening, Major Metherall," she said. "What can I get you?"

"Glass of stout if you have it, please, Blossom," he replied, removing his cap and gloves and setting them down on the bar.

"Course we got it. We got everythin' in this pub. Not like they pubs in Cready."

The comment didn't surprise Charles. Aubrey's commercial contact list appeared to reach directly north into the finest Scottish distilleries and as far south as Bordeaux and Spain, then right across the Atlantic to the Caribbean, if the content of the shelf behind the bar was anything to go by.

"No cracked bottles or breakages here when they fired the gun, I hope."

"That ol' gun'll do for me, it will. Gave me such a fright. I thought as we'd been blitterated by they soddin' Jerries. 'Twas a real fright, weren't it Caleb?"

The gardener grunted something, of which Charles caught "buggers" and not a word more.

"You're quiet in here tonight," Charles said, looking around at the empty seats.

"They'm practising their fighting and stuff up near the church, Major. Mr Chatwynde said it was a proper 'mergency do. Aren't you s'posed to be up there with 'em, Caleb?" Blossom asked, taking a foaming pint mug over to the gardener and raising her voice, though Charles doubted if the gardener was really deaf.

Cottle muttered something, then lowered his beer to the floor for his dog to lick up the creamy froth. Charles took a seat by the empty grate, then the door opened and a small, elderly woman he didn't know came in.

"Evening, Miss Pettit," Blossom said, "drop of your usual?"

"Oh, yes please. That would be most kind. You know where Mr Chatwynde keeps the bottle, do you?"

"Got it right here in my hand, my dear. You sit down an' I'll bring it over."

For a moment the small lady looked around with some embarrassment. Charles got to his feet. "I do beg your pardon," he said. "Have I taken your usual chair?"

"Oh, no matter, no matter, erm . . ."

"Charles Metherall." Charles extended his hand.

The woman removed a kid leather glove. "Maud Lily Pettit," she said in a prim voice. They shook hands while Blossom placed a glass of ruby port on the table where Charles had been sitting.

"Do take your chair," he said.

Miss Pettit sat down, placed her capacious handbag beneath the chair and proceeded to unbutton her navy blue mackintosh. "There's such a cold wind tonight, you see, so chilly and damp for the time of year. And it's always so warm and welcoming here. This is why I come. Fuel is such a problem these days, I've given up trying to get coal altogether. I prefer logs, really, but one has to buy in so much wood and then one has to store it and chop it smaller and so on."

Charles glanced at the empty grate but played along, "Are you short of logs? I can get some for you, and I'm sure Mr Cottle here will lend a hand if you need kindling splitting. You'd do that for Miss Pettit, wouldn't you Cottle?"

"If she pays me," the gardener grunted.

Charles was about to suggest Miss Pettit approach George Braund, the school teacher in Vicky Villas, and ask if his son Roy could do a few odd jobs for her, when the pub door crashed open and a group of red-faced men in khaki virtually fell in. They stopped as one when they noticed Cottle.

"What be you doin' here, you ol' devil?" demanded Alf Plowden.

"You'm s'posed to be lying injured in the church hall. You've been hit by enemy gunfire, you daft ol' fart."

"I was, and I was bleedin' to death so I come down here to save me life," Cottle responded gruffly.

"So there you are!" Aubrey Chatwynde cried, spying Cottle now slurping at his pint. "Not dead yet, then, I see."

"No thanks to you. I could have caught me death this night, lying there on them there bare boards freezing me bollocks off."

Charles coughed in an attempt to cover the vernacular, but Cottle didn't notice, his voice lifting now in righteous indignation.

"What kept you? S'posed to be a bloody 'mergency. I'd be ol' as bloody Thuselah if I'd stayed there, if I didn't die afore'and."

"We had to wait for Billy to wipe the blood out of his van afore they could turn it into a fire engine. All slippery, it was," Alf Plowden explained.

"Ugh," Blossom laughed, setting out a row of half-pint mugs from the bar. It looked as if the first drink was on the house.

The atmosphere and banter were light-hearted. Aubrey Chatwynde gripped a young boy by the shoulder, saying, "Well, you've got him now, Roy. Get your first-aid kit and do your stuff. Cottle, shift yourself over here so the boy can get round you and bandage your head."

"B'aint nothing wrong with my ade now as what another drink won't cure."

"No, I'm sure you are right, but Roy needs to practise his first aid, and I need to see orders are carried out." His voice took on a commanding tone and Cottle reluctantly shuffled round so the boy called Roy could practise medicine.

Aubrey disappeared for a few moments then reappeared, still in his Home Guard uniform, to serve himself a stiff scotch from a bottle under the bar. He nodded in Charles' direction. "One for you, Major?"

"Don't mind if I do, Captain," Charles responded.

For a while there was a hum of chit-chat and then the door opened again and Maisie Rose Hawkins came in. She was evidently surprised to see her employer's husband, but she made her greeting and sat down beside Miss Pettit, who Charles now realised had been waiting for her female reinforcements. Aubrey placed a schooner of sherry on the bar, which Maisie, blushing, collected but did not pay for.

Billy Baxter and Alf Plowden were discussing the saving of Private Caleb Cottle from enemy gunfire when someone said, "Good job they changed it to the church hall. If we'd had to get down through Smugglers Woods to that ol' mine like the CO wanted, we'd be out all night trying to find him."

"Ah, you know why that was, don't you?" Aubrey said, knowingly. Waiting until he'd got everyone's attention, he continued, "You have heard about the tiger – or was it a panther? Big cat anyway."

"Big cat? What big cat?" Alf demanded, placing his glass on the bar for a refill and searching for change to pay for it.

"I thought it was common knowledge," Aubrey said, standing aside for Blossom to pull the next half-pint. "Some private menagerie caught a bomb last week and they haven't been able to round up all the animals yet."

"Where's that, then?" Billy asked. "I didn't know there were private zoos round here. I could be supplying their meat if I'd known."

"Part of London Zoo was evacuated down here couple of years ago. Can't say what animals they sent exactly," Aubrey prevaricated, then added, "Must have been the big cats, anyway. Lions, tigers, and a young black panther, I think it was."

Alf Plowden at the bar was thoughtful. "And you were tipped off that these yer beasts might be in Smugglers Wood down by the mine?"

Aubrey nodded and looked into his whisky.

"Nothing to worry about, then," said Billy Baxter in a loud voice. "If they beasts are anywhere near that old gipsy caravan, Becca Cottle'll see 'em off."

"If she don't strangle 'em with her bare hands first," Mervyn Jones the stationer added.

Caleb, in a turban of loose bandages and back in his usual place, growled a response in a manner not unlike one of the creatures Aubrey had just named. Charles took a swig of very good whisky to avoid laughing out loud.

"That's right, in it, Caleb?" Alf demanded. "Your Becca'll see em off. We could get her a spangly costume for the job."

There was more guffawing at the thought of Becca Cottle emerging like a lion tamer from the run-down gipsy caravan parked in what used to be the Wheal Marie sorting yard.

When the hoo-ha died down, Aubrey gently started again. Addressing Caleb directly, he said, "Joking apart, Caleb, you'd better warn her not to let her little ones out to play until we hear the beasts have been caught. It can't be very nice down there for her, anyway. Why don't we get George Deakin's tractor and move the caravan to somewhere less damp, more open? She'd be safer up near the church. I'll ask Reverend Hughes, if you like?"

Caleb grunted something about it being her life and none of his business, but Charles could see Aubrey's words had planted a rumour that would keep the area around Wheal Marie and the woods alongside Smugglers Mile Hill free of locals for a good while to come. And if by chance unusual noises, bangs or shots were heard in the vicinity, Porthferris would be rife with gossip about the hunting down of big cats, and not drawn to what was actually going on in the disused mine.

Nevertheless, he was annoyed about the Cottle woman: Waterson should have expedited the matter immediately. He had already arranged for Army engineers to create a safe bunker and living area and reinforce concealed exits for Churchill's special Auxiliaries. He silently raised his glass to Aubrey Chatwynde, who caught his eye and nodded.

"Right, then," said Aubrey, slapping a hand down on the bar. "Next on tonight's chaotic agenda is the pig club. Payment of dues to be made by Friday or Pew Pewsey will be roaring in the night as well. Mr Jones, will you do the honours, please? Here's the piggy bank."

Aubrey handed a wooden box to the stationer and caught Charles' eye again, inclining his head in the direction of the gents' lavatory.

Charles made his way to the door at the side of the bar leading to an interior passage and the gents. Before he could speak, however, Aubrey pulled him into the kitchen.

"Quick word. Come in here. That chap Bantry – he's been up at Bayview demanding to see more than just the kitchen and store cupboards. Waterson told him it was being used by the Admiralty, but the fellow insists that makes no difference, that he has the right to make an inventory of all stores, regardless. Wanted to see the cellar as well. The cellar connects to their sea cave by a passage and Waterson got very huffy about it. Said he actually had to shove Bantry out of the way. He's right, isn't he? If it's Admiralty property – even on loan – the fellow can't enter?"

"I don't know. I'll have to find out. It's certainly a bit fishy."

"More than fishy. Looks to me like he's trying to get information about what the Bayview observers are doing."

"Damn it! I'm going back up to town tomorrow. I'll get a clerk to find out about Bantry, and I'll see about jurisdiction as well, but the observers themselves should be able to find that out. What does Bantry call himself exactly?"

"Food Inspector."

"Did Waterson ask to see any form of identification? Delia didn't. She simply took him at his word."

"Doubt it. He hasn't ever come in here, you know, not to check the domestic side or the bar. I wonder why. Waterson says he's a bounder."

"Yes, he told me the same."

Aubrey said, "Thought you ought to know," and started to return to the bar.

Charles grabbed his sleeve. "What's that Cottle woman doing still down at the mine? Waterson was going to evict her."

"He can't get her to leave. What do you think all that nonsense about the wild cats was for?"

Charles sighed. There was nothing he could say or do, so he let Chatwynde return to the bar, made use of the gents then said farewell to everyone. Before leaving, however, he leaned towards Maisie Hawkins and said quietly, "Would you like me to see you home, Mrs Hawkins? No trouble – I enjoy a walk."

Already aglow from the generous measure of sherry, Maisie's faced flushed scarlet. "Oh, no, thank you all the same, Major. I've got my arrangements. He'll see me safe up the hill, thank you."

Outside, Charles pulled on his gloves and checked the weather before deciding which way to go home. A bent, shrouded figure suddenly scuttled across his path. The shape suggested it was Mad Harry, but there was no characteristic whiff and it was getting dark, so it could have been anyone. A pilot had once told him it took up to thirty minutes for eyes to adjust fully to darkness after being in electric light.

Delia was in the kitchen, as always, sitting at the table. "Colonel Waterson has just telephoned again – three times in the past hour now. He didn't leave a message, but it's obviously important."

"I'll call him."

"Charles!"

"What?"

"You can take off your cap and gloves first – or are you not stopping?"

Charles was already at the telephone, dialling the number on the notepad beside the handset. "Colonel Waterson, Metherall here. You called."

"I did. Can you get over here?"

"I'm leaving for London first thing tomorrow, Colonel. Can't you tell me now?"

There was a hesitation at the end of the line, then Waterson said, "There has been an – incident, an intruder. My wife has been attacked. She's badly injured."

Chapter 20

Gladys Fogarty, the Bayview housekeeper, who had reported the intruder, ushered Detective Sergeant Bob Robbins into a room barely lit by a table lamp, saying vaguely, "It's the police." Then she took up a position with her back to a curtained French window, melodramatically wringing her hands.

Dr MacManus, who was folding his stethoscope, looked up and nodded. "Evening, Robbins."

"Good evening, Doctor," Bob replied, then, identifying the victim's husband as he stepped forward, introduced himself.

"Cyril Waterson," the man replied dourly. "I appreciate you coming, Detective Sergeant, but, really, it was quite unnecessary. The doctor has made arrangements for my wife to be taken into hospital."

Bob looked at the housekeeper, waiting for her to speak. She didn't, so he said, "I was called at home, Colonel. Told to come here because your wife had been attacked by an intruder. It's hardly something we can ignore, sir."

The colonel took out a handkerchief and blew his nose, saying nothing. Addressing the doctor, Bob said, "Nothing too serious, I hope."

The colonel now responded before the doctor could speak, "Bashed on the head! Can you credit it? My wife, bashed on the head! We survive postings in all manner of lawless places abroad and the poor girl gets bashed on the head in her own home. Can you credit it?"

Bob looked at Dr MacManus, who caught his eye and shook his head, then said, "Nasty gash on the skull. She might have caught the back of her head on the corner of a wall."

"So an accident? She slipped and fell?" Bob asked.

Ned MacManus grimaced in response. "No, there's more. It looks as if she was pushed, shoved – in the chest with a . . . I don't know, something hard. I'd say the butt end of a rifle if I didn't know that was impossible. Internal bleeding, I fear, and broken ribs. Not breathing too well. Rather serious."

Bob turned to Colonel Waterson. "As I said, not something we can ignore, sir. Miss Fogarty, did you actually see anyone?"

The woman shook her head. "You could ask the people upstairs if they know anything."

"You have guests staying here?" Bob turned to Waterson.

"Not guests. Navy personnel, this is . . ." He took a deep breath. "We were requisitioned in '39 – Navy observation post for the Channel. They have listening equipment and the like. Can't say more – military business."

At that moment the doorbell rang and Gladys Fogarty left the room.

Bob said, "I assume you've asked these people what they know."

"They don't know anything. Two are on night shift; the other two were in their kitchenette drinking cocoa. None of them heard a thing."

"Do you think someone has been looking around, trying to get in? Is it possible for anyone to get up to the top floor undetected? It's not obvious this is a military location –"

"That's the point!" Waterson exploded. "Gladys shouldn't have called you. Ah, good. Metherall, explain to this policeman why he isn't needed."

Bob looked at the visitor, an Army major, waiting for someone to do the introductions. Ned MacManus came to the rescue. Major Metherall shook Bob's hand then stood back. Taking this as a cue to continue, Bob turned back to Waterson and asked, "If this is now a military establishment, are there no guards here? Your gates were wide open. I parked outside in your drive and no one tried to stop me."

"Wrens and Navy people need to come and go. We usually keep the gates closed, though."

"And they use private vehicles – jeeps? Where are those parked?"

"Around the other side of the house. There's only ever one jeep, though. Bit awkward for them – they often complain."

"I see. And there is only one gate onto the road, for cars?"

"Yes, and the gate for pedestrians next to the main gate at the front, where you came in. There's a side gate for tradesmen, of course."

"Of course," Bob responded drily. "How many actual entrances do you have to the building itself?"

"Four, not counting the cellar and the coal hole."

"The cellar can be accessed from outside?"

Waterson evaded the question. "There's the access to the coal house as well. They both open indoors, obviously."

"Hmm," Bob said, leaving the topic of unlocked doors and military security for when he could inspect the property in daylight.

There was an awkward silence. Gladys Fogarty moved to sit at the end of the sofa, rearranging the rug covering Mrs Waterson's legs as she did so.

Waterson huffed, "I'm sorry Detective Sergeant, but Miss Fogarty was in error, calling you. We can manage now Major Metherall is here, thank you."

Bob looked at the major and waited for him to speak, but he was reluctant to say anything, perhaps because of Miss Fogarty being in the room – or perhaps because of her and the doctor. Either way, there was clearly more to the intrusion than an attempted break in.

Ned MacManus picked up his bag and said, "Right, well, I think I've done all I can for now, Colonel. I'll be at the cottage hospital when the ambulance brings her in."

Waterson nodded. "She'll pull through all right, won't she?"

"Oh, I think so. But we need to get x-rays and examine her properly, and I can't do that here, I'm afraid."

"No, of course not." Waterson blew his nose again and turned his back on them.

Bob willed the housekeeper to see the doctor out, but Gladys Fogarty had taken up her position beside the patient with the permanence of a stone saint, so he opened the door himself and led the doctor through to the hall.

"Can you tell me anything else?" Bob said as they stood by the front door.

"Not much. Injuries look pretty serious, though. The ambulance people will take charge, nothing else I can do until we see some x-rays." Ned McManus nodded back towards the sitting room. "Neither of them knows how it happened."

"And the Major, what's he doing here?"

"Family friend, I suppose. Well, goodnight, Robbins. We should try to meet in happier circumstances one evening."

"Good idea."

Bob waited until the doctor's car had left the drive then returned to the morning room and said, "Can you show me what happened, Colonel?"

Waterson looked at Major Metherall, who nodded as if giving permission.

"You need Gladys for that," Waterson said.

Gladys Fogarty looked up. "Olwen – Mrs Waterson and I were in my little parlour listening to the wireless – we like a cigarette of an evening, you see. Not very ladylike, I know, but we each need our little vices, don't we? Well, Olwen – Mrs Waterson – her packet was empty and she remembered that she might have left some in the greenhouse . . . So we came down, and while I put the kettle on in the kitchen for a nice cup of tea, Olwen – Mrs Waterson – went out to the greenhouse . . . and then she didn't come back. When the kettle boiled I thought 'Well, that's strange. She's taking a long time.' So I got the torch from off the shelf and went out to see if perhaps . . . well, I don't know. The fact is, Olwen was lying down across the path by the corner of the house in the dirt – and – oh, it was awful. When I tried to move her I got blood on my hands and – look, it's still there."

"And this was by your greenhouse?" Bob turned to Waterson.

"Yes," he replied.

Bob caught Waterson's expression: he had something to hide. Turning around again, Bob said, "Miss Fogarty, do you by any chance have any idea what this person looked like?"

"No, no. I was in the kitchen, you see . . . but I do wonder if it is – was – the same man who was here before."

Bob intercepted the major looking questioningly at Waterson, who looked away.

"And that was . . .?"

"Well, I hardly like to say." Gladys Fogarty realised too late she had perhaps said too much. "I mean, I have not seen this person in person, if you know what I mean. The person in the dark, that is, with my own eyes, so to speak."

"I have a sort of supplier, if you must know," Waterson huffed. "This being a hotel, we, erm, have – *used to* have – special deliveries of some luxury goods: soap, wine and spirits and whatnot. I still get the odd delivery. Gladys may be referring to him."

"Ah, evading the old excise men and keeping up local tradition, eh?" Bob tried to make a joke of it. Waterson was a fool playing the blithe rogue now his hotel was being used for wartime purposes. "And can I ask how your, er, contact brings in the goods?"

Waterson flushed bright scarlet, then purple, his face so suffused that blue veins stood out like a sinister map. "Ah . . . erm . . . Well, might as well tell you. You'll find out anyway, I suspect. Some come in by boat to the cove, then up the path, obviously. Cottle keeps the cliff steps cut."

"Cottle?"

"Our gardener."

"But Cottle isn't your delivery man?"

"Good Lord, no."

"So that is . . .?"

"Someone local. That is, someone who knows us and most definitely would not have attacked my wife."

Bob rubbed the fingers of his right hand on his jacket. "You'd swear to that, would you, sir?"

"Yes. Ah, but no, it wouldn't have been him. I'd forgotten about . . . Unless he's . . ." One or more unfortunate details had evidently occurred to the colonel. He cast about for support, but if he was expecting any from Major Metherall he was disappointed. Adopting a far more positive tone, attack being the best means of defence, Waterson said, "Actually, Robbins – it was Robbins, wasn't it? I can find out about this myself. I'll get back to you if I think there's something, or someone, that is not quite right."

Bob didn't know whether to laugh or be offended by the man's patronising attitude to the law and himself personally, then decided not to make an issue of it and moved on at a tangent. "As you see fit, sir. You know where to find me. So you haven't been supplied with rolls of barbed wire to block landing craft access or any boats getting into your cove, despite now being a military establishment?"

Cyril Waterson's eyes blinked rapidly. "No."

At this point the Army major intervened. "Actually, gentlemen, I think we should all stop right here." He looked down at the injured Mrs Waterson with genuine compassion. "Colonel Waterson was not wrong to call the police, of course —"

"I didn't!" Waterson interjected.

"And I can see that the matter needs investigating. But as has been stated, this is a military establishment now, not a hotel. I'll take over from here. If necessary, we'll call in the Royal Military Police from Devonport. Miss Fogarty will show you to the door, Detective Sergeant. I'm sure Colonel Waterson would prefer to stay here with his wife until the ambulance arrives."

Bob had a dozen more questions and his fingers were on fire, a sure sign of mischief afoot, but he was being dismissed, and if Bayview was being used by military personnel he couldn't do anything unless the husband wanted a civil prosecution. Which, bearing in mind he hadn't even reported the attack . . . He bade the housekeeper farewell and reversed out of the gravel drive lost in thought.

Bayview had a cove and a sea cave, and Waterson had admitted getting "deliveries" by boat. The cove had been left unprotected, perhaps deliberately, although it was just as likely to be an oversight. Nevertheless, it was all a bit odd, especially since, as repeatedly stated, there were military personnel and no doubt sophisticated equipment on the premises.

As Bob drove up Church lane and passed Maisie Hawkins' cottage, he realised he hadn't even noticed there was no barbed wire or anything in her small cove, and he'd been there several times now. The Hawkins' cove was open and unprotected as well. If someone could attack an elderly woman like Olwen Waterson, were Maisie Hawkins and her daughter at risk as well?

Chapter 21

Charles Metherall waited until the police detective had left the room then without preamble said, "Has no one from the Admiralty inspected your cove?"

"No."

"And you have not adhered to invasion prevention strategies?"

"Oh, come on, Metherall. Jerry is hardly likely to invade England via our little beach path!"

"No, but individuals can easily come ashore, and do, it would appear. You have a lot of vulnerable radio equipment here, not to mention the charts and maps. Do I need to spell out what is happening on your top floor? You are jeopardising a vital listening and observation post."

Waterson hung his head, then he brightened. "But it wouldn't have been any of my chaps, would it? Stands to reason whoever has taken over from Hawkins – and I assume it's one of his chaps – he wouldn't go bashing Olwen about." Caught out by his own admission, Waterson's voice rose with righteous indignation. "Why would he?"

Charles sighed. "No. Perhaps it was someone checking to see what goods you were receiving or keeping here, or in your greenhouse."

"That blasted Bantry fellow? God almighty. Yes, it could have been him! He's not Customs and Excise as well, is he? It's just the sort of thing he'd do. He was here demanding to see our cellar. I sent him off with a flea in his ear, I can tell you. By God, that would be too much."

"I have never met the fellow, but I really can't believe Mr Bantry would be capable of hurting your wife, or have any reason to come onto your property at night. Don't jump to conclusions. If he did have *suspicions* though, he'd be obliged to pass them on through the proper channels. Notwithstanding . . ." Charles thought for a moment about what was best then said, "Show me your cellar, where you bring goods in."

"But Olwen . . . I can't leave her like this."

"Only take a moment, Colonel." Charles grabbed the older man by the elbow and ushered him out of the room.

Reluctantly, Waterson took a key from a row on the kitchen wall. Steps led down from the passageway under the stairs to a door which he unlocked and opened. Entering first, Waterson lit a kerosene lamp on the wall. Charles stepped in. The cellar was not unlike the one at Cleve, but far, far better stocked.

Staying by the door, Waterson said in a low voice, "We have been robbed three times recently, once in March and again in April, then again last week. I put it down to the Deakin twins, to be honest."

Charles swung round. "The Deakin twins – why? How do they get in down here?"

"Not from here, no. That's the strange thing. They've been taking lettuces, carrots, peas . . . from the garden. Last week it was new crop potatoes. It's jolly annoying, especially given their involvement with Hawkins and his other sources. I hate to tell tales, Charles, but I expect you already know about that."

"About Hawkins? More or less. But not about your garden thief. Do they take just a handful of this and that, or more?"

"Oh, more! Much more. They pulled up a whole bally row of potatoes. Stripped the vegetable patch bare one night, they did – every single beetroot went, ripe or not."

"But you didn't report it?"

Waterson gave a small shrug. "Didn't want to draw attention. To start with I thought it was the Wrens and the chaps upstairs. But I kept a watch and got Gladys to have a peek in their kitchenette. It isn't them."

"No. I see. Anything else you think I should know?

"Yes, but this is even odder."

Charles waited, his anger giving way to resignation. He would call Devonport as soon as he got back to Cleve House, and try to speak try to speak to his contact there in the morning as well. The Bayview observation post needed uniformed guards as fast as possible. "Well?" He tried to be civil, but it was difficult. Waterson was an ass.

"It's all the water. Gallons and gallons, and I can't explain where it goes. We only use the regulation four inches in the bath, you know. And at any one time there are never more than seven – sometimes ten – on the premises. But some weeks we use huge amounts of water. I've got a freshwater pipe down in the cove – for when we used to have picnics down there, and to wash off the salt after bathing. Pipe leads down through this cellar and into the tunnel. It's over there." He waved a podgy paw. "See? Well, I think – I know – this sounds ridiculous, but I think someone comes into the cove and steals our water."

"Oh, for Christ's sake!" Charles couldn't contain himself. "You have Navy personnel doing vital war work here and you're letting strangers come into the cove to get your blasted water! Why haven't you told us? Oh, I know. All those dratted cigarettes and NAAFI goods that are supposed to be destined for men and women fighting your war on the front line, only you can sell for a petty profit on the side, or use yourself. I'm sorry, Colonel. I should leave before I say anything else."

Charles turned to go then said, "Don't you hear it – the water? Pipes in our house judder like a blessed earthquake when a tap runs full blast."

Waterson looked down. "I think I have, but I thought it was the chaps upstairs having a bath or something. We're on the first floor on the other side of the house so it's hard to tell."

Charles tapped a foot on the floor with irritation, then sprinted up the cellar steps and let himself out of the hotel into the night.

By the time he got home Charles had calmed down, but he was still angry. After putting through the call to Devonport he went into the kitchen. Delia was still there, but this time wearing her pale blue dressing gown and filling a hot water bottle. "It's so chilly tonight," she explained. "Cocoa? There's some fruit pie in the larder if you're hungry."

"No, thanks, but a hot drink would be lovely." As he undid his jacket, Charles said, "Delia, what's this Mr Bantry like?"

"Bantry? Lean, cadaverous: Uriah Heap, or Trollope's Mr Slope. What was the name of the horrible man who was always staring through the window in *Turn of the Screw*?"

"You mean he stares at people through their windows?"

Delia turned and looked at him, "You know, I wouldn't be surprised."

"Bash an old lady on the head, would he?"

Delia laughed. "No! More likely to be the other way round, and I'd join the queue. Do you know, I caught him gazing at Mrs Bristle-Brush the other day, counting her children!"

Charles gaped at his wife, "Mrs Bristle-Brush?"

"One of my sows, the pink one; Mother Hubbard is the one with black ears. Here, take these up, will you, while I do our cocoa." Delia handed him two hot-water bottles, but she had warmed to her theme and it was a few minutes before he could do as bid.

"The point is, the awful man didn't even have the courtesy to ask. I mean, he didn't come to the front door or even the back door – he simply walked onto our property without a by-your-leave and started nosing about in the grounds. What do you think of that? Am I not right to loathe him? And so what if we have more piglets than perhaps we should? My Mrs Bristle-Brush is doing her bit for England, keeping us fed. Although I do confess I can't quite bring myself to ask Pewsey to come and do the terrible again just yet. Her new little ones are so pretty. It puts a very unwelcome slant on Christmas; we'll have a turkey from Billy Baxter, as usual. . . Those hot water bottles will go cold if you don't go, Charles, then I'll have to use more of the nation's precious gas supply."

Charles stayed where he was by the door to the hall, unsure whether to laugh or not. "How is it that I have never met Food Inspector Bantry? I visit the pub and the village; he's reportedly everywhere all the time, and yet our paths never cross. Could you invite him up for drinks next time I'm down, do you think?"

"No I could not!" Delia was surprisingly vehement for such an even-tempered woman. "Besides, he isn't what my mother used to call 'quality'."

"Since when did you become a snob? You are not like your mother, and war, I'll have you know, is a great leveller."

"My mother wasn't a snob. I didn't know you disliked her."

"I didn't dislike her – I barely knew her. It's just . . . Look, I'd better take these bottles – they'll be stone cold otherwise."

Charles beat a hasty retreat, but his pace slowed at the top of the stairs as his thoughts returned to the infamous Mr Bantry. If this so-called 'Food Inspector' could swan into Cleve House grounds during broad daylight to count piglets, what might he do to catch a bit of black market smuggling at night? Or, was the Bayview incident more sinister and related to the top floor observation post, not the content of Waterson's cellar and greenhouses? Or was it in some way connected to the mine?

He stuffed the water bottles into their bed, then sat down heavily on the slippery gold eiderdown to gather his thoughts. When he had proposed Porthferris as a suitable location for an Operation Base, using Aubrey as a Home Guard leader to organise the secret resistance group, it had been with the best intentions. Having an OB and Special Auxiliaries in the community was not without risk, but they were living beside a harbour conveniently located between Plymouth and Falmouth, which would certainly be occupied. In the long run it had seemed as good a way as any to protect the village should – God forbid – the invasion take place. Now it looked quite the reverse: had he brought trouble on the village? Were Delia and the children, and the blasted prep school, in greater jeopardy than before? He sighed. What sort of person would attack a defenceless, timid woman such as Olwen Waterson in a one-eyed village like Porthferris?

Then Charles sat upright, suddenly certain that the Bayview intruder was after what was on the top floor of the hotel, not in the cellar. It wasn't to do with home-grown vegetables, black market cigarettes or Spanish brandy at all. Someone in the community was actually spying. It sounded absurd, a German spy in Porthferris, but it had to be somebody with local knowledge: someone who knew the hotel and possibly how to get in from the private beach, and someone with a reason to supply Germany with the information. But how was he passing it on? And to whom?

And then Charles went very cold as Mad Harry's words came back to him: *I see'd 'em. Up they come – out the water. Trickly, trickly and over the quay, scrambly, scrambly . . .* Was it possible? Would – could – a German U-boat come into Porthferris Bay, or put a dinghy into the tiny Bayview cove?

Chapter 22

Tuesday usually meant an intensive morning in local villages, but this particular Tuesday proved very productive for Archibald Bantry, thanks to oranges and lemons! Nearly three hard years into the war and housewives still wanted lemons; and it was outrageous how grocers and fruiterers found supplies. Boosted by a successful morning of identifying wrong-doers and a late afternoon stroll round the outskirts of Trebelzue airfield to see how the runways were being extended, he drove slowly back in the direction of Porthferris. Parking some distance from the village near a tourist look-out point, he checked in his rear-view mirror for traffic and waited until a motorcyclist going well over a safe speed overtook him, then got out to spend a few minutes on the cliff. An asphalt path took him down from road level to a bench where, using a pair of good binoculars, he panned the horizon, ostensibly enjoying the oncoming sunset, but in reality doing rather more. After a while, he checked his watch. It was tempting to go straight home. He'd had no supper, but there was still one more task to be completed. Rumours that Rebecca Cottle had been forcibly moved from the grounds of the old mine had reached him: he needed to get down to Wheal Marie to find out why, and whether it merited including in his next dispatch. He returned to his car, stowed his binoculars in the glove compartment, and set off for his last visit of the day.

Ancient oak trees, elms and beeches lined the steep, narrow lane, forming a thick canopy overhead. He switched on his hooded headlights. A rabbit caught in the sudden glare stopped in its tracks and sat upright. Archibald Bantry put his feet on the brake and clutch, grabbed the gearstick and cursed as the big Austin saloon swerved into the high-banked hedge. A branch of hawthorn, sharp as the finger of fate, screeched across the newly repainted chassis. He muttered another curse, righted the vehicle and started the long descent of Smugglers Mile Hill in first, then second, gear.

A short way down, he put his foot on the brake again. The incline was even steeper here. The car did not slow. He crashed into first gear; the engine groaned. But the car did not slow. It did not slow at the half-mile bend nor further on down at the gate to Glebe Farm. He grabbed the handbrake and pulled with all his might. Nothing happened. The car did not slow. It gathered pace. At two hundred yards before the tight, right-hand bend leading to the entrance of Wheal Marie Mine, the Austin was doing over sixty miles an hour. Archie Bantry gripped the wooden steering wheel with white-knuckled hands, willing the vehicle to halt. It hurtled on, intent on disaster.

A bare few yards before the turn, he yanked at the wheel, pulling hard to his left. The Austin veered into the high bank and bounced back, gathered momentum and hurtled head on into the bole of a vast oak at the bottom of the hill.

The front of the car crushed in like a cardboard box. The driver's head and shoulders smashed into the windscreen.

Within seconds, night closed in, cloaking the mortal thud of the impact, complicit in its silence.

J. G. Harlond

The driver of a vehicle going uphill, away from the gate to the long-closed copper mine, noticed the Austin immediately. He pulled into the bank as best he could, switched off the ignition and turned to his passenger, "Bit of a mess," he said.

"Looks like Bantry's car," the passenger replied, tonelessly.

The two men got out and stood in the gathering darkness, waiting for their sight to adjust to the canopied gloom. Then, without a word, they stood absolutely still and listened. An owl hoo-hooed; a farm dog barked in the distance. They waited a while longer, then, satisfied no human sounds were to be heard, they looked at each other again and nodded in unspoken agreement.

One opened the back passenger door of the Austin with a leather-gloved hand, pulled a battered briefcase from the back seat and took it to their vehicle. Placing the briefcase on his driving seat, he opened it and pulled out a manila folder. Using a pocket torch, he scanned the contents and stuffed the folder under the car seat. Then, working in haste, he pulled out sheaves of typed papers, official forms, and a wad of what looked like personal correspondence. He pushed it all under the seat then searched the internal side pockets. Finding nothing more but a tin of coloured pencils and a local map, he closed the briefcase, wiped it carefully with his large handkerchief and returned it to the damaged vehicle. Then he went back to his car, opened the boot and selected a box containing two bottles of Spanish brandy and two bags of white sugar. Before leaving the box on the back seat of the Austin, he wiped the bottles with his handkerchief then ran it over the blue sugar bags and round the box itself.

The other man checked the damage to the Austin's bonnet with a low-light torch. Content that the engine was sufficiently damaged, he tried to prize open the driver's door.

Local Resistance

It took three good wrenches. The driver's upper body was covered in blood. Taking good care not to stain his brown overalls, he placed two fingers on the driver's neck and checked for a pulse the way he had been trained. Content once more, he reached into the driver's jacket pockets. He found what he was looking for – a small notebook in the inside breast pocket, but in trying to extract it he caught his sleeve on the handbrake. He lowered the brake then made another grab for the precious notebook, getting blood on his hands in the process. Eventually succeeding, he waved the notebook at his companion and shoved the car door closed with his body.

Improvised tasks completed, the two men stood back.

"Bugger," said the man in brown overalls, "the lights are still on."

"Leave them," said his companion, the voice of command. "Did you check the glove compartment?"

"No."

"Never mind, we can't stay longer – let's go."

Without another word, the two men got back into their vehicle and set off for their original destination.

Before they parted company later, the man in the expensive driving gloves said, "Good job. But you should have told me."

The man in the overalls looked at him sharply, "Nothing to do with me."

"No?"

"No."

The Cornish lane returned to its natural order. It was as if nothing had happened, except for the crushed carcase of a man-made metal box on wheels and a solitary Mediterranean lemon, which rolled into the undergrowth around the great oak, ready to be eaten by a curious English rodent.

Part Three
Secret Wars

Chapter 23

"Albert Villas will be down on the right, before the shops and the quay. Their back gardens open onto the path that leads up to Cleve House and the cliff meadow, or down to the village and the harbour. Every path round here links somewhere to somewhere," Laurie Oliver explained.

"Well, it would, wouldn't it?" Bob Robbins replied, tartly. "Right, what number are we looking for? Ah, don't bother there's only six houses. I'll park and we'll find it." Bob pulled on the handbrake and made sure the car was in gear before turning off the engine – it was a steep hill.

Laurie put on his helmet and they walked up the short path to Number Six. Bob rang the bell. A tall woman in black with mud-grey hair in a hairnet answered the door. Bob Robbins removed his hat and Laurie Oliver pulled off his helmet.

"Mrs Hilda Bantry?"

The woman stared at him for a moment. "Yes."

"Sorry to bother you, Mrs Bantry. I'm Detective Sergeant Robbins and this is Police Constable Oliver. I believe

Policewoman Thomas and PC Gates were here this morning. May we come in for a word or two? We shan't stop long."

The woman blinked, bewildered. "Police. Again?"

"Yes, just a few questions. Nothing to get worried about."

"If you must . . ." Mrs Bantry opened the door and led them past the front room down a passage that smelled of stale biscuits.

"We're in here," she said, gesturing to a dismal sitting room. "I'm keeping the front room ready for the funeral."

The wallpaper was a foliage and trellis design in olive green and grey; there were two easy chairs, one brown, one dark grey, both bearing aged antimacassars. Under the window looking onto the back garden was a square "Utility" table with two chairs. Scattered on sundry surfaces around the room were china dogs and glass bric-a-brac. Nothing matched; everything looked old and tired. *A sad, cold house,* Bob thought, *and not only now.*

Two mismatched women were perched on chairs belonging to the table in front of the unlit fire. The first was Mrs Hawkins in a shapeless dress and cardigan. Her cup and saucer rattled the moment she saw him. The other was the dapper little spinster he'd seen in the Fisherman's Boot a couple of times. She was wearing a dinky blue-green cloche hat that reminded him of a shiny pigeon. She also held a flowery cup and saucer. Her hands were motionless but her beady eyes darted from him to the young PC and back, taking in every detail. Maisie Hawkins, who wasn't wearing a hat, which was unusual if they'd come on a tea and sympathy visit, looked worn out. Mrs Bantry waved vaguely in her direction, "Mrs Hawkins from the village, and Miss Pettit who lives at Seabreeze."

"We've met – Mrs Hawkins and I, that is." Bob nodded politely at the ladies then half turned to PC Oliver, remembering his connection to the bungalow named

Seabreeze. He stroked a forefinger across his lips to indicate silence; he didn't want any fraternising relating to family holidays. Although the coincidence did rather prove the boy's daft comment about the pathways in Porthferris. Tucking the coincidence to the back of his mind, he said, "Sorry to intrude like this, Mrs Bantry. I didn't know you'd got visitors."

"I expect you are only doing your job, Inspector."

Before he could correct her, Mrs Bantry looked at the police constable and said, "Please take a seat." She indicated a vacant chair at the table under the window. Laurie Oliver pulled it out but didn't sit down.

Maisie placed her cup and saucer on the tea tray on the table, saying, "Shall I do these for you, my dear? I'd best be getting back. Are you coming, Miss Pettit? I can walk down with you, if you like."

"No, no, Mrs Hawkins, you trot along. Oh, but what am I saying?" Miss Pettit popped delicate white fingers to her mouth. "You are quite right. Mrs Bantry has important matters to attend; we must both be getting along. No need for us here now." She jumped to her feet, put her cup on the tray and reached down for her handbag, then, darting nimbly around Mrs Hawkins, lifted the whole tray in one quick movement, saying, "You get along, my dear. I know you have obligations. I'll do these. Don't wait for me; I'm a perfectly dreadful dawdler."

Belying her words, and before she had even finished speaking, Miss Pettit was backing out through the door to the kitchen, carrying the tea tray like a trophy. "Won't take a jiffy to do these pretty cups," she piped and disappeared.

Bob caught a quick glimpse of the handbag as the door closed; it had a lizard's head on it. He could have sworn the reptile was grinning.

Maisie Hawkins hesitated, but she was clearly anxious to be on her way. "I'll say goodbye, then, Mrs Bantry," she said, heading for the front door. "If you need anything you know where to find me."

Mrs Bantry dithered between the door to the passage and the door to the kitchen then, as if making a decision of any description was the greatest burden, she virtually collapsed on the grey chair by the fireplace.

"Sit yourself down, lad," Bob muttered at Laurie, still standing behind him. The boy did as he was told and took out his notebook and pencil.

For a long minute there was silence. Bob watched Mrs Bantry. She was nervous, apparently waiting for the small spinster to return.

Miss Pettit finally popped her neat hat around the kitchen door and, addressing the widow, said, "That's it. I've left your pretty cups to dry on the draining board. Now, do remember, I'm on my own, so just drop in whenever you feel like it. No need to wait for our usual Friday tea party – any day will do. I'll come up tomorrow to see how you're getting on. Anything you need, any shopping?"

The widow shook her head and the spinster smiled. "You be a brave girl, Hilda. I know this must be quite horrible for you, but . . . Well, never mind – I'm being silly standing here talking like this when these gentlemen are waiting for me to go." She gave the room a parting smile and closed the kitchen door.

Bob Robbins waited until he heard the latch to the back door then began. "Good neighbours, Mrs Bantry. A blessing wherever you are."

"Not what I'd call a blessing." The woman turned her long face to look out of the window.

Bob cocked his head to one side and led in gently, "Why's that, then?"

"Oh, I'm not saying their concern isn't genuine, especially Mrs Hawkins. She has her own trials, what with that missing husband of hers and the simple daughter. Miss Pettit, of course, has tried to be friendly with her weekly tea-parties, as she calls them, although we did think at one time she was . . . It's just that . . ."

Bob waited. There was a brief, laden pause, then Mrs Bantry turned back to him. "My husband doesn't – did not – encourage visitors. We've only been here a couple of years, so obviously we don't know anyone yet, except the vicar and his wife, but she's always busy. I had to put myself on the cleaning and flower rota. She is so disorganised, always drifting off here and there, and forgetting things. One rarely even sees her. Of course, one shouldn't be uncharitable, but one can't help noticing church affairs aren't all they should be in this parish."

"You're not from these parts, then, Mrs Bantry?"

"Do I sound like it?"

"Well, accents can be misleading."

"I don't have an accent, Inspector. I went to elocution lessons. Not that I had an accent to start with. My mother was born in Oxford, my father was from Reading."

"And Mr Bantry?"

"Sonning," there was a fraction of a pause then she added, "Common. He was from Sonning Common. After we married we lived in Henley-on-Thames." She sniffed, satisfied that the name of a town should suffice for her pedigree.

"And that was until recently?"

"Two years ago."

"Nice place, Henley. Can't say I've ever been, but I've seen pictures at railway stations. What brought you down this way? Henley isn't too affected by the war, is it? Not many air raids over there, I should think."

Hilda Bantry took a deep breath and pulled a handkerchief from her sleeve. It was still folded in an ironed triangle. The woman dabbed her mouth and scrunched the white cambric into a fist.

"Perhaps you should know, Inspector, my husband invested in a railway scheme in India. Due to events relating to Indian Home Rule the scheme faltered. Stupid workmen sabotaged their own tracks, put themselves out of work. I ask you . . ." She shook her head at the absurdity of the Indian railway worker, then sighed. "The fact is, my husband spent rather too much money . . . Then the war started, which completely halted operations. I can't see how this can have any bearing on his . . . but I'll tell you anyway. Archibald thought – decided – it would be better if we sold our house and moved to the West Country. I would have preferred the Torquay area, but . . ."

Too expensive. Bob waited a few seconds, giving the woman time to add or retract, but she said nothing more, only scrunched her handkerchief tighter, so he said, "Well it's nice enough round here. Quiet."

"That was another consideration."

"Your husband had retired?"

"Yes and no. He took early retirement from the GWR before we moved, but rather jumped at the opportunity to help out when rationing started. Then a seat on the County Agricultural Committee became available."

"And he was in this line before?"

"Food and agriculture? Good heavens, no. I told you – the Great Western Railway. He was responsible for timetables until the unfortunate Indian venture."

Bob nodded seriously, as was expected, at the weight of responsibility the late Mr Bantry must have suffered. "Not an easy job, Mrs Bantry. Goodness me, no. Not easy, either, coming all the way down here and starting again, I imagine.

Local Resistance

Not easy for him at all, not being local and having to visit shops and farms."

"Initially, it simply meant travelling around the county, sometimes visiting the bigger towns, Bodmin, Launceston. He often goes to – went to – Plymouth for cross-county meetings. His post involved visiting shops *incognito* to verify they were fulfilling the points scheme, coupons and rationing quotas and the like. Checking shop lists against coupons and signatures when required. Unfortunately his face became known, you see, which made it difficult in this area, and *very* annoying at times. People do talk so in these small communities. Word got around, and Archibald . . . He has never been a very patient person . . . The people round here, he found them difficult to comprehend. They *are* virtually incomprehensible, you know. And backward. No understanding of the war situation whatsoever. Wilful ignorance, I call it. He tried to show them how important it is for us to all pull together, make sacrifices, show Hitler a united Home Front. I'm so sorry – would you like some tea?"

"Very kind. A cup of tea would be very welcome, Mrs Bantry."

"I'll put the kettle on."

As soon as Mrs Bantry had gone into the kitchen, Bob turned to Laurie Oliver and hissed, "Tell her you need the lav – outside. See if they've got a shed, and if so, what's in it."

Laurie followed Mrs Bantry into the kitchen and was directed to the outdoor lavatory. Bob inspected the mantelpiece. There was an absence of photographs, and no sign of anything like a letter, not even an electric or gas bill, which made Bob's fingertips twitch.

When she returned, Mrs Bantry placed the tea tray on the table by the window and poured three cups. They were pretty, as Miss Pettit had said, but chipped with age.

Mrs Bantry offered him the sugar bowl. It was brimful of refined white sugar.

"No, thank you. I gave it up when rationing started. Keep hoping my waistline will notice."

The humourless woman blinked. "Milk? We pour it *after* the tea in this house."

Bob Robbins took his cup, trying to keep a blank expression. Sipping the weak, yellowish liquid in silence, he studied the sad woman over his cup, then, when Laurie was back in the room, returned to his seat and began again. "So, let me get this a bit clearer. You're saying Mr Bantry made a few – what shall we call them? – 'wartime enemies'?"

"Quite. Inspector, can you tell me precisely what happened to my husband in the car? That young woman this morning was extremely vague. The brakes failed on a steep hill, is that correct?"

Bob grimaced at the "Inspector" bit again but decided to let it go. If it appealed to her snobbery it wouldn't do any harm. It was a fairly common mistake; people assumed a detective of his age automatically ranked as an Inspector. The fact that he didn't was not a matter of regret. He took a final sip of reused tea leaves, then said slowly, "To be honest, I can't tell you very much. The front of the car is completely bashed in. We've taken it back to Mr Paddon's garage."

"Ezra Paddon!"

"It's the only garage for miles, Mrs Bantry. There's a place in Cready, but the last mechanic joined up and the owner can't manage. We can't tow it all the way to Liskeard, I'm afraid. We're woefully short-staffed ourselves, not to mention the petrol ration." He was going to add "there is a war on, you know", but refrained. Arguments such as these were useless in the face of personal loss. Mrs Bantry had gone purple in the face; no reasoning would serve now, anyway.

Local Resistance

"Ezra Paddon killed my husband, Inspector! Archie's car was there for a whole week and he did a botched job. It's that stupid man's fault my husband is dead! If not him, one of his mentally deficient mechanics. You must authorise an investigation. Alert the coroner or whatever it is you people do with suspicious deaths. Why do you think I have just given you all that information about Archibald's job? I cannot believe it was an accident."

Bob was tempted to ignore her, but what she was saying meant there might be more to it – as he had suspected. Nevertheless, her attitude made him mulish. He had visited Paddon's garage recently himself. The owner's son, Shadrach, was profoundly deaf: that didn't make him stupid. The other boy came from the same school for the deaf, apparently, meaning there could have been a misunderstanding regarding Bantry's car. It didn't explain how the man could have been out and about all week without mishap, though, or why the brakes had to fail on that particular hill.

He rattled a thumb against the arm of his chair then got up, put his empty cup on the tray and remained standing by the table, looking out at the garden. It was a mess. The lawn needed mowing and the flower beds needed weeding, which was all wrong. The garden showed no signs of being turned over to vegetables. No "digging for victory" here. His own garden was neatly planted with beans, peas, carrots and potatoes in tidy rows, and he only had himself to feed. It irritated him and went right against the much vaunted Bantry belief in a "united Home Front". It was also a surprise of another kind: he'd marked Mr Bantry down as a potting-shed type – for the usual marital reasons.

Largely for the benefit of Laurie Oliver, who was waiting with pencil in hand, he said, "Mr Bantry was with the Great

Western – timetables, you said. Responsibility and a meticulous attention to detail . . .”

"Yes. My father was Station Master at Reading.”

"A railway family, then. Was Mr Bantry with the GWR during the Great War or on active service?”

Mrs Bantry looked down at the dull rug beneath her feet. "Archibald was in a reserved occupation.”

"On the railway?”

"No, in the City, well, Paddington Station. He was also asthmatic as a child, I believe. But his post was . . .”

"'Reserved', I understand. Go on, you were saying . . .”

"We met at Christmas, 1920. He was a widower. His wife had died in the flu epidemic in 1918. They lived in Woking, I believe.”

"Ah, yes, the 'Great War irony'. Do you know about this, PC Oliver?” Bob looked at the boy at the table and cocked his head on one side, inviting him to speak.

"What, sir? Men surviving gas and bayonets and returning to a hero’s welcome of the deadly Spanish flu?”

The note of criticism didn’t escape Bob. He looked at the boy with a glimmer of respect.

"Right,” he said, "I think that’s all, Mrs Bantry. Let’s check our times, though, before we go. PC Oliver, you’ve got the notes about the crash.”

Laurie got to his feet and flipped back a couple of pages in his notebook. "Mr Bantry’s car was found by John Deakin of Glebe Farm and Miss Joyce Pewsey around ten p.m. It had crashed into a tree at the bottom of Smugglers Mile Hill.” The boy skipped a bit, then added, "Deakin returned to Glebe Farm. Rang for the police before taking Miss Pewsey to her home about ten-thirty.”

"And there’s another person who needs investigating.” Mrs Bantry couldn’t get the words out fast enough. "Mr Pewsey threatened my husband with an axe last year – on two separate occasions. Said if he ever returned to Home Farm he would kill him!"

"A serious threat, do you think? Or had Mr Bantry been questioning the number of animals not accounted for on the County Agricultural list? This is a country area –"

"Oh, and don't I know it! Mad peasants and greedy shopkeepers who look after their own, and never an extra morsel for . . ."

Bob waited, but the woman realised what she was saying and halted, pursing her thin lips and kneading the crumpled handkerchief into final and absolute submission.

Time for a bit of subterfuge, Bob thought. He put his right hand up to his chin and made an "aghhh" sort of sound, as if in pain. "Before we go, Mrs Bantry, you couldn't let me have drop of brandy, could you? I've got raging toothache and it's the only thing that helps till I get to the dentist."

Mrs Bantry went to an old-fashioned walnut sideboard and opened a door, releasing a dusty, peppery smell into the stuffy room. From where he was standing Bob could make out a bottle of sherry, what looked like a bottle of Johnny Walker whisky and a squarish bottle of French Armagnac. She pulled the Armagnac out and held it up to the light. It didn't look as if it had been opened in years.

"I think there may be a little left."

"That's all I need."

Opening the other side of the cabinet, Mrs Bantry selected a brandy glass, then put it back and took out a thimble-size tumbler. Both looked smudged, greasy and unused.

Mrs Bantry couldn't open the Armagnac, nor could he.

"Ah, well," Bob said, "I'll survive till I get home. Thanks for the thought, anyway."

Mrs Bantry blinked, once more unsure how to respond. Bob didn't like her but he couldn't help feeling sorry for her.

"We'll be on our way now," he said. "Sorry to have troubled you. Did we sort out what time Mr Bantry left here yesterday, Constable?"

PC Oliver shook his head as Mrs Bantry started to speak. "Tuesday is Archibald's busy shop day. He was going to Bodmin, I think. He left early because he had to get extra petrol for the journey. This was authorised, of course, despite what Mr Paddon at that petrol pump he calls a garage says. He refuses to let Archibald have any commercial fuel on Saturdays because he says it is the weekend and, naturally, he is never open on a Sunday – and on Monday, for whatever reason, there was no one there." Mrs Bantry shook her head in despair then paused, as if to gather her thoughts.

Bob looked across the room at Laurie and made a writing signal with his hand; he wanted the comment about Paddon's garage noted down. There was something significant in it, although he didn't know what yet.

In response to his silence, Mrs Bantry reluctantly picked up from where she had left off. "After Bodmin, Archibald was returning via Liskeard, or maybe it was the other way round, I forget. That is why he needed a full tank. He left the house about eight-thirty in the morning. Before the nine o'clock news, anyway."

She paused again and looked at her husband's empty chair then out of the window. "I didn't see him again until this morning when I was taken to identify his body. Please pass my thanks to the young policewoman. I am not ungrateful: she was professional, and kind. I'll show you out." She started to move then halted. "One thing – and this is most important – not all my husband's possessions have been returned. His briefcase was given to me, but it is almost empty. I can't imagine why you police might want Archibald's papers, but I shall have to inform his superiors and so on. They will no doubt request all of my husband's paperwork. Please arrange it."

Bob looked at the woman and frowned, "You're saying his briefcase was empty?"

"As good as."

"I'm pretty certain we don't have anything. It's not our policy to open a traffic victim's personal effects." He turned to Laurie, "Does Sergeant Mallett have anything?"

"Not that I know of," the boy replied.

Bob turned back to the widow. "Have you checked his desk, Mrs Bantry? He may have left the papers in his desk — if he uses one."

Hilda Bantry pursed her lips. "There is a manila folder. Archibald has spent months gathering the information. I helped him . . ." She stopped, started to say something else, then stopped again.

"Try and see what he's got in the house, Mrs Bantry. If it's that important I doubt he'll have been carrying it about with him."

"He did. It was part of his strategy — to show the miscreants the error of their ways. A means of encouraging shopkeepers to follow the rules by showing them their names had been recorded."

Bob looked at Mrs Bantry questioningly but she said no more. "I see. Well, in that case I'll ask about the briefcase the minute I get back to the station. You can call me there if you do find it in the house. Local people — their names were in the file?"

"Depends what you call 'local', Inspector. In this vicinity, most certainly."

"Yes, right. Was there anything else?"

Mrs Bantry shook her head. Bob and Laurie returned in silence down the passage. There was no opportunity for a last word on the doorstep because no sooner was the door opened than it was shut firmly behind them.

Chapter 24

The young police constable and the sexagenarian detective strolled back down the short path, replacing their respective headgear, but as Laurie Oliver opened the gate and waited to let Bob Robbins through, his helmet suddenly tilted sideways. "Hey," he cried, putting a hand up to save it.

Bob looked up and immediately located an impish face in the branches of a neighbour's apple tree. "Good shot," he called.

The imp waved a sturdy homemade catapult in joyful response. At the same moment, the front door to Number Five opened and a pretty, dark-haired woman wearing a frilled apron and a harried expression called, "Simon!"

Bob was out of the gate of Number Six and opening the gate of Number Five before the imp hit the ground. "That's your lad, is it?" he called, addressing the woman on the doorstep. "We need lads like him in North Africa."

Seeing Laurie Oliver's uniform the woman put her hands to her cheeks in distress, "Oh, Simon, now what?"

The boy gave a devil-may-care shrug of the shoulders, but nipped behind his mother's skirt just the same.

"Oh, yes, of course," the woman continued, "you must have been with Mrs Bantry. How is she? I heard all about it in the village this morning."

But you didn't go next door to offer your condolences. "As one might expect under the circumstances," Bob replied. Taking a couple of steps up the path he added quietly, "You don't know Mrs Bantry, then?"

"Well, I do and I don't. We're neighbours, obviously, but I'm afraid I had words with her husband some weeks ago, and with her as well, I suppose. I regret I haven't spoken to them since."

"Broken window, was it?" Bob Robbins grinned in the imp's direction.

"Um – yes."

The woman's reply was doubtful, but the imp's response was a clincher. "I've never broken any of *their* windows, only their back gate, and they haven't complained about that yet. They know, because it's been tied up." The boy spoke with a sense of triumph. Then seeing Bob Robbins' expression he changed his tone and added, "I needed the bolt," as if this justified the damage.

"Oh, Simon," the woman ruffled the boy's springy, ginger hair, "what on earth did you need a bolt for?"

"For my crossbow."

"I didn't know you were making a . . . Oh, well. He's always up to something," she gave a light laugh and patted her apron as if for comfort.

"Don't worry – it doesn't work. I've made a Robin Hood longbow instead," the boy said.

"Mr Bantry wasn't sympathetic regarding boys being boys, I take it?" Bob Robbins asked gently, trying not to smile.

The woman gave a small, feminine moue. "Trivial things, you know. It was nothing serious."

But serious enough to halt diplomatic relations. Bob tried another tack. "Will she get many visitors, do you think?" He nodded in the direction of Number Six.

"I really couldn't say. They keep themselves to themselves, except when they're . . ."

"Poking their noses into other people's business?" Bob knew this wasn't very ethical, but the woman's nod of agreement and apologetic smile were all he needed.

"But living next door you see who comes and goes?" Bob fished for more.

"No, not at all. At least, I don't see them. Our sitting room and kitchen are at the back, and we tend to use the back gate mostly, for Simon to go up to school at Cleve House, and when I go down to the village."

"Our visitor always comes in through the back door," Simon stated stuffing his hands in his pockets and nodding in agreement with his mother. Bob thought he heard the word "visitor" in the singular and waited for a response, keeping an open, friendly expression on his face

"He's not a 'visitor', Simon, he's your tutor!" Two perfectly round, pink spots appeared on the woman's face. Bob waited again and she reluctantly filled the gap. "Simon is referring to his tutor, Mr Booth. He's with the school at Cleve House so he comes down the lane and uses our back gate . . . I expect they'll move back to Saltash once the war is over."

"They?"

"The school – St Dominick's."

"Ah, yes, got you now. Bit lazy, are you?" Bob asked, winking at the boy, who grinned in response.

"As you say, boys will be boys," his mother said, "but this particular boy does rather wear me out. It's boarding school next year."

"That'll hone his skills," Laurie said from the gate in such a matter-of-fact tone Bob wanted to hoot with laughter.

Either the mother didn't hear him or she chose to ignore the comment. "Now then, Simon, into the house, and no more arguing."

Before Bob could ask anything else, and he'd compiled quite a list, the intensive, heavy drone of low-flying aircraft filled the air around them. All four looked up into the sky.

"Oh, wow!" cried Simon, "Supermarine Spitfires! Wow!"

"You know your planes, then, lad," Bob said appreciatively.

"I know everything," the boy drawled.

"Not everything, Simon," responded his mother, tugging him backwards.

Bob was about to ask how he knew so much about the planes but the front door to Number Five was also closed firmly in his face. He looked at Laurie and raised his eyebrows. As he closed the garden gate behind him, he said, "You were a boarding school boy – I forgot. Handle a catapult?"

"One-shot Olly, I was. Lethal with a dried pea."

Bob squeezed in behind the wheel of his Morris Eight, removed his trilby, tipped it behind him onto the back seat, then rested his head on the steering wheel and gave way to chuckling laughter. One-shot Olly folded himself into the passenger seat and Bob put a hand out. "Sorry, I'm not laughing at you. Don't get crotchety."

Eventually Bob Robbins started the engine, did a three-point turn and drove back up the hill. Then, instead of carrying on to Cready, he took the right-hand turn at the junction and stopped a little way along the road from the church hall. Opening the door, he said, "I need a breath of fresh air."

As they ambled along the lane Bob said, "What did you make of the old biddy living in your friends' bungalow?"

Laurence Oliver pulled off his helmet and rumpled his mop of blond hair. "She has a nose like a parrot's beak."

It wasn't the response Bob was expecting but he snapped his podgy fingers with satisfaction nevertheless. "That's what's familiar. I've seen her somewhere before. I thought she looked like a pigeon when we went in, but you're right, it's a parroty sort of beak – and I've seen it somewhere before – with another older lady. Winchester, maybe. When? When was that? Something to do with a life-insurance payment and two widows with the same name, mother-in-law and daughter-in-law, and who the money was to go to. Collins, Collinson, Coulson . . . something like that. The insurance company called me in to do a background check before they paid out. And . . . that woman, Miss Pettit, or someone very like her, was there. Paid companion to the mother-in-law. Then the old woman died suddenly as well, and there were questions about whether it was the daughter-in-law who wanted to get her hands on all the money or natural causes. Open verdict, in the end."

Laurie wasn't listening. His face had turned green and he made a dash for the hedgerow where he was violently sick. Bob left him retching into the hawthorn and wandered back towards the car, whistling quietly to himself.

After a few minutes the boy joined him, his face now the colour of the white handkerchief he was using to wipe his mouth.

"Something you ate?"

"Must be, but I haven't had anything hardly all day, only a sandwich in the canteen and Mrs Bantry's tea. I was a bit greedy with the sugar. Don't see a bowl of sugar like that very often these days. Sugar doesn't make one sick, though, does it?"

"Not that I know of. Mind you, the whole house has got a poisoned air about it, if you ask me. Speaking of which, when we get back to the station I want you to talk me through what you've seen and heard in the past hour, if you're up to it. Every detail – doesn't matter if you think it's trivial or not. I want to know what was, or what wasn't in the Bantry shed — things like that. What was in the shed, by the way?"

"Old lawnmower, garden tools. Floor was filthy. No sign of footsteps in the dust either. Hasn't been used for weeks, I'd say."

Bob gave an appreciative grunt. "Useful to know. So no confiscated goods going in there, then."

"Not that I could see — briefly, like that." Laurie paused took a deep breath and walked ahead for a few paces breathing deeply. Coming back to the car, he said, "Sarge, is this turning into murder inquiry?"

Bob opened the driver's door and got back behind the steering wheel. "Road accident, except . . ."

"According to the wife there was a village conspiracy to bump him off."

Bob glanced at the pasty-faced boy. "Mm, looks as if there is more to it than an accident. Or, more like, it's a fortunate accident for some." He sighed. "If I've got time, I'll visit the banks in Cready tomorrow, see if he was in financial straits."

"Do you think there was money in the briefcase?"

"Don't know, but if there was, Mallett or someone would have told me at the station. Mind you, if Bantry had rationing reports against local shopkeepers there's probably a good few who'd prefer not to pay the fines, and, given that they're all related one way or t'other, anyone might have copped hold of a bit of paper with a familiar name on it. I wonder if anyone actually got to the car before it was reported."

"Or the two people who found the vehicle, might they have 'acquired' whatever it is Mrs Bantry is concerned about?"

"Not impossible, worth paying them a call, individually, if need be." Bob mused on this for a moment, then added, "They must have come down in the world, though, the Bantrys, if they lived in Henley-on-Thames." He pronounced the name of the place with an exaggerated la-di-dah accent and regretted it, fearing the young PC might take umbrage again.

Laurie Oliver was evidently still feeling too queasy to notice, however, so Bob said, "Did you notice they'd got a 'Utility' table and chairs? That's only for newly-weds and bombed-out Blitz refugees, as far as I know. *Of course*," he mimicked Mrs Bantry's sharp use of the phrase, "him being 'in rationing' and 'on the County Agricultural Committee' means he'd have access to all sorts of stuff. Even so, it's a bit fishy. Damn it! I should have asked her about his insurance company, to check his life insurance."

"Will they pay out on a murder victim – if he is?"

"Yes, depending on prior circumstances. But not – at least, they didn't use to – if it's suicide."

PC Oliver's head snapped round. "Suicide? But the car –"

"Is bashed up. Yes, I know, so we ought to check the brake shoes. See if they were in good nick. Ezra Paddon's son, the by no means mentally deficient one, is a whiz with car innards. I'll stop by tomorrow, if I'm allowed."

"Supposing it is a murder designed to look like an accident, not suicide?"

"Well, in the old days that was what the CID were for. Nowadays, with the station at half strength and my boss focussed on thefts of explosives from local quarries and now the trouble at the bomb factory as well, and you uniform lads spending more time organising school crocodiles and pulling people out of craters than doing any policing, it'll be a miracle if we're allowed to follow it up."

"But the CID –"

"Write infernal internal reports and that's about it these days, as far as I'm concerned, anyway. It was nice to get out for a change. Not for you today, though – pity. You still feeling queasy?"

Laurie nodded and put the handkerchief to his mouth.

"Shout if you want me to stop."

They drove through the narrow Cornish lanes in silence. As they approached town, Bob said, "Feeling better?"

"More or less. Serge, can I ask you two questions?"

"Long as they're not personal."

"Oh, sorry," Laurie lapsed into an embarrassed silence.

"Go on, ask," said Bob.

"The first – what about the brandy and sugar in the car?"

"What brand was the brandy? Where was it from?" Bob quizzed.

"Spanish, I think."

"Rot gut or good stuff? Genuine question, I need to know."

"Goodish stuff, I believe." Laurie turned in his seat. "Mr Bantry had Armagnac as well, and that's jolly expensive, I think."

"So they may have wanted some cheaper Spanish stuff for the Sunday coq-au-vin? I doubt it very much. Getting hold of anything alcoholic for private consumption these days is close to impossible, so he had a private supplier somewhere. Or he was being paid off in kind to turn a blind eye. Or he made use of confiscated goods." Bob went quiet, then asked, "And the other?"

"Question? Um . . . it's about your name. You said mine was a bit –"

"Only because of Laurence Olivier, the actor."

"Were you actually baptised Robert?"

"No-o, it's a nickname. You get them in the nick, if you're not careful. I picked it up when I joined the police – about your age."

"I don't get it, why 'Bob'?"

"No idea," Bob lied, wanting to keep his ornithology to himself. Even so, he couldn't help himself whistling the opening bars of the popular song that had actually come after he'd acquired the name: 'When the red, red robin goes bob, bob, bobbing along . . .' Laurie Oliver still didn't pick up the connection.

As Bob parked in the Cready Police Station car lot, Laurie tapped the crown of the helmet on his lap. "But why was he found at the bottom of that hill if he was returning from Liskeard? It only goes down to Wheal Marie mine. It's a dead end."

"It certainly was for him. Sorry. Good point. Could he have been meeting a boat? Those moorings I looked at had been used recently. What do you know about the cliffs around there?"

"You mean are there sea caves like in Hawkins' cove? Or do you mean do tunnels lead into or out of the mine to the coast?"

"Both, yes, anything."

"There are tunnels in the mine that lead out to the cliffs. Some open out in the woods, as well, or that's what people used to say. They're probably air ducts or vents or . . . I don't know, but for ventilation, I suppose. Some tunnels must be for the trolleys they used in the old mine. They're probably just old mine shafts, though, not smugglers' tunnels. We thought the old mine was to do with smuggling when we were boys, naturally, but now I think that must just be local legend."

"And you never had any sort of adventure trying to find out?"

"Laurie grinned. "We certainly did. In fact we were trying to get into the Bayview cove and its sea cave the day Mr Hawkins saved us. There are some nasty cross currents along there and we . . . But how could this relate to Mr Bantry?"

"Not sure." Bob switched off the engine and started to get out, intending to bring the conversation to halt, but Laurie was obviously feeling better and keen to be on his way to Scotland Yard.

"And what about what Mrs Bantry said regarding the farmer warning him off with an axe. Shall we talk to him?"

"Not unless I can help it. There was another complaint a couple of weeks ago – a spot of bother with a couple of Land Army girls at Home Farm. Pew Pewsey carries an axe the way you carry a notebook."

"What's he so defensive about?"

"His pigs. Hey, where you going? We've got work to do yet."

Bob received no reply. Laurie Oliver, clutching his middle and bent double was heading straight for the outdoor lavatories. Bob watched the boy disappear then stood for a moment, tapping the bonnet of the car with both hands. His fingertips were itching like mad.

Chapter 25

The day after next Bob Robbins passed Laurie Oliver in the police station corridor. "You feeling better, lad?" he asked.

"Yes, thank you, Sarge. Must have been something I ate, like you said."

"Good. Come up to the office when you can be spared."

"I've got ten minutes now. I was going down to the canteen for a cup of tea."

Laurie Oliver turned in his tracks, and Bob listened to the boy's polished boots click up the scuffed steps behind him on the way to his first-floor office. When they got there, he handed Laurie two sheets of typed up notes clipped to a report for the Coroner's office. "Glance over that for me, will you? See if I've missed anything."

It didn't take the new constable long to get to the key words. "Death caused by injuries sustained in a road accident."

"That's right: the car crash killed him."

"So what am I supposed to be checking? I don't follow – sorry."

Bob held up a palm to prevent the boy from saying more and closed the door. "Look at what the autopsy says."

Laurie scanned the page then whistled. "Arsenic poisoning. He was poisoned. How did you guess?"

"I didn't, the pathologist did."

"So he was poisoned, murdered."

"Not necessarily poisoned as such, although I'd like a full toxicology report." Bob drummed the fingers of his right hand on his desk. "It's all a bit 'yes and maybe no'. I've spent a bit of time in Porthferris lately, fishing. Went out in one of the boats the local boys keep for anglers and had the odd half in the pub now and again. You can't help but pick up local gossip, even when they know you're a copper."

"And you've heard things about this Mr Bantry."

"Certainly have. Not a popular man. Got the idea?"

"His wife was right then, somebody – or various people – wanted him gone," – Laurie rattled the papers in his left hand – "But why say: 'due to injuries sustained'?

"The car crash killed him."

"But?"

"But, what? I didn't say 'but'."

"No, but – sorry, Sarge . . ."

"But you thought I was going to say – oh, heaven save us, this is turning into a Laurel and Hardy talkie."

PC Oliver grinned. "But can you act on it, if the local doctor signed the death certificate saying it was a car accident and the autopsy confirms it? I mean, supposing it was set up to *look like* an accident, but it wasn't – because if he was dead *before* the crash happened due to arsenic, making it actually murder, or attempted murder – if the crash killed him but he was *also* being poisoned." Laurie spoke the last word as a whisper.

"Don't get melodramatic, Constable. I can't act on it because DI Small wants it all wrapped up so we can focus on the explosives thefts."

Laurie's eyes opened wide. "But the car could have been tampered with *and* he could have been poisoned, causing him to collapse at the wheel."

"Possible, but every Tom, Dick and Harry's got arsenic in them round Porthferris way. We've all got arsenic in us living around here, in small quantities. Chickens thrive on it."

"Do they? Crikey. Glad I don't like boiled eggs." Laurie was perfectly serious.

"We live in a high concentration area that's all. It's in the tin mines and the copper deposits, so the ground's full of it. That's why I can't ask for a full enquiry. Arsenic's normal, you see, except he maybe reacted badly to it. My pal at the hospital suggested kidney problems and liver not processing the toxins like it should, so the chap was definitely a sick man before the crash and likely to die sooner than he should have."

"Then why are you telling me about the arsenic, Sarge, if it's normal and we can't find out what happened? I don't follow."

"Well we can investigate, obviously. I've written down my suspicions and the evidence as I see it, to go on record. You'll have to learn that. *Everything* has to go on record. You leave one thing out by accident or on purpose and they'll have you by the short and curlies the second there's the merest hint of misconduct or a suspected oversight. I should know: I've paid the price." Bob plonked himself down behind the desk. "Always watch your back, and if you think something needs to go in writing get it done at home if necessary. Then make sure someone else knows about it." Bob pointed at the report, which Laurie handed back to him. "Now, what makes *you* think this was not an accident but designed to look like one?" From under hooded eyelids, Bob studied the young man standing beside his desk. "What makes you think that?"

But Laurie had lost his confidence. Bob watched him do an almost perfect imitation of Stan Laurel scratching his head, followed by a foolish, rueful grin. Bob put a hand to his mouth to cover his amusement. "Watch it, PC Oliver. You're not in the schoolyard now, you know."

"Sorry, Sarge, I'd better go."

"Yes."

Laurie was almost out on the landing before Bob looked up and said, "I'm going into Porthferris this afternoon about the missing contents of the briefcase. See if you can swap duties or speak to the desk sergeant and come with me."

The boy gave a joyful grin and loped off downstairs. Bob leaned back in his creaky bentwood chair, tapping his twitchy fingers on his laden desk.

At precisely four-thirty Bob Robbins manoeuvred his Morris out of the Cready Police Station car park with Laurie Oliver in the passenger seat and set off through country lanes for the coast. As he drove he said, "Tell me about Porthferris Bay before the war."

"That's what I was going to tell you earlier. It slipped my mind reading that report. Then I had to sort out my driving lessons and I didn't have time to come back up. My mother thinks it's very odd that the Oakleys have actually sold Seabreeze."

"Because?"

"They live in Croydon, so it's possible they could be bombed out and need the bungalow. If, on the other hand they have been bombed and – dreadful thought – but if they have lost their lives, it goes to their son, Graham – who's in the Navy – and his sister, Maggie, who's my age. She's become engaged to one of his pals."

"So?"

"It's not logical to sell or even rent out Seabreeze. Maggie can use it for her honeymoon, and if the Oakleys have been bombed out they can use the bungalow to live in. Mother reckons it's very strange, and she's never heard of a Miss Pettit, though it could be she's some needy old dear who they've let the bungalow to for the duration. Or she's some sort of housekeeper. She says she can write to them, if you like."

"No!" Bob brought the car to a halt behind a herd of cows. For a few moments he watched their box-like frames swing this way and that ahead of him, trying to damp down his anger and set his curiosity aside. There was something amiss with the whole Porthferris set up, but the lad should not have discussed it with anyone. Before he started to speak, however, Laurie supplied the words himself.

"I shouldn't have said anything, should I?"

"No, you shouldn't. Not ever. Police business is not for family chats."

"Sorry, Sarge."

"It's your ma who'll be sorry if you get booted out before you get a stripe and you end up in khaki after all."

Out of the corner of his eye, Bob watched Laurie stroke the high-domed helmet balanced on his knees. So the boy liked being in the Force. Well, that was a start.

When they got to the Porthferris crossroads, where the signpost had been removed as part of the invasion prevention measures, Bob took the sharp right turn and drove on as far as Paddon's garage.

Laurie said, "Sarge, why are we visiting the garage? I thought you said we were going to see the widow."

"The contents of Mr Bantry's car."

"Oh, the missing reports, or something else? A rogue Rationing Inspector – was he working the black market, do you think?"

"Maybe. Mrs B mentioned the briefcase at least three times when she was with Policewoman Thomas. Got really agitated, apparently. Now, keep your eyes open. I want you to watch who looks at who while I'm speaking, in case one of them has helped himself to something he shouldn't, then make a fuss of looking over Bantry's car. Let them see a uniform taking a keen interest. Pull out anything in the back seat area that's loose and have a look underneath – see if the duty bobby missed anything on the night of the accident."

Bob edged his round body out of the car, then, all bonhomie, made straight for Ezra Paddon, who was watching them. Laurie unfolded himself behind Bob and followed, arranging the chinstrap of his helmet as he moved, then paused to ogle a shiny motorcycle propped near the workshop wall.

The garage owner's face was etched in a permanent scowl. Apart from that, he showed no expression. Bob touched his hat and said, "Mr Paddon?"

"What you want?"

"I'm Detective Sergeant Robbins. I was here recently about new tyres, you may remember." Ezra Paddon stared at him blankly. "No matter – can I see the late Mr Bantry's car?"

"It's over there."

Bob followed a greasy, oil-ingrained finger pointing in the direction of a green and black saloon in a small paddock next to the garage forecourt. This had evidently once been the local smithy. "Bit of a mess, is it?" he asked.

Ezra Paddon sniffed but otherwise made no response. A younger man, in brown overalls, came out of the garage workshop wiping something on a rag, then, seeing PC Oliver's uniform, turned and went straight back in.

"That your son, Shadrach?" Bob asked.

"Could be."

"Just you and him working here now, is there? I'd have thought the war would have given you more work, what with all the blackout accidents and army lorries breaking down on every damned bend from here to Land's End."

"We get by."

"Wasn't there another boy here?"

"Joe Smith. He's doing an oil change. They're both deaf, so's no point talking to them."

"Not necessary, Mr Paddon. PC Oliver and I only need to check there's nothing personal been left in the Bantry vehicle and we'll be on our way."

There was nothing personal in the vehicle except for a cardboard tube with a tin lid rolled in waxed cotton and tucked in the crack between the bench seat and the backrest in the rear of the car. Bob watched Laurie pull it out in silence and turned to see if Ezra Paddon was also watching. He was and he didn't bat an eye.

"Mrs Bantry tells us the car was in for repairs last week," Bob said.

"No."

"But the car was here?"

"Oil change and a paint job on the off wing and passenger door, not what I'd call repairs."

"So you didn't need to do a road test before Mr Bantry got it back?"

"No."

Bob pulled at one of his rather hairy ears and said, looking away, "I was wondering – only conjecture, mind – if perhaps the brake fluid had leaked, or the handbrake cable might have snapped."

Ezra Paddon stared at the crumpled car. "We'd have noticed if the brake fluid was leaking. I'll ask one of the boys to check the handbrake if you want."

"Could they do it now?"

"No, they're busy. Come back tomorrow."

Bob turned to see where his young constable had got to. Laurie was wandering around the untidy yard tapping the tube in his right hand against his leg. Bob turned back to the garage owner. "This is police business, Mr Paddon. I'll come back about six-thirty, tonight."

His words were drowned out by the heavy-bellied rumble of a cargo aircraft flying back to the RAF airfield near Liskeard. Ezra Paddon grunted again and walked back to his shed.

Bob stopped the car in a lay-by under a stand of trees. "Let's see what we've got, then, young Laurie. What do you reckon's in the tube?"

"Posters, I expect. 'Mend and make do' reminders. Or, no, it could be maps," Laurie replied, getting out of the car. "Shall I open it?"

Bob leaned over the warm bonnet of the police Ford and watched Laurie pull the protective waxed cotton from around the tube then extract a tightly rolled series of maps.

"Maps it is," Bob said.

"Are these normal Ordnance Survey maps?" the boy asked.

"Looks like. Not tourist maps, though – no folds. They've been rolled from the start. Could be military issue. No fancy covers for these."

Laurie carefully spread the A3-sized sheets of thin paper out over the bonnet of the car. "This top one's for this area, East Cornwall," Laurie said. "Look, Looe to Saltash. He's written on it, made symbols. This bit's Wheal Marie, I think, and this is the copse on the Porthferris to Cready road. He's marked both of them with the same symbol."

"He? Who?" Bob demanded.

"Bantry, I suppose."

"But your chaps in uniform didn't see these maps when they found the box with the brandy and sugar in the car boot. I wonder why not?"

"They were hidden. Stuffed into the gap under the back seat."

"Or they've been put there since. Either way, it doesn't mean they're Bantry's maps."

"But . . ."

"But you think they are because he sounds like an unpleasant character and these look suspicious. Suspicious in what way, eh?"

"Well," Laurie held the maps down against a gust of wind then said, "I mean, Germany has marched into sovereign nations in Europe and North Africa. It's only logical that we're next in line. Couldn't these maps be information for the enemy? They're not road maps showing streets and shops to visit, not even farms for his agricultural role, if that's genuine? You'd expect him to have maps like that, but these look . . . I don't know, but they aren't what you'd expect a rationing or food inspector to have."

"Could be he goes hiking."

"Hiking?"

"No, I don't think so, either. But keep an open mind. Let me have a better look at that one."

Bob placed his hands on either side of the flimsy paper and peered at the symbols that Bantry or someone had drawn in coloured pencil.

"Do you think the coloured pencils were in his briefcase?" Laurie asked.

"Now there's a thought. And did the widow think he'd got maps in the briefcase?"

Laurie opened then closed his mouth.

"Precisely," Bob responded.

"She did say she helped him. Sarge, would you say Mr Bantry's wife . . ."

"Ain't too pretty, either. Doesn't mean we can jump to any sort of conclusion, though. First, I need to find out about these maps. What else is there, while we're here?"

The next one was Bodmin Moor and Trebelzue airfield. Bantry, if it was Bantry's writing, had written *now called St Mawgan, US aircraft expected* and drawn lines suggesting runways. The next map was of Camelford and there were symbols around an area at Davidstow. Bob tapped the map, "They are making an airfield there as well."

While Bob peered at the map and symbols a car passed, slowed then reversed. It was a cream 1939 Alvis in beautiful condition. Laurie whistled his appreciation and got a stern look from Bob.

The car driver rolled down his window. "You chaps lost? Need a hand?"

"No, thanks all the same." Bob moved his body to mask the maps. "Just taking a breather."

The Alvis driver laughed. "Be a bit much if a local bobby needed directions, eh? Not having road signs is a nuisance, though, if you don't know the terrain. Are you from Truro or Plymouth?"

"Cready," supplied Laurie. "We're –"

"Just checking our whereabouts." Bob gave Laurie another stern look.

The Alvis driver nodded. "Ah, nearly locals, then?" he said genially, but giving the young bobby a scrutiny that suggested he wasn't sure.

Bob twigged. "It's all right, sir. Here, PC Oliver, hold this for me." He waited until Laurie had a broad hand on the fine maps and took out his identity card. Offering it to the driver, he said, "You're quite right to question us, sir. We can't be too sure of anybody nowadays, sad to say."

The Alvis driver offered up an ochre-yellow gloved hand – expensive and unnecessary, to Bob's mind. "Just checking, don't you know. As you say, strange times, and what with being so near the coast and Plymouth and whatnot. No hard feelings, I hope?"

"None whatsoever," replied Bob. "And you are . . .?"

"Aubrey Chatwynde. New landlord of the Fisherman's Boot. Well, newish – been here a year now. Still feel a bit of a newcomer, but that's the way with Cornwall if you aren't born and bred here. If you do need directions I can probably help, though."

Bob smiled, "No need to apologise. I've been in your pub, sir, a few times, although a young lady was always behind the bar. I do a bit of sea angling in Porthferris."

"Ah, excellent, well come on down to my hostelry and I'll offer you a pint of the best, on the house."

Bob gave a small salute. "I'll take you up on that, sir. This very day, most like."

"Excellent. Well, toodle-oo. I have a bar to tend."

Bob waited until the car was out of sight and turned back to the maps, saying, "This country's turning into a bloomin' comedy turn."

"But he was right to ask, sir. To check who we are. It's not difficult to get hold of a uniform like mine." Laurie's use of the 'sir' had slipped out automatically, probably in response to Chatwynde's clipped delivery.

"No, you're right, lad. And he's right, too, unfortunately. Spies and invasion plans – not a *Boy's Own* comic or a Henty story anymore. German parachutists landed near Falmouth recently, did you know that?"

Laurie Oliver's pink mouth made a perfect O.

"They didn't get very far. I heard one asked a local where he could get a pint of beer. Gave him right away."

"I don't follow."

"It was nine o'clock in the morning."

Laurie laughed. "Is that true?"

"True as I look like a Toby jug. Right, let's get this lot rolled up and get on our way before another nosy devil comes along wanting to know my inside leg measurements. They're short enough without having to tell anyone."

As Laurie rolled the maps up to replace them in the tube, he paused. "Look, crosses and coloured pencil marks around Penzance. And this is Newlyn. There are two airfields there now, I think."

Bob peered at where Laurie was pointing and sighed. "I'll have to take all this to the Chief soon as we get back."

"Shall you ask Mrs Bantry about them?" Laurie asked quietly.

Bob scrunched his piggy eyes. "Not sure – not until I've got an inkling one way or the other."

"About what?"

"Friend or foe."

"Oh, glory, look, Lundy Island, and these two marks here must be landing stages. He *is* a spy!"

"Calm down. We'd better poke around a bit before we go putting police size nines in what may prove a delicate bit of military business. One thing's for sure, these maps don't have anything to do with Mr Bantry's role as a food inspector. Not many shops on Bodmin Moor."

"Could they be for his Agricultural Committee work – fields given over to the Air Force perhaps?"

"The Bodmin one might be, but there's not much of what you'd call agriculture on Lundy Island, unless you're partial to stuffed puffin of a Sunday. Nah, let's get back to the station. DI Small will want to contact the MPs straight away, I expect."

"Why?"

"They'll have to be informed. Same as that ruddy business at the hotel. Oh, no – MP means Military Police, not Members of Parliament or Members of the Public. *Royal* Military Police, I should have said. The Redcaps. Mind you," Bob scrunched up his round face again, "I'll have a pint later on with mine host in the pub as a member of said public. He seems to know what's what around here, even if he's a newcomer himself. Then I'll have another bit of a think."

"The Fisherman's Boot in Inner Harbour?"

"Mm, not the sort of landlord you'd associate with a quayside pub, I agree. Who was there before?"

"No idea, Sarge. I was under age."

"And you're not anymore?" Bob laughed.

When Bob returned to Paddon's garage that evening the mangled hood of Bantry's crumpled vehicle was open. There was no sign of anyone, but it was getting on for seven now and the garage was likely closed for business. Bob buttoned his jacket and leaned over the open bonnet. The oil pump and battery had been damaged, but the engine was surprisingly clean and in one piece. He poked a finger down to hook up a loose rubber tube, but he knew nothing about motor engines and this wasn't a good time to start guessing and showing his ignorance: Ezra Paddon had appeared at his shoulder.

"Nothing wrong with the engine – you can see for yourself," the taciturn garage owner said.

"Brake fluid – brakes – both in order?"

"Brake shoes are a bit worn. No more'n you'd expect with these roads and hills, and Bantry covered a fair ol' distance of a week."

"And the handbrake?"

"My boy says the brake was down when he looked in the car when we towed it up here."

"Logical, I suppose," Bob was non-committal. "Can I have a word with him? If he was here when they towed the vehicle in, I've got a couple of questions."

"No point asking Shadrach, he's stone deaf. They both are. What d'you want to know?"

"There was a briefcase —"

"We don't touch the contents of vehicles. None of our business what's in a car."

"No, but . . ." It suddenly occurred to Bob that Laurie's theory wasn't so far-fetched. The driver could have had a sudden stomach cramp or some sort of convulsion and lost control of the vehicle. "You say the handbrake was down; is there any way to know if had it been pulled up before the car crashed?"

"If there is, I don't know it," Paddon said.

"Right, well, thank you, Mr Paddon. I shan't keep you from your supper and slippers any longer."

Ezra Paddon sniffed, then lowered the hood as best he could and stayed where he was until Bob was off his premises.

Chapter 26

Bob was wondering whether it was worth asking the local doctor about Bantry's general health when he met him by chance later that evening in the Fisherman's Boot. Dr MacManus was standing at the bar when Bob entered. He half turned to see who was coming in then grabbed his tweed cap and slapped it over a squat bottle. Bob's first thought was *twelve year-old malt*; his second, was *lucky devil*. Scotch whisky went almost entirely to the United States: payment in kind for weapons and ammunition. A form of government-sanctioned Wild West liquor trading.

"Evening, Doctor." Bob made a fuss of closing the door behind him, giving the doctor time to transfer his booty to the sturdy medical bag on the floor.

"Evening, Robbins," the doctor said, straightening his back with a grimace. "Sciatica – it's this cold wind. You'd never know it was nearly June."

Blossom Deakin came in, chased by a blustery gale. "Sorry I'm late," she gasped, out of breath from running. "My brothers have joined up and all hell's let loose at home." She paused and scanned the small bar. "Where's Aubrey? – Mr Chatwynde?"

"Just gone out the back," Ned MacManus replied.

"But he is here? I've got to go again, see."

Bob and the doctor watched the girl open the bar top and flounce through to the back. She must have left via the backdoor because she didn't return.

Ned MacManus said, "Landlord will be back any moment. Shall I get you something?" He slid behind the bar.

"Half of mild, if there is any, please."

"Always beer in this pub, no chance the Boot will run dry, although it might, having said that, with the Deakin twins gone." He passed the half-pint mug across the polished bar, saying, "Pay later or stick it in the pot." He indicated a pint mug beside the till. "That's what I do when he's out."

Bob was astonished that a public house could be open without anyone in charge, but said nothing. He took a seat at a low table and the doctor joined him.

"Your health, sir." Ned MacManus raised his whisky glass.

"Your health," Bob replied, and took a long drink. "Good stuff. They haven't anything like that in Cready. Where does he get it?"

Ned MacManus tapped the side of his nose.

"Ah," Bob responded. After a few moments he said gently, "And once the Deakin boys have gone?"

"It was only a matter of time. Bantry's been after them since the week he arrived. They were down as reserved occupation, but he'll have told someone who told someone there wasn't much fish coming into Porthferris anymore. I can't believe they joined up willingly."

"Like that, was he, Bantry?"

"Oh, aye. I don't doubt he sent to Edinburgh to see if I was qualified."

"You're his GP?"

"No, and thank the Lord for that small mercy. They are on my books but I've never been consulted."

Disappointed, Bob said, "Been down here long, have you? I'm pretty new myself."

"I was in Plymouth in the twenties. Came here ten years ago."

"Long way from home, then."

"As far as I could get. Although you'd be surprised how much two villages at opposite ends of the country are alike: fishing nets and gossip."

"So what brought you here?"

"The gossip."

Bob took another swig of beer and waited.

"I helped a widow: her husband was killed in the last week of the war. Took her over to Orkney to see her folks and helped out a bit in her garden. When she started a bairn – eighteen months or so after her husband was killed – the clacking tongues said I was the father."

"And you weren't?"

"No, but she said I was. There was more to it than that, though." It was evidently a painful recollection. "I was young; she was older than me by a long chalk. I got angry and left. Came as far as I could afford by train and got a job in Plymouth at the hospital, then I got married, and then I became the GP here."

"Your wife's a local girl?"

"Plymouth. She left me two years to the day after we were wed. My mother came to live with us, thanks to the clacking tongues, and Frances took off for South Africa with a miner a month later."

Bob looked round the empty pub. "Very quiet in here tonight."

"It's early."

Bob waited a few heartbeats and led in again, "Not so many clacking tongues in Porthferris, or are you impervious by now?"

"Doctors are never impervious to evil words. No, but Cornwall is different to the north of Scotland – people are kinder, less judgmental. It may be the absence of the kirk, not that the Wesleyans hereabouts aren't strict regarding living a spotlessly clean, utterly blameless life. Ezra Paddon being a fine example. You'll have no doubt met him. He runs his garage with an iron fist, as they say. In general, though, there's a more sympathetic, caring attitude here. Of course, I'm leaving out what happened to Mrs Waterson, which is a baffler."

"Military Police matter."

"Aye, I was forgetting."

"How is she?"

"Still in a coma."

"Puts a dark mark against your kinder, caring community," Bob said.

"I doubt it's anything to do with anyone around here. But things have not been the same since the Germans invaded Poland. You'd think a place like this would be off the map, not affected, but the war has come to Porthferris and that's a fact. It's even found the Deakin twins!" The doctor laughed, but there was a wry edge to his voice. "Why Jerry needs to bomb Cornwall is a mystery to me. What have we got: china clay, tatties, fish, sheep and cows? Do they think they can starve us out by murdering livestock?"

"There's some vital industry. The explosives factory on the Bodmin road is a big concern – for these parts, anyway, and the quarries and mines."

"Ach, the mines are mostly dead. Look at Wheal Marie. Covered in creepers and infested with rats, I wouldn't wonder." Doctor MacManus put down his glass and smoothed his hands down his trouser legs. "I've warned Rebecca Cottle a dozen times about letting those children play there. It's not safe. Mind you, that sort usually land on their feet."

"So the mine shafts are open down there?" Bob asked quietly.

"The seams run into the hill, so it's more like a warren at ground level. There are some deep drops where iron ladders are still in place – or so I've been told. Another reason Becca shouldn't have those bairns down there." Dr McManus picked up his whisky looked away.

Bob sipped his malty beer, watching the doctor over the brim of the mug; waiting to see if he'd move the conversation away from Wheal Marie.

The change of topic came at a tangent, and was not what he was expecting.

"Have you ever been in a coal mine?" MacManus said.

"Not me. I'm not good in confined spaces. I'd rather be outdoors digging ditches than underground – if I had to make the choice." Bob gave a genuine shudder at the thought of being trapped in utter darkness and surrounded by rock.

"I was in a coal mine once. Like you say, pity the poor devils having to work underground. I'd rather be in a steel mill, and they're bad enough, I'm told."

Bob took another swig of his beer then asked, "Who owns Wheal Marie?"

"Belongs to Olwen Waterson's family. Might even be her property."

"So there'll be a tunnel of some sort under the house going into the mine? Bayview wasn't always a hotel, was it?"

"It isn't now. I do hope the Redcaps have it in hand."

Not wanting to set off alarm bells, Bob said, "No one's come forward with any information about the fisherman Hawkins, either. And now this chap, Bantry . . ." he bit his tongue. There was no evidence of any kind to suggest any of the events were linked, yet as he sat here talking to the local doctor he felt there was a connection. "You know, when men disappear – and women, for that matter – without a trace, it's often their choice. They've upped and left for a reason, but I'm not sure about Mr Hawkins. What do *you* think has happened to him, Doctor?"

Ned MacManus put his empty glass on the round table in front of him and rubbed his hands together. "I can tell what I *don't* think has happened to him."

"That'll do."

"I don't think he's run off to sea, joined the merchant fleet or gone for a soldier. I don't think he fell in the sea by accident, either."

"Me, neither. I was studying the currents in the cove under his cottage. If he'd slipped and gone in there, he'd have been washed up along the coast within hours, or a couple of days at most."

"You've been in Hawkins' cove, then?" The doctor's tone was sharp. "With Mrs Hawkins, were you?"

Bob heard the warning and was about to fabricate an answer but at that moment Aubrey Chatwynde came into the bar wearing his Home Guard uniform.

"Evening, gentlemen. Need a top-up, either of you? Ah, our lost policeman," he extended a soft palm across the bar and Bob got up to shake hands and introduce himself again.

"Aubrey Chatwynde," the landlord drawled amiably, "Captain Chatwynde, in this disguise."

Bob laughed, "And you've got other disguises?"

"Whole wardrobe full, including a wooden leg. I'm particularly fond of the tricorn hat."

"For the pirate or the excise man?"

Chatwynde eyed Bob sideways. "Now why would I tell a policeman a thing like that?"

Bob grinned in response, but he'd heard the edge in Chatwynde's repartee and made a mental note.

Chatwynde refilled their glasses. "On the house, sirs – we're celebrating. Two Sten guns and ammunition for the

Lewis gun have arrived. I bet there isn't a village Home Guard unit in the whole of Cornwall that's got *two* Sten guns!" He turned to the doctor, "Ned, can you hold the fort for a while? Blossom has promised to come back, but I've got to play soldiers for an hour or two, make sure my platoon know which is the business end of our new toys."

"No problem," the doctor replied and made his way behind the bar once more.

Bob downed his beer without undue haste, then put his empty glass on the bar, made his farewell and left for a lonely supper. Outside, a southerly wind was gathering reinforcements for a proper storm. Bob turned up the collar of his tweed jacket and made a dash for his car. Turning out of the quay car park, he chose Church Lane and drove up past Bayview Hotel and Maisie Hawkins' cottage. Something suggested she was home, but even with unaccustomed ale inside him Bob couldn't think of an excuse to knock at the door so he drove on up the hill and past the church.

A small figure suddenly darted out in front of him from the churchyard. He slammed on his brakes and glared out at the tiny figure dithering in the middle of the road. "What the devil . . .?"

Leaving the engine running, he got out of the car.

"So sorry! So sorry! So sorry!" It was the elderly spinster he'd met in Mrs Bantry's sitting room. She was carrying a sort of open bag like a leather bucket.

"Miss Pettit, isn't it? What the devil are you doing rushing across the road like that without looking?"

"Oh, yes. Sorry. I am . . . er . . . just on my way home. Goodbye."

Before Bob could say another word, she disappeared around the back of his car. He turned and walked after her a few paces then stopped, took a couple of deep breaths and got back into his Morris. Then he switched off the engine and got out again, curious to see where the woman had been, because something told him it wasn't choir practice.

As he crossed the narrow lane a strong gust of wind nearly knocked him sideways and sent the lych-gate crashing against its hinges. He pushed it open and fought like the devil to get to the church door. It was locked, which surprised him. Taking advantage of the respite from the blast in the shallow porch he looked around, catching a sliver of silvered angel wing as he did so. The cemetery. The batty little spinster must have been in the graveyard.

What in God's name is she doing here all on her own and on an evening like this? Pigeon – parrot – completely cuckoo, more like.

Chapter 27

On Bob's second visit to Albert Villas, Hilda Bantry looked different. Her sallow skin had turned a ruddy, blotchy shade of red, and as he followed her into her drab sitting room he noticed that she'd abandoned her hairnet and it looked as if she was pulling what little hair she had out in clumps.

This time there were no visitors, but there was a tea tray on the table, with a heaped plate of rock buns and another of shortbread as if she was expecting callers. Laurie Oliver's eyes lit up. Bob took another look at the plate, wondering how much butter and sugar went into rock buns and shortbread. He made a mental note to ask his wife, then remembered Joan was dead.

Mrs Bantry sat down with a thump on her grey chair and indicated vaguely that they should also sit. Bob sat down in the other armchair, saying, "Constable Oliver, get yourself in the kitchen and see if you can get Mrs Bantry a fresh cuppa. She's not looking quite herself."

Laurie reached out a hand to the cake plate as he passed the table and disappeared into the kitchen as bid.

The woman sighed with gratitude. "Thank you, Inspector. I do not feel at all well."

"Have you not got anyone who can come in and look after you for a few days?"

"Not really. We don't have any family, so to speak. Miss Pettit has been up each day since Archibald's accident. She brought me those buns and the shortbread today, and an apple pie and some chutney yesterday. Far too much for one person. Mrs Hawkins' daughter – the simple one – is a good little cook. She's Miss Pettit's live-out maid, but Miss Pettit says she does all her baking. Have to say I'm grateful. It's all I can seem to eat. Mother would have a fit if she knew I was eating cake all day and pie for breakfast!"

"But your mother . . .?"

"Is also deceased."

There followed a minute of awkward silence. Bob silently drummed his fingers in the air above the arm of his chair and tried to think up a gentle way to convey what he had to say and then ask questions regarding the maps. He decided to start with chit-chat and take it from there.

"It's been very cold again over the past few days – for the time of year. You might have picked up a flu bug. Strange sort of spring, and winters do go on longer than they used to, it seems to me, probably because we can't get the coal like we did before. My brother says the cinemas round his way give half-price tickets for returners and they're always full – people trying to keep warm, I expect. Mind you, last summer was a scorcher if I remember right."

Hilda Bantry looked at her empty grate. "I use an electric fire."

"Yes. Good idea." Bob looked around. "Portable, is it?"

"I only use it upstairs."

Bob was about to give up when Laurie finally came back into the room with a fresh pot of tea and crumbs around his mouth.

"There's an apple pie in the scullery safe, if you'd like some," Mrs Bantry offered.

Laurie looked sheepish. "That's all right, Mrs Bantry, thank you. I'll have one of your buns, if I may? I love rock buns. Anything for you, Sarge?"

Bob shook his head. "Just the tea, and no sugar. I've been rationing my rations so long I don't even like sweet stuff anymore."

They sipped their tea in silence, then Bob started again. "I moved down here a couple of years ago myself, from the Midlands, which was home for me, although we moved about a bit as well – when I was in the force the first time round. I was in the insurance business after that, for a few years, until my wife became ill and . . . Well, one thing led to another and I was looking for a bit of a change, and a place to settle at the same time, if you know what I mean? Thought I'd take up sea angling, something a bit more exciting than slow rivers."

This wasn't strictly true. He did spend a lot of time by rivers and walking along the coast, with a pair of binoculars and a notebook to hand because his hobby was bird-watching, but he let people assume he was going fishing; it had a more masculine ring to it than sitting under a tree waiting for a woodpecker to pop out and say 'how do?'. "Mr Bantry a fisherman, was he?"

Mrs Bantry frowned. "No, whatever gave you that idea?"

Bob shrugged, "You moving to Porthferris from being by the Thames; just wondered if we'd had the same idea."

Mrs Bantry pursed her thin lips in apparent disapproval at such familiarity but made no reply. She really did look very unwell.

"Just a thought. So we both got called back to work – for the government, king and country – time of war and need. I suppose that's what we've got in common."

There was still no response, but the policeman in Bob made him have one last go. "I never expected to be called back into the Force, though, that's for sure. Still, it's a minor sacrifice compared to what some have got on their plates. I expect it was the same for Mr Bantry, wasn't it, looking for a way to serve his country?"

Mrs Bantry now turned and looked him full in the face. Her eyes were red, but, he thought, not from crying; at least not with grief.

"My husband was a true patriot, Inspector. He offered his services for anything, in any capacity, the moment war was declared."

"Of course he did. It's what our generation was brought up to do, not that young PC Oliver's lot aren't doing their bit now. Hats off, eh? Joined the Home Guard, did he? Local Defence Volunteers as they were called."

"No. Not the Home Guard. He was asthmatic as a child. I told you. A delicate chest . . . not suitable for being out in all weathers. Especially down here where it is so very damp all year."

"Worse than being by the Thames?"

"In my opinion." Mrs Bantry closed the topic.

Giving the visit up for lost, Bob gave Mrs Bantry the information on the missing rationing reports. "We haven't found anything in the way of documents that might belong to your husband, not even a notebook, I'm afraid. If you give me a list of shops and farms that your husband visited I could go round and see if he left anything behind somewhere. It would help if I knew what I was looking for, though – folders, envelopes, what sort of papers are missing."

"I don't have that information."

"Well, can I see his diary so I know where to go?"

Hilda Bantry looked about her dowdy room vaguely, then said, "I believe Archibald kept a small notebook as a sort of diary. I haven't got that, either."

Bob studied the woman's face. "Pity."

"I don't think he ever made actual appointments. Surprise was his policy, you see – to catch shopkeepers red-handed."

"But his committee work – he must have had meetings."

"Oh, yes, all the time. Now I think about it, he did keep a small notebook in his breast pocket, for agendas and so on. It wasn't in his jacket. It may be at the hospital, if they haven't thrown it away because it was covered in . . ."

"I see, yes. I'll ask."

"Inspector, why can't you locate Archibald's papers? Who on earth would want anything from his briefcase?"

Bob could think of a list of people in the near vicinity alone but made no reply and got to his feet. "I'll ask at the station again and call in on a few local shops, see what I turn up, all right?"

Hilda Bantry wiped a hand across her blotchy forehead. "I'm sorry, I think I must have some sort of flu."

"We'll see ourselves out, my dear. No need for you to trouble yourself – you stay there. I'll just nip upstairs and get that electric fire for you."

"No! That won't be necessary."

But Bob was out of the room and up the stairs before she could finish speaking. The landing was as cold as the hospital morgue. There were four doors. He peeked through each: a bathroom over the kitchen, clean and plain; a double bedroom with a somewhat feminine air, hairbrush set on the dressing table and a two-bar electric fire in what had once been a fireplace; a second bedroom, gentlemen's hairbrush on a dresser, man's carpet slippers by the bed, photograph in a frame. And a third bedroom – with a padlock on the door. "Well, I'll be blowed," Bob murmured to himself, "in his own home."

He returned to the main bedroom and collected the electric fire.

When he got back to the sitting room he plugged it in and said, "Shall I call the doctor for you, Mrs Bantry? You've got a phone here, haven't you?"

"Yes, we have a telephone, but I don't want to see that Scottish doctor – don't call him."

"Is there someone else I can call?"

"No, please don't trouble yourself."

Bob looked at Laurie Oliver who was waiting by the sitting room door and shrugged his shoulders. There was nothing more to say or do so they left.

They were nearly at the garden gate when the sad woman opened the front door again. "Inspector! One moment! About my husband's belongings – I shall have to inform his superior. There may be papers they need urgently. Would you do as you said, call in and ask people, please?"

"No problem, Mrs Bantry. Glad to be of help. You get back into the warm, now."

On the way back to the police station Laurie was sick again.

"Serve you right for being greedy," Bob said. But he thought it was a bit of a coincidence, even at the time.

Chapter 28

"The Acting Chief Constable of the Devonshire Constabulary wants to see you."

"It's well past April first, Mallett." Bob shrugged off his raincoat and shook it across the already slippery linoleum floor.

"No joke – he called this morning, first thing. Before you were up, obviously," the desk sergeant looked at Bob meaningfully. "You're to drive down to Plymouth. He wants to see you before he goes for his *luncheon*. And take anything related to the Bantry business, except he doesn't want the brandy and sugar. I told him about that m'self but he already knew anyway."

"Bantry?" Bob turned and stared at the man across the desk. "Have you got this right, Mallet? Plymouth, not Bodmin?"

"Plymouth, not Bodmin. Correct."

"Whatever for? Plymouth's got nothing to do with Cornwall Police."

"How should I know? You been a naughty boy again?"

Bob ignored the innuendo that was not entirely without foundation, and folded his wet mackintosh so it didn't dampen the frayed lining. "Where've I got to go? I don't know Plymouth. I'll need a map."

"Map won't be much use these days. There's more holes than streets, thanks to Jerry, or had you forgotten?"

Bob carried on up the stairs to his office, wondering what he'd done or not done this time, and how Sergeant Mallett had heard about his previous misdemeanour.

"Maybe they'll send me back into retirement," he mumbled to himself. "I should be so lucky."

He swung his mackintosh onto a hook and wound a half-written report back into his ancient typewriter, then stared at the keys for inspiration. "Sod it all," he grumbled and got up again, put on his mackintosh and picked up Bantry's tube of maps from beside the filing cabinet. He'd have to get a move on if he was to drive all the way to Plymouth before *luncheon.*

The Acting Chief Constable was a tall, fair-faced, elegant man. It had occurred to Bob Robbins on more than one occasion that the popularity of Mr Churchill with the man in the street had much to do with his lack of height and shape. Men in authority, like Acting Chief Constable Clarence Soames, were generally tall. *So we have to look up to them,* he thought.

Soames came round his vast desk to greet him, which came as a bit of a surprise and bode ill, extreme courtesy being an effective means of dismissal. The thought made Bob realise he didn't want to be dismissed. His stomach did an unexpected dip and dive, but he managed to keep his expression open and shook the offered hand firmly.

The Chief Constable indicated the chair in front of his desk and returned to his position of authority on the other side, saying, "Detective Inspector Small tells me you have found some maps showing military installations and you are interested in a car crash in Porthferris."

"Yes, sir. It's all a bit odd, but I don't think it was an accident."

"And why's that?"

Bob grimaced. "The garage owner says the car has slightly worn brakes because the victim did a lot of miles and because of all the hills around our way, but otherwise it was in good nick – condition. The constables who went to the scene when it was reported say the handbrake wasn't on before they towed it away. They'd have had to put it down, obviously, but it wasn't necessary. But there's another aspect I'd like to look into."

Bob paused, wondering whether to risk saying he'd requested a second toxicology report and not mentioned it to his superior, Detective Inspector Small. Unless his doctor friend had, which wasn't impossible – he hadn't said it was a secret. Before he could say anything further, however, Soames interrupted him.

"It was an accident: close the book on it and get on with more important issues. We'll give the maps to the Military Police and let them handle it all." The Acting Chief Inspector's face was expressionless. He steepled his hands as if in earnest prayer and continued, words evenly-paced, "You need to be careful, Robbins: 'careless words', mm? *Prima facie* there is no evidence to suggest this was anything more than an unfortunate misjudgement of a narrow bend involving a respected member of the community. Regrettable, but what can we do? Nothing."

Bob couldn't believe he had been summoned to Plymouth to be told this; Cornish police matters for the Cready area were dealt with in Bodmin. Using Laurie Oliver's frequent phrase he said, "I'm sorry, sir, I don't follow."

"Good, because I don't want you to follow."

"You mean I should drop the case?"

Glad now that something had warned him to leave the tube of maps in his car, Bob decided to risk mentioning the notion that Stan Hawkins' disappearance was somehow linked to Bantry's accident.

"As you say, sir, we're pretty overworked and understaffed in Cready. It'll give me more time for the missing fisherman. I've a hunch he hasn't drowned, you see. There's a disused mine –"

"Robbins, Cready has neither the manpower nor the resources to undertake investigations based on a *hunch*, and we certainly don't need you to go poking around in that old mine. According to what Detective Inspector Small tells me, you have already looked there and found nothing."

"Not in the mine itself, sir – we've only looked around the outside."

Soames got to his feet, then, changing back to his earlier, politer manner, said, "I'm sorry about this, but there's a war on and we have to deal with matters of greater importance. Do you have the maps with you?"

"In my car, sir."

Soames turned and stared out of his window. Bob wondered if he should stand, but stayed put.

"Poor Plymouth, poor old city," Soames murmured. "Have you heard what happened Tuesday night?"

"The queue for the ferry was buzzing with it when I crossed the river."

"Hundreds of innocent people have been killed in this city alone since the war started. Bombers missed our house but the rest of the road is a shambles." Soames turned back to face him. "The Hawkins case is still open? No leads at all?"

Bob shook his head. "I've spoken to just about everyone in the village – butcher, grocer, his crew . . . Nobody has any idea. The two lads that crew for him were pretty cagey, but it's got more to do with perishable goods off the back of a lorry than the whereabouts of Stan Hawkins. They were genuinely concerned – everyone was.”

“So he must have fallen into the sea?”

“Must have, but the rope for his boat was cut right through, which nobody can explain.”

“Curious. Well, don’t abandon the missing Mr Hawkins entirely, but I do insist you focus on his fishing connections – offshore, if you follow me? This is the type of thing to focus on, Robbins. Helping people, not meddling in wartime threats.

Bob sat perfectly still. *What ‘wartime threats’ were these – in Porthferris?* Then the maps suddenly made sense. He took a gulp of air. *Bloody hell, could Bantry have been sending information on airfields and harbours to the Nazis?* The skin on the back of his neck crawled.

Bob had an inborn inclination to dislike tall men in authority, but that didn’t mean they were stupid: far from it in this case. He glanced up at Soames wanting clarification, wanting to know more. “Wartime threats, sir? That would be preventing Jerry getting in?”

“Nothing secret about that, Robbins, although I can’t give you any details, obviously.”

“Obviously,” Bob repeated, thinking: *What the hell’s obvious here?*

“Military observers are in place in Porthferris. Did you know that? At the hotel. They monitor shipping. There are also plans afoot to use the harbour for MTBs.”

“MTBs, sir?”

“Motor torpedo boats.”

“But how does this relate to the road accident, sir?”

“Quite. This is why it is a Military Police matter now. All I can say is that the old mine has been taken over . . . for special purposes. I have been asked – instructed – by people in London to keep the local community away from the mine called Wheal Marie. I am not at liberty to say why."

Soames crossed his wide room in four strides and opened his door. Bob scrambled to his feet.

"You have been most efficient, Robbins, for which we are grateful, but this is as far as we can take the Porthferris incidents. Bring me the maps, would you, then get back to Cready and carry on. The business of the missing explosives is still on your books. That needs tidying up as fast as possible. We don't need explosives circulating on the black market, do we?"

Bob Robbins collected the maps and handed them to the Chief Constable's secretary like a schoolboy. Returning to his car, his surprise turned first to annoyance and then to suspicion. "What is going on?" he muttered, drumming his fingers on the steering wheel before starting the engine. "All the way here just to be told to stay out of an old mine: he could have phoned and sent a rider for the maps. What is this all about?"

As he drove through the broken streets of the old city, Bob was forced to halt at a vast crater that had once been a row of terraced houses. Staring at the tragic debris of ordinary people's lives, he slammed a hand on the steering wheel. "Sod it! That's what I should have done in the first place," he said aloud. "Hawkins' tunnel leads into the mine – MacManus said there were steep drops. He must have gone in there to put stuff in or take it out and met with an accident."

Bob was angry with himself, knowing he should have looked behind the bricks in the Hawkins' sea cave when he was down there fishing and had the chance, but hadn't because he hated being in small dark, shut in places and . . . He gave a wry grin, *because I didn't want to know, because I like Mrs Hawkins and she'll cop it one way or another if it's war profiteering.*

Once back at Cready, Bob went into the station with an assumed jaunty gait and stopped at the desk. Constable Oliver was on duty.

"PC Oliver, do you have any idea where the box that was brought in from the Porthferris car crash has got to?"

"The brandy and sugar?"

"That's it. Hasn't been half-inched by anyone in uniform, I hope."

Laurie gave Bob a questioning glance, unsure whether it was a joke, then opted for a jovial response. "No, Sarge, I don't think we drink the evidence in this station, unless it's Christmas."

"Now why did you say 'evidence', constable?"

Laurie gave him another worried look. "That's what I asked you the other day, Sarge. It is, isn't it?"

"Black market goods, do you think?"

"Could be, or he could have confiscated them."

"So his friend Miss Whatsit could make him some cakes?"

"My mother says getting sugar is like getting gold dust these days, and brandy's disappeared altogether." Laurie Oliver paused.

"You been chatting to your ma over a cuppa again, haven't you?" Bob asked, not unkindly.

Laurie bit his lower lip, but Bob smiled. "Never mind – tell me what you've learned at your mother's knee."

"She says the rationing is not so bad for us because there are three of us, so she can put our sugar and butter rations together to make a proper cake, or use margarine if she has to."

"And the brandy?"

"Good stuff, Sarge. But – and this is what I do know – everything imported is difficult to get because of the merchant fleet being given over to troops and armaments. And two bottles . . . it does make me wonder."

"Good. Have you been shown how to do fingerprinting yet?"

"Yes, Sarge. I was pretty good on the test."

"Better still. When you can get away from the desk, find the box for me and let's see if it leads us to The Cready Gang of the Black Hand."

Laurie Oliver's eyes opened wide.

"Joke, constable: that was a joke. Mind you, given the ancient and respected tradition of smuggling in this area, I'd be very surprised if there wasn't an organised gang of some sort. Somebody took the papers out of Bantry's briefcase for a reason. From now on we're after black-marketeers, and if one of them's not wearing a bloody tricorn hat, I'll eat my trilby."

"I'll get the box the moment Sergeant Mallett gets back from his tea break," Laurie said with distinct enthusiasm.

Bob smiled, satisfied that a bit of thinking on the hoof meant he could continue poking around the Bantry case without disobeying orders from on high. Cready had all the necessary time and resources for a rationing fiddle and Mrs Bantry had requested personally that he ask around in the local community – which was helping people, as instructed.

Chapter 29

Bob Robbins knocked gently on the cottage door. Maisie opened it, wiping her hands on her apron.

"Mrs Hawkins, sorry to trouble you of an evening but can I have a word?"

Maisie Hawkins led him into her sitting room, pulling off her apron as she went. She was wearing a dark green summer dress with boxy sleeves and looked as if she'd lost weight.

"Sorry, love, are you going out?"

"I was, but to tell the truth I'm that weary I can't face it. We've got a Mother's Union meeting at the church about the summer fête, but I really haven't got the energy." She sighed and sat down by the remains of a fire.

Bob sat opposite her then got to his feet again as the daughter came in from the kitchen. She took a chair at the table, picked up a *Girl's Own* annual and beamed at him.

He smiled at her and said, "Mrs Bantry tells me you're a great little cook."

The girl's face lit up. "I'm Miss Pettit's 'little treasure'."

Maisie Hawkins looked at her daughter. "You didn't tell me you were doing cooking for Mrs Bantry?"

"I'm not."

"Do you cook for Miss Pettit?"

"Yes."

"You haven't said anything about cooking at Miss Pettit's."

"You didn't ask," the girl responded.

"What you cooking then, her meals? You can start cooking mine if you like." Maisie's tone was dry, impatient.

"I make cakes. Two weeks ago I made chutney."

Maisie sighed again, this time with annoyance, and before Bob could think of anything to say Ginny launched into a recipe.

"One pound of plain flour, four ounces of margarine, six ounces of caster sugar, two eggs, one quarter teaspoon salt and three teaspoons of fairy dust."

"Fairy dust?" Bob asked.

"She means baking-powder," Maisie explained.

"No. It's Miss Pettit's magic fairy dust. She keeps it in a special tin."

Bob and Maisie exchanged glances. Pleased with her audience, Ginny continued. "Mrs Beaton's Apple Chutney. Peel and core six pounds of cooking apples and chop into small pieces. Miss Pettit keeps all the pips, Ma. You don't keep apple pips."

"No, but I do know how to make chutney, thank you."

"This recipe has 'witch's mushrooms'. They aren't in the recipe book but Miss Pettit says they give an extra flavour so we put them in."

"Mushrooms? You're not going up to the spinney again, are you?"

"No, they come out of a jar."

"A jar – of mushrooms – what you on about?" Maisie Hawkins lost her patience. "Ginny, take that book up to your bedroom. Mr Robbins hasn't come here for a cookery lesson."

Ginny gathered the fat compendium into her arms and quietly left the room. Maisie turned back to Bob. "Sorry. She is a worry. I don't know what to do for the best: whether to keep her here with me, let her stay up at Cleve, or send her off for the Land Army. Mr Bantry was on at me about her not doing any war work and she's courting."

"And that's a problem?"

"Certainly is. We've already had one scare. He was away for a while but he's back now and there'll be a baby on the way before the end of summer if I don't do something."

"Local boy? I thought they'd all joined up."

"Not this one. He's joined us! Sorry. You haven't come here to listen to me frettin'. It's just that I'm worn out with it all, and that's the truth."

Bob smiled. "I'm not surprised, Mrs Hawkins. You've a lot on your plate. Who's the young man, by the way?"

"Works up at Paddon's Garage; moved in with the family as well, from what I can tell."

"He's one of the deaf boys?"

"Deaf? Not him. Nothing wrong with *his* faculties."

Bob filed the information and drummed his fingers on his knees.

"I am sorry," Maisie repeated. "You haven't come here to listen to all this."

"Don't you worry about me. Look, if your meeting's important I'll come back tomorrow."

"No, it's all right. I don't have to be up there till seven and the church hall's no distance. Come in the kitchen while I make a pot of tea. I need something to get me going again."

Maisie filled a kettle, lit the gas then sat at the small kitchen table and put her head in her hands. "You haven't found him, have you?"

"No." Bob cleared his throat. "What would you say if I told you I was going to knock out all the bricks in your sea cave and have a look at what's behind?"

"I'd say I'm amazed you haven't already done it, specially as the job's been half done for you. Wasn't that why you were fishing from our cove?"

"No, actually. We looked around the mine area, in the copse in the grounds and down along the quay, then round the old engine house. The parts we could get into. The woman in the caravan said her brood would know if there was anyone around. Which I can believe – they're as close to being wild things as you see these days. I wouldn't wonder they don't lay mantraps alongside their rabbit gins. They certainly don't seem concerned about the wild cats supposedly lurking in the woods."

Maisie laughed. "Becca Cottle – she's a case. I wouldn't cross her, though. She put up a hell of fight when they tried to move her caravan. They've shifted her now, but Benjie didn't dare go down to her new place for days in case she blamed him."

"Ah, so there is a husband."

"Sort of."

"Maisie, what will I find in that old mine?"

"Well you won't find *my* husband there. Aubrey would have told me."

"Aubrey?"

Maisie looked away.

Bob waited a moment, then led in gently, "If you're worried about me finding tins of treacle and bars of soap via Devonport docks you can stop worrying. Everyone's finding ways round all these blasted shortages. I'm looking for a man, your husband, not a packet of tea."

Maisie attempted a smile in response, but tears welled up in her eyes. She took out a folded handkerchief from her dress pocket and wiped her eyes. "I'm that weary of it all. I killed 'em both – both of them . . ." The tears started in earnest.

Bob turned off the gas and sat down again. "Tell me," he said quietly. "Start from the beginning and tell me everything. Take your time – your Mother's Union can do without you for one night, there's no hurry."

Gradually, in fits and starts, Maisie told him of her husband's temper, blaming it on the trenches and gas in the Great War. Then she told him about how she thought she'd killed her father-in-law with an overdose of cough medicine – which Bob thought very unlikely – then about how she'd coped for years with physical abuse and the strain of trying to protect her daughter. After a pause, while she wiped her eyes and tried to get herself together, Maisie returned to something earlier in her story.

Her voice almost a whisper, she said, "There was a man on the quay. I wanted to cross the footbridge but the tide was right up and coming over the rails. I slipped – nearly went in – but he wouldn't help me. He was watching but he wouldn't help me. He knew I wasn't at Cleve House. I've been waiting all this time for him to say I wasn't there. Every day, every week I've been waiting for him to tell and the police to come for me, and then I hear he's dead as well and . . ."

"Who, Maisie? Who saw you, love?"

"Mr Bantry. He used to look at me like . . ." Maisie's shoulders shook with sobs. "I'm that glad he's dead, and that's a dreadful thing to say. If I didn't arrange for Ginny to go into a factory he said he'd tell the authorities himself and we'd be in trouble. I'm glad he's dead and I'm so ashamed . . ."

Bob quietly got to his feet. Patting Maisie's shoulder, he said, "I think we need that cuppa now." While he fiddled about with a match and relit the gas he asked, "Who's Ginny's boyfriend?"

Maisie took a deep breath. "That's something else I shouldn't have done. I took him in; he was hurt. I thought . . . I don't know what I thought."

"He's not from round here?"

Maisie shook her head. "Foreign. Says he's French. Yan or Jan he calls himself. I don't know – could be true."

The fingers of Bob's right hand tapped the wooden draining board of their own accord. "Which cupboard for the cups, love?"

"That one up there."

"And he works around here, you said?"

"Paddon's garage, I told you."

After they'd drunk their tea and Bob was satisfied Maisie Hawkins was feeling better, he said, "I'll come back later in the week during the day. What time's high tide, any idea?"

"It was up about ten-thirty this morning. The bridge was still wet when I crossed to come back down to the shops from Cleve."

"Why don't they get stuff delivered?"

"They do, but there's always something we need."

"And Mrs Metherall can't get it?"

"Not now. She's helping with the school. She does music and singing lessons with the older ones, and she's looking after the garden and the pigs and everything."

"So it's you that does all the fetching and carrying?"

Maisie gave a half-smile. "She's asked me hundred times to go back and live at Cleve to save the walk every day."

"Why don't you?"

"Because of this cottage. If I move up there the Major might want it back. I mean, it's Delia's by rights, but the Major looks after everything like that now. It was meant only for my mother's lifetime, you see – and I'm still here."

"So you don't pay rent?"

"No."

"Mrs Hawkins, if you don't pay rent and your husband was making money from the fishing and his *other* business, where did his money go? What did he spend it on?"

"Drink, mostly. I don't know where the rest went – not in our Post Office book, anyway. He used to pay for some of the stuff he got in cash."

"And was he always involved in moving imported goods, or just since the war started?"

"His family were always up to something. His uncle got blown up on his own barge ferrying stolen explosives from the Cready works to Ireland."

"Explosives . . ." Bob's voice was a whisper. Then Laurie Oliver's comment about the paths in Porthferris came back to him: "Every path round here links somewhere to somewhere".

When Bob got into the police station next morning there was a message on his desk from Dr MacManus. Hilda Bantry had died. Bob dialled the number on the message.

"MacManus speaking."

"Bob Robbins here, Cready CID."

"Ah, Robbins, I left a message about Mrs Bantry. The milkman raised the alarm. Milk hadn't been collected off the doorstep for three days and she didn't answer the door. He told the vicar and they broke in through a back window. I think you'd better ask for an autopsy – could be food poisoning. Could be self-administered arsenic, but that's a dreadful way to go. There are signs of excessive vomiting . . ." The doctor paused, choosing his words, "I'll be in and out of the hospital during the next couple of days. Oh, and Mrs Waterson has come round from her coma."

"The woman who was attacked at the hotel? That's good news. Have the RMPs been informed?"

"Not by me, not yet. I shall have to do it later today, though, if Waterson doesn't call them himself."

"Of course. Thanks for letting me know. I'll speak to Inspector Small and come to the hospital as soon as I can, but I'll go to the Bantry's house first, have a look round, if that's all right?"

They said their farewells and Bob sat down to gather his thoughts, but a girl's voice interrupted them, saying "magic fairy dust" and "witch's mushrooms". He opened his desk and selected a bunch of keys collected during a lifetime of investigations. One of these would fit the padlock on Bantry's spare room. Exploring Hawkins' tunnel into the old mine would have to wait another day.

Crossing the landing, Bob knocked on Detective Inspector Small's office. "Can I have a word about Porthferris, guv?" he asked, tucking the keys deep into a pocket where they wouldn't jangle. "There are a couple of things I need to tell you."

Chapter 30

Much to Bob's relief the Bantry's back door was open; saved wasting time on finding a key, and wriggling through a window was no fun anymore. He shut it silently behind him and turned the key so he wouldn't be disturbed.

The kitchen was a mess. Cats had got in by the look of it, or mice. A plate of what may have been Mrs Bantry's last supper was on the wooden draining board. He peered at a brown sticky mess that could have been plum jam, then remembered the chutney Ginny Hawkins had mentioned and went to the pantry.

A white face peered out at him, halting his heartbeat and making him jump. It was Simon Prior.

"What are you doing in here?"

"Just looking."

"For what?"

The boy shrugged then slithered out of the dark space. "You're a policeman, aren't you?" he said. "Have you come to find the evidence?"

Bob frowned. "Of what?"

"Of what old Bantry did at night. It was very suspicious. I think he was a spy."

"Do you? And what gave you that idea?" Bob indicated the door to the sitting room. "Come through here and tell me what you know."

Simon Prior grinned and took a seat at the table by the window. Bob sat down in front of him. "Well?"

"He used to go out at night, very late. After midnight. He took a big torch and he carried things."

"Things?"

"I couldn't see very well. He climbed over his gate. It's tied up with string – that's how I got hold of the bolt without him knowing."

Bob frowned again. "Why climb over the gate? I don't get it."

"So it looked as if it hadn't moved, I suppose."

"Maybe. And was he carrying things when he came back?"

The boy sniffed and licked his fingers. "I'm not sure . . . I used to fall asleep."

"And why were you looking out of the window that late at night and not tucked up in bed fast asleep like a good boy?"

"I keep a diary – it's for my father – it shows what time Mr Booth leaves after my lessons. My mother says he's my tutor but he doesn't come to teach me – only for twenty minutes, anyway. After my lessons he stays and stays and stays."

"I see." Bob folded his short arms and leaned back. "So this was every week, when Mr Bantry went out?"

"No, more like once or twice a month. I tried to follow him one night but I only got as far as the bridge over to the quay."

"He heard you?"

"The battery on my torch ran out." Simon licked the fingers of his right hand again.

Bob sat bolt upright and snatched the boy's hand from his mouth. "Have you been eating anything?"

"Only a rock bun and some sugar. We don't get sugar at home, hardly."

"Sugar!" Bob was out of his seat. "Stick your fingers down your throat – make yourself sick. Do it! Now!"

Grabbing the boy by the scruff of the neck he frog-marched him to the back door and out to the privy. "Stick your fingers down your throat and make yourself sick, boy, quick!"

"Yoo-hoo, Simon, are you over there? Is that you?" It was the boy's mother.

Bob left Simon in the privy and dashed through the weeds to the fence. "Mrs Prior, get your bag and meet me out front. I'm taking your son to the hospital."

"Oh, heavens, an accident? Is he all right?"

"Don't panic, we're in time. My car's right outside. Come round to the front gate."

They stopped three times on the way to Cready Cottage Hospital for Simon to be sick – to Bob's relief. A greater relief was seeing Dr MacManus getting out of his car just ahead of them as they arrived. Bob rapidly explained what had happened – skirting round details while in the mother's hearing – then left the rest to the doctor.

The drama now out of his hands, he made his way to the canteen and bought a large cup of spoon-rot tea. Half an hour later Dr MacManus joined him with Colonel Waterson from the one-time hotel, Bayview. They shook hands, then Bob turned to the doctor and asked hastily, "The boy's all right?"

"He'll live: I've left him in good hands. No solids for a few days, but he'll survive. Did you bring any samples with you?"

"Sod it, didn't cross my mind. I'll go back and get them soon as I can."

"Right, if you'll excuse me, I'll leave you two to chat while I check up on my other patients."

Bob was anxious to get back for the food samples but didn't want to miss an opportunity to speak to the colonel.

He made a point of looking at his watch and said, "Just got time for another cuppa. Care to join me, sir?"

Bob collected their tea at the counter. As he put it on the table, the colonel said, "I have wanted to contact you a couple of times, Robbins, to be honest. This business with my wife, nasty affair – all my fault, I suppose. But what with the Navy upstairs and the Army in the mine and Metherall insisting it's all hush-hush, and Military Police nosing about all the time now . . ." He puffed through his cheeks like a children's picture book west wind. "Frankly, I'm never certain I'll be allowed back in my own home if I go out, or who's listening to my telephone calls, and Gladys has been acting *very* strangely. I should have insisted we stay in Simla, as I wanted. Far better life all round, but there you are."

Bob eased his collar. The bit under his chin was tricky to shave and usually began to itch about this time of day. Casually, he said, "Wheal Marie, the old mine – it belongs to you, sir, doesn't it?"

"My wife's family. She inherited it along with the house."

"Her father owned it?"

"Father's father and further back."

"So your house was built after the mine was started?"

"This one, yes. There's been a dwelling of some sort in the grounds for centuries, though. The tunnel between the house and the mine predates the current building by at the very least a century or more."

"And do you have a sea cave, like in Mrs Hawkins' cove?"

Colonel Waterson looked at him, his eyes red-rimmed and blurry. "Oh Lord, I'm rumbled," he said. "Yes, there's a cave, and, yes, there's a tunnel leading into the mine – but I haven't bought in anything new for weeks, not since the Hawkins business, if that makes any difference? The RMPs haven't bothered with the cellar at all."

"You surprise me. I wonder why."

"Domestic environment not their concern – more interested in what's going on upstairs – I really couldn't say."

"Look," said Bob, "tell me what you wanted me to know, and we'll talk about your cellar and the tunnel later – perhaps."

But Waterson had gone coy. "Not sure I should now, actually. You'll have to square it with Metherall, first. Or speak to Aubrey Chatwynde."

Chatwynde again, and now Metherall. Square it – for what? For the duty-free goods or something else? What is going on? There's even a Chief Constable involved somewhere along the line. Bob's stomach lurched – *No: an 'Acting Chief Constable' . . . Had he been taken in? Was this all some elaborate, conniving scheme with everyone running rings around him, an entire village laughing up its sleeve?*

This had to be more than a bit of smuggling or black-marketeering. And Aubrey-blasted-Chatwynde was a darn sight more than a village pub landlord.

"Did you say the Army is using the mine now, Colonel?" Bob asked.

"Ah, did I? Yes – no. Sorry, can't say. Shouldn't have mentioned it."

Bob tried to make light of the issue. "So it's a bit more than 'baccy for the parson and brandy for the clerk, and the odd tin of NAAFI jam, is it? Never mind, someone'll tell me something sooner or later. Remind me what happened to your wife, sir. As you said, that was very nasty. I understand she has been in a coma."

Missing the more sinister connection in Bob's apparently benign questioning, Waterson was only too happy to discuss his wife now, and recited everything Gladys Fogarty had told them previously. Bob formulated a few questions as he went along.

"So whoever it was – the intruder – you think he was looking for something upstairs, not downstairs, or under the stairs?" Bob grinned making it sound like a joke, which it was not.

The retired colonel blew his nose loudly then said, "Actually – I think it might be to do with the greenhouse."

Bob kept his features blank. "Greenhouse, really? How so?"

"Oh, well . . . I have a few boxes of this and that in the greenhouse and – er – if you must know, Hawkins, the missing fisherman, used to bring me a bottle or two of brandy and the like, sometimes cigars and cigarettes – for our own personal use. Cigarettes aren't rationed, of course, so there's no harm in that, is there? Just getting round shortages, don't you know. And sometimes little extras I could use when we were a hotel. I told Metherall all this, more or less."

"And the tunnel, sir?"

"Ah, yes. Well, as you have rightly detected, there is a tunnel from our sea cave. It joins into Hawkins's, and they both . . ."

"Lead into the mine – got you. So there's a network of tunnels that come out under your cliff, along that bit of the coastline?" Waterson nodded. "But the intruder was trying to steal something from your *greenhouse*?"

"This is the part I cannot understand, Robbins. This is the key. Who in Porthferris would be in our back garden and push poor Olwen around and bash her on the head? None of my – erm – contacts, I can tell you that. I mean who would do such a thing? And the vegetables and lettuces? Someone has been stealing from Olwen's vegetable patch for heaven's sake! I told Metherall about it, but he dismissed it. The thing is the Deakin twins get their own special supplies from any number of locations. I can't see them wasting an hour in the dead of night pulling up beetroot, and they're the only ones I can think of. Unless it was a ruse, a sort of decoy, and the objective was upstairs after all. And, there again, all the locals know about the WRNS and the Navy observers working there, even if they don't know what they're up to."

Bob looked at Waterson. "So it's nothing secret going on at the hotel?"

"No – well, we don't need to talk about it, but as far as I know they're only using the rooms as a sort of listening and observation post: monitoring shipping coming in and out of the Channel. I sometimes hear Morse messages and I know they are listening and transmitting on radio equipment – although perhaps I shouldn't have said that. Bit hard *not* to hear what's going on, to be honest."

"But would Jerry like to know about it, I wonder."

Colonel Waterson's fleshy jaw dropped. "Good Lord, do you think it's a spy? In Porthferris of all places."

"I wouldn't go as far as that, but –" Bob was interrupted by a drab little couple pulling chairs out from under the next table. He half turned and they all nodded a polite "How do you do."

"Can we talk about this later, Colonel?" Bob said quietly. "If I come to Bayview could you at least show me the tunnel you mentioned?"

"Have to clear it with someone first and get permission."

"Hmm – I was rather hoping to have a quiet recce, to be honest. I've got a couple of ideas – theories, if you like – about the sea caves and the mine. And along the way we might uncover what happened to your wife."

The colonel held up a soft paw and shook his head. "No can do, Detective Sergeant, sorry."

"I thought you said the Redcaps weren't interested in your cellar and what's under your house."

"They aren't, but you'll have to speak to Metherall first."

"Major Metherall, from Cleve House? He's still here, is he? Or has he returned to his unit? Or is he with the War Office, now?" Bob asked lightly, fishing for information.

Waterson was deliberately vague, "He might be back in London, but his wife will have a number for him."

Bob sighed again: the conversation had taken him in circles, and the vicious tea had given him heartburn.

Simon Prior was lying green-gilled against a starched white pillowcase in the men's ward. His mother was sitting in the waiting room. She refused Bob's offer of a lift back to Porthferris, for which he was grateful, so he made his farewell and left the cottage hospital on his own.

His mind buzzing with a dozen unanswered questions and more possible outcomes, Bob climbed into his car, turned on the ignition and cursed out loud, "Damn and blast and sod it all!" There wasn't enough petrol to get back to Albert Villas then return to Cready without calling in at Paddon's garage on the way. Then he tapped the steering wheel jauntily: a nice little excuse to nosy out Ginny Hawkins' beau – the one with all his faculties. The foreigner nobody ever mentioned.

Chapter 31

Ezra Paddon pulled the pipe round to Bob's petrol tank without taking his eyes off him. "I don't hold with vurriners. Cause too much trouble. If people stayed where they belong we'd all be better off for it." He eyed Bob meaningfully.

"So you are still managing on your own, with just your two boys? Can't be easy, what with your Home Guard duties and all."

Ezra Paddon delved into a pocket of his overalls and pulled out a rag. "We manage. There's a war on you know."

As Paddon screwed the petrol cap back into place, Bob glanced around. The flashy motorbike Laurie had admired was parked beside the workshop again. It wasn't the sort of machine a man like Paddon would use. But was it his son's or son's pal's bike? Or the foreign boy's? "Nice little machine over there. Belong to your boy, does it?" Bob pointed at the motorbike.

"No," said Paddon, and that was that.

Bob drove the half mile up to the crossroads then parked outside the Bantry's villa for the second time that day. His stomach grumbled and he looked at his watch. "No bloody time to get a meal in this job," he moaned. Then he remembered the dubious contents of Mrs Bantry's kitchen, stopped feeling hungry and groped among the many and varied objects stuffed in his glove compartment for a pair of rubber gloves. As he closed it, he wondered if Laurie or any of the other constables had checked in Bantry's glove compartment. Nobody had mentioned it.

Returning to the Bantry's kitchen, Bob picked up a shopping basket and lodged in the suspect jar of chutney and the sugar bowl, then popped in a couple of uneaten buns and the remains of the woman's supper. Then he took everything out again, made a fist of putting them in paper bags, which he had noticed folded neatly on a shelf, and set the basket by the front door. Taking it slowly, because this time there was no need for haste and his knees had been playing up of late, he headed upstairs.

The padlock to Mr Bantry's study was easy to open. Simon Prior could have done it with a penknife. It was a box room over the stairs, furnished like a monk's cell. The thin, colourless curtains were closed so he opened them. On one wall was a map of the southwest of England, but without pencil markings. There was a small, plain table and a chair and a narrow bed. Rolls of blank paper lay on the bed beside two cardboard tubes and a roll of waxed cloth. Bob looked around for a cupboard of some description. There was nothing, not even a small wardrobe. He looked under the low bed. "Aha!" Two leather suitcases: one large, one small.

He pulled the small one out. It was locked, but not for long. A fine little stiletto picked both catches and the top swung up. Inside was a radio transmitter. It looked brand new. He closed the lid and pulled out the other. This one was unlocked. Inside were neatly stacked rows of ration books without names; coupons for everything from overcoats to eggs, and two neat bundles of money. A fortune for a working man in five- and ten-pound notes.

Bob lifted them out and sniffed, then flicked through them to see if they were counterfeit. They seemed like the real thing. He put the paper money on the floor and ran a hand along the back of the case, searching for a pocket of some kind. Then he ran his fingers along the paper lining under the hinges: there were small bumps like lumps of glue. He felt lower down. There was something there. Something flat. Using his pocketknife, he prized the striped-paper lining from the leather backing. Passports. Five passports in different men's names – but no photographs.

"Well, well, well – the boy's right, and so's the colonel. Or are they? Whose side are you on, Mr Bantry?" *Is all this for our chaps working undercover or foreign bodies arriving via the airfields?* Bob wondered, closing the lid and pushing the case back where he'd found it.

He tried to stand up but his knees wouldn't take his weight, so he sat back on the floor again and had a think. It was as good a place as any to plan his next move, decide who to question about what and in what order. The big question, though, the overriding question, related to what he'd just found.

"Friend or foe, Mr Bantry? What are you?"

And then a word the Chief Constable had used came back to him: "invasion".

Was all the paraphernalia under the bed to help invaders coming in – meaning "foe"? Or was it in preparation for personnel to be stationed in the area in the near future – meaning "friend"? The passports suggested "foe", but he needed more evidence.

Rolling over in much the same way his son used to at the crawling stage, and with the aid of the bed, Bob finally got himself to his feet, then cursed aloud, "Oh, damn it all, I'll need the bloody cases."

Mumbling to himself, he bent down and heaved the two leather cases out from under the bed and then out of the room. Leaving the big one on the landing, he clumped the smaller, heavier one down the stairs. His leg muscles screamed at him as went back up for the second case and then again because he'd forgotten to padlock the door behind him.

Leaving the cases with the basket in the passage, Bob wandered into the sitting room looking for letters, photographs, anything that might shed light on Archibald Bantry's life. In one sideboard drawer there was a pile of utility bills, in the other the couple's own ration books. He glanced through them but could see nothing amiss so he moved to the middle of the small room and looked about him. There had to be *something* that would inform on Archibald Bantry apart from what he'd found upstairs.

For a moment he stared at the shabby furniture. Either they had sold their house with furniture and fittings in Henley-on-Thames or they'd been coming down in the world for quite a while. Thinking about their relocation reminded him that before he himself had moved down to his cottage in Kerrith Cross after Joan died, he'd spent hours, days, sorting through all manner of papers, old letters, concert programmes, school reports for their son Jimmy, now somewhere in the Far East on an aircraft carrier . . . and other long-forgotten mementoes – a lifetime reduced to one cardboard soapbox. The knick-knacks had gone to the church jumble sale; ancient bills and cheque stubs had gone on the fire; the rest had gone into other boxes . . . So if the Bantrys really had moved from Henley-on-Thames, their past life was probably still in boxes in their attic. Bob went back into the passage and stared up the stairs, then decided against it. There was no dire rush now the people in question were deceased. Deciding to return later, he edged the cases towards the door with a foot, to save picking them up.

But something insisted he do another quick check in the house itself. Opening the door to the front room, the room respectable families kept for best, Bob caught a strong whiff of camphor and un-cleaned chimney. Recent high winds had sent a fine layer of old soot across the fireplace and onto the linoleum. Mrs Bantry had said she was keeping it clean for her husband's coffin, but she'd either been unwell for several days or she was a poor housekeeper. There were no photographs, and no sideboard or bureau where papers might be kept.

He returned to the front door, and had his hand on the latch when he remembered the brown and beige masculine room upstairs. Struggling once more up the steep staircase, grumbling on every tread, he finally got to the landing and opened the door to the second bedroom. A dust-filled ray of sunlight caught the top of a silver frame.

"Bingo!"

A signed photograph of Mr Archibald Bantry in the uniform of a Black Shirt shaking hands with Sir Oswald Mosley, who was staring mad-eyed at the camera.

"Traitor!" Bob spat out the word. "Hitler-lover."

There was no date with the signature on the image so he peered at the background, rubbing his sleeve across the glass to clean it first. There was nothing to suggest where it had been taken, only a brick wall and the lower ledge of a high window. He turned the frame over. Tucked into the back was a slip of paper with type-written words: "Courage, action, loyalty, the gift of service. BUF 1935".

The BUF was the British Union of Fascists. Bob let out a sigh. "'Loyalty and the gift of service' . . . Who to, eh? Who to?"

He put the photograph back on the tallboy and left the house via the front door lugging the two cases, then went back for the basket of foodstuffs, making no effort to hide what he was taking away.

J. G. Harlond

Gulls called mournfully from above. A melancholy sound for a warm afternoon. He stood by his car for a moment and studied the village scene below, filling in what could be seen with the naked eye with what he knew to be there: white-washed, terraced cottages; the Fisherman's Boot with its welcoming red step; the row of shops on Main Street running between Porth Hill and Church Lane. Butcher, baker, candlestick-maker . . . the grocer, stationer and the post-office, and they none of them had a good word for Archibald Bantry.

Somewhere down there among quiet streets and closed doors, the recent and perhaps not so recent goings on in Porthferris were all coming together, he was certain of it. Despite the London connection with the fascist, Oswald Mosely, and the ill-fated Indian railway scheme, something in the labyrinth of old family ties and local village history had to be linked to his — and possibly her — demise.

And what of the other newcomers, little Miss Pettit and the cheesy Mr Chatwynde? Had they added their past histories to the mix? Where did the latest arrival, the foreign boy who *wasn't* working at Paddon's garage according to its owner, fit in? Somewhere here, but where? Bob tapped the bonnet of his car with his stubby fingers. Somewhere, somehow, all their aspirations and private desires formed a chain of petty motives leading to a dragging anchor on something much bigger than any of them perhaps imagined. All the age-old motives of greed, spite and revenge were coming together. Sex would be involved somewhere along the line, but quite where he had yet to fathom.

Bob looked back at the non-descript Bantry villa, then climbed into his faithful little Morris and drove back to Cready to deliver the food to be analysed, and to apprise DI Small of the contents of the box room.

Much later that same day, Bob was back in Porthferris. The closed curtains twitched as he opened the gate, but there was a considerable delay before his knock was answered.

"Miss Pettit, isn't it? I'm Bob Robbins, driver of the car the other night. I nearly knocked you over, remember? I was wondering if you were all right. It was a near miss."

"Oh, oh, yes." The spinster's hands fluttered dramatically over her high-necked, mauve dress. "I'm quite all right, thank you."

She evidently remembered him, and perhaps what he was and where she had seen him previously. She also wanted to shut the door, so Bob said, "You're friends with Mrs Bantry, aren't you? Have you heard the sad news?"

Miss Pettit met his eye, "About poor Mrs Bantry? Yes, everyone is talking about it – the milkman found her. So sad."

She wasn't going to let him in, so he was forced to say, "You were visiting Mrs Bantry when I called a few days ago. I'm a policeman – detective sergeant."

"Yes, I remember."

"Would you like me to come in and tell you what has happened? I could do with a cup of tea – if you can spare one?"

"I don't have any tea left, I'm afraid."

The spinster edged the door forward and was about to close it, so he said, "I'd like to talk about Ginny Hawkins, Miss Pettit. She works for you, I believe. Makes your cakes and looks after the house."

The spinster's eyes flickered. She dithered for a moment, then said, "Come back tomorrow, in the afternoon – so I can get some tea for you."

"Bit difficult, love. You never know in my business where you're going to be from one hour to the next. Can you not tell me something about her now?"

"It's getting late, Detective Sergeant. I don't like to admit visitors after dark."

"It's not dark yet and you're all right with me, Miss Pettit, I am a policeman. Look, here's my card."

Before Bob could reach the identity card in his jacket pocket, Miss Pettit said, "All the same, come back tomorrow," and shut the door.

Bob leant against the peeling, green-painted wood and banged his head three times in desperation.

"Come back tomorrow," was the muffled response.

He laughed out loud and walked back to the quay. Pulling out of the car park, he was in two minds to call in on Maisie Hawkins. She'd give him a cuppa and a sandwich, but he had nothing to tell her and, regrettably, it was no time to start poking about in her sea cave and quite by accident find himself in the tunnel leading into the mine he'd been expressly forbidden to enter.

Never mind, he thought, the fast-banter, comedy programme ITMA was on the wireless this evening – he'd head home for a decent supper and a chuckle or two before bed.

Chapter 32

Next morning Bob went straight into his boss's office to ask if PC Oliver could be relieved of his village school duties: "never pick up shrapnel" . . . as if any schoolboy was ever going to listen to that advice. Getting a more positive response from Detective Inspector Small than he expected, he tried out a bit of theorising he had omitted from the previous day's factual report.

"The thing is, everyone in Porthferris, from what I've heard, hates – hated – Archibald Bantry, and his wife was pretty much loathed, as well."

DI Small, a compact man appropriate to his name, looked up from his laden desk. "I can't say I liked him, either, but I wasn't tempted to kill him."

"You knew him?" Bob was surprised.

"Oh, yes. He was always in here with his tittle-tattle, wanting us to chase up shopkeepers who'd fallen into his nasty rationing traps, reminding us 'Weights and Measures' was part of our job as well. Ask Mallett, he'll tell you all about the charming Mr Bantry."

Bob sat down in the nearest chair. "Of course, I hadn't thought of that side of things. So we've got a file on him."

"Not *on him*, exactly, but, yes, on his depositions. They'll be in Mallett's filing cabinet. Mallett detested him, especially after the business with the vicar's wife."

"Tell me."

"Poor woman went a bit mad after her baby died – picked stuff up in shops and forgot to pay for it, that sort of thing. Most of the local shopkeepers made a discreet call to her husband at the vicarage and he returned the goods as fast as he could. Then one day last year – whenever clothes rationing first started – Bantry was in the big haberdashers and outfitters in Cready High Street. It was tipping with rain and he said he'd got his feet soaked and could he have a pair of socks. The girl serving checked with her father and he said of course he could have a pair of socks. Anyway, Bantry sits down, takes off his shoes and puts on these dry socks, and while he's doing it, Mrs Hughes comes in, drifts around a bit, picks up some handkerchiefs from the counter and wanders off without paying. Bantry puts on his shoes and he's round here like a shot denouncing the shopkeeper for letting him have socks without demanding coupons and the poor vicar's wife for shoplifting. John Crouch, he's the haberdasher, came round later to turn himself in – like he'd committed a crime."

"'Struth."

"Exactly."

"What did you do about it?"

"Oh, it's all in Mallett's cabinet, waiting for us to – deal with it."

Bob grinned, but his superior's face gave little away.

Inspector Small shuffled his chair back and said, "But Bob, I don't think Bantry's mean-spirited nastiness justifies a non-accidental road accident. Not really."

Bob grimaced. "I know, but what about those leather cases I brought in yesterday? That's a much bigger issue: a radio transmitter, for heaven's sake, false passports, and all that cash. What's that for? And the maps we found . . ."

"I know, and too big for us to handle at present. That's why I called Bodmin and they handed it on to Plymouth. Now the Devon Chief Constable is handing it over to the Military Police, perhaps in connection to the Bayview business. We cannot – must not – get in their way."

"Even if it looks like we've got a ruddy fifth-columnist on our hands, not to say German spy."

"That's why it's their business, not ours. I know, I know – you found the stuff, but it's out of our hands. This is for intelligence specialists like Metherall."

"Metherall – Major Metherall, the chap at Cleve House?"

"Yes, and don't ask me any more, because I can't tell you."

Bob wanted to ask a lot, not least why DI Small had never mentioned Metherall's name before, but it was not the moment to ask.

"So do I start with Mrs Bantry, then?" he asked. "Dr MacManus says Mrs B was chock-full of arsenic, like her husband, but the actual death suggests something else killed her. I took the chutney, sugar and cakes she'd been eating for analysis. We should hear the results later today."

"Oh, it's confirmed. They sent this over late last night. The chutney contains small pieces of a type of amanita mushroom, a particularly lethal little white-cap that smells like vanilla. It grows in this part of Cornwall, all along the warmer south-western coast down to the Scillies. It has a delayed effect, causes vomiting and pain one day then victims get jaundiced and there's complete kidney failure or other complications within a day or so."

"Stone the ruddy crows."

"The fact to bear in mind is that this little fungus can't be mistaken for a field mushroom. It's far too small to bother with for a start. It's not flashy like fly agaric or a death cap, but picking one of these is not going to be accidental in a normal adult. It grows in tiny clumps and you'd have to know where to look because I think they only grow under deciduous trees and in damp places. *Amanita fragrans* – if this is the one."

"You're well versed in the subject, guv." Bob was impressed.

"My wife's a bit of an expert. She compiled a pamphlet on Cornish fungi, toadstools and unusual plants in the area a couple of years ago. Local printer published it for her and all the hospitals and medics from here to Land's End seem to have bought a copy. Dr MacManus is a bit of an expert, too. Did you know he was a pathologist in Scotland?"

"No, I thought he was just a local GP."

"Ned MacManus keeps himself to himself, but he knows his stuff."

Bob gaped at Inspector Small. Something he'd just said had struck home: *not accidental in a normal adult.* "God Almighty, Ginny Hawkins! I was worried about that – tried to speak to her employer yesterday, in fact. She's poisoned them. Well, Mrs Bantry anyway. Ah, but no, can't be. *He* had got more arsenic in him than the usual traces found round here, as well. If somebody was putting stuff in his food, not his wife in this case, it seems, it's been going on longer than . . ."

DI Small waited for Bob to say more. When he didn't, he said, "Go on – talk it through. Let's see where we get to."

"The autopsy report on Bantry said he'd got more arsenic in him than is normal, but that could have been due to his particular constitution; he wasn't eliminating it like most of us do. PC Oliver suggested, in fact, that Bantry could have had a stomach spasm while driving down Smugglers Mile Hill and passed out, and that could have caused his car crash.

"Ginny Hawkins," Bob continued, "who's not a hundred per cent in the head, has been working for Miss Pettit, making the cakes and chutney et cetera that Miss Pettit has apparently been taking up to Mrs Bantry. The Bantrys were also visiting Miss P once a week for tea. Ginny was telling us – me – about what she was making. She actually mentioned the mushrooms, in fact."

"You'd better get her in, then."

"Yes. But I honestly don't think Ginny could have acted on her own."

"Get them both in and interview them separately. Better still, take someone with you and interview them in situ first, then bring them in."

"I will. But what had Pettit got against the Bantrys, assuming she directed the cooking?" A dreadful thought washed over Bob like a chill wave. "It won't matter, though, will it? Because it was Ginny who made the chutney and the cakes."

The lovely Ginny with the face of an angel, who was not a 'normal adult'. *Had she sprinkled fairy arsenic dust in the Bantry's sugar bowl as well*? He had to find out fast. If the Pettit woman had got Ginny to do her dirty work for her, she might find a way to get rid of the girl to stop her telling tales. "Damn it, I should have talked to her last night like I wanted to."

"Who?" DI Small asked

"The Pettit woman."

Inspector Small pursed his rather girlish mouth and said, "You'd better get onto this right away. Take young Oliver with you."

Bob got to his feet but Small raised a hand and went to his filing cabinet, saying, "Take this before you go." Running a tidy fingernail along the alphabetical labels, he stopped at 'H' and pulled out Stan Hawkins' file. "Small-town crimes usually take us round the houses one way or another, and in this case it's the man's daughter we're interested in as well," he said, handing some sheets of paper from the file to Bob. "Speak to the girl then bring her in, all right? We don't want the village gossiping about arrests, though, so play it down if you can. Do the same with this Miss Pettit, and make sure you've got someone with you at all times."

Bob had learnt the wisdom of that advice the hard way. Doing things *his way*, on his own, had got him into a lot of hot water in the past. A bunch of crooks had once twisted his inquiries and turned his words against him to implicate him in fencing their vicious thefts. He'd cleared his name, but it had dogged his steps until he'd given up any hope of promotion and resigned. After that, he'd worked for an insurance company, but he'd never acted entirely alone again.

Inspector Small then handed Bob a toxicology report on hospital paper. "Have a look at this before you go. Don't take it with you – we'll need it for the prosecution. The Bantry woman was almost definitely murdered, but why and by whom you'll have to find out."

"Right you are. I'd better take a search warrant. Miss Pettit wouldn't let me in last night when I tried to talk her."

Chapter 33

By half-past eleven Detective Sergeant Robbins and Police Constable Oliver were standing outside Seabreeze. The sitting room curtains were closed. Bob's heart sank. He'd been hoping Ginny would be working in the bungalow so he could have a chat about this and that and keep an eye on how Miss Pettit and her Miss Mop interacted before he interviewed them individually.

No one answered his knock.

"Tell them I came, and no one answered," Laurie quoted after Bob knocked more loudly the second time.

The detective looked up at the young constable. "What's all that about?" he demanded, not best pleased that his plan had been thwarted.

"It's a poem I learnt. It's called 'The Listeners' . . ." Laurie's voice petered out as he noted Bob's glowering expression.

"Well, get yourself round the back and listen there. You know the layout of the place better than me. If you don't hear or see anyone, come back and tell me." Bob took out his bunch of keys and selected one for the front door. As he did so, the slow clip-clop of a horse's hooves halted by the gate.

Laurie hovered, shifting from foot to foot.

"Go on. It's only the milkman. Get round the back," Bob snapped, stuffing the keys back in his pocket. "Morning," he called as an aged milkman opened the gate.

"Her not in then?" the milkman asked. "We'm very late – 'spect she's gone to get her milk down the shops. Wouldn't wonder." The old man wearing brown overalls placed a bottle of milk on the doorstep. "Who be you, then?" he demanded, straightening his back and trapping Bob with a disconcerting blue-eyed stare.

"Bob Robbins – um – Miss Pettit's usually in at this time of day, is she?"

"Ooh, can't say one way or t'other to that. We'm very late, see. Had a bit of bad news last night and what with one thing and another I didn't get started till – ooh, can't say."

Bob watched the old man's eyes start to well and knew without asking why. "One of your sons?"

"Walter, our youngest. Unexploded bomb down in the dockyard. Went off while he was on night shift. Killed three of 'em on the spot. You got a boy working there, too?"

"No, Jim's on an aircraft carrier out east. Same fears, though. I dread receiving that telegram more than anything in this world."

The milkman nodded, "Nobody's safe nowhere these days. Well, best be getting on. We'm very late, see."

Bob escorted him to the gate, where the horse was munching its way through a tussock of wild flowers and uncut grass.

"If you're looking for Miss Pettit," the milkman said as he lifted the horse's head from its snack, "she might be down the shops or mayhap in the Boot. They say she goes in there of a dinner time, now and again. Can't say it's every day, but my Peg's seen her go in more than once."

"And Virginia Hawkins?"

"Ginny? Oh, she'll be with her mother up at Cleve House, I 'spect. Good day to you, sir, and thank you."

"For what? I haven't . . ."

"Ah, but I can see. You know how it is. They'm all precious, and my girl's working and we worry about her as well, but it's the boys that get it mostly. You only got the one, have you?"

"Yes." Bob felt himself choking up with emotion.

"May the Lord keep him safe. Good day to you, sir."

Side by side, the aged horse and milkman plodded on down the lane and Bob went back to the bungalow, all the bounce sucked from him.

"Damn it to hell," he suddenly shouted, kicking a surprised gnome across a stretch of ill-kempt lawn.

Laurie Oliver appeared at a run. "Did you call, Sarge?"

"No." Bob went back to selecting a key and began waggling it in the front door lock.

Laurie watched him for a moment, then said, "We can get in through the back. There's a ladder in the outhouse and a window open over the sink."

"You play Tarzan if you like; I'm going in through the front door." Bob was trying another key.

Taking this for dismissal, Laurie sprinted off again and three minutes later opened the front door from the inside. Bob was on his fifth key. He looked up at the young PC, who at least had the sense not to grin, and pushed past him into the small hallway.

The sitting room was neat and tidy, cushions plumped up on the sofa. But even without opening the curtains Bob could see the doors of an ornament cabinet were open and the shelves bare.

"She's gone: done a runner. Check the bedrooms," Bob said, pulling a pair of gloves from his jacket pocket. "I'll do the kitchen."

Laurie left the room and Bob ran a finger along an empty shelf in the glass cabinet. It was dusty. He went to the mantelpiece and ran another finger along that. It was not dusty. "Hmm," he said. "Laurence, come back here a moment." The boy appeared at the door. "Was this cabinet here when you used to visit?"

"I think so. Actually, I don't think much – if anything – has been changed. The sofa was there and the table over there. The kitchen's exactly how it used to be."

"Can you remember what was in this cabinet?"

The boy shook his head. "Ornaments, I suppose."

"Valuable? The Oakleys are well off, are they?"

"I doubt it was anything of value, Sarge. They only used this bungalow for holidays."

"Hmm . . ." Bob grimaced and started opening the drawers of a sideboard. He pulled out a set of framed photographs and held them up to Laurie.

"Mrs Oakley, and those are their children when they were small. That one's Mr Oakley. I remember that photo. He caught a huge sea bass. Look, you can see Hawkins in the background. They must have used one of Hawkins' boats."

There were more photos and some family snaps. Bob smiled and pulled out a picture of four youths with milk-white legs sitting on the beach beside a sandcastle. "That one's you, isn't it?", he asked pointing at a youth grinning like the infamous Cheshire cat.

Laurie went slightly pink. "Why would the new owner keep all these pictures? I mean, even if she was only renting . . . it's a bit odd. Unless she's one of the family – an aunt, perhaps?"

"I doubt it somehow, and it's more than a bit odd. I did you a disservice, lad," – Bob blew through his cheeks – "I got cross that you'd mention the bungalow to your family – looks like you did exactly the right thing. There's a phone in the hall. Call your ma right now and ask her what she knows, and ask her to get in touch with the Oakleys. Where did you say they lived, outside London? Ask her to find out how they came to let the bungalow to Miss Pettit, and what they know about her."

Laurie went into the hall and picked up the heavy black handset. There was no signal. "I think the lines been cut off, Sarge," he called.

"Because the bill hasn't been paid. Why am I not surprised?"

Bob wandered into the kitchen and sniffed. It didn't smell as if a meal had been cooked recently. The gas oven was spotless, the table bare. He opened the pantry. Rows of crockery jars and some empty jam jars lined the shelves. There was some cheese and butter in a wire safe on a marble slab and a generous stock of tinned goods in boxes on the floor. If the fairy arsenic dust and vanilla toadstools were here, they were well camouflaged. He stood back, removed a glove and scratched his head, wondering what to do next.

Returning from the bedrooms, Laurie said, "I think some clothes have gone, belonging to Miss Pettit, that is. But it looks to me as if the Oakley's clothes are still here, the sort of thing they'd use for holidays, anyway."

Bob gave a wry laugh, "A bloomin' cuckoo in the nest."

"There's something else. You'd better come and look."

Lying flat, unrolled, on a single bed in the second bedroom was what looked like the deeds for the bungalow. Bob peered at the parchment without touching it and laughed again. "Cheeky madam – look what's she been trying to do."

Laurie gazed at the document. "I don't see anything. What am I looking for?"

"The name of the owner, boy. In red ink – except it's not the right red ink. Our Miss Pettit has made herself the owner of Seabreeze with a few strokes of the old pen. Cheeky madam."

"Glory!" Laurie gasped. "Should I mention this to my mother as well?"

"No, not for now." Bob picked up the parchment and rolled it up carefully. "I'll keep this safe till we need it."

"Should we get samples from the kitchen, like you did at the Bantry house?" Laure asked.

"We should, but . . . Oh, damn it all, I made an appointment to visit Bayview today as well." Bob let out a sigh. "We'll call in and I'll make my apologies. I want to get to Ginny Hawkins first. Waterson can wait another day, and Stan Hawkins' tunnel, as well. There's an awful lot of crime going on for one small village, if you ask me."

"I was going to, actually."

Bob looked at Laurie Oliver sideways to see if he was being sarcastic. He wasn't.

"Is this normal?" Laurie asked. "Missing persons and poisoning –"

"And a possible German spy and illegal occupation, and don't forget the smuggling. Or shall we call it by its less romantic modern name: war profiteering? No, it's not. And it's our job now to find out why, precisely, it's all going on in such a small place."

"So you think things are – sort of – linked together?"

"Sort of, yes."

"What do we – you . . . I mean, what needs to be done now?" Laurie stumbled over his words, trying to contain his enthusiasm, a young hound straining at the leash.

"I'm going to do what the milkman suggested – I'm going down to the pub, and you're going to use the public telephone outside the post office. Where did you say you lived?"

"Just outside Cready, Sarge."

"Right, no problem with long distance, then. Ask your ma what she knows then meet me on the quay. After that we're going up to Cleve House to talk to Mrs Hawkins' daughter – assuming the girl's there. Waterson will have to wait. This is more important. Got it? Or do I need to go over it all again?"

"No!" Laurie held up a clean palm. "I can find a telephone on my own, Sarge, but won't there be one in the pub? I could use that."

"Oh, no, you can't," Bob replied, shaking his head. "Nothing said in a pub stays secret for two minutes, lad."

Aubrey Chatwynde, wearing a yellow silk cravat that set Bob's teeth on edge, was leaning over his bar reading a copy of the Daily Telegraph. The pub was empty. Bob rapidly enquired whether Miss Pettit had been in.

"Little Miss Maud? No, she's gone up to London. I ran her into Cready last night. Her niece telephoned to say her sister had been rushed into hospital – Maud's sister, that is."

"The niece telephoned her at Seabreeze?"

"Must have done. Miss P was in quite a state, damsel in distress and all that, so I drove her into Cready for the first train."

Bob drummed the fingers of his right hand on the bar.

"You're friends with Miss Pettit, then? Have you known her long?

Chatwynde shook his mane of white hair and folded the newspaper. "No. Curious old biddy, though. She started coming in for the fire, I suspect, during the coal strike. Said she couldn't get fuel. Anyway, we got talking as you do, and she let on that she needed to sell the odd knick-knack to stay afloat. She'd got some nice bits of jewellery, and as I have a couple of acquaintances and family contacts in that line . . . well, I obliged as a sort of intermediary."

"Knick-knacks? Valuable ornaments, that sort of thing?"

"Rings and brooches, and a very nice set of pearl earrings with a three strand necklace . . . I'm sorry, is this a police inquiry? Has she . . . ? Oh, Lord, have I become mixed up in something?" Chatwynde gave a winning, what-a-silly-billy smile.

Bob ignored it. "London, you said. She didn't mention where in London?"

"Not the city – Potters Bar. Her sister lives in Potters Bar. They used to live in Epsom as children, by the racecourse. She told me all about it. Jolly well-heeled young ladies I'd say, in their day."

"Hmm." Bob grimaced, not for the first time in the past hour and for the same reason. He'd failed to act as soon as he could have done and missed his chance. Rapping the bar a couple of times with his right hand, he came to a decision. "Could you write down the name and address of your contacts and acquaintances for me, Mr Chatwynde, please? It'll save us a deal of time that way."

"So this is a formal inquiry. That – um – makes it a bit tricky."

Bob heaved a sigh. "Mr Chatwynde, I tell you what, write me a detailed list of what Miss Pettit has been selling and drop it in at the Police Station in Cready. Then, when we find Miss P, we'll ask her about it and put her in contact with an agency that helps the elderly in need, so she can keep her keepsakes if she wants to. How does that sound?"

"That sounds perfectly acceptable," Chatwynde drawled, setting Bob's teeth on edge again. "Can I offer you a drink now, on the house?"

Bob was sorely tempted but refused; he wanted to get up to Cleve House as soon as he could. As he left the pub he looked at his watch, checking to see if it was legally opening time. It was, but he suspected the Fisherman's Boot had flexible opening hours to go with a rather too flexible landlord.

Chapter 34

"Keep stirring until the bubbles start then turn the gas down low as you can before it goes out, and keep on stirring it now and again after that – don't stop or it'll get lumpy again like it did yesterday."

Bob could hear the tension in Maisie Hawkins' voice from across the large kitchen. Maisie herself was draining a huge pot of something at the sink, her reddened hands clamped on oven cloths over a tilted lid. He wanted to take the weight of the over-sized saucepan, tell her to sit down. He didn't; he said nothing, only watched.

Charles Metherall stood behind him, and behind him stood PC Oliver, helmet in hands. A fair-haired woman rushed into the kitchen from a side door.

"Is that the little ones' potatoes?" she asked, lifting a big, empty dish from the dresser and taking it to the sink. The two women could have been sisters, although Maisie was older by a number of years.

Resting the heavy pot back on the draining board, Maisie wiped a stray hair off her forehead with the back of her hand and indicated the oven with a foot. "Get the pie served first. I'll do the potatoes. Ginny, you still stirring or has that custard turned to cheese?"

Ginny looked up vaguely then caught sight of the men at the door. "Hello," she said and waved a hand like a five-year-old on a merry-go-round.

Maisie looked across the kitchen and caught Bob's eye. Silently he shook his head. She went back to the potatoes without a word.

"We've come at a bad time," Bob said, giving Ginny an embarrassed half-wave as she gazed expectantly at him.

The fair-faced, fair-haired woman came forward and shook his hand.

"My wife, Cordelia," Metherall explained.

"I'm sorry," she said, "we can't stop at the moment. There are forty-five starving children to feed, not to mention their teachers. Is it urgent?" She looked at Laurie Oliver, who shuffled from one foot to another, unsure whether to say anything in reply or not.

"Always a bad time in this kitchen," Charles Metherall said. "Come through to my study, Detective Sergeant. You can talk to the cooks as soon as the boys have got their nose bags on."

The study was a haven of leather chairs and crowded glass-fronted bookcases: the result of generations, not one man. Metherall, in faded fawn slacks and open-necked shirt, seated himself in a chair by the empty grate; Laurie Oliver took his now accustomed place at a table. Bob looked out of the window. A row of archery targets had been assembled on what had once been a lawn. The wind had knocked two to the ground.

"Learning to shoot arrows, are they? That'll make Hitler think twice if he lands down this way," Bob grinned.

Charles Metherall looked at him with a poker face then burst out laughing. "Quite right. Teach them useful skills, that's what I say. Take a seat, Detective Sergeant. Let's see if *I* can be of any help to you."

J. G. Harlond

Bob played for time at the window; he hadn't expected to meet Major Metherall, and although he had a good few questions to ask him, right at this moment his mind was on a neat little spinster who was almost certainly not the person she claimed to be. Nevertheless, remembering the hint Inspector Small had dropped about Metherall being in Intelligence, and desperate to know how this connected to Porthferris, he was not going to pass up the opportunity for an informal chat. The problem was where to start. The whole Porthferris affair was getting out of hand: he needed an afternoon in the woods, sitting quietly watching Mother Nature feed her young to get his thoughts together.

To his surprise Metherall made the opening move. "Chatwynde at the Boot tells me you are interested in the old mine."

"Did he, sir? And how does he know that?"

"Are you?"

"Yes."

"They have looked, you know, extensively. If Stan Hawkins went into the mine, or got in through his sea cave tunnel, Chatwynde's Home Guarders would have found him. They used the search to practise all manner of skills and – sorry to say – found not a single trace."

"Is Colonel Waterson in the Home Guard unit, sir?"

"Game old boy – yes, why?"

"So they would have looked in his tunnel as well?" Metherall ran a long hand down an un-pressed trouser leg and cocked his head to one side. "I'm going over to visit Colonel Waterson later," Bob added.

A dark look crossed Metherall's face. "Waterson – why?"

"I met him in the cottage hospital. His wife has come round from her coma."

"Yes, he rang us. Very good news."

Metherall hesitated a second too long, to Bob's mind, but he was a smooth operator. He certainly didn't interview like a man in the street. It made Bob nervous, but he persisted. "Colonel Waterson invited me over to Bayview to take a look around the grounds. He seems to think that whoever their intruder was, he was more interested in his greenhouse than the military goings on upstairs. I know the RMPs have got it all in hand, but I'd like to have a look in the sea cave and the Bayview tunnel regarding another matter."

"No longer possible, I'm afraid. You can get into his cave or into his cellar and *see* the tunnel from there, but the mine has been taken over by the military. As I said, if there was any chance of finding Hawkins in the mine they would have done it by now."

"And your opinion, sir – what do *you* think happened at Bayview?"

"Oh, one of two scenarios: someone was after extra rations in the kitchens or, possibly, someone was interested in what is going on in the rooms upstairs. Navy personnel are doing vital monitoring work, or they were: the project has been terminated. That's all I know."

Bob stared at an archery target, then began, "I was at Mr Bantry's house. You may have heard his wife has died."

"Yes, I know all about it."

"*All* about it, sir? Including what I found?"

"Yes."

Bob waited for the major to say more. When he didn't Bob said, "Do you know who I should approach, sir, for permission to get into the mine?" Bob had changed tack fast, but not fast enough.

"Yes – me." Metherall's voice had a decisive "don't cross me" timbre.

Bob sat down in the chair opposite him and rubbed his chin. "As it happens, sir, I'm not actually here regarding the missing fisherman, Hawkins."

"No? When I saw the constable's uniform at the door and you asked to speak to Mrs Hawkins I assumed it was to do with her husband."

"No, sir, I asked to speak to *Miss* Hawkins."

"Ginny! Whatever for?"

"It's rather a long story, but I need to know a couple of things from Miss Hawkins about the lady she was working for, Miss Pettit."

Charles Metherall backed down now. He clearly had no idea who Ginny Hawkins worked for. Bob decided to risk a tit-for-tat information exchange. Metherall was a bigwig in Porthferris and could be useful one way or another.

"Major, I don't wish to sound uppity or anything like that, but if you could tell me a bit about what I need to know regarding the mine so I can cross it off my list for good . . ."

"You'll fill me in on what's going on in Porthferris that I don't know about?"

"Something like that, yes."

"Not possible, I'm afraid. Not within my powers to reveal military information. But please believe that I'm not trying to be uppity, either. It's the way it is, and I think you had better follow your instructions and drop the whole issue of the mine."

Bob squinted at the Army major: *you're in contact with the Acting Chief Constable Soames.* He turned to Laurie. "PC Oliver, if you've written anything of that down, be a good chap and tear out the page."

Laurie pulled a page from his notebook and handed it to Bob, who tore it in pieces and dropped the bits in the empty grate.

Then Bob started again, outlining as succinctly as he could what had happened to Mrs Bantry and adding the details relating to Ginny making the cakes and chutney.

The major was silent for a moment then said, "You've seen for yourself just now what Ginny's like. She's in her twenties, I think, and she can't be trusted to make custard on her own. You surely cannot believe she was responsible for poisoning Mrs Bantry? It's unthinkable. Impossible. Unless – God forbid – it was a ghastly accident."

"That's what I'd like to believe as well, but the fact remains, she was the person who – apparently, and this has not been verified yet – put some un-named compound into the cakes and the toadstools into the chutney."

"Are you going to arrest her?"

Bob shook his head slowly. "Not if I can help it." He looked over at Laurie. "Don't write that down, either."

"No, Sarge." PC Oliver's expression was blank.

Bob turned back to Major Metherall. "Can you give us a reason why you don't think Miss Hawkins acted on her own, sir?"

He caught Laurie Oliver's eye and indicated he should take this down. The constable nodded and turned to a fresh page in his notebook.

Charles Metherall needed a moment to think about what he was going to say. "Ginny's a sweetheart, but she's not quite right in the head. That's not to say she does strange things on her own. Quite the opposite. She can't do anything without being told to first. Frankly, the girl gets on my nerves, but she's harmless. I mean, if that custard starts to boil over she won't react by turning off the gas unless someone tells her to. That's a bit of an exaggeration, perhaps, but I've never seen her do anything useful of her own accord."

"And you've known her since she was . . .?"

"Twelve years now. No, more – fourteen. Since I started coming to Cleve House. It's my wife's family home. I used to visit when we were courting. Ginny was always here with her mother, in the kitchen and around the house – same as now. Pretty thing and always cheerful, but, as I say, definitely not the full pound note. Except, and this is curious, she can read quite well. Although I doubt she understands what she's actually reading. She forms syllables and words, and reads aloud. Spends hours with our copies of *Picture Post*. And she has amazing recall: phenomenal memory for irrelevant details. If she reads the contents of that tin of custard powder, she'll be able to reel it all off, exactly as it's written, a month hence – next year."

"So she could have *read* about arsenic and – or – the mushrooms, toadstools whatever they are – and *remembered* this information when she was making the cakes and chutney?"

"I suppose so. Can't see why; but, yes, I suppose so."

Bob sighed. "The problem here is that Ginny goes out to pick mushrooms. Her mother told me that. They found an injured foreign boy once in the church spinney and took him back to their cottage because Ginny had gone looking for mushrooms. If she's not that bright, she might decide to pick the poisonous sort . . ." Bob was going to say more but the major's body language told him he'd touched a chord. What was it? Mention of the spinney, which was directly over the mine, or the boy, or Ginny picking poisonous mushrooms? "You were going to say, sir?" He left an opening for the major.

"No, nothing." Charles Metherall got up. "I'll go and see if the coast's clear. They should have sent in the pud by now." He left the study, closing the door behind him.

Bob drummed his fingers on the shiny back of a leather chair then sat in it.

"What spooked the major, Sarge?" Laurie asked, coming to stand by him.

"Wish I knew. But something spooked him, didn't it?" Bob looked up at the lanky PC and smiled. "I reckon I can turn you into a pretty good copper, you know."

Laurie grinned, but before he could reply Maisie Hawkins came into the library, pulling off her apron. She was followed by Ginny.

Bob jumped to his feet and went to greet them. "Come and sit down, if that's all right with Major Metherall? I've got a few questions. It shouldn't take long."

Maisie and Ginny sat down in the chairs he and the major had vacated. Delia Metherall hovered near the open door then closed it but remained where she was.

Bob stood next to Ginny's chair and said quietly, "Did you go to Miss Pettit's this morning, love?"

Ginny looked at her mother before she spoke.

Maisie Hawkins said, "Miss Pettit's had to go to London."

"And you know that because . . .?"

"Mr Chatwynde told me – last night."

"I see. So Ginny didn't go to the bungalow today, but she has been going regularly before today."

"Yes," Maisie was still answering for her daughter.

Bob turned so only Ginny could see him speak, "And you do Miss Pettit's cleaning and cooking, do you Ginny?"

Ginny gave him one of her luscious smiles. "I'm her little treasure."

"Can you tell me what sort of cooking you do, sweetheart?"

"Cakes for Miss Pettit's tea parties."

"Not her meals, then, just cakes?"

"I made chutney. Apple chutney. Peel and core six pounds of cooking –"

"And who comes to Miss Pettit's tea parties, do you know?"

Ginny shook her head.

"She sometimes delivered cakes and things to Mrs Bantry," Maisie said behind him. "Haven't we talked about this before?"

Ignoring the question, Bob said to Ginny, "Why do you take things to Mrs Bantry, sweetheart?"

Ginny responded with one her vacant smiles. Her mother supplied an answer of sorts. "I suppose Mrs Bantry didn't cook or they shared their rations. Maybe Mrs Bantry gave Miss Pettit her sugar and dried egg and they let Ginny make up a batch of cakes. Perhaps that's why she made the chutney."

Bob scratched his chin and turned back to Ginny. "Does Miss Pettit help you when you're cooking, Ginny?"

"She tells me what to do."

"Of course she does. Excellent." Bob rubbed his hands together. "Got that, PC Oliver? Miss Pettit tells Miss Hawkins what to do. Right," Bob addressed Delia Metherall, still standing by the door, "next thing we need to do is take a look at Miss Pettit's kitchen. Can Mrs Hawkins and Ginny have time off this afternoon? Won't take long."

Delia Metherall's eyes were the same blue as Maisie Hawkins' and they were alive with curiosity. "I'll drive them down. What time would suit you?"

"About four-ish. We've got to get back to Cready or I'd say now."

"Not now," Maisie said hastily. "We got to clear up after the kiddies' dinner and I'll have to do their tea before we can leave. Can you manage that on your own?" She was looking at Delia Metherall.

"Of course, but I won't be able to take you down to the village."

"We'll manage on our own, won't we Ginny?"

Ginny looked at her mother. Her face was clouded and she bit her lip.

"It's all right, sweetheart, no need to look glum," Bob said then looked at Maisie Hawkins, but she was lost in her own thoughts. "We'll see you later, then."

Bob drove out of the Cleve House drive onto the main road and turned sharp right. Before Laurie had time to speak, Bob pulled into the kerb in front of Albert Villas but made no move to get out.

"Sarge . . ." Laurie began.

"Wait! Here he is." Staring into his rear-view mirror, Bob pointed a finger as a car passed going downhill. "Major Metherall in a hurry, and where do you reckon he's going?"

"I don't know – post office? The pub?"

"Me, too." Bob started the engine but coasted downhill to save petrol. "Is there a back way into the Fisherman's Boot, do you know?"

"No, sorry."

"Must be. Chatwynde's roadster is undercover somewhere – he wouldn't leave that on the quay to get salted. The gents are out the back in the yard so . . . Look, I'll park here." They were on the quay by now. "You stay put and keep an eye on the front door of the pub. It'll be closing time soon. See if Chatwynde comes out with the major, and, if he does, where they go. I'm going to take a recce round the back."

Bob slipped out of the car and strolled towards the shops as if out to get a packet of cigarettes. But instead of turning left, he went right, nipping along the blind side of the pub at a sprightly half-skip for a rotund man, then down an alley beside a wooden-fenced garage that must once have been a stable yard. A few yards further on there was a tall gate. He lifted the latch and sidled in. The back door to the pub was open and someone had come out to the gents because that door was open, too. He turned into the gents and came out adjusting his clothes, then wandered into the pub via the back door. The door leading into the bar was open, but there were voices coming from the kitchen. Raised voices. Bob paused and leaned against the wall.

"You should have told me!" It sounded like Metherall.

"It wasn't hard to guess. You're in Intelligence, not me. Foreign boy – speaks French and Italian – I gave you enough clues."

"He's your fancy boy. That's why he's here. All that nonsense about being a car mechanic and being ferried over from France."

"That is true, as it happens. He worked in the Fiat factory in Turin before he came to England. And when the war started he crossed the channel to get back home."

"I thought you said he was an Italian waiter."

"No, Charles," Chatwynde's voice was cold, "that was your prejudices inventing details. Aren't you people still trained to avoid that?"

"But you knew him London. I'm not inventing that, am I?"

"No. I knew him in London."

"Well it was bloody idiotic bringing him here. Get him out of that garage and send him packing."

"He's not there anymore. Paddon kicked him out."

"I'm not surprised. Look – no – you can't send him packing. He was at Coleshill. He's had the training, knows far too much. He knows about the mine as well, doesn't he? How to get in, how much ammunition you've got there, the grenades . . . Damn you, Aubrey, you've dropped your men right in the muck heap. I'll have to close this down now. After all the effort that's gone into setting up the Operations Base – damn you."

Local Resistance

Chatwynde started to speak. Bob couldn't make out the words but he was certain it was Chatwynde's drawl. Then he did hear something.

". . . according to the good doctor. So if anyone asks about Bantry's accident we can say he was ill, lost control of the car because his wife had been poisoning him . . ."

Metherall responded, his clipped English plain to hear, "Don't try to sidetrack me. I'm not interested in the Bantry business. That boy is a liability – I'll get the RMPs to arrest him and keep him somewhere safe, where he can't talk to anybody. You said yourself he's unreliable – and dangerous. Was it he who attacked Mrs Waterson?" Chatwynde must have shaken his head because Metherall's response was a scathing. "So you say."

There was a lull in the exchange and Bob looked up, suddenly aware he was being watched. A young man with uncut, bottle-bleached hair, wearing only a white vest, loose trousers, and expensive leather slippers without socks, was on the stairs, gazing at him with folded arms.

Bob's throat went dry. "Afternoon," he said. "Feeling a bit dicky. Too much ale on an empty stomach . . ."

The boy shrugged, turned and went back upstairs. A chill ran down Bob's spine. He backed out and returned to the gents feeling genuinely sick. He'd seen expressions like that before – on merciless young villains with flick-knives and nothing to lose.

He leant over the toilet but brought up only a spit of bile. More slowly now, he left the gents and walked back up the alley.

As he sank into the car seat, Laurie said, "No one's come in or gone out, Sarge. Did you see anyone?"

"Yes, I saw someone; and he saw me."

Laurie was about to ask who but caught the look on Bob's face and looked out of the car window. "It's a nice day."

After a while Bob said, "There are too many players in this game for my liking. I can't face the hotel business now. Let's get back to Cready."

As they entered the town, they were caught in a small traffic jam caused by a herd of spindle-legged ewes trotting tipper-tap the wrong way down a one-way street. It was Friday, market day. Bob's favourite day of the week: he liked to call in at the market bar and listen to the locals. Catch up on the gossip and enjoy a glass of warming rum, or two. It suddenly struck him that he'd never wondered where Jack the bar owner got his liquor. He looked at his watch: too late to call in now.

"Next week," he said aloud. Laurie looked at him questioningly. "Take no notice," Bob said. "Thinking aloud as usual. I'll drop you off at the station and go back home. If anyone asks, you don't know where I am, which is true in the strict sense, and don't mention anything about Ginny Hawkins unless you're tortured by DI Small. I'll talk to him later, once I've got it clear in my own head. Ginny Hawkins isn't going to do a runner – I hope. Are you on duty over the weekend?"

"I've got Sunday free."

"You got transport?"

"Yes, my brother's motorcycle. Why?"

"Take a run down to Porthferris and ask about hiring a boat – say you're taking up sea-angling for the summer. It'll do as an excuse. If the Deakin boys really have joined up we may have to take ourselves out, though. You up to that?"

"To be honest, no."

"Tough. Ask about a dinghy with an engine and make sure it's got oars, just in case we can't sort out the sail between us."

"A winkboat? Like Hawkins had? What are you planning, Sarge?"

"I'm planning to make a corned beef sandwich and have a cup of tea. I'm planning to have forty winks in my chair and then I'm going to dig up a dish of worms."

Bob let in the clutch as the traffic began to move. Once the car was moving, Laurie said, "Was that a metaphor, sir?"

"A meta-what?"

"Metaphor – figure of speech. About the dish of worms."

"Can of worms, more like. I keep them in a tin with a handle. Why?"

"Ah – got it. You're going fishing."

"Tomorrow – if the sun stays out long enough. I'm having a thinking day, if DI Small will let me."

"That's when you sort things out, while you're fishing?"

"In a manner of speaking." Bob glanced sideways and risked a personal revelation, "I use it as a bit of an excuse – fishing. I just like being outdoors, really, watching wildlife. On my own."

"I used to have a secret tree house," Laurie said, "to get away from the teasing and squabbling. Then I got to like being there for the sake of it. If you stayed still long enough you could see all sorts of birds and things that most people never . . . well, you know."

"I know."

A bit later on Laurie said, "It is a bit of muddle, isn't it? And I thought nothing ever happened in places like Porthferris."

"Nearly forgot – what did your mother say about little Aunt Maud?"

"She wasn't in. I'll try again from the station."

"Ah, well, we'll find out sooner or later." Bob pulled into a street that ran beside the police station and stopped. "Right, hop out here, I'm going home for an hour or two so mum's the word, as they say. I'll pick you up here about half-past three. Tell Mallett I've booked you for another visit to the den of Cornish crime so no school crocodile duty, all right?"

Chapter 35

Maisie Hawkins went in first, then Ginny, then Bob and Laurie Oliver. The bungalow already smelt stale and fusty, unoccupied. Maisie opened the curtains in the sitting room and Ginny noticed the cabinet immediately.

"All the little boxes have gone," she said, pointing at the top shelf. "Painton, Scarborough and Whitney Bay; Skegness and Eastbourne." She pointed at the lower shelf. "The Rock of Gibraltar, Ifracombe." She spoke the name slowly, pronouncing each syllable. "Blackpool and Llandudno — that's got two 'l's, but you say Clan-dud-no. And Alton, Ham*p*-shire."

Bob stared at the girl.

Maisie came to stand by him. "Miss Pettit kept souvenirs from places she'd been to, shell-boxes and the like."

Bob didn't move. "PC Oliver, get your notebook out. Write these names down. Underline *Alton, Hampshire.* I thought it was Winchester, but it wasn't — it was Alton." Laurie looked at him and frowned. "Just thinking aloud again," Bob said. He turned back to Ginny, "Could you start again, sweetheart, with the top shelf? Go slowly so PC Oliver can write down the place names?"

Ginny Hawkins recited the place names and Laurie committed them to his notebook.

"How do you know all this, Ginny?" Bob asked gently.

Ginny looked confused and turned to her mother for help.

"Tell Mr Robbins what you told me about the first day you worked for Miss Pettit and you tried to clean the boxes."

"She said I mustn't clean them." Ginny looked as if she were about to cry.

"Never mind," Maisie said, "I'll tell him. Each box was a place, you see."

"I do see. And each box contained . . . what? Can you tell me what was in the boxes, Ginny? The ones Miss Pettit didn't want you to touch."

"All of them. They all had bits in. Or powder. Scarborough and the Rock of Gibraltar had bits of old leather, like the dried mushrooms in the pantry. The rest had a sort of talcum powder, only it was grey, not white."

Bob rapped a tattoo on the back of the sofa. "Hmm. Show us the pantry now, love," he said to Ginny. Then, turning, he said *sotto voce* to Laurie, "Start a new page, label it 'kitchen' and get every word she says."

Ginny went into the kitchen and opened the pantry. Maisie followed them in and paused at the door, saying, "I think Ilfracombe is something to do with the Bantrys."

Bob swivelled round. "Why?"

"I can't remember exactly, but they were talking about it at church one day. I wasn't really listening. I think Mrs Bantry recognised, or thought she recognised, Miss Pettit from a hotel in Ilfracombe."

"And Miss Pettit said she'd never been there."

"How do you know that?"

"I don't, but I'd like to find out why she might have said it. You can't remember which hotel?" Maisie shook her head. "If you remember, call me, immediately. PC Oliver, circle Ilfracombe in your notes." He turned back to Ginny standing at the pantry door. "Can you tell us what's in the jars up there?" He indicated a row of crock jars with lids.

Ginny pointed as she spoke: "Plain flour, white sugar, special sugar, salt, sultanas, currants, raisins."

"Special sugar? What makes it special?"

"Don't know," Ginny responded.

"Do you make the cakes with the flour and currants from here?"

"Yes."

"With the ordinary white sugar or special sugar?

"Special sugar is for when Mr and Mrs Bantry come to tea, and for when Miss Pettit goes to their house. I make rock buns and Scottish shortbread for when she goes to Mr and Mrs Bantry's house. There's no currants in Scottish shortbread. It's in *Mrs Beeton's Household Management* book, over there."

Ginny pointed at a much used volume on a shelf above the kitchen table.

As Bob reached for the book, Ginny recited: "Scottish shortbread. Eight ounces of flour, two ounces castor sugar, four ounces of butter. Put the flour and butter in a pile on a pastry-board. Gradually knead the sugared flour into the butter. It is important not to let the butter –"

"Ginny, Mr Robbins doesn't need to know how to make shortbread," Maisie interrupted.

"Actually, yes, I do. But only the ingredients. There's no magic fairy dust in shortbread, then, Ginny?"

"That goes in the rock buns."

"And where do you keep that?"

"It belongs to Miss Pettit. She puts it in."

"That's what I wanted to know! Good girl. Got that, PC Oliver? 'She puts it in'."

Ginny beamed with delight and started on the recipe for rock buns. "One pound of plain flour, one quarter teaspoon of salt –"

Maisie Hawkins stopped her daughter with a hand on her arm. Looking at Bob, she said, "Can you tell me what's going on here?" Her voice was sharp.

"Yes, as soon as we get the contents of those shelves analysed. Ginny, where does Miss Pettit keep the labels for the jam pots?"

"In here. I use the ones with stripes for the chutney, I like the stripes."

Bob removed a packet of labels from the table drawer and got out a pen. *Special sugar*, he wrote. "Now show me again, which is Miss Pettit's special sugar?"

Ginny showed him and he popped the label inside the pot.

"Now show me the chutney you made."

Ginny searched the shelves. "It's all gone."

"All right. Show me the mushrooms you put in it."

"I didn't. Miss Pettit said they were magic mushrooms for a special flavour. They smelled like ice cream. They were in a jam jar on the window sill, there. They've all gone now. They are pretty, but I don't like those mushrooms. They smell like ice cream but they aren't nice."

"Do *you* ever pick them when you go looking for mushrooms?"

Bob caught Maisie's eye. She had gone white. He tried to nod in a positive way, but she obviously knew where this was going.

"Tell Mr Robbins what you pick in the spinney, Ginny. Tell him exactly what you look for and what you find."

"Edible fungi," Ginny was reciting again. "Fungi grow in woodlands of all kinds, mainly on leaf litter and rotting wood. If you are not sure that a mushroom is safe to eat and not a poisonous toadstool, do not pick it or taste it. Edible fungi: Saffron milk-cap, common under conifers; Paxil, very common under birch trees in summer and autumn, edible when well cooked . . ."

Bob let Ginny recite everything she could remember: Wood Blewits and red-brown Deceivers; Chanterelle smell like apricots; Wood Mushrooms smell like almonds. After she mentioned the almond smell he interrupted gently, saying, "What about the little white ones that smell like ice cream?"

"*Amanita fragrans*. You mustn't eat those. It says in Mrs Chenoweth's book. But Miss Pettit said hers were different. They were vanilla, not ice cream."

Bob looked at Maisie for clarification. "Mrs Chenoweth was Mrs Metherall's mother. Her books are in the library at Cleve House."

"So Ginny has studied this book on mushrooms and toadstools."

"Ginny, when did you read this book?" Maisie asked.

"Lots of times. When I was little. There are ever-so pretty pictures. I like the Fly Agaric, but you mustn't eat it. It's in Mrs Metherall's children's picture books, but you mustn't ever eat it. Ma, why's it in children's books if you mustn't ever eat it?"

"Good point," Bob said. "Right, well I think we've established the fact that young Ginny here knows the difference between a mushroom and a toadstool, and a darn sight more as well." But to be on the safe side he asked her again about the chutney. "You don't need to tell me about what you put in the chutney, or how you cooked it, just tell me, who put in the mushrooms?"

"Not mushrooms: toadstools. Miss Pettit. She chopped them up and dropped them in. They were a bit soggy from being fresh. I was stirring the pot, like I do with custard at

Cleve House. And Miss Pettit put the ingredients in. Have I done wrong?" Ginny's lower lip was trembling.

Bob patted her shoulder. "No, sweetie – you were Miss Pettit's little treasure, weren't you?"

The girl's face brightened but Maisie Hawkins looked deeply worried. Bob rapped his fingers on the table twice and said, "Got all that, PC Oliver?"

Laurie recited back what he'd written.

"That's what I said." Ginny was delighted. "He wrote down what I said."

"Yes, dear," said her mother. "Can we go now, Mr Robbins?"

Maisie Hawkins was eager to be off and Bob could understand why, although he was rather disappointed that she didn't understand his sense of relief: they had effectively established her daughter was not guilty of murder.

As they left the bungalow, Maisie let Ginny walk ahead to the gate then came back to him at the door. "You didn't tell me you were going to accuse my daughter of poisoning," she hissed.

"Why do you think I came to speak to you at Cleve House?"

"You didn't say it was this serious."

"But you knew Mrs Bantry had not died of natural causes. I told you. And now you tell me Miss Pettit knew the Bantrys before they came here, so there might be a motive for what's been going on."

"I didn't say that. I only said I thought I remembered something. And you didn't tell me you thought my daughter was too stupid not to know the difference between a field mushroom and a flaming toadstool." On the defensive now, Maisie was getting angrier and angrier.

"She didn't mention field mushrooms, as it happens," Bob said.

"Ah! Men!" Maisie snapped and flounced off.

Bob watched her go then did a few Charleston steps on the spot. Maisie Hawkins had been talking to him as if he were a friend – an ex-friend now, admittedly. Nonetheless, she would never have spoken to a policeman – on duty, what's more – like that. Especially one who had made a point of not asking where the dubious Miss P got her extra sugar and raisins.

Unable to keep the smile off his face, he danced back into the kitchen to find a basket or box for the crock jar exhibits.

Driving back to Cready, Bob screeched to a halt, nearly sending Laurie's head through the windscreen.

"Alton, Hampshire, two women with the same name: Collins. Mother-in-law and dead son's wife: the Martha Collinses. I was right, that's where I saw her. She was the old lady's paid companion!"

"Miss Pettit?" Laurie ventured.

"Maud Lily Pettit, indeed. But what's her connection to the Bantry couple?"

"And why would she want to kill them?" Laurie added.

Part Four
Home Defence

Chapter 36

Laurie Oliver loped into Bob's office while Bob was speaking on the phone. He was obviously bursting with news, but Bob held up a palm and finished his conversation on the handset: "Chatwynde, yes. With a 'Y', yes. It's on the pub licensee name plate. Could be an alias, but, if it is, I reckon he's been using it for a long time. Could be he's legit . . . Yes, with a 'Y' in 'wind' – where else would you put it? . . . Yes, that's right. Also, can you have a browse through any files in the naughty boys section? See if you've got a Chatwynde there. Go back about five years . . . Was there? What? 1939, same name? . . . Well, dog bite me – so that's why he's holed up in a one-eyed Cornish village. Give me a date." Bob scribbled something on the edge of a typed sheet among the papers littering his desk. "Thanks Tom. I'll follow it up in old newspapers in the library if I can . . . No, no, it probably wasn't . . . Mm . . . I'll return the favour one day. There's bound to be something down here on the empty moors and the mined beaches that you're dying to know about . . . No, not much. Weather's improving. I've started doing a bit of sea angling . . . You got to be careful, mind. It's not like Brighton. Waves down here come in sideways ruddy fast, knock you off your feet and pull you in before you've got a tiddler in the bucket . . . Yeah . . . Regards to your Meg. Bye."

Bob put the phone down and rubbed his hands. "Our Mr Chatwynde's been in a spot of unseemly bother, if it's the same chap. You look as if you're about to wet yourself with excitement. What's to do, PC Oliver?"

"The Oakleys – their house was hit during the Blitz." The boy's face changed. "That's the sad bit. Mother hasn't been able to contact them, but she rang my aunt and she said she thought both the Oakleys had been killed. She hasn't heard from them, anyway. Ma's trying to find Graham and Maggie – the son and daughter – to see if they have a spinster aunt. But she thinks not, because Mrs Oakley's family were overseas and Mr Oakley was an only child, so if there had been an aunt –"

"She'd have been in the wedding photos."

"Er, yes, something like that."

"So our Miss Pettit comes across the deeds for a nice little bungalow by the seaside after an air raid. It's named Seabreeze – very evocative. There's no one living there, so she settles in like Goldilocks. And why not, eh?"

Laurie's jaw dropped.

"In a People's Socialist Republic a surplus second home like that would be divided up among the needy." Bob was only half joking. "Only I don't think Miss Pettit was needy at all. I think she's another one with a record, except it won't be in the name of Pettit, I'll bet you that." He suddenly launched himself from his chair and rushed for the door.

"Where are you going, Sarge?" Laurie asked, caught sideways in the draught.

"To talk to the local vicar. You want to know anything about a parishioner, talk to the vicar. Mrs Hawkins said she remembered the Bantrys talking to Miss Pettit at church about somewhere they'd met – or not met. Good job they're not Methodists like Ezra Paddon or we'd never have heard a word."

"I don't follow."

"No need to, lad. Look, I want to keep this informal until it's decided what's happening with Ginny Hawkins – and possibly her ma."

"Is Mrs Hawkins involved?" Laurie couldn't keep the surprise out of his voice.

"Her husband has disappeared, remember."

"But, Mrs Hawkins seems so nice."

"Agreed, but as Major Metherall said, the girl Ginny can't do a thing without being told to – except read books. And Mrs H told us herself that the girl went up to the spinney to pick mushrooms . . . So what else were they being used for, eh?" Bob paused. He wanted to believe what Maisie Hawkins had said about her husband's disappearance, but he was a policeman, and right now he had a few doubts. "Let's say I think Mrs H knows more – or has done more – than she's told me. I hope I'm wrong. But it's not impossible your 'angel' Ginny is the 'angel of death' acting on her own, either. She does go picking mushrooms at odd times. That's how they found the boy who I now think may be lodging in the Fisherman's Boot with Mr Aubrey Fancy-pants, and there's various other bits that are beginning to stick together. You stay here and keep Sergeant Mallet sweet today, and don't forget what I asked you about renting a boat."

Bob drove the now very familiar back-lane route to Porthferris and parked outside the vicarage, wondering if he should have called to make an appointment first. He got as far as the gate to the house, then changed his mind and crossed the road to the church; he'd said he wanted to keep it informal. It would be better if he could speak to the vicar as if in passing, get him chatting casually about the Bantry couple and Miss Pettit, about Ginny Hawkins and the missing father, without giving too much away, and find out what he could about Charles Metherall as he went along. The Bayview incident, which was never his business anyway, could wait another day.

The church door was open. He didn't know much about churches but the square tower told him it was probably Norman, and the worn flagstones told him it had been in constant use for centuries. He paused to look up at the stained-glass window over the altar and the tiny choir stalls. Christ the Shepherd surrounded by fat, fleecy sheep; behind them a seascape and a ship on the horizon. How little life had changed in this area: generations of humble people scraping a living from the soil and sailing into danger and, if they were lucky, coming back to give thanks for a safe haven. He gave a deep sigh; Joan would have liked it here. She could have joined the Mother's Union, gone on the flower rota . . .

Aware of the aggressive clip-clip of his oft-repaired shoes in the soft atmosphere, Bob sauntered down the short aisle until he noticed a woman polishing the lectern. She looked up.

"Good morning," she said as if she recognised him.

"Bob Robbins," he said, going up to her and offering his hand, and sending her into a flurry of indecision about what to do with her duster. "I'm a newcomer," he added, trying to put her at ease.

"Oh, welcome. Welcome to St Chad's. It's always nice to see a new face. If you are looking for the vicar, he's preparing his sermon over the road. I'm Rosemary Hughes, the vicar's wife."

The woman's hand was warm, her handshake surprisingly firm. Bob quickly trawled his memory. The vicar's wife had been reported for petty larceny by Bantry and let off with or without a warning at DI Small's discretion because . . . *why*? As she moved he noticed the shape of her figure: she was pregnant – and her previous baby had died. He smiled, pleased to see her round bulge. "I'm just having a look-see, getting to know places. That sort of thing."

"Then you must join us for the service tomorrow. Perhaps your wife would like to come along to some of our social events. We have quite a lot going on for a small church like this. I'm sure she'd be made very welcome."

Bob shook his head slowly.

The woman understood immediately. "I'm so sorry," she said. "Well, feel free to wander where you will. The churchyard needs clearing out badly, but it shows our history, graves going back to early . . . Sorry, you're perhaps not interested in local history."

"No, on the contrary, I'm fascinated. I was reading up about the harbour in the library. About how they shipped copper round to Looe or down to Falmouth direct from the mine. And about the fishing in Porthferris: place used to be thriving, apparently. It goes back centuries, doesn't it?"

The woman picked up her duster and gave the top of the lectern a final wipe. "My husband has become quite an expert – you should talk to him."

"I'd like that, yes. But he must be busy all the time."

"He is, but he always finds time for people from somewhere. If you'd like to, come over and have a cup of tea or what passes for coffee these days – but could you give us an hour? We ought to finish our chores before we can chat."

"Lovely. Thank you. I'll take a turn in the churchyard."

"The spinney's a bit muddy, but it's still full of flowers – do have a look. They lift the spirit." The woman suddenly blushed. "Sorry, bit girlish."

Bob smiled. "Not at all. I know exactly what you mean. I could do with a bit of 'lifting'."

Local Resistance

As he left the church, Bob remembered how little Miss Pettit had come hurtling out of the lych-gate that evening. What had she been up to? He wandered along a gravel path then slowly made his way over muddy grass between irregular graves, ancient and modern, until he came to a low wall. Flat, weather-worn headstones cushioned by soggy daisies and clusters of small, white toadstools leaned against the softer, rounder stones of the old wall. Age and the salty air had etched away names and dates, but they bore witness, nevertheless, to what he'd been thinking: the sense of continuity, of a community that had lived and died together on the edge of history and the British Isles – nicely out of reach of world events. Until now. This was exactly what Churchill said they were fighting for.

Bob felt an unaccustomed surge of emotion and was suddenly anxious to get away. Looking around, he spied a limp gate propped half open. It led into the glebe-land spinney. A half circle dug into the path showed it had been used recently: lifted open and closed often enough to create a furrow in the mud. Curious, he tapped his left pocket to check he'd got his little binoculars and followed the path into the trees. It joined another path coming from the road.

Walking carefully around ruts and puddles, tree roots and sopping ferns, Bob reached a steep drop where the path disappeared down towards the sea and the old mine. Rain had obliterated tracks, but he had a pretty good idea the path was in use.

Somewhere to his left a man's cap appeared in the undergrowth, the head and figure revealing themselves a few inches at a time until a man came into view, pushing briskly up through brambles and ferns as if from a trapdoor in a pantomime forest glade.

The figure stopped when he saw Bob, then bent double and fiddled among the undergrowth. Bob couldn't make out what he was doing, but the action was definitely furtive. Then he realised it was the Army major from Cleve House.

"Detective Robbins," Charles Metherall said as he came onto the path, somewhat out of breath.

"Setting rabbit gins, are you, Major?" Bob kept his tone light.

"Not a bad idea. Make a change from bacon and pork pie."

Bob looked out at the view. From here they could just see the edge of Wheal Marie quay and the open sea. "Lovely view," he said.

"But you're not here to look at the view, are you, Mr Robbins?"

"As it happens, I was looking for late-blooming bluebells."

Charles Metherall guffawed.

As they gazed out to sea, a trawler appeared on the horizon.

"They're taking risks, going out that far these days. German U-boats must be lurking out there like sharks," Bob mumbled.

Charles Metherall lifted a hand. "Trickly, trickly, scramble, scramble," he said slowly and quietly.

Bob turned and looked at him.

"Trickly, trickly, scramble, scramble," the major repeated. "Mad Harry Deakin. I didn't twig at first. U-boats. Submarines. As they come up, the water runs off them: *trickly, trickly*. Then the crew set out inflatable dinghies and – *scramble, scramble* – climb in and row ashore."

"Ashore – here!"

"Right under the nose of our so-called surveillance team at Bayview."

Bob's jaw dropped open. "You *know* – *knew* about this?"

"It's only just dawned on me. I'll do something about it right away, though. Don't discuss it, please: we don't want a stupid invasion scare."

"Hardly stupid, sir. Could it be linked to Bantry's suitcases and the maps, do you think?"

"It's possible, isn't it?" Charles Metherall removed twigs and foliage from unseasonal thick, green corduroys. Then he looked at the place he'd come from in the brambles and back at Bob. "Were you looking for me?" he said.

Bob frowned, "For you, sir? No. I wanted to talk to the vicar. He's busy so I came for a walk."

"And caught me red-handed."

Bob was completely flummoxed. Then it dawned on him there might be a bunker hidden in the hill; that the mine might have become the new observation post, if the Bayview location had been closed down. He decided to give Metherall a way out and said, "A U-boat, here? That's a frightener."

"You're telling me. Perhaps they put men ashore at night to get fresh water . . . *and fresh vegetables*. Of course!"

"Vegetables?"

"Waterson's garden. Someone's stealing their lettuces and beetroot, and it isn't Peter Rabbit. It makes sense. Crazy, but it makes sense. There was a standpipe running on the quay early in the morning a few weeks ago, too. Just after Mad Harry told me what he'd seen. I turned it off, didn't take any notice. They must be coming in and filling up with fresh water. Waterson told me about their water, too, and I was rude to him." Charles Metherall paused and took a deep breath. "I'm talking too much. Forget it, please, Detective Sergeant, and please don't repeat what I've said to anyone."

Bob nodded. "No need to worry on that score, sir. But if Jerries have been coming in for fresh water, maybe they found out *by accident* you'd got an observation post set up right there in Bayview – so then they wanted to see what was to do and – that would explain what happened to Mrs Waterson, if she disturbed them. Or did *someone* tell them about Bayview, do you think?"

Charles Metherall studied Bob's face for a moment. "Such as?"

"A local man."

"Archibald Bantry."

"If enemy sailors are actually coming ashore here, sir, on a regular basis – perhaps they are also collecting secret information, or putting agents ashore."

"We can't say 'regular', yet, but, yes, it's horribly possible. Trouble is we don't have one single person who's actually seen anything except Mad Harry, and he's not what one could call a reliable witness. There's nothing to incriminate Bantry apart from what you found in his house, either. Well done, on that."

"There's a signed photo with Moseley, which is pretty damning. And it has to be a German sub – there's no reason for a British sub to surface and put in for water this close to Devonport. They get all their victualling in the docks there."

"We were warned Cornwall was on Hitler's invasion plan. They could already be here for reconnaissance." Metherall stopped abruptly and they were silent for a few moments, then he said, "Robbins, can I insist again you say nothing about this discussion, or meeting me here?"

"You can. But as a policeman I'd like to ask why you can't take a stroll in the woods when you fancy it."

Charles Metherall turned to face him. Looking him in the eye, he said, "You know what, as you're right here, I'm going to show you why. Come with me."

Bob followed the younger, fitter man through a mass of dripping undergrowth that soaked and tugged at his trousers until Metherall stopped and pulled a pair of field binoculars from under his sports jacket.

Panning the surrounding area, Metherall said, "Just checking for bandits." Then he pushed the binoculars back inside his jacket and took a pair of thick gardening gloves from a pocket. Bending down, he began to pull at a tangle of brambles. Underneath, was a thick, brown-painted metal trapdoor. He opened it slowly: it was evidently heavy. "Follow me down," he said. "There are twenty rungs and we do it in the dark. I've got a torch, but there's a couple of lamps once we get inside."

Bob felt a worrying loosening of the gut as he turned his back and lowered his left leg into the abyss, feeling for the first rung.

"Pull the door shut as you come," Metherall instructed.

Bob swallowed hard then leaned out and grabbed a handle. The moment the metal door came vertical it slammed down over his head with an ear-splitting crack, shutting out every vestige of light.

"Let's tell the whole of Cornwall, shall we?" muttered Metherall.

Bob was too wrapped up in self-preservation to care about the sarcasm. He started to count, but the ground took him by surprise before twenty, jolting his spine as he sought another rung. A light flickered on in a kerosene lamp behind him.

He blinked. He was in some sort of square living quarters: six bunks built into two walls; a table and three chairs against another; three Sten guns leaning against the open wall, with a pistol and what looked like a box of ammunition on top of a metal cupboard with fuse wire or something for explosives; and two frighteningly dangerous knives.

"This is our OB – Operation Base," Metherall said, opening what Bob could now see was a reinforced steel door. "Leave the door open behind you this time – I'll show you one of our observation posts."

Metherall led the way into a wide tunnel, bent double. Even Bob had to crouch to avoid bumping his head. After a few paces, there was a hint of daylight – a crack in the earth. They stopped at a sharp turn in the tunnel and Metherall moved aside, revealing a ledge and a horizontal lookout with a clear view of the old Wheal Marie sorting yard and quayside.

"Sappers have created a safe network for us to get down into the mine shafts, but anyone trying to get in from outside will come up against dead ends, unless they know the route. They've also made it look as if the tunnels have caved in, so there's loose rubble about. Adits off the main gallery are safe enough but some shafts are rotten right through and really are caving in, so don't get lost. You know what this is, don't you?"

"Not exactly, sir. I mean I can see it's a hideaway and you've got weapons. Like a French Resistance hideaway, I imagine."

"That's it, except we are the British Resistance. If the Nazis do invade, we are ready to go underground. Certain people – I shan't say who – will use this place as a base to cause as much havoc as they can."

"You'll shoot from here?" Bob indicated the open ledge.

"No. We'll use this as a secret base for carrying out sabotage. We've stockpiled enough food and supplies to last months, if need be. Men will come and go secretly – life as normal – except we'll be organising sabotage and discreet assassinations from here. If push comes to shove, our chaps can come down here permanently."

Bob felt his stomach churn. The major was deadly serious. "God almighty," he whispered.

"The reason it is so bloody secret is so no one can tell the enemy what's going on. Nobody should know *who* we are or *where* we are. That way no one with a petty grievance can give the game away. And – if the worst comes to the worst and our Auxiliaries do start hindering the enemy as they should . . ." Metherall paused then said, "there are bound to be reprisals. We've seen that in France. The less anyone knows the better. We can't ignore the possibility of torture, you see. It's the same all around the country."

"Was this why Bantry had a car accident so close to the mine?"

"I'd like to think not, but Auxiliary Units and bases have to be kept secret at all costs."

"And you are coordinating these Auxiliaries and OB secret bases?"

"Not me. As it happens, various Chief Constables are in charge once the balloon goes up. They've got special orders that even I don't know about, and I was in on the plan more or less from the outset. It was Churchill's own idea, you know. Then that rogue Brendan Bracken got involved. That's how I came to meet Chatwynde."

Bob was only half listening. *Chief Constables . . . and Acting Chief Constables? Was this why he'd been warned to stay away from the mine?* The need for absolute secrecy made sense. Then the word 'reprisals' hit home. That and the idea of local men and women, Maisie Hawkins for instance, being tortured to reveal information.

It wasn't impossible – a phrase he'd started using too often of late. He and millions of other British men and women had spent the past three years getting on as best they could. Not ignoring the Nazi threat – how could they? – but trying to keep life as normal as possible. And here was the action plan for what would happen if and when the enemy landed in airfields and came ashore.

That was the information Bantry was supplying: the airfields, and, no doubt, safe harbours. *And this was why he'd had to go all the way to Plymouth.* "I'm sorry, sir," he said. "You did say County Chief Constables?"

"Not all, but yes, a few. Some other members of the Police are involved, but I cannot say anything more."

Such as DI Small? Bob drummed his fingers on the stone ledge. "I have to make you an apology, sir."

"For what?"

"I was fussing about the old mine, certain it was being used for profiteering – contraband, if you like. I see why you were anxious to keep me out."

"Oh, you're probably right. There are two ancient tunnels running in from sea caves. They're both bricked up now, but bricks can be moved. You only have to tap away at certain places and they'll fall in – or out, if you're this side of them, of course. Hawkins and his pals could easily be storing their stuff there."

"But Chief Constable . . . wanted to keep me out of this place not for the smuggling but so I didn't –"

Metherall held up a warning hand and peered out of the horizontal slit, "Looks like Chatwynde has arrived, and, hell's teeth, someone else, on a motorbike." Metherall pulled out his field binoculars and Bob scrabbled in his pocket for his little pair.

The major laughed. "Opera glasses?"

"Work a treat, sir, at certain distances."

While Bob adjusted his lenses and panned the esplanade below, Metherall hissed, "Is the man completely stupid? They've been expressly told to stay away in daylight."

Two men, an older man with a mane of white hair and a younger, much lither figure, were now making their way across the open space between the quay and the main entrance to the mine. It was Chatwynde and the boy he'd seen on the stairs in the pub.

Metherall sighed. "As you suspected, this place is probably being used for untaxed or illicit goods. We've also got a stock of grenades and dozens of weapons hidden in various places."

"But if Mr Chatwynde is one of your team you can't be worried about that?"

"Can't I?"

"But he wouldn't be taking the weapons, would he?"

"Not Chatwynde, no. The boy, though, he's a different kettle of fish."

"Maybe they've got their own stuff tucked away in a tunnel and they've come to take it out. Does Chatwynde know how the mine is being used?"

"That's why he's down here – to organise local cells. He knows exactly what's here, and where. He also has a plan of the mine and the booby traps – helped design them himself."

"'Struth," Bob was genuinely surprised. "So who's the boy?"

"His catamite."

"Catamite!"

"I'd like to be wrong, but I don't think I am. He's a foreigner, as well, ally, technically, but – well, who's to say which side he's really on."

"Ah, the boy they call Johnny or Jan or Jean? So he swings both ways."

"I've been totally duped. Worse, really, because I had my doubts – I did have my doubts." Charles Metherall was clearly furious. "He's supposed to be our vehicle expert – worked in a Turin car factory, or so he's told them."

"You know about him?"

"This and that."

More parts of the jigsaw that was Porthferris in wartime started to fit together. Bob said, "Is this is the young man Mrs Hawkins found and looked after?"

"Maisie Hawkins? I don't know anything about that."

"He'd been injured – had taken quite a beating, from what she told me."

"I bet he had. And if this is the same one that was in London there's a queue who'd like to have another go, believe me. No, you're right. He was or is walking out with Ginny, I was told."

Partly seeking clarification and partly wanting to confirm his instinct had been right about the old mine, Bob said, "What do you think they're doing here?"

"Getting Chatwynde's liquor, if I'm lucky. Helping themselves to our weapons, if I'm not. Either way, one or both of them are racketeering. Look," Metherall began buttoning his jacket over the field binoculars, "I haven't got time to talk right now. I'm going down. You'd better go back. I know the route and I want to do it without a lot of fuss. You'll make a noise and frighten them off."

"What do you want me to do?"

"Get back to the entrance where we came in. Make sure the lamp's out, and don't forget to cover the door again."

"Yes, sir," Bob nearly saluted. "I'll see you outside somewhere, all right?"

Metherall had gone.

Bob stayed where he was for a few moments, staring through the slit, then, doing as he'd been told, passed through the living space, put out the lamp, located the steps and felt his way back up to blessed open air and sunshine.

After taking care to pull the bramble cover back over the trap door and nearly shredding his hands in the process, he slithered down across the steep, wooded cliff as fast as he could, heading for the path. No sooner had he found it than he fell flat on his back as a smooth stone shifted beneath him.

"Bollocks!" he shouted and tried to sit up. He was winded and lay back down to catch his breath. He closed his eyes. When he opened them again he was surrounded by a group of merciless outlaws.

"It's the Sherriff," one called.

"Stay where you are, villain," another voice piped.

"What the . . ." Bob squinted through a shaft of sunlight, straight into the shaft of an arrow aimed at his heart.

It was Simon Prior and his merry men in green jumpers.

Bob started to scramble to his feet.

"Down, villain!" Simon shouted, pulling the bow taught.

"I thought you were in hospital," Bob said, levering himself onto his elbows.

"I was. I'm not now. Stay where you are. You're the enemy."

"Don't be stupid, boy! I've got things to do."

Simon drew his arrow arm back.

"Oh, come on, lad: I saved your life, now you save mine." Inelegantly, Bob rolled onto his knees. The arrow thwacked into a tree behind him. "You stupid little bugger!" Bob was suddenly on his feet and shifting fast for his shape. "Give me that bow. I'll have you on a charge for this." Simon dodged behind a tree. "What do think you're doing?" Bob demanded.

"We're hunting the panther. It's loose in these woods," said a small urchin by way of logical explanation. "They moved my mum's caravan 'cuz it's here, and we're going to kill it."

Three other boys of various ages joined the small spokesman. "It might be a lion," one said.

Bob sighed and wiped the dirt from his hands on the back of his trousers, but he didn't feel inclined to laugh. Just then a portly, lopsided figure came steaming down the path, crying out, "George, are you here, boy?"

"It's my dada," the urchin said, dropping the stick he'd been holding.

The man, huffing and puffing, caught the urchin by the back of his neck. "Your mother'll flay you alive if she finds you've been down here. It's not safe. I told you a dozen times, there's wild beasts down yer."

The urchin put a hand to his collar but the father held on. Turning to Bob he said, "Beg pardon, sir. Are these boys with you?"

"No!"

"Then I'll be going, sir." He headed off towards the mine.

"Not that way!" Bob called.

"It's quicker to get to the road this way. We'm up at Glebe Farm, see."

Bob didn't see, but set off after them. Simon and his merry men followed.

Once they got down to the grassy esplanade, Bob stopped and took stock of the situation. It could be that Chatwynde was doing nothing out of the ordinary – for a man who arranged secret Resistance hideaways. But Metherall had been pretty certain he was up to something. Bob wanted to know what. Above all, he wanted to know more about the French-Polish-Italian car mechanic.

Chatwynde's fancy car was parked with its boot towards the entrance to the mine. The high-powered motorbike Bob recognised from Paddon's garage was now fitted with ample panniers and propped next to it. Of the two men, there was no sign.

The urchin's father was hovering near the open gate, obviously curious about the car and what was going on, and Simon Prior and gang were loitering somewhere behind him.

Bob wondered what to do. Go in? Stay here? First, however, he had to get the boys out of the way. He went over to the man at the gate. "I'm a policeman, sir, and I must insist you take these –"

As he spoke there was a deep, ponderous boom from inside the mine. "Run, go! Get away as far as you can!" Bob screamed at the boys. Nobody moved. "Go – there's been an explosion!"

Without thinking, he turned and headed for the mine entrance at a run. When he was halfway there, Jean-Gianni came of the open doorway and rushed towards his motorbike carrying an armful of small boxes. Ammunition. Bob quickened his pace, but before he could get anywhere near him, the boxes had been stuffed into the bike's panniers and Jean-Gianni was revving the engine. Bob turned back to look at the man at the gate. "Close it!" he shouted, gesturing with an arm. "Close the gate!"

The man didn't understand, but Simon Prior did. His gang joined him, pushing the old five-barred gate to a close just as the motorbike reached it.

The foreigner skidded round and drove hell for leather back to the entrance, then he swivelled round and revved the bike, ready to crash through the gate. Simon Prior stood to one side and fitted an arrow in his longbow.

"Christ almighty . . ." Bob was running towards him as fast as his short legs could carry him, chest heaving at the effort. "Get away, you fool," he gasped, trying to reach the boy.

The bike crashed into the gate, swerving to the ground.

The rider lifted the machine, skidded round once more, and raced for the entrance to the mine, ready to make another run and ride over the broken wood.

On his second run, Simon Prior's arrow hit the rider's thigh, but he didn't stop and raced on up Smugglers Mile Hill.

"Well, I'll be . . ." said the man in the greasy cap with the urchin.

Bob bent down, hands on knees, trying to get his breath. As soon as he could speak he said, "Look, Mr . . ."

"Benjamin. Benjie, they calls me."

"Right, Mr Benjamin – Benjie – do me a favour. Get these boys out of the mine area and call Cready Police Station."

Benjie Benjamin shook his head and drawled, "Can't do that."

"Why ever not?"

"We bain't got no phone."

"God, give me patience! Then go somewhere that has."

"Glebe Farm's got one."

"Good. Call Cready Police and tell them there's been an explosion in the mine. We might need an ambulance as well."

"How will I know that, sir? To call the ambulance?"

"Oh, for God's sake! Leave one of the boys with me, I'll tell him and he can run up to the farm." Bob turned to Simon Prior. "You fit enough to run yet?" Simon nodded eagerly. "Right then, Benjie, you make that call and Simon here will come up as soon as we see what's what. But don't tell anyone. I don't want gawpers down here as well."

As Bob approached the mine entrance this time he was aware of an ominous silence. The earlier boom had died away completely. He'd never been behind the large metal double doors and didn't know what to expect, but the silence combined with the utter blackness after leaving bright sunshine totally unnerved him. He waited, wondering if it was safe to call out. Didn't shouting trigger avalanches? Might his bass tones bring further trouble?

He listened hard. The silence was broken by a gathering, low, rolling rumble, not unlike a train entering a station. Bob was terrified but he forced himself not to back out into the daylight. He took a step forward, and another, and another and tripped. Arms extended to break his fall he came flat against a cold wall. He moved his feet forward and back then to the side – there were raised trolley lines. Metal tracks. As far as he could tell there was only one set, and they led into nothing. He struck a match, holding his breath, half expecting to die as the blue flame lit a tiny area around him and went out immediately. The noise was getting closer, louder. *It's all right*, he thought, *it's only a trolley coming this way.* But he wasn't certain. Lighting another match, he moved towards the sound, following the tracks – forcing himself to walk into the ancient, disused mine.

From somewhere inside the earth around him there came another boom, then a series of thumps and a drumming sound, and through it all, unmistakably, came the rolling rumble. Certain he was going to be buried alive beneath this Cornish hill, Bob stopped, frozen to the spot. And the rolling rumble came nearer – and nearer.

Then, black on black, a shape appeared before him and the noise ceased.

"Jean?" It was Aubrey Chatwynde's voice. "Jean, come and help me."

"It's me, Bob Robbins." Bob's voice cracked and he had to repeat himself.

"Oh, thank God. Stay where you are, I'm trying to get Metherall to the door."

The trundling noise came closer. It suddenly dawned on Bob that he could turn back and open the doors wider to let in more light.

As he was doing so, Chatwynde pushed a wooden trolley into the main entrance. Metherall was doubled up in it like a broken doll.

"Help me get him out," Chatwynde said, "and be quick, there's a fire behind us and an adit stacked full of explosives. Jean's been using it for his . . ." Chatwynde stopped speaking, overtaken by a paroxysm of coughing.

Bob rushed to his aid and between them they half-dragged, half-lifted the victim out of the trolley. Before they could get near the open doors, though, there was a tremendous cracking sound and a deafening blast. Everything about them shook. A dense shower of dust followed by lumps of earth fell from the natural roof above. Bob could hear the very rocks around him creak and groan.

"Quick," said Chatwynde. "If we hurt him, we hurt him."

Each taking an arm over their shoulders, and with Metherall hanging perilously between them, they reached the doors and staggered outside, then staggered further to get to a safer distance. Once they'd found a soft area of grass, they stopped, and gasping, lowered Metherall to the ground. Then both bent double, coughing and coughing.

Slowly, Bob got his breathing back to normal. Kneeling down, he put a hand to the major's neck. He was still warm, the pulse strong. Apart from a deep cut across his brow, there were no other wounds to the head – that he could see – but Metherall was covered in black earth and his clothes were in tatters. Through the rents in the thick corduroy of his trousers Bob could see his legs were bleeding profusely.

The major opened his eyes and tried to speak but Bob said, "Keep still. Don't try to move." Taking off his jacket, he dropped it over the major's upper body.

"It's all right – I can see to him," Chatwynde said, joining him on the grass and pulling off his cravat. "One of my youthful aspirations was to be a doctor. I got as far tourniquets," he said by way of explanation, and began examining the major's legs. "It was when we started on the female of the species I had to stop. Women are so messy?"

Bob gaped at Chatwynde. There had just been an almighty explosion in the mine – he and Metherall had damn near been blown to smithereens – and here he was chatting as if they were leaning against the bar in the Fisherman's Boot.

As if to exemplify the thought, Chatwynde said calmly, "Do you have a clean handkerchief, Mr Robbins?"

Bob pulled himself together. "Yes, yes, sorry." He tugged a crumpled but clean handkerchief from a trouser pocket.

"I've got one, too." It was Simon Prior. "Shall I tell them to send an ambulance now?" he asked, hunkering down to inspect the major's wounds.

"No need. It'll be quicker to get him into the hospital in my car," Chatwynde said. "You still with us, Charles? I'm taking you to the hospital, all right?"

The major tried to reply, but his eyes rolled up and he fainted. Bob loosened his shirt collar and pushed the boy aside. "Out of the way, boy."

"You take his shoulders," Chatwynde said, then turned to Simon, "and you open the back door of my car. Clear anything off the back seat."

Simon rushed to obey and Bob gently lifted Metherall's shoulders. "Poor chap's torn to pieces," he said.

As they edged the injured man into the back seat there was another deep rumble from within the mine.

"Oh, God," Chatwynde gasped, "the whole place could blow up. We'd better move and fast!" He gave Metherall a less than gentle shove, ignoring the blood seeping into his ochre yellow upholstery, and jumped into the driving seat. "Get in!" he yelled.

Bob did what he could to organise the injured man's legs so they could close the back door. "Hop in the front, Simon," he ordered.

Chatwynde crashed into first gear and as they pulled away there was another booming sound. A vast tongue of flame flashed out the horizontal lookout slit, where Bob and the major had been standing less than ten minutes before. Chatwynde drove over the collapsed broken gate and turned up Smugglers Mile Hill, heading for the cottage hospital. There was no doubt in Bob's mind as to who was in charge here.

"What happened in there?" Bob asked.

"Bloody fool threw a live grenade."

"At you! Why?"

"Not directly at us – he was trying to block a side adit or gallery, whatever they call them. My young Jean has been running a sideline in explosives, not ours I hasten to add, not that that improves matters. Must have been bringing it in for weeks – had it all stacked neatly in our OB, though, bloody fool."

"Ah, right." Bob struggled to find a way to respond. The 'my young Jean' phrasing had set him a quandary, despite confirming his suspicions about the young man on the stairs in the pub. He tapped a knee with his fingers and waited for Chatwynde to either explain or take the conversation in a new direction. He was somewhat surprised at what Chatwynde said next, though.

"We've saved Metherall, thanks to you, Mr Robbins, but I rather fear Jean has done for me this time – if Metherall reports what's been going on here as he should. Not that I blame him. Only got myself to blame – as usual. One day I'll learn, I suppose. The Army takes a dim view of my choice of friends, and what Jean has been up to will put the kybosh on what's left of my career that's for sure."

Belatedly remembering the ongoing Cready explosives case, Bob got his thoughts in order. "How long has this Jean been in the area, sir?"

"In Porthferris itself, a couple of months. He has been nearby, coming and going for quite a lot longer."

"But why would he try to harm you, sir? If you're his . . ." Bob grasped rapidly for a word, "friend?"

"Buggered if I know. Literally, in this case."

Bob glanced at Simon Prior's face, wondering if he'd understood. The boy was grinning from ear to ear.

"Shame about your bow and arrow," Bob said.

Local Resistance

"I can make another one."

"No doubt you will."

Chapter 37

As soon as Charles Metherall had been delivered to the Cottage Hospital emergency department Bob told the nurse in charge there was no need for an ambulance, then called Cready Police station to tell them what had happened – they had only just received Benjie Benjamin's call. Anxious to get back to the station to talk to DI Small, Bob then remembered where he'd parked his car and asked Chatwynde to drive him back to the church. From what Metherall had said, Archibald Bantry's road accident was very likely to be buried as a military matter, but possibly not all the explosives in the mine, and DI Small had been on that case for weeks.

They collected Simon, who had been deposited in the waiting room, and set off back to Porthferris. Despite the boy's flapping ears, Bob took advantage of the journey to find out more about the mysterious pub landlord.

"I know these lanes like the back my hand now," Bob started. "Seem to spend every blessed day, to-ing and fro-ing between Cready and Porthferris. I came here to retire, get away from travelling all over the place, and what am I doing? – belting round blind bends every twenty minutes."

Chatwynde chuckled. "If you came here for a quiet life, you came at the wrong time. You should have come ten years ago."

"Yeah, well, some of us have to earn a living."

"Indeed we do, more's the pity. I would have been a dab hand at motoring down to Antibes – cocktails on the deck as the sun passed the yard arm, but it was not to be." Chatwynde slowed as a cock pheasant stalked out of a hedge at leisure, king of the road. "This lovely jalopy is the most I'll ever be able to afford, and nowhere to show it off."

"Have you always been a publican?"

"Heavens, no. I've been quite a lot of things, but, up until now, never a publican. You'd like to know what and who I am, wouldn't you, Detective Sergeant?"

"Yes, sir, that would help enormously. Off the record like this you can tell me whatever you like – if I can then ask you a couple of questions?"

Chatwynde grinned and looked in his rear-view mirror. "That suit you, young man?"

There was a rustle of paper behind him and Bob looked over his shoulder. To Bob's surprise, Simon Prior wasn't listening. The boy was engrossed in a comic he'd pinched from the waiting room. "You all right, lad?" he asked. "Not feeling queasy with your head down round these bends?"

Simon looked up. "What?"

Bob turned back to Chatwynde, "I don't think you need to worry about our passenger," he said.

Chatwynde smiled. "Very well – so what is it you are burning to know?"

"Whatever you want to tell me, sir."

"Well, starting at the beginning, my step-pa is a silverware expert in Hatton Garden. Mater was an actress until I ruined her figure. They sent me to a good school, wanted me to take up one of the professions. I tried two of them: Medicine and the Law. The first gave me the heebie-jeebies, the second sent me to sleep. So I joined the Army to become an officer in one of the flashier regiments. That would have suited me quite well, but during officer training they discovered I was good at languages and bad at following orders. Then there was a bit of an incident, while I was off-duty, I hasten to add. And I was sidelined into unofficial special ops and sent to Germany, undercover, to get me out of the way. I've stayed out of the way on and off for the past fifteen years."

Bob closed his eyes. Chatwynde spoke fluent German. Was he involved with Bantry? Was it he, the conveniently located pub landlord, who was getting information off or onto a U-boat? He said nothing, but listened more carefully.

" . . . Claiming absurd expenses was entertaining, but the salary was disappointing. Finally, I came back to London, started looking for a niche and a new occupation. Followed up a few contacts, got in touch with a few old pals, and then, unfortunately, the week after war was declared there was another little incident with another member of the great and good. So I came down here to help the war effort in less conspicuous surroundings. That's about it, really. Except for Jean – you'll want to know about him, of course."

Chatwynde halted at the crossroads, then drove in silence and stopped at Albert Villas. "Which one?" he asked, leaning round to look at the boy.

"This one," Simon replied and slipped out of the car.

"Oy!" Bob called. "Shouldn't you be saying thank you to Mr Chatwynde?"

"He should be saying 'thank you' to me," Simon replied. "I was the one who shot his Johnny."

So the boy had been earwigging. Bob tried not to laugh.

Chatwynde shrugged, raised a yellow-gloved hand in farewell and drove on. "His name is Jean Blanc, or Jan Kowalski, or Gianni Bianco, depending where he is. They may all be false names, of course. He was born in Paris, though, I'm pretty sure about that. I also know he worked in Turin, became a communist then went back to France to spread the word. That's how I met him. When I came back to England he followed, said he wanted to see Karl Marx's grave. He used my flat. This is what he's told me, anyway. It's probably a pack of lies. However, I do think he has been in constant contact with an Italian communist cell, and I also think he's involved in a plan to overthrow Mussolini. He's certainly no Nazi spy so don't judge him too harshly. "

"You can say that, can you? – after he's just tried to kill you?"

"No! Come on, Detective Sergeant. He was trying to block the tunnel where he's been storing his gelignite. Poor boy was in a total frenzy while the sappers were reinforcing the tunnels, moving it in and out of one place, then another. I suppose he's been sending it to Italy, though heaven knows how – via neutral Spain, perhaps, by boat to Vigo, then on to Barcelona . . ."

"By boat, it would be. The mooring rings on the Wheal Marie quay were shiny. I noticed that weeks ago." Bob fell to wondering if Jean-Gianni was responsible for taking Stan Hawkins' boat out of his sea cave, but decided to say nothing until he'd spoken to DI Small.

"Well, if it was by boat – and I suppose it had to be – how else, except by plane? – I should be pleased. He was always wanting to borrow my car. I did wonder if he'd take off in it one day and I'd never see it or him again. That's why I bought him the motorbike."

Chatwynde passed the quay car park outside his pub and drove on up Church Lane, past Bayview and Maisie Hawkins' cottage towards the church. Bob looked out of the window. It had started to rain. Seeing Maisie Hawkins' cottage made him reverse his earlier decision to hold back on the missing boat mystery. The more he learned, the faster he could eliminate an unpleasant nagging doubt. "Was this French chap using the sea caves, do you know?" he asked.

"You're asking about Hawkins' tunnel? Could have been. Probably. He was certainly using the girl. Yes, actually, he could have been stashing his explosives in the mine via Hawkins' tunnel. I knew we'd have to wall it up completely pretty soon, but he could have got in that way."

"Did you know he'd been staying in Mrs Hawkins' cottage, and walking out with her daughter?"

Chatwynde sighed, "I found out – he'd been filching cigarettes and . . ."

"It's all right. I know all about that."

"Yes, I rather feared you did."

Bob rattled his fingers against the leather panelling under the window. "Was he taking explosives from your OB store in the mine, or from elsewhere? The Cready works, for example?"

"Cready, yes, I'm afraid so. We didn't keep much gelignite in the mine – for the OB. I don't know what he's been taking from our stores, to be honest. And we won't know now, either."

"You said he'd been in the area a while?"

Chatwynde changed gear and passed a cyclist. "He had a supplier, one of the workers. You ought to check it out. Might be someone from his lodging house, from when he first came down here – before I could risk letting him stay with me. I can't give you an address, but he rented a room in the town."

"Thanks, I'll see to it. Did he use the Bayview sea cave instead of, or as well as, the Hawkins tunnel? You know what happened to Mrs Waterson, I suppose."

"Yes, but that wasn't him, although I can't prove it. He was using Ginny as a way to hide his goods, and make a bit on the side from what her pa had stockpiled. There was someone from Plymouth who collected Hawkins' goods and they struck some sort of deal. That happened by accident, apparently. He was down on the Hawkins' beach when a

Plymouth racketeer arrived and assumed he was down there to meet him. Waterson dabbles a bit on the side as well. But I honestly don't think Jean was their intruder. He wouldn't bash an old lady about – not without very good reason."

"And if he had a very good reason?"

"No. What reason could there be? He had Hawkins' stuff – didn't need our scotch as well."

Bob registered the word 'our' and filed it.

"Here's your car, Detective Sergeant. I hope I've been of more use than a mere taxi service."

Bob waited until Chatwynde had pulled in behind his humble little Morris, then said, "Thank you, sir. I may be seeing you again, but thank you for what you've told me. You won't forget the list you were going to make for me – Miss Pettit's jewellery?"

"Already compiled. I'll drop it in, as you requested. One thing, Detective Sergeant – you will keep what you know about the mine to yourself, won't you? I don't know if we'll ever be able to use it again for what we planned, but . . ."

"Mum's the word, and let's hope there's never any need to use it. I shall have to follow up the missing gelignite, though. We've been on the explosives case too long to overlook it."

"I doubt you'll catch Jean – not now."

"Personally, I'll be happy if the thefts just stop, but it's for my boss to decide." Bob opened his door, but before he got out he turned back and said, "How well do you actually know Miss Pettit?"

Chatwynde laughed. "I don't think anybody really *knows* Miss Pettit."

"Any idea why she would have taken the contents of her glass cabinet up to stay at her sister's house?"

Chatwynde frowned. "Can't have been much. She only had a carpet bag and a small case, and they weren't particularly heavy. You'll have to ask Maisie Hawkins and Ginny about that."

"You don't happen to know how she knew the Bantrys?"

"Did she? No, she never mentioned it to me."

"Well, thanks again."

Bob closed the car door and Chatwynde drove off. Strolling leisurely round to his economy-version vehicle, he paused at the driver's door then straightened up and crossed the road at a quick march. Entering the ancient churchyard, he made straight for the broken gate into the spinney. Then he stopped and backtracked a few steps. Sitting snug but damp in the lee of a leaning gravestone was a patch of pretty white toadstools. Bob pulled out a second handkerchief and used it as a glove to pick one. It smelt of vanilla ice-cream. He picked another one, then, folding them carefully into the cotton, tucked them into his jacket pocket.

Returning to the car Bob remembered Mrs Hughes' offer of coffee. It was very tempting. He was feeling very cold with a post-trauma chill down his back, but the information he needed could wait until the toadstools had been identified and DI Small informed about the explosives.

Chapter 38

The weather on Sunday morning was as bright as a Cornish summer morning can be, but Bob and Laurie prepared for a change in the weather and took the planned boat trip. Bob showed Laurie what the Deakin twins had shown him a few weeks earlier – how to set up a rod and line in a moving boat. Laurie showed him how to get out of the tiny natural harbour, past the rocks and along the short stretch of coast with the sea caves.

It was quite chilly out on the water so they didn't waste time. They stopped the engine when they were facing the narrow cove below the Hawkins' cottage, and, despite the bobbing boat and tugging current, managed to test Bob's theory about sight lines to get in, at what points lights might have been set at night or signals given from the road or cottage above. Then, using oars, they pulled back around the rocks, into the wider private beach belonging to Bayview.

As Laurie had warned him, the currents were very strong and the water very choppy. Nevertheless, Bob confirmed his idea that anyone with a working knowledge of boats and tides, and who knew this area of the coast, could get into either cove and deliver or collect goods at high or low tide, day or night.

Laurie was starting the engine to get out of the Bayview cove when Bob said, "No, wait. How deep is it out here, do you think?"

"At high tide? It'll be pretty deep further out, I'd say. But over there – not very. There are rocks a good way out at low tide."

"So a large vessel couldn't get in?"

"Like a trawler? No. Although the sea lane is extremely deep – that's how ships come into Devonport and the Barbican. Back in the old days sailing ships moored out there and the local smugglers went out to them in skiffs. They'd have had to bring their goods in that way, off the cargo ships anyway."

Bob rubbed his chin. "Or a submarine." Laurie looked at him. "I know, you don't follow. Look, if a submarine surfaced out here and inflated one or more rubber dinghies they could get into these coves and into Porthferris harbour without too much trouble, or any noise, couldn't they?"

"Yes. You'd need more than one man to row, perhaps, but yes. Why, Sarge?"

"Something Maisie Hawkins told me, then Major Metherall told me something else, and I'm trying to put them together to make something to go in a report that sounds plausible and a lot less like an adventure story. Maisie Hawkins told me the night her old man went missing there was a tall, dark stranger lurking on the quay. Metherall told me *he'd been told* a submarine was surfacing off Porthferris Bay. Now, suppose our tall, dark stranger is meeting – and delivering something to a German sub . . ."

"Like a waterproof tube of maps, Sarge?"

"For instance."

"You're saying Bantry was definitely a German spy? That's why he had all that gear in his house? So men could come ashore as well, and get identity papers?"

"Possibly, yes."

"And that's why he was killed, and his wife?"

"Not necessarily. But I don't think the car was an accident. He was done for in the car by person or persons unknown, but somehow connected to Mr Ezra Paddon, or I'm a Chinaman. Although – and this is where it gets stickier – he was also poisoned. The poisoning – the poisoned sugar and chutney – are Miss Pettit's doing and something separate. I don't have to prove anything related to the Bantry incident, the Redcaps are dealing with it. But we both know there are a good few people in Porthferris who had a reason to want Bantry out of the way. Not that we can do anything – it's out of our hands. No, I'd like to nail the black marketeers, and find out what Miss P was up to."

"Why are you still worried about the Bantry case, Sarge, if the Military Police are on it?"

"Because Mrs Hawkins says she saw Bantry the night her husband disappeared."

"And you think Bantry killed Stan Hawkins?"

"You don't think it holds up?"

Laurie shrugged. "Doesn't sound very likely. Hawkins was a big chap. I'd back him in any fight, even if he was drunk. Why should Mrs Hawkins need to testify to seeing Bantry, anyway? More to the point, why may she not want to? I don't follow."

"She's got her reasons. We need to find her old man's body first, anyway. Forget it. You're right; we need to focus on *Mrs* Bantry and our friendly neighbourhood poisoner."

"I thought all that was tied up. Ginny Hawkins has explained about the sugar and we've got the lab report on the chutney and the pie, and buns as well. And you've found the toadstools. No wonder I was sick those days."

"Comes of being greedy, I told you."

Laurie Oliver looked out at the surging water, then back at the Bayview cove. "No, wait, suppose *Mr* Hawkins saw what Bantry was doing. Could Bantry have attacked him – taken him by surprise? I mean if Hawkins was so drunk he couldn't defend himself . . ."

"Or not Bantry, but a German . . . Listen, if a Jerry sailor comes ashore prepared to meet trouble – knife in hand, for example, and Hawkins sees him and he's in the way . . . Yes, Hawkins might have died for being in the way. But it was a stormy night. What would they have been doing trying to get into Hawkins' cove? That he was obtaining and selling rationed goods and liquor, I'm prepared to believe, but Hawkins as a spy or vigilant citizen prepared to risk his life to save his country, nah. And I'm pretty certain he didn't follow his wife down the hill that night – he'd have surely tried to help her or get her to come home – no, he wouldn't have been on the quay when Bantry was there. Whatever happened, it happened in that blasted cove or the sea cave itself."

"Perhaps the German dinghy couldn't get back to the sub from the harbour. There was a storm – perhaps they got blown round here and pulled in for shelter. Inflatable dinghies are the devil to manoeuvre, they float *on* the water not *in* it, you see."

"I see. And Hawkins was down in his cove trying to get into the sea cave to get dry."

"Why?"

"Because he hadn't got a door key."

"It's possible then. He might have seen them. Although Chatwynde said it was well past ten-thirty when he left the pub, so it was pitch black."

"The U-boat might have had a light – to signal, at least, so they could get back to it."

Laurie stared out to sea. "There must have been a light on Hawkins' little beach. He'd have had a torch – everyone carries them these days. Yes, that's possible. That's how the Germans got into the cove. They saw a light and thought it was a signal . . . and why they – or someone – cut the rope of Hawkins' boat." Laurie Oliver had got the bit between his teeth. Seeing the event in his mind's eye, he began a running commentary: "The tide pushes the German dinghy into the cove, like it did to us when we were kids and we were out sailing – and that was summer. They pull their boat up out of the water. Hawkins is using a torch. He sees a boat coming in, even though there's a storm, and assumes he's getting a delivery. Goes out to help them, sees they are in uniform or something like that, and they cut his throat – or shoot him, but that would make a noise. They put him in his boat – so he won't be found on the little beach, cut the rope, and set him adrift. No, they use *his* boat with its engine to get back to the sub, towing their inflatable dinghy, which is much lighter in the water. Not sure about that. Then they tow Hawkins' boat out even further and set it loose, with Hawkins in it. That's why neither he nor the boat has washed up on the coast round here."

"Bloody hell!" Bob said, then went very quiet.

After a while, Laurie said, "We haven't caught any fish."

"Haven't we? I'd say *you've* got a ruddy great big one!"

Bob, grinning from ear to ear, gazed at the young policeman sitting by the propeller with paternal satisfaction. The lad looked about twelve, wearing civvies. Laurie caught his eye and gave his Stan Laurel hunch.

"Right, get that engine going," said Bob. "I'm freezing the family jewels off sitting here. Get us back and we'll have a warming drop of scotch in the pub, and we won't ask where it came from. Then we're getting straight back to Cready to tell DI Small your theory. Bit of luck, we'll tie up the Hawkins mystery and find Miss Pettit before the end of next week, and have a real day off."

"Won't you have to go up to Ilfracombe?"

"Certainly will. D'you want a stick of rock?"

Chapter 39

Despite it being Sunday, DI Small was in his office. "Do you have a moment, guv?" Bob asked.

"I do. Come in. Give me a break from all this paperwork. I wish I'd never accepted promotion now, all I ever do is admin and nag people about things I can't do myself." DI Small indicated chairs by his desk. "I thought you two were off duty today."

"We are. I was showing PC Oliver a bit of sea angling and the lad's – PC Oliver – has come up with a pretty convincing theory about the missing fisherman, Stan Hawkins."

"I see. Pull up another chair."

Laurie pulled a chair in front of the detective inspector's desk, sat down and folded his hands in his lap like a nun. Bob wanted to laugh; instead, he sat down in the other chair and reached over to squeeze the boy's arm.

DI Small studied their faces one after the other and said, "Right, let's hear it. But start from day one, even if you've told me before."

Bob drummed his fingers on his knees, wondering how much to reveal about Stan Hawkins. Maisie hadn't sworn him to secrecy, and he didn't want to cause her any more trouble than was necessary. She'd had a barrel load most of her life, from what he could see. And he didn't need to build his career on dramatic arrests and successful convictions, either. In a year or two he'd be back in his deck chair, God willing. It was, perhaps, why he'd let the Stan Hawkins issue drag on: initially certain they were going to find the body washed up on a beach, then later, convinced the man had got trapped in the old mine. He'd always been certain in his own mind that Hawkins hadn't gone off of his own accord, but . . . and much as he liked Laurie's interpretation and really didn't want to accept an alternative, alternatives did have to be examined. Hawkins *could have* been in cahoots with Jean-Gianni, and for whatever reason, the vicious Frenchman *could have* cut Hawkins' throat to conceal what he was doing with stolen explosives. Maisie *could have* contrived a nasty accident for her husband, she had good reason. And charming Mr Chatwynde, having had the appropriate training, *could have* done away with Hawkins himself. Chatwynde *could also be* a double agent or something equally dramatic linked to the German sub theory . . .

Bob blew through his cheeks, wondering where to start. Opening with the dodgy Frenchman, meant he could get to the Hawkins affair via the black market goods and the stolen explosives, circumventing mention of the wife. He quickly ran through a running order: what to present first, second and third, and how to lead into Laurie Oliver's colourful but perfectly plausible solution, that Hawkins had been killed and dragged out to sea by the crew of a German U-boat. It tallied with what Maisie had told him about Bantry being on the quay that night, and Metherall's theory about the U-boat coming in for water, the Watersons' missing veg, and Bantry's maps showing new airfields and Navy installations for the Nazi war machine.

After all that, he'd start on the Miss Pettit saga and ask for a couple of days to go up to Ilfracombe. He'd called the police station there, but they'd been less than willing to take on extra work. There was a "search and arrest call" out to all the other seaside resorts and similar watering holes for the well-heeled that were represented in the Oakleys' cabinet.

Twenty years in the Force and another ten investigating insurance frauds had provided Bob with ample contacts. One way or another, he'd make sure they found the mad spinster before she baked another poison pie, and keep Ginny Hawkins from being charged with the Bantry woman's murder.

"Well?" prompted DI Small. "Come on, out with it. Start from the beginning and let's go through all we know about the crime haven of Porthferris, then you can let PC Oliver give me his theory himself."

Bob began with Stan Hawkins' sea cave. As he was talking, DI Small took notes. When Bob finally came to the end of his convoluted story, Small tapped the paper in front of him. "You're overlooking something here, Bob. In a village like Porthferris everybody knows everybody. They know *all* their secrets because their knowledge of each goes back generations. You say there's a 'bit of illicit buying and selling' going on, what some may call profiteering and some call contraband or smuggling. It's not romantic, it's racketeering in wartime – but it will have kept most of them quiet because they can't risk blowing the gaff on each other. They may not have told you anything, but I guarantee they all know what's what – except perhaps what happened to the fisherman that night."

"This also relates to Bantry," Bob said. "He had some sort of file on people in the village. His wife told us that in so many words. It went missing the day of his accident."

"A file – reports?"

"I think so. It might only be a list of fraudulent coupons and extra rations, but somewhere along the line he knew what was going on and either wanted in, was already part of it, or he was hated sufficiently for one or more of them to . . . But that's for the MPs sort out – if they choose to. Except someone stole papers from Bantry's briefcase for a reason."

"The whole village, I wouldn't wonder. All right, let's set that aside and hear what PC Oliver thinks about the missing Mr Hawkins."

Laurie Oliver, speaking quietly and modestly, related what he'd told Bob in the boat. In clear, concise language he explained how and why a number of unknown enemy sailors had been coming into Porthferris harbour, how their dinghy could have been dragged by the tide around the cliffs, how they had seen a light in Hawkins' cove and killed the man on the beach beneath his home; how and why the rope on Hawkins' small boat had been cut; and how and why they then towed said boat out to sea and either sank it or set it loose, with the body of Stan Hawkins inside.

Bob sniffed, satisfied in a slightly envious manner that he'd just heard a future Superintendant or Chief Constable speaking. He'd tied himself in knots trying to sort out the links in the Porthferris business and explain it in plain English, and young Laurie Oliver had just delivered an utterly convincing scenario without a moment's hesitation.

DI Small caught Bob's eye and raised his eyebrows. "Type it up. I'll give you till Tuesday to finish it. Not that we can do anything to close the Hawkins case without the body, or the man turns up live and well – you know that, don't you?"

Bob nodded. "And the Bantrys?"

"Well, he at least is out of our hands, as we keep saying. We're following up the connection with the explosives. We've started asking at lodging houses in town – thanks for that. I'll continue with that until it's closed. Let's see if we can run this Frenchman to ground and get the chaps who've been supplying him. Bloody nuisance that mine's not safe to go in anymore."

"Is it worth bringing Chatwynde in for questioning on that?" Bob asked.

"We can, but we'll need permission, Chatwynde's protected in high places."

Bob scowled and DI Small held up a hand, "Don't ask me to tell you how I know, I can't and shan't. Look, Bob, let Constable Oliver do the Hawkins report so you can focus on the *Mrs* Bantry business. We need that poisoning sorted out as fast as possible, before she gets involved in anything elsewhere."

Bob took a deep breath. "I've already got everything Ginny Hawkins can tell us written down. I've been ringing round to follow up the seaside souvenirs."

"Do you have a motive as to why a perfectly respectable little spinster wanted to murder a perfectly respectable member of St Chad's parish?"

"No – but . . ." Bob was tired from the boat trip and the events of recent days and wasn't thinking clearly.

"Martha Collins. Alton," Laurie Oliver mumbled out of the corner of his mouth

"That is, yes. I'm onto it. I have to contact Hampshire CID again, but it's moving." Bob caught Laurie's eye and gave a nod of thanks.

DI Small leaned back in his chair, "Find the Pettit woman," he said. "Forget the bottles of whisky and the NAAFI jam; we're not likely to put a stop to that and they're too small fry to take up our time now. Mind you, if you do come across names to show there's a wider network of suppliers behind the Porthferris locals, let me know. We'll have to find out about who supplied Hawkins, eventually, and we'll certainly have to inform Devonport about the NAAFI goods."

"Anything else, guv?" Bob asked.

"No. Just find the Pettit woman, and fast."

"I need to go up to Ilfracombe first. It'll take a couple of days, counting the journey, and I'll need a bigger petrol allowance."

"Granted. Smile, Bob. You can retire again when this is all over."

Bob gave one of his wry grins and got up.

Laurie hastened to his feet beside him and started to move his chair back to its original place, but DI Small stopped him. "Not you, Constable. I'd like a few words before you go."

Bob hovered at the door.

"Off you go, Bob. PC Oliver's safe with me."

Bob did a mock salute and went back to his office. Then changed his mind and went down to the canteen for a hot cuppa and a bun. He was going to need some energy before he called an insurance agent in Alton, Hampshire, then packed his bag for the wilds of North Devon.

Chapter 40

Not long after setting out, Bob regretted not bringing a compass, and not asking for Laurie Oliver. The boy could have nipped out at junctions to ask locals which road for Launceston, then which road for every other town he needed to go through. "'Tis a fair old treck," Mallett had warned, and he'd ignored him, to his detriment. There were barely enough sandwiches to get out of Cornwall, and certainly not enough tea in the thermos to see him over the Devon border.

More by accident than map-reading skills, Bob reached the rugged north coast of Devon and deliberately turned off the main road onto a coastal track. Parking at a safe distance, he walked a short way to sit on the springy grass of a cliff top and watch brutal rollers churn between giant rocks below. This was a part of England he didn't know, and, sitting alone, perched above the wild Atlantic, was a strange and moving experience: utterly peaceful, yet exhilarating at the same time. The sea here had a special sort of excitement. Joan would have known the right word. Joan would have loved it.

Still thinking of Joan, silently pointing out blooms in hedges, russet-red cows, the way moorland changed to cattle pasture and led into single-street villages, then small country towns, Bob reached Barnstaple and stopped for a tea break. It was getting dark when he finally drove down through genteel ivory-yellow brick terraces into Ilfracombe harbour. He was starving, visualising cheese on toast, and knew the best he could hope for was a landlady's scorn. So he was tickled pink to find a small booth selling fish and chips on the quay.

Wandering around the harbour with his precious package wrapped in greasy newspaper, Bob was as content as he had been for a long time. Except this wasn't a place to be on one's own, either. It was somewhere to be with a wife and kiddies, to share your thoughts and laugh at naughty postcards.

When he found the bed and breakfast he'd booked by telephone, the landlady had gone to a council meeting, but her husband was "on duty" – his words. Mr Watts, a retired shopkeeper who evidently missed his customers, was very happy to talk to someone new.

"Policeman, eh?" he started as Bob showed him his card in explanation as to why he was visiting Ilfracombe. "Can't say we've ever had a policeman here before. You investigating a crime in Ilfracombe? Can't say as I remember seeing anything about a crime in the paper this week, not a proper crime, if you know what I mean? Not in the local paper. Not in the North Devon Gazette, neither. That I know of."

Bob ran his fingers down a set of imaginary scales on the table that served as a desk and counted himself blessed. "It's nothing very recent, but if it was in the paper it's something you'd likely remember. There were two ladies staying in a hotel here. One was a widow, I believe, the other was her companion." Bob wasn't entirely sure about any of this but it made a good start.

"We got a few like that between the wars. Still here, some of them. Widows who lost their hubbies in the Great War, they come down here for a change of scenery. Some of them stay on as long-term residents in the hotels. I was in ladies outfitting so I met a good few war widows, especially when I went up to the Rock Hotel or over to the Gables or the Grand with deliveries."

Bob smiled. "You may have met the lady we're looking for, then."

"The widow or the companion?"

"Well, I'm not sure she was a companion, but it's likely. Small, neat, spinster-type. Beaky sort of nose. Perhaps with a wealthy widow."

"You're not talking about the Gables jewel murder, are you? Not that it was a proper murder, of course, but, oh my goodness, that was a to-do. Whole town was talking about it. Oh, yes, I remember that, all right. In all the papers, it was. The companion stole her employer's jewellery and all her money and left the poor woman for dead."

"Left her for dead?"

"Well, I don't know all the facts, only what was in the papers. They'll tell you at the police station – best you ask there."

"Yes, I'm going there first thing in the morning. So . . ." Bob measured his words, "presumably a waitress or a chamber maid heard what had happened and . . ."

"That's right. All over town, it was. The big mystery was where the companion had got to. There's only one bus of a morning into Barnstaple, you see, and another that crosses the moor for Taunton, but none of the drivers or conductors remembered seeing her, and there's no railway station here to catch a train. I think, and I told my wife at the time, while the police were in and out of the hotel for days on end, the companion must have been hiding right here – in the town. I don't reckon she went anywhere at all. How could she, unless she'd got a car? Course, she could have had a car. Not usual, but she could have. What d'you think of that, eh?"

"You don't happen to remember the woman's name?"

"Which one?"

"Er – either."

"The widow had a funny double-barrelled name." Mr Watts screwed up his face and pursed bluish lips. "No. Don't recall. They'll tell you up at the station. Proper to-do, it was."

Bob didn't go to the police station next morning as he had originally intended – he made straight for The Gables Hotel. Choosing a chair on the front terrace with a good view, he ordered a cup of coffee then sipped at a cup of brown liquid while apparently perusing the morning paper. It looked as if the hotel hadn't changed in years, and neither had the staff. Getting the waitress, who had likely witnessed the laying of the foundation stone, to chat to him was no problem at all. The disappearing companion had been with a Mrs Crabtree-Gatwood or Crabtree-Attwood.

"It was definitely Crabtree-something-or-other, though, because I'm afraid we used to joke about it, sir. I'm ashamed to say that, but it's true. She was always making a fuss over her food, you see. Couldn't eat this, wouldn't eat that. 'Crabby old woman, give her crab apples,' we used to say." The waitress touched her starched cap as if to check its fixture, then shook her head slowly from side to side. "It was awful, sir. And it wasn't *natural*. I know they say it was, but I can't believe it. She was a big woman, you see. She didn't like our food much, but she must have been eating cream teas and ice-cream sundaes down on the promenade because – well, she wasn't thin, sir. I think she liked to make a fuss, that's all. There wasn't really anything wrong with her tummy. Not in my opinion. Not that anyone ever asked."

"And her companion? Do you remember her?"

"I do, and I wish I didn't. Nice lady. Small, very clean. Nice. She'd wink at me sometimes when Mrs Crabtree made a fuss over her soup. I liked her. We all liked her. It was a proper shock when we found out it was her that had taken the jewel box and the money. At least that's what they say.

Then when I thought about it after and we talked together, it wasn't a shock at all, not really."

"But the police didn't find her."

"No! She disappeared, sir. That showed, we said, she must have been guilty. And like as not she'd planned it. Not that she knew that Mrs Crabtree was going to pass away or . . ." The waitress looked about her and lowered her voice. "It *might* have been *murder*." She touched her cap again then nodded her grey head knowingly. "We did wonder, sir, at the time."

Bob left a generous tip under his half-full cup and set off to call in at the police station, knowing he almost certainly wasn't going to learn much more about the incident than he'd already been told.

He spent a fruitless half-hour with the officer he had spoken to previously on the phone, learning only that Mrs Crabtree-Gatwood had died of a heart attack brought on by shock, and there had been no toxicology report. Uniformed police had searched the local area, but they had never located the missing companion. The officer was very cagey about the so-called search and reluctant to tell him anything further. *Because* thought Bob, *they were neatly out-witted by a little spinster-woman.*

Chapter 41

The following evening, Ned MacManus settled into the one of Bob's old easy-chairs and magicked a twelve-year-old single malt from between his stethoscope and tongue-depressors in the depths of his medical bag.

Bob's eyes lit up and he fetched the appropriate glasses. "Are we drinking to anything special?" he asked.

"Depends. For my part, it's Dutch courage, I'm afraid. There's something I should have told you and for one reason or another I haven't with all the goings-on in the village, and what happened at the mine. That's all over the place, by the way, thanks to young Simon Prior." He poured liquid gold into their tumblers. "Ach, I don't know if you'll think I'm just being daft."

"Try me." Bob sipped his whisky and sat back to listen.

"It was a few weeks ago. I'd had a bad day, took a couple of tumblers of this stuff and turned in pretty late, and the telephone rang, as it always does on the nights you're most tired. It was the midwife, Nurse Brown. She was struggling to bring another little Deakin into the world in Inner Harbour. I got my bag and set off straight away. As you know, my cottage is in the terrace near Paddon's garage. I was low on petrol, so when I got to the top of Porth Hill, I coasted down to the harbour and parked on the quay. There's no way you can get four wheels into that Inner Harbour labyrinth."

The doctor was nervous; he took another gulp of whisky. Bob waited.

"Now here's the thing. When I got out of the car . . . It's the smell, you see: that special night-time-by-the-sea smell, the lap-lap of a turning tide, always takes me back to Caithness. I went over to the edge of the quay to spend a moment. Just a wee moment, breathing in the night, listening to small boats clinking on the water and . . . and there was something else. I couldn't make it out at first because it seemed so out of place, but it was the low, heavy chug of an engine out in the bay. Then it stopped and there was silence, except the boats clinked more because there must have been a strong wash. The entrance to the harbour is narrow, but something set the boats moving." He paused.

"And?" Bob asked, gently.

"And then I – I thought – I wasn't sure, but . . . No, I was sure, but I was scared, to be honest. Someone else was on the quay; someone else was standing there – waiting for me to move first, to leave. How do I know that? I don't." Ned McManus laughed. "You'll say it was a foolish fancy – the whisky, the cold night."

"No, Ned. I shan't say that because you aren't the only one to tell me this."

"Am I not? Well, there was someone. But it was a full-tide, a clear sky – a smugglers' night if ever there was one, so I didn't want to see any of it. I kept my head down to avoid embarrassment. It's a small community here and being the local doctor I . . . you know what I mean?"

Bob nodded. "I'd probably have done the same, and I'm a policeman."

"So I headed for the alleys. I got to the Deakins' row, located the cottage where I was needed and put my hand out to knock at the door." Ned extended an arm to show what happened. "But before I actually knocked, I turned around; I had the distinct sensation that there was someone behind me. I looked back the way I'd come and caught sight of a sort of angular figure crossing the entrance to the alley. Tall, male. On his own. He was holding something – a length of pipe, a telescope, perhaps. I called out, "Good evening to you!" He halted, then he shot off at a run."

Bob slowly nodded his head in understanding and gestured for the doctor to continue.

"The midwife hadn't been wrong to call me. It was a difficult birth – twins. Another set of boys to keep the Deakin name and their remarkable ability to breed identical twins going. Afterwards, I joined the father and various uncles and cousins to wet the babes' heads and didn't give the incident in the alley another thought until you said something recently and planted an idea in my mind. And even then I didn't connect it to bringing those Deakin bairns safely into a world at war."

Bob put his glass down. "Can you say who you think it was you saw?"

"I can, but there's more. And I think it's connected in some way. When I was on my way back home there were lights on in Paddon's garage. I mean, with the blackout, seeing any light on at night is strange these days. It was a very low light, candles maybe. I don't want to drop him in trouble, but I couldn't help noticing because it seemed odd. Ezra Paddon's a righteous-living, tee-total Wesleyan; he's the last man to be up and about in the small hours. I'd coasted back down the hill and I had to slam on my brakes, switch on the engine and reverse. 'Everything all right, Ezra?' I asked. 'Do you need me?' He was still in his brown overalls. I think he sleeps in them. Anyway, he came out of his workshop even angrier than usual. 'Who's asking?' he shouted. You know what he's like. 'It's me, Ezra,' I said. 'I saw your light on. Have you a problem? Someone ill?' There was a big motorcycle I didn't recognise propped against the workshop wall. 'Has there been an accident?' I asked, pointing at the bike.

"The thing is, I could see a younger person behind him. I assumed it was Shadrach, but Ezra – *without turning round* – said something, and whoever it was disappeared. Then he said, 'We'm all perfect, no accidents yer. You get on home'."

Ned mimicked Paddon's Cornish accent perfectly, making Bob smile.

"So I did. And I forgot about it until, as I said, something you told me – and then I heard what Benjie Benjamin told Alf Plowden about what happened at the mine and it reminded me. You see Ezra spoke to the boy behind him – and the boy must have done what he was told – in the dark. So it couldn't have been Shadrach Paddon. Shadrach is stone deaf. He needs to watch your face to lip-read. Then I thought it was the other deaf boy that was working with them. But Alf has been telling me what they are saying in the village about the explosion and some foreign fellow called Yan or Johnny with a motorbike, and I wondered if it was him that was at the garage."

"It almost certainly was. If it makes you feel better, we know all about Jean-Gianni. He's French, by the way. Was that who you saw on the quay?"

"No," – Ned paused – "that was Archibald Bantry."

"Ah."

"You're not surprised? What could the man have been doing, though? And why so suspicious?"

"Would you be prepared to come into the station and report it was Bantry before I contact the Redcaps? And about the sound of a big vessel out on the water?"

"Well, it's as I just explained – I wasn't sure."

"But you are right," Bob said, "and as you're a doctor and you know how to keep a secret, I'll tell you why."

As Bob stood at his front door, waiting for the doctor to drive off, the black sky above filled with the heavy, menacing chunter of unseen aircraft. It sounded like old Manchesters leaving to cross the coast, not coming inland, so almost definitely British. But he wasn't sure. He waved pointlessly in the dark as the doctor's car pulled away and closed the door against the night and the war.

Sitting down again in front of what remained of his fire, Bob mused on what to do next. Ned MacManus had saved Maisie Hawkins from making a statement that would land her in a lot of unpleasantness. It could all go in Laurie Oliver's report, and with a bit of luck the matter would be closed.

That just left the personal matter that had been nagging at him for months now. Much as he liked Laurie's theory about why Hawkins and his boat had gone missing, he wanted to be absolutely one hundred per cent sure Maisie Hawkins hadn't actively murdered her husband.

Chapter 42

One week later, Detective Sergeant Bob Robbins was well away from Porthferris in the popular holiday resort of Weston-Super-Mare in Somerset. Rain lashed the seafront horizontally, sending the more determined day trippers into whatever shelter they could find. The less determined had stayed at home. Bob pulled his collar up, his cap down, and, trying not to run, headed for the doorway of the next hotel.

The girl at the reception desk gave him a dubious look and said, "Can I help you?" meaning she'd really rather not.

Bob pulled his identity card from his inner pocket and said, "Yes, I'm trying to trace a Miss Pettit: Maud Lily Pettit. I'm a police detective."

"Oh," the girl squeaked. "I don't think we have anyone of that name."

But before she could run a finger down the names in her register Bob had swivelled it round and was running his own damp forefinger down the list of guests, blurring names as the ink ran. He flipped back through the days, a week, two weeks, and then, "Here we are."

The girl peered at the book sideways. "That's not Pettit."

"No, but Miss Magdalene Lillian Patton is close. Room nine." Bob looked at the row of keys behind the desk. "She's out."

"Miss Patton generally goes out after luncheon with Mrs Chiltern. They've become good friends." The girl smiled, showing rather horsey teeth.

"And Mrs Chiltern is staying here for the summer?"

"Mrs Chiltern has been with us since the Blitz. She was bombed out and has taken up residence here."

Bob rattled his fingers on the polished wood. "And Mrs Chiltern comes from . . .?"

"Oh, I can't reveal information about our guests. That wouldn't be correct."

Bob sighed. What was it about receptionists that turned them officious and la-di-dah the moment you asked for anything useful? "No, of course not. I'll come back with a search warrant, shall I?"

"Oh!" The squeak was a tone higher. "I better fetch Mrs Walters – she owns the hotel."

"It's all right, love. I'll come back later, if need be. Just tell me where I might find . . ." he peered down at the book, "Miss Patton on this damp and dreary afternoon."

"I believe they go to the tea rooms on the promenade."

Bob picked up his waxed-cotton cap and smudged the wet circle it had made on the counter with his sleeve. Giving the girl a grateful grin, he made his way back into the rain and walked along the sea front in the direction of the town. Weston-super-Mare on a wet day. It was the end of the world.

Miss Pettit or Miss Patton was sitting at a small table with a woman wearing a burgundy outfit and flowered hat that resembled an overstuffed armchair and matching lampshade. Their cups were empty and the cake plate bare. Bob watched them for a moment or two before approaching, wondering what Miss Pettit would remember from their previous meeting. Eventually, chivvied by a waitress to take a seat, he removed his cap and made for her table. "Miss Patton?"

The bright pigeon eyes looked up. She gave a vague, blank smile.

"I thought it was you," Bob said.

Miss Pettit continued smiling then looked at her companion. "Victoria, this is Mr . . ."

"Detective Sergeant Robbins. Pleased to meet you. Would you excuse us a few minutes, Mrs Chiltern? I'd like a word with Miss Patton. It's a private matter, but I expect you'll hear all about it later." He put a hand on Miss Pettit's chair, giving her no alternative but to get to her feet.

The immediate problem was where he could talk to her, inside or out. He decided on out and propelled her past the coat rack to collect her mackintosh then across the road to a glass-sided shelter on the promenade. Miss Pettit, or Miss Patton, sat primly on the damp, cold bench, her lizard-skin handbag gripped between her small hands on her lap, her toes barely touching the floor.

"You know why I'm here, don't you, Miss Pettit? Or is it Miss Patton?"

"Neither. I was christened Marion Pauline Pratt but I never liked the name."

"And in Ilfracombe you were Myra Lavinia Priestley."

"You've been to Ilfracombe? Such a nice place."

"And a pleasant hotel. The Gables, wasn't it?"

Miss Pettit cocked her head to one side and gave him an appraising look. "Oh, dear, well, it was bound to come out eventually," she said. Then after a moment's thought added more brightly, "The policemen in Ilfracombe aren't very quick, you know."

"No, I agree with you on that one."

"Would you like me to tell you something about Ilfracombe?"

"I would indeed. But before you do, remember I am a policeman so I may not keep it a secret."

"Secrets are always difficult to keep," Miss Pettit's replied.

"But you are good at them aren't you?"

To Bob's surprise Miss Pettit gave a girlish, almost flirtatious laugh.

"Tell me about Mrs Crabtree," he said.

"Mrs Crabtree-Gatwood – ooh, she was a gorgon; dreadful accent as well. Her husband owned a chain of jewellery stores in the north of England. He left her *very* wealthy. She wasn't a nice woman, and no children. Nobody to miss her. So selfish. Do you know, she never, ever left a tip for the waitresses, and they had to put up with her being rude to them every single day about the food, which was perfectly acceptable in my view."

"And what's in your Ilfracombe box, Miss Pettit?"

"Oh! You know about my little boxes. My souvenirs."

"To remind you of . . ."

"Where I have been, obviously. I'm not fond of the ones that say 'A present from Southend on Sea' or wherever – rather tasteless, but sometimes I make do."

"And your Ilfracombe box?"

"Shaggy ink-caps. Dried to nothing by now, but they might be useful in a pinch. I think that's a joke, officer."

"Shaggy ink-caps, eh? And how do they work?"

"Well they don't, unless mixed with alcohol. Mrs C-G liked a sherry mid-morning before luncheon, and always had a tipple of gin in her room on the quiet before dining. No one knew, naturally, but I did."

"And Mr and Mrs Bantry stayed at The Gables as well, did they, while you were there? They connected you with Mrs Crabtree-Goat . . . what was it?"

"Crabtree-Gatwood. It might have been because I miss-timed the extraction from her jewellery box and foolishly couldn't resist the extra wallet she kept in her corset drawer."

Bob watched a mountainous wave break along the side of the pier. "I didn't expect to see waves like this in the Bristol Channel."

"One can miss a great deal by accepting assumptions."

"Accepting assumptions – Hmm, I'll have to remember that. Tell me about Mrs Collins in Alton. Was she not very nice either?"

"Mrs Collins senior? Dreadful! Do you know she prevented her own daughter-in-law from having anything that belonged to her husband when he was killed? She even tried to stop her getting the life insurance payment due to her. A road accident. Terribly sad. The daughter-in-law, poor dear girl, had the same name, you see. Both of them were Martha Collins. And the gardener, his little boy was ill, and Mrs Collins senior wouldn't do anything to help them pay for the doctor or the medicine he needed. Dreadful. Ah! But you know – it was you who came to visit Mrs Collins senior about the insurance money, wasn't it? I thought your face was familiar, but then I went to Gibraltar, you see, and one meets so very many people on one's travels. And then, again, you are quite an ordinary-looking man, so you could have been anybody."

"Right, yes . . ." said Bob, somewhat taken aback. "And was there a lady in Gibraltar you didn't care for?"

"No, no, on the contrary we got on very well. She had a brother, though. Nasty fascist sort. Had some sort of arrangement with General Franco. I didn't *really* care for him. As it happened, it was an accident, falling like that when he was getting on the ship. Then I found he hadn't left anything to me because we were not officially married, so in the end I was in a tricky situation again."

"And then you went to live in Croydon?"

"I did!" Miss Pettit turned her beady eyes on him. "You have been checking up on me. You're the first one, you know. Nobody has ever noticed me before."

"Except Mr and Mrs Bantry." Bob kept his voice low and looked away.

"Archibald Bantry was a nasty bully. He was upsetting everyone in Porthferris no end. They are such nice people, too. Do anything for anyone, and he comes in with his silly rules and regulations. And Hilda Bantry – such a snob. She was even horrid to the poor vicar's wife." Miss Pettit gave a shudder. "Nobody liked her. Nobody had a good word for either of them. Poor Mr Plowden the grocer was going to be fined, you know. Mr Chatwynde told me he could be fined as well, and it was an awful lot of money, over three hundred pounds, Mr Baxter, the butcher told me . . ." Miss Pettit paused and looked back at Bob. "But you know all this. You are a policeman."

"I know some of it, yes. You'll have to come with me now, my dear."

"Are you arresting me?"

"In a manner of speaking."

"Why?"

"Well, to start with I need you to tell my boss about your magic fairy dust . . . and Ginny Hawkins."

"Oh, yes, I see. The girl is simple, you know. Even a little bit mad."

"*She* is!" Bob spluttered, but stopped himself from saying more.

"Although, now I think about it, she's somewhat more than simple, intelligence-wise. The strange girl knows the names of all the fungi in the churchyard and roundabout."

"She knows the names, you say. What else does she know about mushrooms and toadstools, do you think?"

"You mean does she know which ones are edible and which ones aren't?"

Bob nodded, "That's right. You've said yourself she's a bit simple."

"Yes."

The neat little spinster looked out across the promenade and Bob felt his hands clench with tension. Was the woman going to use Ginny to get out of a prosecution?

Miss Pettit remained silent. Bob decided on an alternative approach.

"What I'm curious about, Miss Pettit," he said, "is how you know about them."

"My father was a dispensing chemist in a rural area. I learnt all about poisons and prescriptions in the shop where he worked."

"But you didn't want to be his assistant?"

"It wasn't his shop, although had he lived he might have persuaded the owner to take me on. He died just after the Great War – angina. My beau had been killed in France, and my mother passed away from the Spanish flu a few weeks after my father. After that, I had nowhere to go. Our flat was over the chemist shop, you see. I did try being a governess, but I don't like children. So I had no choice – accept being a waitress or shop assistant, or become a lady's companion."

"So all this time, you've never actually had a home of your own until you moved to Porthferris."

"Well, technically, Seabreeze doesn't belong to me. I mean, I came across the deeds to the property after an air raid. Houses had been bombed and everything – furniture and knick-knacks, papers and the like were all over the street. I took a bit of a risk, but no one came to tell me I couldn't stay, so I rather thought, 'Jolly good, a home at last.' Until those nasty Bantrys threatened to – what is it you say, blow my gaff?"

Bob swallowed a smile. "Something like that. But you knew a way to avoid being connected to the Ilfracombe business – the cakes and chutney . . ."

"Yes, it was so easy – greedy people, the pair of them."

"This is exactly what we need to know in Cready, Miss Pettit – Pratt. You come with me and we'll talk to a woman police officer here in Weston, then she'll come with us on the train. We ought to put a few things down on paper at the police station first, though. You tell us all about your souvenir boxes, then I'll arrange for us to get back to Cornwall."

Miss Pettit's small hand flew to her throat, "Oh, my boxes. I shall have to go back to the hotel to fetch them."

"Exactly what I was about to suggest." Bob got to his feet and offered Miss Pettit his arm. "Ready?"

Chapter 43

Delia Metherall and Maisie were putting skipping ropes into a box on the terrace, tidying away the bits and bobs that got scattered around the garden each day. Maisie picked up a stray rounders bat and weighted it in her hands.

Delia looked across and said, "She'll be all right, if it's Ginny you're worrying about."

"Ginny and Aubrey . . ."

"Oh, 'Aubrey', is it? You didn't tell me it had gone that far."

"*It* hasn't gone anywhere, but he has." Maisie dropped the bat into the PE box. "Gone back to London, where he belongs. Blossom's looking after the pub. She'll do a roarin' trade once all those sailors get here and take over our harbour for their new-fangled motor boats. Pass me that loose rope over there."

Delia pushed at a muddle of rope with her foot, saying, "Come and live up here, Maisie. It'll solve your problem with Ginny. I won't ask her to go into the village if I can help it, and she won't have to go past the pub to get home. It could avoid a lot of trouble. Might even prevent an *embarrassment.*"

"What, like me?"

Delia's head shot up. "I didn't mean . . . I've never thought of you that way."

"No, but it's true, and we both know it. Everybody in Porthferris knows it. Maisie Rose Hawkins has got her cottage because the people up at the big house owed it to her ma."

"That's awful. I never knew you felt like that."

Maisie could see Delia was distressed but she pressed on anyway. Properties were being requisitioned all over the place. The Navy was taking over the harbour for motor torpedo boats – MTBs – or whatever they were. Sailors had been billeted on Bayview. Sooner or later, someone was going to mention the Hawkins' cottage and that she had no rights or deeds to a stick or stone of it: she and Ginny would be homeless.

Maisie tried to stay firm but she couldn't bear to see Delia unhappy so she put her arms around her, like she used to do when Delia was a child and she was Mrs Chenoweth's tweeny. "I'm sorry, my heart," she mumbled. "I didn't mean to snap at you. But it's all such a worry."

"Maisie, your mother's cottage is yours now." Delia's voice was muffled with sorrow.

"But who's to say so?"

"I'll tell Charles to sort it out with our solicitors."

Maisie felt awful but held her breath, determined not to show weakness. Then she remembered what Delia was suggesting for Ginny. It probably was the safest solution. At least it would keep her in one place; there'd be no need for her to be walking up and down the hill or past the hotel or the pub. She let out a grateful sigh and smiled. Dropping her arms, she said, "Have you got a suitcase I can borrow, for her clothes and the like? I'll ask Ned to bring it over."

"Ned as well, is it!" Delia brightened.

"He's a family friend. He's helped me a lot over the years, one way and another."

"And the portly but intriguing Detective Sergeant Robbins, is he helping you as he should?"

"If you're referring to trying to keep Ginny out of a courtroom, he certainly is. If you're referring to anything else – mind your own business." Maisie couldn't keep a serious tone and started to chuckle. "Talking of 'portly', what you going to do about those porkers outside? There's far too many now. We'll have to eat them sooner or later."

"I know, I know. And Mrs Bristle-brush is due again any day. I'll have to ask Pew Pewsey to keep them at Home Farm like Alf Plowden's pig club pigs."

"Well, get him round quick, and without that blasted axe! If he turns up carrying his axe, those Military Police wandering around will shoot him on the spot."

The two women were still laughing when Charles Metherall hobbled onto the terrace using crutches. "Good to see someone has something to laugh about," he said.

Maisie dropped the last rope into the box. "We're nearly done, Major."

"Anything a cripple can manage?" Charles Metherall sounded peevish.

Maisie prayed Delia wouldn't mention the cottage – this was not the time. She was saved by the jangle of the brass doorbell.

It was Bob Robbins. He doffed his cap, nearly making Maisie laugh out loud; his short white hair was all bristled up like Mrs Bristle-brush.

"Mrs Hawkins. Good, I was hoping to find you here. Can we have a word?"

"Um, yes. You don't want to speak to the major first?"

"Later – it's you I'd like to speak to."

Maisie's heart sank; it wouldn't be good news, whatever it was. "I'll just let Mrs Metherall know you're here. Come through to the kitchen. Take a seat – I won't be a moment."

When she got back, Maisie said, "They're saying in the village Mr Bantry was a spy."

"Yes, Ned MacManus saw him on the quay one night."

"Like I did?" Maisie's voice was a whisper.

"Like you did. Dr MacManus also thinks he saw him on more than one occasion, so there's no need for you to come forward with that bit of information, if you don't want to. I'll talk to you later about your sea cave. But it might be a good idea to get rid of anything – um – incriminating."

Maisie gave a heartfelt sigh. "The cave end is empty and that explosion blocked up the back of the tunnel so . . . Is that why you're here?"

"Not altogether. I've got a bit of good news for you."

Maisie's hand flew to her throat, "Stan."

"No, sorry, it's about Ginny."

Maisie was torn: she wanted to know more, but didn't want to discuss Ginny here if she was going to be living in the house as a full-time maid. "Is it urgent?"

"We can talk later, elsewhere, if you prefer. What time do you finish here?"

"About six-ish."

"I'll be outside in the car – save you having to walk home."

Maisie wasn't sure how to react, then smiled. "That's kind," she said.

Chapter 44

Returning to his cottage next evening, Bob found a large cardboard box on his doorstep. He opened the door first, then bent down to pick it up. It was very heavy.

Staggering through to his kitchen, he dropped it on the table. The box had once contained Sunlight soap, but not now. The flaps had been overlapped so they wouldn't open, but he knew it wasn't soap. Prizing the cardboard apart, he expected to see a message or an invoice. There was nothing. Slowly, he removed the contents: a box of brown sugar lumps, then a grocer's paper packet of raisins, four ounces of tea, and a good-sized slab of cheese – local – probably from Glebe Farm Dairy. Under the cheese, wrapped in layers of newspaper then greaseproof paper, was a knuckle of cooked gammon. Bob began to laugh. He pulled out every last item and found a flat bag of rice, and tucked under that a bottle of very fine single malt whisky.

Gazing at the cornucopia on his table Bob rubbed his hands together and started to laugh again. And he laughed and laughed and laughed.

"Such nice people in Porthferris."

He was interrupted by the sound of a motorbike through the open front door. The laughter faltered. He felt his stomach churn.

Closing the kitchen door firmly behind him, Bob went to see who it was, fearing the telegram no parent wanted to receive in wartime. It was Laurie Oliver.

Staying astride the bike, he waved a small buff envelope in the air. "This came for you at the police station."

Bob swallowed hard, hoping against hope it wasn't about his son, Jimmy. Then he noticed that Laurie was in civvies. "Are you off duty?"

"Yes. DI Small called me at home, asked me to deliver this as a favour."

Bob tried to govern his features. Keeping his hand as steady as he could, he opened the gate and took the envelope. His name was on it, but it was handwritten and without an address. He felt the weight lying on his shoulders lighten. Not a telegram, then.

He looked at Laurie, who must have noticed how the colour had drained from his cheeks at the sight of the envelope.

"Sorry, Sarge. It's nothing official. DI Small asked me to write his message down and bring it myself because he couldn't get you at home. You're out a lot, he says. Here."

"Read it to me, Laurie," Bob said, trying to breathe normally. "I haven't got me reading glasses."

"I've never seen you in reading glasses."

"Just read it, lad."

"All right. I can do it from memory, actually. Scilly Isles police were called out to a remote rocky beach last week. There was a boat trapped above high water and a body in it – large male, aged about forty-five. The boat is registered to Stanley Hawkins, Porthferris. Coroner's report says he'd had his throat cut."

Bob nearly slumped to the ground with relief. Then he registered the final sentence. "So you were right, you young devil. Well, I'll be blowed."

"It closes the Hawkins case, Sarge. Shall I go on up and tell Mrs Hawkins, or should you do it?"

"I'll do it."

"Right, then, I'll be off. Hey, what's that?" Laurie pointed to a wooden box beside the front door.

"Ah, I didn't see that, what with the other one."

"What other one?"

"Oh, you mean *that* box? That's where I put the milk money."

"Ah, right. See you tomorrow – bye." Laurie revved his engine and charged off towards the junction at Kerrith Cross.

Bob picked up the box and took it into the kitchen. The table being full, he put it on the draining board and opened it. A dozen brown speckled eggs nesting in fresh clean straw. There was only one person who could have sent them: a kind, gentle widow who deserved a bit of kind, gentle attention.

Forgetting his hat, Bob grabbed his car keys and slammed the front door behind him.

THE END

J. G. Harlond

Author's Note

During the Second World War, British intelligence officers recruited and trained small cells of civilian saboteurs and assassins throughout the British Isles. Groups called Special Auxiliary Units or Patrols consisted of four to eight local men picked from Home Guard platoons, or supplied with Home Guard uniforms as a cover for their activities. In the event of invasion, their role was to go into Operational Bases that had been established underground near strategic roads and railways. Members of these highly secret groups were sent to a training school in Wiltshire named Coleshill.

Operational Bases were adapted out of old mine shafts; Royal Engineers also dug tunnels and created underground rooms or bunkers in forests and hillsides. Entrances and emergency escape hatches were so well camouflaged that people have been walking over them or farming around them since the 1940s without noticing. The OB in this novel differs slightly to real underground posts in that it is close to the coast, almost all were built a minimum of one mile inland.

Operational Patrols, who consisted of local men such as gardeners, carpenters, plumbers, doctors, farmers, gamekeepers and garage-owners, plotted and prepared for dangerous night time raids to harass and destroy the invaders' mobility, and disrupt vital supply lines. Inside each buried hideout or OB there was an arsenal of pistols, plastic explosives, submachine guns, commando knives, plus food and water to last a month.

The key point to everything related to what became known as 'Churchill's Secret Army' was utter secrecy to protect both the network and civilians. Partisans were expected to shoot themselves first rather than be taken alive. Men volunteered knowing they would be shot if captured. They also knew local civilians were at risk and likely to be executed in retribution for damage to the invaders' supply lines. For this reason alone, it was vital nobody – not even family members – were told about their Resistance roles.

Retired policemen and young recruits such as Bob Robbins and Laurence Oliver in the novel were desperately needed between 1939 and 1945 to replace the policemen and women who had joined the Armed Forces. The German submarine surfacing off the coast of Cornwall to take on fresh water in this story is also based on real events.

Porthferris is a fictional location set between Saltash and Looe in East Cornwall. All characters with the exception of named politicians are fictional, and this being a work of fiction, I have taken a few liberties with historical details here and there. The nature of village life, on the other hand, while being somewhat exaggerated, is based on experience.

J.G. Harlond

The Author

J.G. Harlond

Jane G. Harlond grew up in Devon and studied in Bristol, Portsmouth and the USA before finishing her academic studies with an M.A. in Social and Political Thought at the University of Sussex. She has lived and worked in a variety of different countries and is married to a retired Spanish naval officer. Harlond has two sons and five step-children, all of whom now have their own careers in diverse parts of Europe.

If You Enjoyed This Book

Please Visit

PENMORE PRESS
www.penmorepress.com

All Penmore Press books are available directly through our website, amazon.com, Barnes and Noble and Nook,, Apple iTunes, Kobo books and via leading bookshops across the United States, Canada, the UK, Australia and Europe.

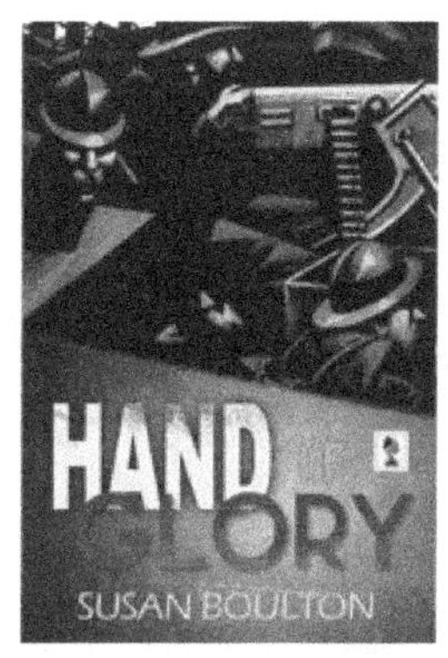

HAND OF GLORY
BY
SUSAN BOULTON

"And all that awake now be as the dead, for the dead man's sake . . ."

In Passchendaele near the end of the Great War, Captain Giles Hardy is trapped on barbed wire, wounded in mind and body, convinced he should be dead. But Giles's true battle begins after he's rescued and sent home. In the small town of Stafford, he struggles with terrifying visions of the atrocities he's witnessed—and a recruit he served with.

The visions lead Giles to a man who exploits the grief of the bereaved with the help of a Hand of Glory, a mythical tool of thieves. A new friend, Agnes Reed, and the ghost of an old one, Corporal George Adams, aid Hardy in his investigation. Now he must catch the thief, destroy the hand, and lay to rest the men who will otherwise never leave the fields of Flanders.

PENMORE PRESS
www.penmorepress.com

THE EMPRESS EMERALD
BY
JANE HARLOND

Stolen: A child, a priceless jewel, and an identity

Abandoned as a child in a Bombay orphanage, Leo Kazan's life takes an unanticipated turn when he becomes the protégé of Sir Lionel Pinecoffin, the city's District Political Officer in Bombay. Under Pinecoffin's tutelage, the boy, adept at learning languages and theft, is trained as a spy and becomes immersed in international espionage, revolutionary politics, and diamond smuggling. In 1918, during a visit to London, he has a brief but memorable affair with a young English woman Davina Dymond in London before leaving for Russia.

Separated, their lives take different turns. As he matures Leo begins to question his family history, seeking to uncover the truth about his parents. A pregnant Davina is married off and exiled to Spain, where she gives birth to Leo's daughter. They are fated to meet again in Gibraltar in 1936, their love rekindled. But a new war plunges Europe into crisis, the Spanish Civil War tearing them apart, leaving, Leo and Davina in a fight to reclaim their lives and their love amid the violent storms of war.

PENMORE PRESS
www.penmorepress.com

Fortune's Whelp
by
Benerson Little

Privateer, Swordsman, and Rake:

Set in the 17th century during the heyday of privateering and the decline of buccaneering, *Fortune's Whelp* is a brash, swords-out sea-going adventure. Scotsman Edward MacNaughton, a former privateer captain, twice accused and acquitted of piracy and currently seeking a commission, is ensnared in the intrigue associated with the attempt to assassinate King William III in 1696. Who plots to kill the king, who will rise in rebellion—and which of three women in his life, the dangerous smuggler, the wealthy widow with a dark past, or the former lover seeking independence—might kill to further political ends? Variously wooing and defying Fortune, Captain MacNaughton approaches life in the same way he wields a sword or commands a fighting ship: with the heart of a lion and the craft of a fox.

PENMORE PRESS
www.penmorepress.com

ROCAMORA

DONALD MICHAEL PLATT

No man is closer to a woman than her confessor, not her father, not her brother, not her husband.

-Spanish saying

Vicente de Rocamora, the epitome of a young renaissance man in 17th century Spain, questions the goals of the Inquisition and the brutal means used by King Philip IV and the Roman Church to achieve them. Spain vows to eliminate the heretical influences attributed to Jews, Moors, and others who would taint the limpieza de sangre, purity of Spanish blood. At the insistence of his family, the handsome and charismatic Vicente enters the Dominican Order and is soon thrust into the scheming political hierarchy that rules Spain. As confessor to the king's sister, the Infanta Doña María, and assistant to Philip's chief minister, Olivares, Vicente ascends through the ranks and before long finds himself poised to attain not only the ambitious dreams of the Rocamora family but also—named Spain's Inquisitor General

PENMORE PRESS
www.penmorepress.com

Local Resistance

Penmore Press

Challenging, Intriguing, Adventurous, Historical and Imaginative

www.penmorepress.com